NEVER GIVE UP ON YOUR DREAMS!

RONALD GRAY

MY CALL

Click For Book Trailer

MY CALL

Ronald Gray

BLACK WALL STREET NEW DREAM PUBLISHING
Owned by
MY PROVIDER PRODUCTIONS LLC
www.myproviderproductions.com

RONALD GRAY

My Provider Productions LLC
My Call
Copyright © 2013 by Ronald H. Gray
Revised Edition: 07/04/2021

Library of Congress Control Number: 2012908556
ISBN-10: 0615743978
ISBN-13: 978-0-615-74397-4
Author: Ronald H. Gray
Second Printing Edition
Cover Design/Graphics: www.oddballdsgn.com
Printed in the United States of America

This is a work of fiction. Any references or similarities to actual events, real people, living or dead, or to real locales are intended to give the novel a sense of reality. Any similarity in other names, characters, places, and incidents is entirely coincidental.

Distributed by Black Wall Street New Dream Publishing
My Provider Productions LLC
www.myproviderproductions.com
blackwallstreetnewdream@yahoo.com

RONALD GRAY

Dedication

This book is dedicated to family and friends who never stopped believing in me and my vision. Their words and attitudes were always the same, "Never give up!" Special thanks to my sister who attended Howard University and Catholic University Law School, both are in Washington DC. She has been directly and indirectly helpful to me concerning getting this book completed, contributing financially, and assisting me with other personal matters. Thanks to Sis and her husband Scott. I can't forget my niece Leslie for making sure I remained focused. Special thanks to some close friends; Ray Quick, whom I have known for some years. He has proven to be a true friend, he designed my company logo and two business cards along with other graphic work, free of charge. He has supported me in many ways. William Ray: this brother and I go back many years, a friend to the end. Terry Franklin: another brother who has supported me and has been part of other ventures with me, CK: a young man to whom I am a mentor, who believed in me and supported this vision. Who said never lose focus because you are capable of accomplishing anything you set your mind to. Hamza Hosein, we have been friends since 1982 when we met in Germany while in the military. He has always been supportive, giving me encouraging words to continue with my goals. Thanks, Hamza for believing in me, and your financial support as well, greatly appreciated. Thank you, everyone.

RONALD GRAY

Acknowledgments

First and foremost, I would like to thank God for giving me this gift and opportunity to share this story, some of which I have lived. Thank you for purchasing this book.

I thank all who stood by me in this journey and all who did not. The betrayal, lies, deceit, pain, and love I have experienced in my life's journey compelled me to write this story. I am still blessed because of the mercy of God and, I *never gave up*.

To the people who crossed my path in life and expressed true kindness and love toward me, I can never thank you enough.

To some of you, this may be just a story, but to others, it may be a mirror of your life. If you are truly honest you can see just a little of yourself or someone you know in one of the characters in this story.

MY CALL will make you laugh, cry, and think about your life and others in various ways.

This book will move your mind and spirit. It is the beginning of what you should look forward to.

This is the real raw untold story…until now!

Prologue

Ron drove his Ash Grey 2012 S600 Benz slowly into the south end of Hustler's Park in Hyattsville Maryland and stopped. He rolled the windows down and felt the morning breeze as he leaned back in his car seat listening to, *A House Is Not a Home*, by Luther Vandross.

Closing his eyes, he began to think...*How did I get into this mess? Ronald Emmanuel O'Neil, aka S&D. I have so much against me. Mr. Bones is a voodoo doctor, the devil's evil servant. If that is not enough, I also have the police, FBI, DEA, and Mr. Victor Augular, a very powerful drug lord against me. My family does not understand me including my lady Diana, who I love deeply, but she won't let me make love to her. I have accumulated millions of dollars in a short amount of time which attracts many women willing to do whatever just to get next to me. I am talking about women who are nothing but FULL SEVEN'S.* He shook his head coming out of his thoughts.

"For those who do not know, a *FULL SEVEN* is a woman who is, pretty in the face, slim in the waist, has hips, full lips, painted fingertips, a big butt, and a pretty smile. Dangerous!

A woman this fine drives a man crazy with lust, making men look at what they have in comparison to what they want. Thinking, what would it take to get a lady like her? And the *FULL SEVENS* usually give most guys a nasty attitude and the look to match and keep it moving." He exhaled and continued his deep thinking.

To add to my problems is my best friend Keith Washington, my crime partner, and someone who I should have stayed away from. I made a deal to stay loyal and protect Keith, but I did not know the full price!

I started out serving God, now look at me. I am serving the devil himself. I went from carrying the Bible to carrying two guns, a 357 magnum, and a Glock Nine. From going to church to going to nightclubs, from working a legal nine-to-five job to contributing to a hundred million dollars a month, illegal business...selling death. Drugs!

"Lord, the beginning of my life was very peaceful and good. My mom and dad's faith gave them their heart's desire for a son. Me! A prophecy from God! Now, the most dangerous hitman the world has ever known, Satan himself is trying to destroy me. I also have Mr. Victor Augular trying to destroy me. I found this out about Victor long after my involvement with him. And this is his story."

When he was twenty-seven years old, Victor was standing in front of his mom and Dad's headstones at Blackbird Cemetery. His mom died of cancer and his Dad was shot in the back while running away from the police for selling marijuana.

He became so emotional at that time looking at his parent's headstones, that he fell to his knees, cried, and yelled out his pain. He spoke the words, "Whatever it takes, I want revenge, I want blood."

A well-dressed six-foot two hundred twenty-five-pound man approached him carrying a black oak cane with a silver wolf head.

He tapped his cane on a tombstone close by to get Victor's attention.

"I can give you what you seek. But would you give up everything you have, for everything you have ever wanted?"

These words, Victor's agreement to do whatever the man asks because he felt at that time, he had nothing to lose, and the stranger's actions caused Victor to say, yes. They shook hands. Victor did not know he was shaking hands with a voodoo doctor named, Mr. Bones, the devil's servant.

On that day, Mr. Bones revealed to Victor a small sample of his powers by making ten thousand dollars appear in his jacket pocket. From that day forward Victor's life would never be the same.

CHAPTER ONE

The O'Neil's

David and Sheila O'Neil live in a two-level, five-bedroom brick house in an affluent neighborhood in Mitchellville Maryland. They own a black Lincoln Navigator and a white S500 Benz. They have two daughters, Christine and Sandra who are six and seven. David is twenty-seven and Sheila is twenty-six. They met at *Arcadia Junior High School* when David was in the ninth grade and a strong connection was established early that is almost unheard of nowadays. They have always known they were meant to be together.

At nineteen, David asked Sheila to marry him, but her parents were against it because they felt they were too young. So, David and Sheila eloped. One year later Christine was born then Sandra the second year. David has been in the construction business for years and is a foreman working for the largest construction company in Maryland owned by Victor Augular, *Augular's National Construction.*

David is brown skinned five feet ten, two hundred thirty-five muscular pounds with a six-pack. He is clean-cut and very handsome. Many ladies try to get his attention, but he is committed to his wife. Sheila is incredibly attractive, five feet seven, one hundred forty pounds with a curvaceous tight body. She has shoulder-length hair, full breasts, and a round firm derriere that David cannot keep his hands off. Sheila is a part-time office assistant at a law firm. David is very playful and enjoys touching and flirting with his wife sensually because he thinks she is the finest woman walking. They work out together at the nearby gym because this is part of their bonding time. They have strong convictions about obeying the word of God and raising their daughters the same way.

It is 4:00 p.m. on a sunny evening in May. Sheila and her two daughters were at home. The girls were upstairs in their room studying and Sheila was in the kitchen. She was wearing the conservative dark blue dress she wore to the office today that hung just below her knees. A white apron fit snugly on her 24-inch waist and she was preparing one of her husband's favorite meals. Southern-fried pork chops, mashed potatoes with dark gravy, spinach, corn on the cob, cornbread, and homemade iced tea and lemonade mix.

While she was cooking and setting the table for dinner, she heard Mary J Blige's song, *I Am*, on the radio. Sheila started singing the words as she worked with the skill of a woman who knew her way around the kitchen. She paused for a moment, turned down the radio, and called out to her girls upstairs.

"Girls, are you doing your homework?"
Sandra was in Christine's room, and they were sitting on the floor doing their homework. Both chorus in.

"Yes Mom, we are." This was followed by hysterical giggling.

With her hands on her hips, Sheila yelled back.

"Don't try to be smart and you better not be playing in

there or your Dad will hear about it. Hurry and finish you're reading because dinner is almost ready." Sheila looked toward the ceiling. "Lord, I thank you for my husband. He is a good man and I love the way that man lays his hands and body on me." She turned the music back up and started dancing but was thinking...*I will hurt a woman over that man the way he put in work. He has a diamond penis and a pearl tongue. I hope my baby is not too tired when he comes home because I got something for that fine, praying, man tonight. Feed him and then drain him.* She looked up again.

"Lord, please give my baby some strength tonight so he can put it on me. I want a son and I do not care what the doctors have told me, I believe in you Lord, and your word. I hope those red pumps I will be wearing for my baby tonight, with my sexy bra and matching thong, will help." She shook her head and smiled. "I love that man," she murmured aloud. The Mary J. Blige song fades in the background and another song comes on.

David drove into the driveway in his white work pickup truck and Christine heard the familiar sound of his truck in the driveway. She and her sister got up from the floor and walked to her bedroom window and they both yelled.

"Mom, Daddy is home, we heard his truck in the driveway."

Sheila walked upstairs into Christine's room and pointed at them. "Ok, both of you put your schoolwork away and go wash your hands and get ready to eat." Sheila walked quickly back downstairs, checked herself in the hallway mirror then walked towards the front door.

David stepped out of his truck wearing his work clothes and boots and had his lunch box and a hard hat in his hand. Before he could unlock the door, it opened, and Sheila was standing there with her hands on her hips displaying a beautiful smile that David loves so much.

"Hi David, come on in with your big fine self."

David stepped inside the house smiling, put his lunch box and hard hat on the floor closed the door, and then walked into the kitchen quickly to wash his hands and then walked toward Sheila. He pulled Sheila into him, wrapped his arms around her waist, kissed her lips, and allowed his hands to slide to her hips and butt, caressing them slowly.

"Baby, I have been thinking about you all day. I could not wait to get home so I could feel all this fine body of yours. You got a big sexy, fat ass."

She leaned back and playfully slapped David on his shoulder.

"David don't say ass, it sounds so nasty, and my butt is not that big thank you. It is round and shapely like it should be from spending hours in the gym, now let me go." She pushed him back playfully knowing she never wanted him to let go. He pulled her into him again and began kissing her neck and face.

"Relax baby, I said you got a big sexy fat ass and that is what I meant. A round tight booty." He smacked Sheila on the butt lightly. "Let me get some of this, hit it from the back," he laughed knowing it would provoke her because she does not like that kind of talk. Sheila pushed him away trying to be serious.

"David, I asked you not to talk to me like that. I am not a woman you picked up in a nightclub. I am your Christian wife so respect me and stop talking like some street thug."

David laughed and pulled her back into him gently, kissing her passionately on the lips. Sheila tried to act aloof, but her body betrayed her while she was thinking...*I feel this man's touch down my spine. Lord, he feels so good all over me.*

David slid his hands underneath her dress caressing her butt until his fingers slide inside her panties feeling her wetness.

"You know it feels good. Now say you want me to hit this." He murmured while sucking on her neck.

Sheila moaned and pressed her body into him thinking...*if he only knew how badly I want him to push me against the wall and take this lovin.* She pushed his hands down, smoothed out her dress, and slapped his face playfully.

"Stop, you are so nasty and impossible David. Now behave yourself." They both start laughing.

David saw his girls walking toward him. He picked them up, hugged and kissed them on the cheek then put them down. He looked at Sheila.

"I am going to take a quick shower and then we can eat." He kissed Sheila and walked quickly to his bedroom and into the bathroom. Fifteen minutes later David was sitting at the dinner table wearing sweatpants and a t-shirt. He blessed the food, and they ate and talked while listening to jazz music. When everyone was finished, the girls hugged and kissed Sheila and David good night and walked toward their rooms.

Sheila yelled.

"Don't forget tomorrow is church night!"

David stood and walked over to Sheila, and kissed her on the cheek, neck, and lips. Sheila stood and faced David and then he picked her up and she started laughing.

"David O'Neil, you better not drop me. Put me down."

He gazed into her eyes.

"I love you Sheila. Tonight, I want to take my time and make passionate love to your entire body until we fall asleep in each other's arms."

Tears come to Sheila's eyes and slide down her cheeks because she can feel the sincerity in David's words.

"David, I love you just as much baby."

"Sheila, you are my best friend." He walked down the hallway toward their bedroom carrying Sheila in his arms.

When they reached their bedroom, David put Sheila down and put his finger to her lips.

"No words Sheila just let me spoil you." He starts undressing and she does the same. David's eyes explore his wife's naked body, and he shakes his head smiling. Even after having two children Sheila's body was still very tight and sexy. He grabbed her hand gently. "Let's have some fun in the shower."

They walked to the bathroom and got in the shower washing each other slowly and then rinsing off and David kissed and licked his wife's body all over. They stepped out and wiped each other off with the towel and David kissed her lips repeatedly then carried her to the bed. He began kissing and licking her entire body again making her moan and climax from his wonderful touch. Before Sheila could relax David moved his body up until he was parallel with Sheila's and slid inside her. Being inside Sheila always feels wonderful, like it is the first time, and he is moving inside his wife deeply but slowly.

Sheila looked deep into his eyes and began to cry.

"Oh David, baby you feel so good inside me. I thank God for you. Ohhhhh you are so hard baby, please, don't stop. It feels so good. I love you David, ohhhhhh David, I am cummming baby, don't stop."

CHAPTER TWO

Construction Site

The following morning Sheila was sitting in front of her desk at work. She picked up the phone to call David.

David was walking to the office trailer on the construction site when he heard his cell phone.

"Hi baby, just for the record, if you are trying to hook me, too late. I am already hooked and last night was good. You tried to hurt a brother." He said and laughed.

"David don't talk dirty on the phone and I did not hurt you. I just put this body on you like I always do. Anyway, I felt some heaviness in my spirit when I was praying this morning."

"Well, things around here have been tense this morning. We have a new site foreman, this guy is mean, and cold, and he has evil-looking eyes, and I can feel his bad spirit. We have the same lunch box, and I grabbed his by mistake earlier and he snatched it out of my hand like I was stealing it. I looked at him like he was crazy."

"People like that need more love in their life. So, let your light shine and be kind to him, God will do the rest. Have a blessed day baby and I love you. Oh, don't work too hard because I need you to save some of that energy for me."

"Yeah, I know. Be nice to him. I will save some energy for you because you got that, do right."

"David, what in the world is, do right?"

"Your loving is so good you make me want to do right." He said while laughing.

Sheila laughed quietly and had a big smile on her face.

"You are so nasty David." She held the phone closer to her mouth and whispered. "Baby, I got some more of this, do right, for you when you get home." She giggled and hung the phone up, thinking...*I have a whole lot more of this, do right. What a man!*

David saw the foreman watching him as he put his phone away. Greg Johnson is the foreman, he has been in the construction business for over twenty years. He is also Mr. Augular's assistant on various matters. Greg is six feet two, two hundred thirty pounds with a very muscular physique and a handsome face. But his heart is very cold, and he cares for no one. He walked toward David extending his hand to him.

"Excuse me, Mr. O'Neil, how are you sir?" Greg purposely shook David's hand hard. "There is some business that we need to discuss. May I have a word with you?"

"Mr. Johnson, yes sir," David looked sternly into his face. "Nice handshake. So, what can I help you with?"

"Please call me Greg."
"No problem, call me David."

"Okay. I have heard good things about you. You have been with the company for years, starting as a laborer and working your way up. I can respect that."

"Thank you. I enjoy my work and God has blessed me."

Greg looked at him and frowned.

"I heard you are very religious and a church-going man." He said with a grin on his face.

"Well, I am a born-again Holy Ghost-filled Christian. There is a big difference."

"Yeah, I know God too. But right now, we need this job completed. Bad weather, equipment breaking, and lazy people have already caused us to be behind and it may rain today. So, you need to make sure everyone is doing their job, which means less talking on the phone and more work. Is there a problem with that?"

"No problem at all."

"Very good" Greg stared at David thinking how much he loved irritating Christians. He shook David's hand and walked away, then stopped, turned around, and looked back at David. "David, since you are born again, ask God to hold back the rain so this job can be completed on time." He walked away laughing.

CHAPTER THREE

Victor's Reign

Victor Augular is twenty-seven years old. He is five feet ten, two hundred twenty pounds. Finely groomed with a muscular physique, light skin complexion, Dominican Republican mixed with Italian. He wore a dark blue Armani suit, a light blue long-sleeved cuff link shirt, and Italian shoes. He was sitting in his office in his nightclub called *Reigns*. His office was spacious with a mahogany desk, two expensive sofas, several soft leather chairs, and a refrigerator.

The club is in Laurel Maryland. It is a two-level building with an exterior made of stone and brick. No expenses were spared in the decorations of marble floors, imported oak, and granite countertops. One million dollars was spent on lighting. The front has an overhang, so customers do not get wet in the rain when they drive up, and lots of greenery around the building.

It is the most popular club in the metropolitan area with a seating capacity of eight hundred. It is not the largest in the area, but it is a very elite club that caters to those who desire to be treated like kings and queens. The club has a strict dress code, no jeans or athletic wear is allowed. It has an elite security team to enforce its rule of zero tolerance for any disturbances or violence.

There are two dance floors, three bars, and plenty of private VIP booths throughout the club. The food is exquisite. Fresh lobsters, crabs, and shrimp are flown in weekly. People brag about how good the food is and all the desserts are handmade.

Victor picked up the phone but stopped moving when he heard the buzzer from his office door. He put the phone down and opened his desk drawer and pulled out two 357 magnums, then moved his hands under his desk.

Stephanie Walker walked in. She is every man's dream concerning looks. Twenty-four-year-old Brazilian and Caucasian model. Stephanie is five feet ten, gorgeous face, slim waist, and curves in all the right places. She causes car accidents while walking down the street. She is wearing a snug-fitting dress that shows her abundant hips, butt, and ample cleavage. Every step she takes makes her body shake with the spirit of lust. Stephanie walked through the door and stood in front of Victor's desk.

"Mr. Augular how are you today? I hope my presence is not disturbing you." Stephanie put one hand on her hip and looked at Victor with a, bend me over your desk look.

Victor stared at her thinking…*damn this woman is fine and if she only knew how badly I want to bend her fine ass over my desk and blow her back out, now.*

"Miss Walker, I was just going to call you, so your entrance is perfect timing." He put both guns on top of his desk and looked directly at her. "Please have a seat."

Stephanie sat in a chair in front of his desk, and crossed her legs slowly making sure he saw her panties. She shakes her head while looking at the guns.

"Why do you have two guns? I did not know I made you so nervous." She smiled and licked her lips.

"Miss Walker, I don't get nervous, but I do get what I want, one way or another. Has anyone ever told you, you have beautiful legs?"

"Yes, but they are not my best feature." Smiling as she spreads her legs slightly so he can get a better look between them.

Victor leans forward staring between her legs.

"Very nice view but let's discuss some business."

Stephanie frowns because she did not get the reaction from Victor she was hoping for.

"Victor Augular, it is always business with you and little time for me. I am about pleasure and a woman who gets what she wants, and I don't have patience when I don't get it. You need to make time for me sir, and very soon." She is thinking...*forget all his discipline. He needs to leap over here and get this ass.* "Break your rules for me and I will show you that I am more than worth it."

Victor stared at Stephanie knowing she was a gold-digging freak, like all the rest of them. She is a high-class freak but still a freak.

"Damn, all of this talking." He walked over to Stephanie, pulled her from her seat, and kissed her passionately.

The moment their lips touched Stephanie could feel herself getting wet. She quickly removed her dress and stood in front of him in high heels, a garter belt, and panties.

"So, do you see anything that you like?"

Victor nods his head and smiles.

"You look beautiful Stephanie." He caressed her back, hips, and butt while kissing her passionately on the lips. Victor reached down and lifts one of her legs gripping her butt while sliding his fingers inside her panties feeling her wetness knowing he is only seconds away from being inside her. His office phone rang.

"You have got to be kidding me." He spoke with instant irritation in his voice and shook his head. "Who in the hell could that be?"

"Victor, please don't answer it. My body is on fire for you right now and I am so wet for you baby." She grabbed Victor's waist and pulled him closer to her.

He kissed her again.

"I have to. This better be good." He walked over to the desk and answered the phone. "Hello...yes, I am interested in your proposal. I can be there within the hour. No, that will not be a problem. Yes, I will see you then, goodbye sir." He put the phone down and stared at Stephanie.

She has her hands on her hips staring at Victor with anger in her eyes.

"I cannot believe you Victor. You are filthy rich, and you stop pleasing me, of all people, to answer a damn phone so you can get some more money. You are a greedy bastard. Men dream, fantasize about touching me and I am standing here, wet and on fire, waiting to get fucked, and you," she waved her hand at him, "forget it." She began getting dressed.

Victor has no choice but to watch her get dressed knowing she is highly upset.

"Stephanie, I do apologize for this, but I have been waiting for that call. It came at a bad time and I realize this is a missed opportunity but I plan on making it up to you."

Stephanie finished getting dressed and walked toward his office door but stopped and turned around. She caressed the inside of her thigh and looked at Victor.

"You have no idea what you missed. Sometimes opportunity only knocks once. You remember that." She walked out still fuming mad and whispered her thoughts. *Greedy bastard, you will pay for that, no man turns me down.*

As soon as Stephanie walked out of the door Victor slammed his hand on the desk.

"Damn, I have been waiting to hit that fat ass for a while, but no piece of ass is worth more than my one hundred million dollars a month business, net income." The phone rang. "Hello...secure this line...good, go ahead. Do you want ten thousand kilos? It will take me a little time but consider it done. It will cost you ten thousand dollars per kilo, which comes to one hundred million dollars, cash on delivery. I will call you tomorrow with the details." He put the phone down and smiled. "No ass is worth, one hundred million dollars. Do you know how much ass a man can get with one hundred million dollars? Multiethnic international worldwide global ass." He laughs.

CHAPTER FOUR

O'Neil's Home

David drove his work truck into his driveway. He stepped out slowly because he was tired after a tough day at work. He left his hard hat in the truck but walked into the house carrying his lunch box and looked around not seeing or hearing anyone as he stood in the living room.

"Daddy is home," he yelled, "Can I get some love in this house?"

Sheila walked out of the bedroom and downstairs wearing a tan color top a light blue skirt that comes just below her knees and tan-colored heels.

"Hi baby and stop yelling in this house." She gives David a loving smile, and a hug, and then kisses him on the lips. David responds by caressing her hips while kissing her with passion.

"I missed you today and these hips always make me come home. Where are the kids?"

"Never mind my hips and don't start something you can't finish." She kissed him again. "The girls are getting ready for church tonight, you know it's revival week and I am looking forward to going. So please hurry and get ready."

"I almost forgot this week was a revival at church." He kissed her and walked into the kitchen setting his lunch box on the counter. "I am going to shower and get ready for church. Would you and your hips care to join me?" Holding his arms out and licking his lips.

"Sweetheart, we don't have time for that. I don't want to be late for church so hurry and get ready."

"Forget all of that talking. Let me shower, grip your hips, and work that body, good! Make you scream my name, oh David, oh David." He started laughing.

Sheila could not help but laugh.

"You are too much, and you are nasty. No, you cannot, so go take a shower. I am going to check on the girls and clean your lunch box." She walked upstairs into Christine's room where the girls were.

Christine and Sandra are sitting on the bed wearing dresses.

"Hi Mom, I heard Dad. Is he getting ready for church?"

"Yes, he is Christine and you and your sister look nice."

"Mom, do we have to go to church tonight? I'm sleepy."

"Yes Sandra and you will feel better once we are in church praising God. Your dad should be ready soon, so you two stay in your room until we are ready." She kissed them on the cheek and walked downstairs and into the kitchen. Sheila opened David's lunch box and stared at it and then walked to their bedroom carrying it.

David was dressed wearing a polished black pair of Stacy Adams shoes, grey triple pleated pants with a quarter-inch cuff, and a black Gator skin belt with a long-sleeved white shirt with grey lines in it. He looked at himself in the mirror and saw Sheila walking in.

"Have you ever seen a man this fine in your life? Talk to me and don't be a hater."

Sheila has a concerned look on her face.

"David, look at this please." She stepped closer to him holding the box out so he could see inside.

David looked inside.

"Baby, this is not my box."

He took the box from her, walked over to the bed and sat down. Sheila sat next to him. David removed a yellow envelope that was six inches thick with rubber bands wrapped tightly around it. He unwrapped the envelope and saw stacks of hundred-dollar bills.

"Good God almighty." He rubbed his eyebrow.

"Lord have mercy. David, that's a lot of money."

David nods his head and removed a brown sandwich bag that he opened and removed six plastic bags with a white powder-like substance in them. He stared at Sheila.

"Oh my God David, is that powder stuff what I think it is?"

"I am no expert, but I am sure it is drugs of some kind. I grabbed the wrong box and I know this is the beginning of trouble."

"David, what are you going to do and what do you mean by trouble? This is not your lunch box or the money and drugs that are in it." She put her hand on her heart looking at him with worry.

"Sheila, I think I know who it belongs to or who had it."

"Who David? Who does this box belong to?"

"I believe it belongs to Mr. Greg Johnson the new foreman on my job. Well, it has to be his or someone that he knows."

"David this is a serious situation. What are we going to do?" She looked up. "Lord help us."

"I know this is serious and I am not sure what to do about the money, but I do know what to do about the drugs in the plastic bags." He stood up.

Sheila touched his arm.

"Baby, please don't do anything stupid. We should talk to God about this and call the police." She stood up, stared at him, and put her hand on his shoulder.

"Get real Sheila. You watch too much TV and calling the police, please give me a break. We would be under investigation, the drugs would end up back on the streets, and the money in their pockets. Forget the police but I know how to handle these drugs."

"Baby we need to pray and pray now."

David stepped closer to Sheila.

"We can pray later, I need to handle this problem now." He said raising his voice.

Sheila pointed her finger at his face.

"Let me tell you something, David O'Neil. Do not ever tell me when or when not to pray. I am your wife, not your slave." She said with conviction and anger.

David looked at Sheila with a smirk on his face then smiled.

"Well, I guess you told me. I think you are very sexy when you become emotional and it turns me on. Can a brother get a quickie? You know, five minutes of quick-moving rabbit sex. To release some stress." He started smiling and moved closer to her.

"Get away from me," holding her arms out, "you are impossible David," she said laughing and then became serious. "At a time like this and you are thinking about sex? What are we going to do baby?"

"I already know." He kissed Sheila and took the plastic bags to the bathroom flushing their contents down the toilet and walked back into the bedroom. He put the money back in the lunch box and put the box under the bed.

Sandra and Christine walked downstairs and were standing in front of David and Sheila's bedroom.

"Sandra and I are ready for church." Christine said.
David and Sheila turned to look at the girls. David cannot help but smile.

"You two look very pretty. My two beauty queens and I love you." He walked over, hugged, and kissed them. "We are going to have a very blessed time in church tonight, so let's go." He turned around and looked at Sheila. "Baby you always look good. You are a walking fashion model." He smiled and winked at her.

"Oh, you finally noticed thank you for the compliment and your love dear." She placed her hands on her hips.

"I always notice baby, always." Staring at Sheila he walked over and kissed her lips softly. "Now it's time to go and get our praise on."

They all walked out of the house and got in the Navigator and David drove off.

CHAPTER FIVE
The Church

David and his family attend church in Hanover, Maryland. It is a nice brick building with a seating capacity of six hundred people. Thursday night revival the church is full, and music is playing. David and his family are sitting together close to the front of the church. Mr. Cleo Williams is the Pastor. He is thirty-seven years old, African American, five feet eleven, dark skin complexion, two-hundred twenty-five pounds with a baritone voice. He walked out to the pulpit wearing an off-white and red robe and raised his arms high in the air.

"Praise the Lord Saints, praise the Lord, everybody. I do believe tonight is the night. I know Betty Wright sang the song, but I am talking about a mighty move of God, not a sex thing. Can I get an Amen?"

The church says. "Amen."

"I thank God for blessing us to gather in his name one more time. I believe the Lord will move tonight in a mighty way. He is a friend that is closer than a brother. I feel like praising him, but I have a message for the house tonight. Church, you cannot live the life God has called all of us to live unless you have the word of God on the inside of you. I am not talking about church attendance, Bible reading, telling people about Jesus, and speaking in tongues. By the way, the devil can speak in false tongues."

"Fasting is an important sacrifice but most people are dieting. Eating pork and meat or neglecting to eat it will not get you into heaven either. No, I am talking about being born again by the Holy Spirit of Jesus and walking in the spirit of obedience to his Holy word. This is the only way heaven will be your home, Jesus Christ being your Lord and master, living a Holy life." He looked up. "Yes Lord, have your way." He looked at the people in the church. "Saints, God is going to answer a long-sought-after prayer." He waved his hand.

"David and Sheila O'Neil, will you come to the altar please."

Sheila and David stood, and David looked at his daughters.

"Christine, you and Sandra stay here. We will be back."

They walked to the altar and the Pastor stepped from the pulpit to meet them and stood directly in front of them.

"Praise the Lord David and Sheila."

"Praise the Lord Pastor." They said while nodding their heads.

Pastor Williams placed his hands on David and Sheila's shoulders.

"David, you and Sheila have been praying for years for a son. Well, your prayers have been answered and a lot more." He stared at Sheila. "Sheila, you are three weeks pregnant with a boy. A miracle birth because physically you could not have any more children, according to the doctors. This child is special. Before God formed him in your belly, he knew him before he came out of your womb, God has already sanctified him to be a mighty evangelist. God will give him spiritual gifts to prove the unlimited power of God and defeat the works of Satan. But beware, the devil himself will try to destroy this child and his end is not known. But you and David keep the faith and hold on no matter what happens."

The entire church stood and began clapping their hands and praising God. Because the people in the church are praising God from the depths of their hearts and soul God reveals his power by showing up as a thin light colored cloud at the ceiling of the church. It was impossible for anyone not to feel the awesome peace and glory of God. Everyone in the church looked up and stared at the cloud. The Pastor fell to his knees praising God and Sheila and David did the same. Now, every knee in the church is bowed down thanking and praising God for what he has done and was about to do.

CHAPTER SIX

The Belly of the Drug Beast

Victor has one thing on his mind this morning, getting his drug shipment out. He was sitting at his desk in his office in a large warehouse in Bogotá Columbia which happens to be the main location for the production and distribution of his daily death, cocaine. This was Victor's big multi-million-dollar empire. He is wearing ostrich skin shoes, slacks, and a shirt with a gun in his shoulder holster. Two of his bodyguards are dressed just as nice and are standing on both sides of his desk carrying guns in their shoulder holsters. Many men are working in the warehouse loading pallets with stacks of tightly wrapped Cocaine. A workman is standing in front of his desk.

"I don't care what it takes or how much work, I want this shipment ready. Use three shifts if you must but this shipment will be ready. This is worth one hundred million dollars cash on delivery and I will kill anyone who gets in my way, their mother and their entire family." He pointed at the man in front of him. "You are my shop foreman, make this happen. Do I make myself clear?" He said staring at the guy with eyes of death.

"Yes Sir Boss, it will be ready, no problems," he is nodding his head as he walks out of the office. Once he was in the warehouse he looked up. "This man is crazy, no mistakes. He ain't killing my family and I love my mother." He continued to walk away.

Another workman walks into Victor's office removing his mask that protects him from the drug fumes and stands in front of his desk. Victor looked at his men and then at the man standing in front of him.

"What is it and this better be important and quick. You are messing with my money fool."

The workman quickly began sweating and stuttering when he spoke.

"Mr. Augular, I jjjjust, received a very urgent phone call. I must g-g-go back to the States to take care ooof some vvvvery important personal business."

"Look at this stuttering fool. You are wasting my time and risking your family's life. I have a large shipment that must go out and I need everyone working until it is complete. You can leave when it is finished, stupid stuttering idiot."

The workman was incredibly nervous and was sweating so badly he could feel the sweat dripping down his leg and back. He swallowed hard before speaking again.

"You don't understand, Mr. Augular. My wife iiiis about to have our ffffirst baby. I must ggggo now, sir."

Victor laughed, and then his entire demeanor changed into anger.

"You are one foolish stuttering idiot. I don't care about your wife or your new baby fool but go ahead. This must be your lucky day. If you must go, then so be it."

The workman was so scared he thought he would piss on himself and nodded his head repeatedly.

"Thank you Mr. Augular, thank you vvvvery much sir." He turned and began to walk away.

Victor shook his head and pulled out his 357 Magnum. He walked in front of his desk and aimed the gun at the workman.

"There is one more thing fool."

The workman turned around.

"Yes sir boss."

Victor shot the workman in the chest and head then looked at his bodyguards.

"He said he had to go, so I sent him on his way." He put his gun back in its holster. "Now get this garbage out of my office."

Three of Victor's warehouse guards came into the office quickly with automatic weapons drawn. They looked at the man on the floor, then at Victor. Victor pointed to the guards who came in.

"Get this dead body out of my office, now. Then find out where his fat pregnant wife is and kill her and his family."

They put their guns away and dragged the body out of the office. Victor's office phone rang, and he walked over to his desk, sat down, and picked up the phone.

"Hello, yes send him in." He put the phone down and pulled his gun out but kept his hand under his desk.

Mr. Bones walked into the office wearing all black and carrying his black cane.

"Mr. Augular, you can take the gun from under the desk and put it back in its holster."

"Mr. Bones, you continue to amaze me," he put the gun in its holster. "I called you for some information and direction."

Mr. Bones leaned his head back then looked at Victor.

"Ahhhh yes, you want the bones." He pulled out a black pouch from his pants pocket and held it in his hand. "Ask the question Mr. Augular."

"I'm working on a hundred-million-dollar deal. Will it be a success and on time?"

Mr. Bones shook his black pouch, walked over to the desk, shook the pouch again, and dumped the bones on the desk. He stared at the bones and then looked at Victor. "The bones say, yes and yes."

"Are you sure?" Victor said while rubbing his chin. "This is too important for anything to go wrong and I don't give a damn about killing people in the process. Are you certain?" He stood up and his bodyguards slid their hands towards their holsters.

"Mr. Augular, the bones never lie, and I have never been wrong about anything. So yes, I am very sure."

"No, you have not but there is always a first time." He smiled at Mr. Bones.

"The first time we both know will be the last time, but you should never question the bones, Victor." He backed up and mumbled some words tapped his cane on the floor twice while looking down then looked directly at Victor. "Victor, open your desk drawer."

Victor opened his desk drawer and saw a black snake that started sliding out. He jumped back quickly and kicked the desk drawer shut smashing the snake. His bodyguards pulled their guns out and aimed them at Mr. Bones.

"You made a mistake." Victor pulled out his 357 Magnums and aimed them at Mr. Bones. "I will see you in hell." He unloaded the guns on Mr. Bones and his bodyguards did the same.

All the bullets hit Mr. Bone's dead center in his chest ripping through his flesh like paper. He fell still holding his cane and blood was pouring from his wounds. Victor and his men looked down at Mr. Bones and smiled. Seconds later blood stopped flowing from Mr. Bones' wounds and they began closing. His eyes opened, he mumbled some words and the end of his cane tapped itself on the floor twice. The bones he put on the desk began to shake and they floated off the desk over to Mr. Bones, landing in his hand, his body stood straight up.

"The bones, you can't beat the bones." He said yelling pointing his finger at Victor.

Victor's bodyguards stepped back with their mouths open in total amazement but aimed their guns at Mr. Bones. Victor stepped back as well but still held his guns. He can feel his heart rate increasing and feels fear, but he hides this well.

"Well, I'll be damned. There is no way you could have survived all those bullets. We shot you over thirty times in your chest, big holes and all that blood, no damn way. How in the hell did you do that?"

"Victor, you will be damned and in hell, if you ever go against the bones," he said with a very deep voice and his eyes turn blood red. He stepped closer to the desk. "When will you fools learn? I run the whole earth, I am hell. Tell your men to put their guns away before they piss me off and I kill their whole stinking sinning family today. Now, is there anything else Mr. Augular?"

The bodyguards put their guns away and stepped back.

Victor looked at Mr. Bones and put his guns on top of his desk as he sat down.

"Yes, there is. Tell me about my future."

Mr. Bones walked over to the desk and put the bones back in the black pouch, he shook it mumbled some words threw the bones on the desk, and then stared at them.

"Ahhhh." He screamed with his eyes opening very wide and he stepped back. "Never have I felt or seen such a powerful spirit."

Victor's bodyguards stepped back, and Victor stood up quickly and looked at Mr. Bones.

"What is it? What did you feel and see? Tell me." He said with a trembling voice.

"Remember you asked. There is one that will be born soon, and he will be given great powers. He will be a serious threat to you but fear not, because you have me on your side and no one can beat the bones." He walked over to the desk and grabbed his pouch and bones and threw his bones down on the ground. A cloud of black smoke appeared, and then he and the smoke disappeared.

Victor wiped his forehead.

"What have I gotten myself into?" He sat down. "Who did I make a deal with? This man has got to be the devil incarnate to do all that he does." He slid down in his chair and stared out into space. Victor stood up with a look of confidence on his face and looked at his men. "The hell with Mr. Bones and his threats, we will find a way to defeat him when the time is right, but in the meantime, let's make this damn money." Victor smacked his fist with his hand. "Damn, I feel like killing someone." He walked out of his office and into the warehouse with his men following closely behind him.

CHAPTER SEVEN

Grandma Harris and Diana

Grandma Harris lives in a small three-bedroom brick house in Largo, Maryland. She is sixty-three years old and has been serving God since she was twenty-three and she is known as a prayer warrior. Everyone in the church calls her Grandma Harris out of respect for her strong walk with the Lord and not her age. She is wearing a long paisley print dress and sat in her living room on the sofa watching TV with her two-and-a-half-year-old granddaughter Diana Brown, who was next to her on the sofa sleeping. She is singing the song "Jesus Can Work It Out." She stopped singing and waved her hand in the air.

"Talk to me Lord." She got on her knees beside the sofa and began to pray, then sat back on the sofa and looked at her granddaughter.

"Baby Diana, let me tell you what my Lord just revealed to me. You are a chosen child, a prayer warrior, and a protector. You must remain clean and pure and stay away from no good men with one thing on their mind, sex. Most of them do not know what they are doing anyway, ten minutes if that long, and it is over. All that jackrabbit fast humping like a dog. That is nothing and then they want you to lie to them later. Asking you, baby was it good? Was I the best?" She leaned her head back and laughed. "What we should say is no, you jumping up and down fool, it was lousy. Now, my husband was a real man, and he knew how to love me. He loved the Lord, but you talk about lovin. Child, that man knew his job. He would talk softly to me, you know, get me in the mood. Then caress me, stroke me, rub me, hold me, and make love to me like it was all about me." She looked up. "Oh, I am sorry Lord, please forgive me." She looked back at Diana. "The Lord said I was going too far and to finish telling you what he said. Anyway, God is bringing someone into this world that's also chosen. He will experience many things, but God will take care of this too. You and his path will cross in a big way." She pointed at Diana. "Now you must be careful about that one. God does have his hands on that child but so will the devil. No matter, the Lord is in control." She stopped talking and began singing again.

CHAPTER EIGHT

Sherry Wilson and Victor

Victor is in his office at his club sitting at his desk doing paperwork. He is wearing custom-made soft leather shoes, a tailored suit worth eight thousand dollars, a Rolex watch worth forty thousand, and a pinky ring valued at over two hundred thousand. Ever since Victor returned from Bogotá, he has been extremely focused and determined to gain wealth and enjoy the fruits of his labor.

It was eleven o'clock and the club was already full because it was Thursday night, lady's night. There was a line of people outside waiting to get in.

His club manager is Miss Sherry Wilson, a Brazilian beauty. She is twenty-four years old with a master's degree in business and she is five feet six and incredibly attractive with a figure that would make any man turn his head in her direction. She has ample breasts, a small waist, just enough hips to get your attention, and a round shapely derriere.

The song is playing, *How Deep Is Your Love* by Keith Sweat. Sherry walked into Victor's office wearing black high heels, an expensive white low-cut blouse revealing her breasts, and a tight black skirt that comes just above her knees. Sherry has a walk that would cause a man to wreck his brand-new Benz, after watching her hips and butt move in perfect harmony.

Victor looked up at her and smiled.

"Miss Wilson, please come in and close the door. The music is loud." He stood up before Sherry could close the door and waved his hand at her. "Wait, leave it open." He removed his suit jacket and put it on the back of his chair and walked over to her and put his hand behind her neck, kissing her lips gently and rubbing her back, butt, and hips. "I like that song, so tell me, how deep is your love?" He smiled at her.

Sherry is very interested in getting to know Victor on a personal level but does not want to cross the line with him concerning business. However, his touch always melts her heart and makes her sexually desire him.

"Victor, if you did not travel so much and were not so busy, you could find out." She kissed him passionately.

"Your lips and skin are so soft, and you smell so good, you make it hard for me to concentrate on business, but business it is. For now my dear," he tapped her on the butt lightly with his hand and kissed her then walked back to his desk and sat on it. "Please close the door and come in, we need to talk."

Sherry stared at Victor with irritation thinking…the nerve of this man, getting me all hot and bothered, and then just walked away. If he wasn't who he is, I would slap the taste out of his mouth. She closed the door and added an extra bounce in her step as she walked over to the sofa and sat down.

She looked at Victor and rolled her eyes at him.

"Fine Victor, would you like to know how the club business is doing?" She said with much attitude in her voice and stared at him with controlled anger.

Victor was laughing on the inside because he knew how irritated Sherry was with him right now, but he could care less.

"Business is my favorite subject, and yes, I would like to know how things are going. Have there been any problems?"

"No problems Victor, everything has been going smoothly. The supplies and employees have been arriving on time, there have been no fights and all inspections have gone well concerning the club and..."

Victor stood from his desk and waved his hand at her to stop talking.

"That's fine Miss Wilson everything sounds good. As always, your work is excellent. Now where were we, oh yes, you mentioned how busy I have been. I am not too busy now." He licked his lips and stared at her.

His office phone rings.

"Damn it." He picked the phone up quickly.

"Hello, can this wait? Where are you? In the club, no problem. Give me five minutes and come to my office." He put the phone down and walked over to Sherry. "I need to take care of this, but it should not take long."

Sherry looked at Victor giving him a fake smile and attitude.

"Promises, promises Victor." She stood and kissed him on the cheek. "Victor, you don't know what you just missed." She grabbed his crotch gently, caressed it, and walked out.

Victor's eyes were fixated on Sherry's butt and hips shaking as she walked out.

"Damn, that woman is sexy. I was about to spread those legs, but true gangsters always stick to the number one rule in business; *A.M.O.A,* always money over ass. Only suckers choose ass over money. The ass may be great, but money will always buy you some ass and anything else you want," he laughed, "if you got enough money, you can have a woman suck a monkey's dick, sorry sluts."

Greg Johnson sat at the bar wearing twelve-hundred-dollar shoes, a four-thousand-dollar tailored Italian suit, and a Rolex watch. He has been patiently waiting to see Victor while looking at the people dancing in the club.

An incredibly attractive, well-dressed lady with a figure that makes men dig in their pockets has been watching Greg all night. She walked towards him making men and women turn their heads in her direction.

"Hi, my name is Rachael. I could not help but notice you from a distance. Your strong handsome facial features, impeccable attire, and well-toned body. What's your name handsome and are you waiting for some woman in particular?"

Greg noticed her long ago. Very sexy but looks like a vulture waiting to strike for its next available meal. A certified gold digger he has no use for. He looked at her with a disdained look on his face.

"My name is Greg, and I am here on business." He spoke with a serious attitude.

"Well, maybe I can entertain you while you are waiting." She was thinking…another sucker I am about to drain, men are so gullible for a woman with a pretty face and a hot body.

"Thank you, but I am not interested in you. So, go find you a sucker somewhere else." He stepped within inches of her face and stared into her eyes. "Don't say another word to me or I will put a bullet in your brain." He pulled his coat back revealing his gun tucked in the waist of his pants and then walked away. Rachael watched Greg walk away and realized she had never been so afraid of anyone in her life. She walked over to the bar and asked for a strong drink.

Sherry walked through the club and saw Greg walking toward her. She was always uncomfortable around him because she felt nothing but evil from this man.

"Hi Greg, Victor is all yours but don't take too long because we have some unfinished business." She smiled but hated to be next to him.

"Hi Sherry, it is good to see you again, and as always you look nice. My business with Mr. Augular will be brief and he will be all yours."

"Okay, no problem, and thank you very much." She was happy to walk away from him.

Greg watched her walk away and spoke to himself. "She is pretty and got hips and a nice ass, but she talks too damn much, stupid female." He continued walking towards Victor's office and rang the buzzer at the door.

Victor was sitting at his desk when he heard the buzzer. He checked the monitor on his office wall hidden behind a painting. He can see every angle of his club from his monitors which only his bodyguards are aware of. He takes his security very seriously and desires to know what and who is around him at all times. He pushed the button underneath his desk to let Greg in.

Greg walked over to Victor's desk, extending his hand to him.

"Mr. Augular, how are you sir? I know you are busy so I will be brief." He stood in front of Victor's desk looking at possibly the only man that he has respect for, but he does not fear him, Greg fears no man.

Victor shook Greg's hand and stared at him. Greg is the only man he would not want as his enemy, but he would never tell him that.

"Greg it is good to see you, please make yourself comfortable."

He sat in a chair in front of Victor's desk. When dealing with Victor he was always on guard because he was taught long ago, never to slip up.

"Thank you Mr. Augular. We have a problem sir, money and merchandise landed in the wrong person's hands."

This news got Victor's attention quickly because regardless of how much money he makes, he wants more.

"Okay, how much money and merchandise?"

"Two-hundred thousand in cash and five-hundred thousand dollars of product is missing."

This amount of money is nothing for Victor, but his spirit is greedy, and he will not lose one dollar.

"Okay, so you owe me seven hundred thousand dollars. Now, what happened?"

"No problem. One of the workers in your construction company grabbed my lunch box by mistake as he was leaving. I notice one day we have the same lunch box. His name is David O'Neil, a very outspoken Christian man. He has been with your company for years, a great worker. How do you want me to handle him sir?" Greg hopes Victor tells him to kill David and his whole family because he hates Christians.

Briefly, Victor feels bad for what he is about to tell Greg because he likes David, but no one gave a damn about him and what he went through in life. Losing his parents made his heart ice cold. His mindset is, to show no mercy and care for no one. Money and fear are all he needs in life and the rest of the world can go to hell.

"Kill him, but if he has not gone to the police, spare his family. Do this quickly, quietly, and with no witnesses. Is there anything else I need to know about?"

Greg was looking forward to killing David and is hoping he can kill his entire family.

"No sir, that's it and I will handle David's demise personally. I will leave you to your business." He stood up and walked over to Victor extending his hand.

Victor stood and shook Greg's hand and looked into his eyes feeling the joy from his spirit knowing he would get pleasure from killing David. This allows Victor to see Greg is just as evil as Mr. Bones. He wondered why Greg was part of the deal that he had to accept from Mr. Bones, years ago. He had to have Greg as part of his team no matter what, but to this day he never understood why. Maybe one day he will find out.

"I thank you for coming by and keeping me informed of this situation. Remember Greg, no trails."

"No problem sir." Greg walks out of the office and runs into Sherry again.

"He is all yours Miss Wilson. Enjoy the rest of your day." As Greg walked away, he looked back at Sherry and thought…*Stupid female, I would put dick in her and then kill her.* He continued to walk out of the club.

Sherry watched Greg walk away and realized more and more just how much she feared and disliked being around him. She walked back to Victor's office and walked in.

Victor was sitting on the edge of his desk talking on the phone and then hung up when Sherry walked in.

"Miss Wilson, please just walk into my office." He said sarcastically.

Sherry was not in the mood for any games or distractions at this point. She walked over to Victor and placed her hand on his chest and slowly rubbed it. The fabric of his expensive shirt felt good to her, but she desired to feel his flesh.

"Sir, production and demonstration beat conversation and now it's time," she slowly licked his lips, bit his neck, and whispered in his ear, "I must warn you, I am not a twenty-minute lady, and we could be here all night."

Victor leaned forward and sucked Sherry's neck then stared into her eyes.

"Some things in life are worth taking your time for Miss Wilson."

Sherry walked away from him stood in the middle of his office, and then turned to face him.

"Remember you asked for all of this Victor." She undressed slowly, removed her blouse and skirt letting them fall to the floor. She is standing there in her heels, black bra, and black thong. Sherry's body is very sexy and tight. She walked over to his desk and put one leg on top of it looking directly at him. "Well, what are you waiting for? You asked for this, now come and get it."

Victor stared at her.

"You are gorgeous Sherry." He began removing his shoes, socks, and shirt and stood directly behind her and stared. "Sherry, you are truly breathtaking, and you are right. We will be here all night." He leaned forward to kiss her upper back and slid his tongue down her back to her butt, kissing and sucking on it. Victor placed his hands on her hips and pulled her to him so she can feel how strong his desire is for her by placing his erection against her butt.

Sherry stood up straight pressing her butt into Victor to feel him even more and cannot help but respond to him.

"Victor, you feel so good against me, you know I want you badly so stop teasing me." She turned around, hugged, and kissed him slowly, sliding her tongue into his mouth.

When their tongues touched it set off waves of desire that had been building between them for some time. Their hands caressed each other's bodies, building their sexual desire for one another. Victor picked her up and carried her to the sofa, gently laying her on it. He removed his pants and T-shirt. He is wearing black silk boxers with his erection staring her in the face.

Sherry leaned forward and grabbed his penis gently through his boxers feeling how hard and thick it is and was getting ready to put her mouth on it to show Victor her great oral skills, but he backed away from her.

"Sweetie, tonight it is all about me pleasing you, so relax, I got you."

Victor got on his knees and began kissing Sherry's soft lips again moving down to her bra which he quickly but gently removed. The moment Sherry felt his warm mouth and tongue on her breast and nipples she almost climaxed on the spot. Victor kissed and licked down to her stomach, placing his hands underneath her butt and pulling her forward so he can have total access to her the way he desires. He slid her panties off with his teeth and placed the palm of his hands on both of her knees, pushing them slowly apart as he lowered his head between her legs and licked from her inner thigh to her wetness.

Sherry was trembling at Victor's very touch but when she felt his tongue hit her spot, she gripped the sofa with her fingers, pushing her body into his face.

"Oh Victor, baby please don't stop. You are driving me crazy, make me cum Victor."

That is all Victor has been waiting for. He buried his head between her legs and slid his tongue inside her, tasting her juices and kissing and sucking on her with great passion and skill.

Sherry could no longer contain herself and she exploded in his mouth.

"Victor, ohhhhhh I am cumming baby, don't stop, please don't stop. I am cummming, ohhhhh Victor, Ahhhhhh Victorrrrr."

As she climaxed, his hands are on her legs and he gripped her clit with his tongue sucking on it, making her shake wildly as she climaxed in his mouth, and he tastes and sucks every drop. Before she could even recover from her orgasm Victor removed his boxers quickly and slid his hard dick inside her.

Sherry jumped the moment she felt Victor inside her because this was a dream come true for her. His size was exactly right and so hard just the way any woman wants a man. She wrapped her legs around his waist quickly to pull him into her deeper and her head fell back as she was in the throes of passion.

"Ohhh Victor, you feel so good inside me. Fuck me baby, I want it harder."

Victor removed Sherry's legs from around his waist grabbed her ankles and lifted her legs high in the air, pushing them back a little so he could give her what she so desired. Holding her legs in the air he began pumping in and out of her, slowly at first to get her used to it, then faster and deeper making her wetter. She felt so tight and hot inside.

Sherry was in total sexual bliss because no man had ever pleased her like Victor was doing now and she felt another orgasm building quickly.

"That's it baby, harder just like that, I am so close Victor, ram that dick in me." She screamed. "Victor, ohhhhhh it feels so damn good, fuck meeeeee, I am cumming so hard again baby, ohhhhhh Victor fuck me, I am cumming, ahhhhhh Victor."

Sherry was so hot and tight he could no longer hold it. Victor was ready to explode inside her, gripping her ankles even tighter, pulling her into him more. You could hear their bodies slapping together with every thrust.

"Sherry, I can't hold it baby, you are making me cum, ahhhhh, Sherry you are so wet and tight, ahhhhhhh. Damn Sherryyyyyy this pussy is so good."

Sherry throws her body into him hard with great desire and passion.

They soon relax and cuddle together. Sherry has never felt this way about any man, and she cannot help but speak her feelings.

"That was beautiful Victor and truly beyond words. You were incredible, emotionally, and physically. I love you Victor," she instantly started thinking...*I may regret saying those words. I do not want to be just another piece of ass for this man, but it came from my heart.*

Victor was not expecting to hear those words from her, and it touched his heart. He turned to face her, looking into her eyes, and saw something that he had not seen since his mom was alive. He saw real love and it scared him. He knew this woman loved him for him, not his money or his power, but for him. This brought tears to his heart that she would never see. He stared into her eyes and leaned forward kissing her lips softly.

"This is new for me, and my words are not just words, but I love you back Sherry, and I will always protect you no matter what. I got you." He pulled her closer and they lay together holding one another until falling asleep.

CHAPTER NINE

Greg's Deception

David was at work walking around the construction site making his inspection checks. There was a slight breeze this morning, so he is wearing a light jacket. He pulled his cell phone out but saw Greg walking toward him, so he put it away.

"Greg, this is a wonderful day the Lord has made. Is there anything you need? My call can wait."

Greg stares at David with a great dislike because he is so happy all the time but that is about to change real soon.

"Not now David, but we have a lot of work to do today. So, don't spend too much time on the phone." He walked away thinking…*it will not be long now Holy man.*

David called Sheila but while he was on the phone, he saw Greg watching him from a distance.

Sheila is home by herself and is close to delivery time. She was sitting on the sofa reading her Bible when the phone rang.

"Hello David."

"Praise the Lord miracle lady."

Sheila's entire face lit up when she heard David's voice.

"David, hi baby, and praise the Lord because God deserves all the praise. He is the miracle maker, and we are just the vessels God uses to show his mighty hand."

"Spoken like a true child of the Lord Sheila. So how are you and my son?"

"Both of us are doing fine but just in case you forgot David, I did have something to do with making this baby. So, it is not just your son but *our* son, Mr. O'Neil."

"Okay, you did have a little something to do with it. Girl, you got some sweet loving, and you know how to throw that ass back good. Can I hit it slow when I get home? Because you need my good, deep dick loving." He knew this would set her off which made him laugh.

"David, you should be ashamed of yourself, and I have asked you not to talk to me like that. And no, you cannot hit it slow or otherwise because it is too close to delivery time. You know this but you want to talk dirty to me." She is smiling because deep down inside she likes it.

"Okay, Sheila, but can I get some throat action, head wobble? Do not be selfish with the loving baby. I want hands, fingertips, and lips. Wobble, wobble." He started laughing, visualizing the expression on Sheila's face.

"David, we need to talk. Your mouth has gotten disgusting, but I might show you I still got it if you are sweet to me."

"I am always sweet to you, and you are something else. Sheila, I am concerned about you being home by yourself when it is so close to your delivery time."

"Don't worry about me David. I am fine and the girls will be home from school soon, but I will call Grandma Harris and ask her to come over."

"That is a good idea, along with you getting some rest and kissing the girls for me and tell Grandma Harris, praise the Lord. Well, I have to go because the evil foreman is watching me, so have a blessed day."

"Same to you David and be nice to your foreman."

"I will Sheila. Oh, by the way, since I can't hit it when I get home, can I get a taste of your tongue and mouth? And stop faking you know you want to get your freak on." He was laughing knowing she would playfully slap him right now if she could.

"David, you are a very nasty man. I love you. Goodbye David." She hung up the phone. "I can't believe this man sometimes, but he did speak the truth and I miss his mouth. He has skills that make me want to pay the bills. I need a quick orgasm right about now, release some pregnancy stress."

David put the phone away and smiled knowing he made his wife smile, but he noticed Greg was still watching him and he began to walk away but Greg waved at him to come over.

"Greg, what can I do for you?"

"I need to show you this area inside a building that could be a problem if it is not handled properly."

They walked to a secluded part of the site and entered a dark room that was used for storage. Greg walked in first to the far corner of the room and bent down looking at a very deep hole in the ground.

"David, come over here so I can show you this hole that was dug too deep."

He walked over to Greg and bent down next to him.

"What do you want to do about this and…?

Before David could finish his sentence, a man walked up behind him and hit him in the head with a board. David

fell to the ground unconscious. Greg smiled and stood up and looked at the man who hit David.

"Perfect timing Wallace. The only thing that would have made it better was if I could have hit him myself."

"Greg, why do you hate this man so much?"

"He is too happy all the damn time and is always talking about Jesus Christ is God manifests in the flesh and the Holy Ghost. Well, if he does not have my money and merchandise, I am going to find out how much he loves Jesus. Put the handcuffs on him and shoot him up so we can get out of here."

Wallace walked over to David and put his hands behind his back and put handcuffs on him. He removed a small case from his pocket, opened it, and removed a needle. He slid David's jacket sleeve up stuck the needle in his arm and looked over at Greg.

"How long will this stuff keep him out?"

"I was told this would keep him under for several hours but I am no doctor so stop asking me questions and hurry the hell up so we can go."

Wallace was thinking…*Greg is one evil man*. He put the needle back in the case and put the case in his pocket. "I am finished, so we can go."

"Good, it took you long enough." They walked out but Greg knew when this was over, he was going to put a bullet in Wallace's head, dumb fool, no witnesses.

CHAPTER TEN

The Appearance of Mr. Bones

Grandma Harris, Christine, baby Diana, Sandra, and Sheila are at Sheila's. Baby Diana is sitting on the sofa and the rest are on their knees next to the sofa praying, with Grandma Harris leading the prayer.

"Lord, we thank you for this day and to gather in your name. Lord, forgive us this day for all our sins and we bind every spirit contrary to the resurrection spirit of Jesus Christ God manifests in the flesh. We cast it away right now."

Sheila smiled because she always enjoyed Grandma Harris's prayers.

"In the name of Jesus, that name that God has highly exalted and given him a name which is above every name, that at the name of Jesus, every knee should bow of things in heaven and things in earth and things under the earth and that every tongue shall confess that Jesus Christ is Lord. Christine, you pray."

"Yes Mom. Oh Lord, your Holy word says, if thou shall confess with thy mouth the Lord Jesus and believe in thy heart that God has raised him from the dead thou shall be saved. Thank you Lord. Sandra, it's your turn."

"Father, your Holy word says, for with the heart man believeth unto righteousness and with the mouth, confession is made unto salvation. Lord let thy will be done."

Sheila is so proud of her girls.

"Lord, we thank you for your miracle baby, my son…" she suddenly grabbed her stomach and cried out, "Ohhh my stomach, oh God it hurts, it feels like my stomach is on fire, help me Lord."

Christine touched her mom.

"Mom it will be alright."

Sandra touched her mom as well.

"Lord, help my mother."

"That is right children pray because I feel an evil spirit, but it is just the devil, and he is a liar. I rebuke you devil." Grandma Harris said waving her hand in the air.

A cloud of smoke appeared behind them suddenly and they stood up and turned around and saw Mr. Bones standing there dressed in all black holding his black pouch and pointing his cane at them.

"It will do you ugly people no good to pray. I come for the pregnant one and I will get Grandma and you ugly crumb snatchers later." He said with a voice that seemed to echo throughout the house.

Sandra stepped forward.

"Who are you?"

Christine pointed her finger at him.

"He is the spirit of the antichrist."

"Shut up child," he yelled. "And don't point at me. You are a rude ugly crumb snatcher." He pointed his cane at her. "My name is Mr. Bones."

"I rebuke you devil, now get out of my house." Sandra pointed her finger at him.

"Be quiet," he yelled. "Stop pointing at me, you ugly monkey child." He mumbled some words. "Tonight, the child will die." He pointed his cane at Sheila's stomach.

Sheila grabbed her stomach.

"Oh Lord, the pain, it hurts." She was holding her stomach dropped to her knees and looked up. "Submit yourself therefore to God, resist the devil and he will flee from you, in Jesus name, I rebuke you Satan."

Mr. Bones stopped pointing his cane at Sheila and screamed.

"Nooo," he dropped to his knees but only for a few seconds and then stood up laughing. "You are no match for me, and your pregnancy has put you in a weakened state." He took his hand off his cane but it stood up by itself. He mumbled some words, shook his pouch, and dropped the bones in his hand. "Now you will know why they call me, Mr. Bones."

Grandma Harris stepped closer to him.

"I am not in a weakened state devil, I am born again in Jesus' name, Holy Ghost filled, and I have been fighting you a long time." She pointed her finger at him. "In the name of Jesus be gone devil."

"Ahhhhh no, not again," he yelled as he pointed his cane at Grandma Harris "Shut up old woman I will be back. I will be back." He tapped his cane on the floor and it sounded like thunder. Smoke appeared around him and he was gone.

Grandma Harris turned around towards Sheila and the girls.

"The Lord doesn't play and neither do I. Sheila, we need to get you to the hospital because it is time for God's miracle to come forth."

Sheila touched her stomach.

"Lord have mercy since the devil appeared like that, I know this child is going to be used by God to do great things."

Christine stepped closer to her mom and touched her hand.

"Mom, what just happened? It was like something you see on TV, but this was real. I felt his evil spirit and I was scared but I felt strong at the same time."

Sandra stepped to her mom and touched her other hand.

"It was something that you see on TV and I was scared too but I knew God would do something."

Grandma Harris walked over to Sheila and put her arm around her waist.

"Be strong baby. The flesh is no match for the devil. We wrestle not against flesh and blood, but against principalities, against powers, against the rulers of darkness in this world, against spiritual wickedness in high places. The only way to defeat the devil is you must be washed in the blood of Jesus, born again." She raised her arms, "Lord, we thank you for this victory."

Christine tugged on her mom's hand.

"Mom call Daddy please, I miss him."

Sheila kissed Christine on the cheek. "Okay baby, I miss him too." She picked up the phone and called David but there was no answer, so she hung up. "David did not

answer and that's not like him, but I will leave a message on his voicemail." She left a message and then sighed heavily because she was concerned about David.

Grandma Harris hugged Sheila.

"Come on Sheila, we need to hurry. That baby is on its way. Christine, you and Sandra help your mother and I will get baby Diana and we can ride in my car." She picked baby Diana up from the sofa and all of them walked out of the house got into Grandma Harris's blue Mercedes GLK 350 and drove off.

CHAPTER ELEVEN

The Unstoppable Prophecy

Christine, Sandra who is carrying baby Diana, Sheila, and Grandma Harris walk through Providence Hospital's emergency entrance in Washington, DC. It is ten miles from Mitchellville MD. Sheila was holding her stomach because she was in great pain and Grandma Harris walked next to Sheila helping her walk in.

Grandma Harris yelled and pointed to the nurses and doctors she saw walking around when they walked in.

"Nurse, doctor, somebody help this woman, she is ready to give birth."

Several nurses rushed over. One has a wheelchair and she helped Sheila sit in but the nurse pushing Sheila was thinking…*some people are so dramatic.* She stopped pushing Sheila and leaned slightly over her.

"What is your name, and do you have a doctor here, Miss?"

Grandma Harris could feel this nurse's bad spirit and nasty attitude, so she spoke to her with a little attitude of her own.

"Her name is Mrs. Sheila O'Neil and yes, she does have a doctor here and a good one, he is good-looking too. His name is Dr. John Hardy." She said staring at the young girl.

This nurse knew this lady was not to be played with, so she changed her tone and attitude quickly.

"Yes, I know Dr. Hardy and he is nice looking. Now let's get Mrs. O'Neil up to the delivery room."

Sheila turned toward Grandma Harris.

"Grandma Harris, please call David. He should have been here by now. I am worried about him. He has always been by my side." Spoken with great worry in her voice and on her face.

"God has blessed you with a good man baby, but God said, *he will never leave you nor forsake you.* So, lean on him and he will see you through." She rubbed Sheila's shoulder to relax her.

The nurse was pushing Sheila toward the delivery room and Sheila grabbed her stomach again.

"Ahhhhhh, Grandma Harris, please call David." She said while looking back at Grandma Harris.

The nurse pushed Sheila into the room and the doors closed.

"Girls, let's go to the waiting area and keep praying for the Lord's miracle."

They walked to the waiting area of the hospital and sat down, and a few other people sat in the area as well. Christine sat on one side of Grandma Harris and Sandra sat on the other. Grandma Harris held baby Diana.

Christine tapped Grandma Harris on the arm.

"Grandma Harris, is mom going to be alright?"

"Yes, baby she will be just fine, don't you worry."

Sandra tapped Grandma Harris on the arm.

"I know mom will be alright because I have been praying and God said he would take care of her, and God

cannot lie." Sandra said as she looked at Christine and Grandma Harris and smiled.

"You are right Sandra. Your mom will be fine, and God cannot lie baby."

Grandma Harris began to pray about David to herself because she felt something was wrong. A dark evil spirit touched her, and she lightly shook and then quietly spoke her thoughts.

"Now I know what it is, or shall I say, who it is. That devil Mr. Bones came into this hospital somewhere, but he is no match for my Lord." She got her cell phone out and called David, but he did not answer. Everything inside her was saying something was very wrong with him. "Lord, where is David?"

CHAPTER TWELVE
The Faith of David

David was in a dark storage room unconscious sitting in a chair with his hands handcuffed behind his back. Greg Johnson and his partner Wallace were standing a few feet in front of David. Greg has a small black leather case attached to his belt. He looked over at Wallace.

"Wake the Holy man up and make it painful."

Wallace looked at Greg and walked over to David and was thinking…this guy is sadistic, but I better do as he says because he might kill me just for something to do. He slapped David's face hard.

"Wake up Holy man." He said as he walked back to Greg.

David woke up and was slightly dizzy. His eyes begin to focus in the dark storage room when he looks up and sees Greg and a stranger. It takes him a few seconds to realize he is handcuffed and how much his wrists are hurting because the cuffs are so tight.

"What is this and why am I handcuffed? What in Jesus name is going on Greg?" David was shaking his arms trying to get loose.

Greg looked at Wallace and smiled and then looked at David.

"You see, even in David's situation of despair and confusion he still calls on God. Well, God cannot help you now Holy man, and playtime is over. Where is my money and merchandise that you stole from me, you fake Christian?"

"I knew there was something evil about you. I felt your demonic spirit and I did not steal anything, but you are talking about the lunch box with the dirty money and the devil's product that was in it."

Greg shook his head.

"Now we are getting somewhere Holy man but allow me to tell you something. I did not like you even before we met. You Christians are fools, always talking about repenting of sins, and being born again in Jesus' name. Your kind is weak and refuses to accept the world as it is. Sex, drugs, and money make the world go around boy, and people like you use God as a crutch for all of your problems."

"Do you know of a better crutch, Mr. Devil?" He said smiling at Greg.

"Teach Holy man some manners and wipe that stupid smile off his face." Greg said looking at Wallace with hate in his eyes.

"It will be my pleasure." He walked over to David and hit him in the stomach, and his ribs, and he hit him so hard in the jaw that he fell out of his chair. He helped David get back in the chair and then walked over to Greg.

David started coughing. His ribs hurt so bad he thought they were broken, and it was hard for him to breathe. His teeth were loose, and his mouth was bleeding. He spat blood out then lifted his head and smiled, refusing to give Greg and his partner satisfaction they were getting the best of him.

"Is that the best you can do devil?" He said smiling.

Greg walked toward David.

"So, you think you are a tough guy? Okay, tough guy. You have two girls, you are married, and your wife is ready to deliver any day now. Have you told anyone about the drugs and merchandise? If so," he pointed to Wallace, "I will have him cut both of your girls' heads clean off. Your wife is very pretty, and she got a fat ass. I will take pleasure in bending her over a chair and hitting that fat ass of hers from the back. I know she got some good, tight, loving. And then I will feed that new baby boy of yours to my pit bulls for a snack. Now, where is my money and merchandise?" He yelled.

David's blood was boiling, he was so angry. Listening to this man degrade and talk about his family like they are nothing. He believed every word of what Greg said he would do to his family, but he must remain strong. David looked directly at Greg.

"I flushed your drugs down the toilet where they belong and put your money away, and I fear no flesh."

Greg stepped back and looked at Wallace.

"You see partner, he is not so Holy after all. This hypocrite is a thief, he stole my money. Enough of this, playtime is over hypocrite." He looked at Wallace again. "Make him bleed."

"I love this part." He smiled pulled out a razor walked over to David and ripped his shirt open. He slides his razor slowly and deeply across his chest.

"Ahhhhh," David screamed. He had never felt such intense physical pain, but he looked directly at Wallace. *"The Lord is my shepherd I shall not want."*

"Cut him again, harder this time." Greg said with frustration.

"This is so good," Wallace said looking at Greg smiling. He cut David across the chest two more times so deeply he felt his razor scrape David's chest bone and then walked over to Greg.

"Ahhhhhh, my chest," David screamed so loud he was shaking. Blood was pouring from his chest and his pain was beyond words and felt like he was about to pass out, but he still refused to give in to them. He looked up. *"Blessed are they which are persecuted for righteousness sake, for theirs is the kingdom of heaven."*

"Wow, this guy is something else." Wallace said staring at David.

"I am sick of this," Greg waved at Wallace, "Step aside and let me find out who David loves." He pulled out a Glock 19 handgun from behind his back and aimed it at David. "I will give you credit for one thing Holy man. You have strong convictions, but so do I, and I am a man of my word. I want you to curse God, denounce him, or you will never see your wife and children again."

David looked up with tears falling from his eyes and then looked at Greg with confidence and conviction.

"Mr. Johnson, I love my wife and children beyond words but not more than God. Jesus said...*whosoever deny me before men, him will I also deny before my Father which is in heaven,*" He looked up, "I will never denounce you Lord, but I pray before I die you allow me to see your prophecy, my son, not as I will but your will."

Greg laughed.

"He did not hear you, Holy Man." He pointed the gun at David. "See you in hell, you thief and hypocrite." He shoots David in the stomach.

David experienced the strangest thing. When the bullet hit him, he felt it but not like he thought he would, and he knew he was going home to be with the Lord. He lowered his head then slowly lifted it back up with tears running down his face and smiled.

"Lord, I did not denounce you, now take me home." David dropped his head and fell to the ground dead.

"I can't believe it. Not even for his wife, daughters, and unborn child. The man was a true warrior. Leave him there and we will bury him in some cement later. Oh, remove the cuffs." Greg said.

Wallace has never seen such commitment from anyone about anything. He is truly shocked. He removed the cuffs and looked at Greg.

"I could not have done that. God would have to forgive me for denouncing him. He had so much to live for." He shook his head.

Even Greg was astonished. He has tortured many people and learned if you put enough of the right pressure on people, they will always give in and do what you ask. David was different and it was at this moment that he had great respect for the man. He would never admit this to anyone. He looked at Wallace.

"The man was a true believer. So many people talk about being real, but few are. He died as he believed. Let's go."

Wallace walked in front of Greg and while he walked, Greg looked at the back of Wallace's head. He snarled, gritted his teeth, and his eyes turned coal black. He was still holding his gun when he raised it and shot Wallace in the back of the head twice, his head exploded. He put his gun away reached down and removed Wallace's wallet. Greg removed a small bottle from the case on his belt. The bottle was full of strong corrosive acid that he poured on Wallace's face, which began to melt the flesh off. Then he poured the acid on all Wallace's fingertips which instantly burned his fingers down to the bone. He then poured the acid on Wallace's teeth and the acid ate all his teeth down to his gum line. Greg put the bottle back in the case dragged Wallace's body over to the deep hole and pushed it in. The hole was three feet wide and fifteen feet deep. Greg grabbed a shovel and put enough dirt in to cover the body. "This hole will be filled with concrete tomorrow. No witness, no identification." He walked out of the room laughing. "Stupid idiot, did he think I was going to let him live? What a fool." He continued to walk away laughing.

CHAPTER THIRTEEN
Back at the Hospital

Sheila was lying on the bed in the delivery room with the nurses by her side when Dr. John Hardy walked in with his white lab coat on. He is Caucasian, thirty-seven years old five-feet-eight, one-hundred and ninety-five pounds. He is a nice-looking, clean-cut man with a nice build, and you can tell he goes to the gym regularly.

"Mrs. O'Neil, I see you and David have been busy." He smiled at Sheila to help her relax.

"Dr. Hardy, it is good to see you again. Now stop trying to flirt with me and help me deliver my son." She said and laughed.

"You don't need my help. After your two girls, you should be a pro at this." He stepped closer and held her hand.

"You are right," she said smiling at the doctor then grabbed her stomach, "ahhhhhh my stomach, oh my God this hurts. It is more than labor pains, it feels like my stomach is on fire. Dr. Hardy, help me," she said with fear written all over her face.

One of the nurses monitoring the equipment noticed a change in Sheila and checked the equipment.

"Dr. Hardy, her blood pressure is rising and so is her temperature."

In the waiting room, the girls are asleep, and Grandma Harris is reading the Bible when her body shakes.

"Oh Lord Jesus, that devil is back again. I feel his evil spirit trying to get Sheila's baby." She looked around and saw a lady in the waiting area who had been reading the Bible since they had been there. The lady looked toward Grandma Harris and smiled.

"Excuse me, but I will watch the children for you if you have to go to the bathroom. I cannot explain it, but the spirit of the Lord revealed to me that you need to go and handle something quickly. And God said to show no fear of the enemy."

"Thank you so much sister. You are such a blessing, and I will not be long." She said smiling at the lady.

"Take your time. This battle is not ours to fight, and I will pray as well."

"Well, praise the Lord and I thank God for his on-time help." She stood and looked at the girls sleeping lightly touched their heads walked toward the lady patted her on the shoulder and walked to the bathroom. She looked around to make sure she was alone.

"Alright, you devil. I know you are in this hospital, so show yourself."

A cloud of smoke appeared in the bathroom and Mr. Bones appeared, dressed in all black holding his cane in one hand and his pouch of bones in the other.

"We meet again old woman. I come for the child, Sheila, and you're old wrinkled dried up looking ass. You know you are an ugly old woman. By the way, you know I killed your husband. All that praying he would do but he got weak and then I busted his weak heart. I gave him a heart attack. He is in hell right now burning. Playtime is over, ugly Grandma."

"You don't scare me devil and you are a liar because *greater is he that's in me than he that's in the world.* For Jesus has overcome the world when he rose from the grave on the third day just like He said he would."

"Shut up about this Jesus. He does not exist, he is dead. We killed him and now it is your turn." He mumbled some words, tapped his cane on the floor twice and the floor began cracking and he threw his bones at her feet. Fire appeared on the floor, and it made a circle around Grandma Harris' feet. He tapped his cane again and the bathroom walls caught on fire.

"Help me Lord." She looked up, "I rebuke you devil, heavenly angels, fight my battle." She raised her hands. "Lord, I thank you for the victory. Now show your mighty hand Father." She waved her hand and the circle of fire around her feet went out and the walls that were on fire went out as well.

"Noooo," Mr. Bones screamed, "what is going on? This does not happen, no one can defeat me, no one?" He pointed his cane at Grandma Harris. "You are no match for me or the bones, you stupid female." He mumbled again and threw his cane on the floor in front of her and it turned into a twenty-foot-long king cobra snake. It rose with its hood spread facing Grandma Harris and ready to strike at any second.

"Oh my Lord Jesus," she cried out while looking at the snake but did not move, she looked up. "I will lift up my eyes unto the hills from whence cometh my help, my help cometh from the Lord which made heaven and earth." She pointed at the snake. "Death and life are in the power of the tongue, in Jesus name, burn snake."

The snake immediately caught on fire and burned up, leaving nothing but ashes on the floor. Mr. Bone's cane reappeared in his hand, and he tapped it on the floor repeatedly cracking the floor even more with every strike.

"No, no, no. Damn you woman, damn you. You ugly old dog, I hate the ground you walk on."

"You are the one who is damned for serving a false God who is the antichrist and is deceiving the world, now be gone devil." She said pointing at him.

"Stop pointing at me, you rude old dog. And shut up. I hate you born-again people. You have been nothing but trouble, but you are no match for the bones," he mumbled more words. "I will get the boy, maybe not tonight but I will get him, damn you old woman." He tapped his cane on the floor, smoke appeared, and then he and the smoke disappeared.

"Thank you Jesus." She started dancing and walked out of the bathroom toward the waiting area. She stopped walking and placed her hand over her heart, "Lord, where is David? Bring him here to his family, protect him father. Thank you Lord."

CHAPTER FOURTEEN

The Construction Site

Back at the construction site, David was lying on the ground on his back when his eyes opened. It is so dark in the room that he can barely see.

"Lord, I thank you, now help me. Give me the strength to see your prophecy come alive. Your word will not return unto you void, it must come to pass." He stood up slowly and touched his stomach where he was shot and saw all the blood. "Father, you did not let me die and I know you do not half bless. Now give me the strength to see my wife and son." He pulled his shirt together and zipped up his jacket, pulled out his cell phone from his jacket, and called home, no answer but he heard Sheila's message on his voice mail. He put the phone back in his pocket. "Lord, help me reach Sheila." He looked up with a smile on his face and walked out of the room in pain with every step he took but was determined to make it.

David walked across the construction site stumbling at times and dizzy but managed to make it to his truck. He sat in his truck for a few minutes thanking God. "When I am weak, you have made me strong, oh Lord. I will make it." He started the truck and smiled then drove away.

CHAPTER FIFTEEN
The Hospital

Back at the hospital, Sheila was delivering her baby. Dr. Hardy has delivered many babies in his career, but that is vastly different. No matter how hard Sheila pushed, the baby would not come out and he did not understand it.

"Push Sheila, push, it is almost out, don't give up."

"Ohhhhhh, this hurt, and I am tired of pushing. Where is David? Where is David?" Sheila continued to push and go through the delivery procedure and then the baby finally came out.

Dr. Hardy is holding the baby, but it is not moving.

"Sheila, it's a boy." He looked at the baby and then at the nurses.

Sheila knew something was wrong, she looked at Dr. Hardy.

"What is wrong with my baby? Why is he not moving?" Sheila gripped the bed sheets for support trying to lean forward, she yelled. "What is wrong with my baby?"

Dr. Hardy looked at the baby and would never be prepared to say what he was about to say to Sheila or any mother.

"I am so sorry Sheila, but the baby is dead."

"Noooo," she screamed, and tears flooded her eyes, "this is not what God promised me, his word is true, he can't lie." Sheila held her hands out toward the baby. "Give me my baby, give it to me."

Dr. Hardy shook his head but understood her grief.

"Sheila, I am so sorry, but we did all we could. There is nothing else we can do; the baby is dead. I am so sorry."

"No!" She hits the bed with her hand, "I don't accept this, give me my baby, give him to me now. I want my baby now."

Dr. Hardy hands Sheila her baby and shakes his head feeling her deep grief and pain.

"There is nothing you can do Dr. Hardy, but all things are possible with God." She kissed the baby and looked up. "Is anything too hard for the Lord? Father, you said, *if thou can believe, all things are possible to him that believeth.* Jesus, give life to my baby." She laid both hands on her baby. "Now let thy will be done."

About five seconds passed then the baby shook a little and then cried. All the nurses in the room and Dr. Hardy's mouths dropped open in total amazement at what they just witnessed. The nurses began crying and clapping their hands.

Sheila was crying and kissed her baby repeatedly.

"Thank you Jesus! Thank you Lord, thank you. I know your word is true, thank you."

Dr. Hardy stared at Sheila and the baby. He was without words. A baby is born dead then it comes to life, after prayer. What can he possibly say after such an event? He stepped closer to Sheila.

"Sheila, I have seen many things, but this was amazing, a miracle. Truly unbelievable and only God could have done this. Wait until the medical journal reads this story."

Sheila kissed her baby, held her close, and looked at everyone. "This is just the beginning."

David walked toward the emergency entrance of the hospital, adjusting his clothes to look presentable. He looked up.

"Lord, I thank you for my strength." He walked through the hospital doors to the waiting area and saw his girls, Grandma Harris, and Baby Diana. David rubbed his stomach. The girls looked up and saw David, then ran toward him and Sandra got to him first. He bent down to hug them, and Sandra hugged and kissed him on the cheek.

"Daddy, where have you been? Mom is in the delivery room."

Christine hugged and kissed David.

"Hi Daddy, where have you been? Mom needs you.

The girls are so excited to see David their faces are glowing.

"Hi girls," David said holding back his tears because he was so glad to see them. "I miss you more than you know." He hugged and kissed them repeatedly.

Grandma Harris stood a few feet away from David holding baby Diana, giving him time to be with his girls. Carrying the baby, she walked over to him.

"Don't just stand there, come over here and hug my neck and kiss me, I feel left out, kiss baby Diana too. I don't know what to say about you young people."

David stood and laughed then grabbed his stomach and slightly bent over feeling pain, but stood upright, smiled, and stepped toward them.

"Hi Diana, I miss you." He kissed her on the cheek.

"I miss you." She said smiling and laughing.

Grandma Harris put Diana down and David moved closer, hugged, and kissed Grandma Harris on the cheek.

"Praise the Lord Grandma Harris. You don't know how glad I am to see you and I thank you for everything."

Grandma Harris stared at David because she felt something was very wrong with him.

"Praise the Lord David." Moving closer she whispered so the girls could not hear her. "Now where have you been and what is wrong with you? Don't lie because I see your physical pain."

Dr. Hardy walked into the waiting area saw David and walked toward him.

"Mr. O'Neil, I am glad you made it sir," placing his hand on his shoulder. "It is good to see you. Your wife has been calling for you. Congratulations, you have a healthy miracle baby boy, and you don't know half of it."

David shakes the doctor's hand.

"Thank you Dr. Hardy, but what do you mean by, I don't know the half of it? Are Sheila and the baby alright?"

"Oh yes, they are both fine, doing well. Come with me and we will get you dressed to go in, and your wife will tell you all about it." They walked away and through the doors.

David got dressed in a hospital gown and walked with Dr. Hardy. One of the nurses was in the room with Sheila when David and Dr. Hardy walked in.

Sheila was holding the baby when she looked up and saw David walk through the doors.

"Oh David, baby, where have you been?" Sheila could not hold back the tears as they flowed down her cheeks. She looked at the baby and then back at David. "Look at our son, God's miracle child. David, I have so much to tell you about what God did today in this room." She began to cry even harder, but tears of joy.

David's feet seemed frozen to the floor as he stared at Sheila and his baby boy. The emotions he was dealing with now were overwhelming. What does he do? Fall on his knees and begin praising God? Grab his baby and pick him up, kissing him over and over? Kiss Sheila and tell her except for God, she is the love of his life? He calmly walked over to Sheila, bent down on one knee, and kissed her on the forehead and lips. The moment their lips touched his emotions got the best of him and he began to cry, he caressed the side of her face slowly and stared into her eyes.

"Sheila, I know this may sound very odd, especially at a time like this, but you have never looked more beautiful to me than you do right now, with that glow on your face holding our son."

"David, I love you so much. Now come over here and hold your son." She smiled as tears rolled down her face.

He stood and reached for his son, but a sharp intense pain hit his stomach causing him to bend over slightly. He touched his stomach and then placed his hand on the bed to steady himself. His hand was bloody now because his stomach was bleeding again.

"Sheila, praise God Baby," he said staring into his wife's eyes.

Sheila looked at David's bloody hand and then at him. "Oh my God, David, what happened to you?" Her facial expression went from complete joy to instant worry and sorrow.

David smiled at Sheila with tears running down his face.

"Sheila, God has truly blessed us and has answered my prayer to see his miracle child, my son. I thank him for that. Baby, always stand on the word of God no matter what." David leans closer to her, "I love you so much Sheila O'Neil." He lowered his head praying silently...*Lord let me hold my son, please oh God, just let me hold him.* He stood erect and reached for his son slowly with a smile on his face when the pain hit him so hard, he coughed up blood and some of it hit the floor. Suddenly, David's pain goes away, and he feels at peace. He fell to the floor.

"David," Sheila screamed. "Oh God David, Dr. Hardy, help my husband. David, oh God please no, let him be alright."

Dr. Hardy rushed to David, kneeled, and shook his shoulder.

"David." He examined him and saw the gunshot to his stomach. Checked his pulse and then looked at Sheila.

Sheila began shaking her head slowly.

"No, no, please don't tell me. Make him get up doctor, please make him get up. David, oh God Dr. Hardy, do something."

He stood up slowly and looked at Sheila.

"Sheila, David has been shot. I am so sorry but he's dead."

The nurse that's in the room puts her hand up to her mouth.

"Oh Lord no." She said with tears in her eyes.

Sheila goes numb inside instantly at what the doctor said. This was supposed to be one of her and David's happiest days of their lives. Everything hit her and she began kicking her legs against the bed up and down. Sheila screamed with so many emotions and so loud you could feel her pain in your heart and soul.

"Noooo! God no! Not David, not my husband. Oh God, don't let this happen. Not my husband." Tears flowed from her eyes like a river and her heart felt like it was going to explode from such emotional pain. She leaned her head back and screamed. "Nooo!" Sheila passed out still holding her baby and the baby started crying very loudly. Screaming as if he knew something was wrong.

The baby was screaming so loudly you could hear the screams down the hall. For ten seconds, you felt the entire hospital shake like it was an earthquake, but it was not. This action was not caused by anything in the physical realm of things, but by the hand of God. One soul goes on to glory and another begins his mighty journey. If people only knew what was coming!

CHAPTER SIXTEEN

Attorney James Reed

This was one of those beautiful summer mornings, with a light breeze. A day you expect to hear some good news or expect something good to happen. This was not going to be one of those days for Mr. James Walter Reed. He is twenty-seven years old African American, five feet ten, two hundred twenty pounds, and is a very handsome man with a muscular physique. He is an incredibly good defense attorney and a close friend of the O'Neil family. Mr. Reed was standing by his desk in his office in Bethesda, Maryland looking at paperwork when his phone rang, and the receptionist answered it.

"Good morning, Attorney Reed's office, may I help you?" Yes ma'am, Mr. Reed is in, hold on please and I will transfer you to his office." She calls his office, "Mr. Reed, good morning sir, you have a Mrs. Sheila O'Neil online."

He picked up the phone smiling.

"Hello Sheila, it has been a while. How are you, David, and the girls doing?" He stopped smiling and sat down very slowly. All the color seems to drain from his face. "Oh my God, Sheila how did this happen? And the police, they have no clues? Do you know the detective's name who oversaw the investigation? Mr. Rick Matthew yes, I know him, and he is good, very persistent. I will give him a call and do all I can to help. God, I can't believe this. When is the funeral? Yes, of course, I will be there Sheila, and keep the faith and stay strong. Alright and goodbye." As he puts the phone down, tears fall from his eyes, and he slams his hand on his desk. "I can't believe this, David is dead." He called the receptionist. "Will you get Detective Rick Matthew on the phone for me, please? His number is in the file, thank you." He hung up the phone put his hands over his face and cried. James slowly removed his hands, and his expression was one of anger. "Lord, I will not rest until I find out who is responsible for killing David."

CHAPTER SEVENTEEN

The Funeral

There were a lot of people in the cemetery at David's funeral on this bright and sunny day and everyone wore white. Pastor Cleo Williams wore a white and gold robe. Many people were standing around but there were chairs for the immediate family and close friends to sit on. Sheila, her baby, her two daughters, Grandma Harris, baby Diana, James Reed, John Hardy, and Greg Johnson were all sitting together. Grandma Harris sat next to Sheila. David's body was put in a solid Mahogany wood casket with the words, *Never Give Up* etched on top.

Pastor Williams stepped forward to speak.

"I thank everyone for being here on behalf of the O'Neil family and for embracing Mrs. O'Neil's request for everyone to wear white instead of the traditional black. She will speak on this matter later. There are no words that I could say now that would even come close to describing David. The man was walking, talking love. I have personally known him and the family for many years. He showed love to his wife and daughters daily and to anyone whom he encountered. David loved the Lord deeply and his lifestyle revealed this love in all he did. The O'Neil family needs all our love and support now. Again, I thank all of you for coming here today. At this time, Mrs. O'Neil would like to say a few words." He turned toward Sheila and motioned for her to come forward.

Sheila stood and faced everyone.

"Praise the Lord everyone. I give honor to my Lord Jesus who is the head of my life and for giving me and my family the strength to deal with this great and sudden loss. I asked everyone to wear white because it is a very bright color, and the foundation of my husband's belief and faith was all about *brightness*! The Lord said, *I am the light of the world.* Yes, I miss my husband beyond measure, but he is with my Lord now. I thank all of you for your love, your support, for coming, and for wearing white. Except for God, I do not know how my family and I will get through all of this. My husband David was my best friend and I miss him so very much." She sat down and began to cry.

The pastor stepped forward.

"We all need to remember the O'Neil family in our prayers. Right Now, for those who desire to, you can come around and greet the O'Neil family. Again, the family thanks you for coming and being supportive in this time of great need."

People began to form a line and one by one they embraced the O'Neil family. As each person greets Sheila, they hand her a small envelope. Grandma Harris was holding Sheila's baby and Christine and Sandra were holding baby Diana's hand. Greg Johnson approached Sheila.

"Mrs. O'Neil, my name is Greg Johnson. Your husband worked for me, and he was a good man. If you need anything, please don't hesitate to call me." He hands her a small envelope and extends his hand to her.

Sheila stared into Greg's eyes as she shook his hand and felt the cold, hard, evil spirit of this man's heart.

"Thank you Mr. Johnson. I appreciate that and for the company paying all of my husband's funeral expenses."

"No problem. It is the least we could do. Also, you will be receiving David's insurance paperwork from the job and a check soon. Mr. Augular did not want you and the family to suffer any financial woes at a time like this, so he is sending you an extra three hundred thousand dollars now to hold you over until the check arrives."

Sheila stared at Greg and was surprised at the financial gesture from the company.

"Wow, I don't know what to say but thank you for the money. We can sure use it."

"David was a good man." He walked away grinning. Grandma Harris moved closer to Sheila and touched her on the arm.

"When that man walked by me all I felt was darkness and a very strong evil spirit, evil." She shook her head.

Sheila leaned into Grandma Harris.

"I felt it and he is the man David spoke about who was so mean and he may have had something to do with his death."

Pastor Williams approached Sheila.

"Sheila, I have to go but if you need anything please call me, and you know I mean that. I will keep you and your family in my prayers."

Sheila stepped closer to the pastor and hugged him. "Pastor Williams, I know your heart is true and I thank you for everything and I will see you in church."

The pastor walked away. Christine, Sandra, and baby Diana walked up to Sheila who was standing close to the casket now staring at it. Tears began to fall from her eyes. She touched the casket with the palm of her hand.

"I will always miss you my husband, but you are in a better place now." She stepped away and nodded her head at the burial personnel standing by to let them know that they could lower the casket into the ground now.

Christine catches up with Sheila and touches her on the arm.

"Mom, who gave you the name for my brother?" Sheila looked at her daughter and the baby.

"God did. His name is Ronald Emmanuel O'Neil." Sandra walked up to her mom carrying all the envelopes that were given to her for Sheila.

"Mom, there are a lot of envelopes here and there is money in them, I can see it."

Sheila looked at her daughter and smiled.

"Sandra, you hold on to them and I thank God for the money, we will need it."

James walked toward Sheila and hugged her.

"Sheila, there are no words I can say. I am still in shock at all of this. I can't believe it."

"Oh James, I miss him so much." She started crying and hugged him.

"I know you do Sheila so do I. He was a good man and a good friend to me. We need to talk so I will walk you to the car."

"It is time to go." Sheila said looking around. They all began to walk toward the car with Sheila and James walking very closely together and behind everyone else.

"Sheila, I talked with Detective Rick Matthew and there are no solid clues at this point as to who shot David or where he was shot but he was shot with a thirty-eight-caliber. Also, I know this may not be the greatest time to mention this, but I took the liberty to investigate David's work insurance policy and it is very substantial. He has a two-million-dollar policy. It will take a little time for the insurance company to pay but it will be done I can assure you of this. I will follow up to make sure they do. This is the least I can do for now."

Sheila embraced his arm as they walked.

"I did not know this. Greg Johnson told me Mr. Victor Augular is sending me an extra three hundred thousand dollars until the insurance check arrives."

"Wow, that's a nice gesture," he rubbed his chin, "interesting."

"James, thank you so much for everything you are doing for me. I do not understand any of this. One day I have my husband and the next day he is gone. Lord, give me strength." Sheila lowered her head trying to keep her emotions in check.

"I promise you we will find out who was responsible for his death and the information you gave the police about the lunch box with drugs and money in it is a big help." He stopped talking because he noticed a man dressed in all black standing far off pointing at Sheila.

Mr. Bones stood there pointing his black cane at Sheila and shaking his pouch of bones. They stopped walking and Sheila looked at Mr. Bones, then waved at Grandma Harris who was looking at Mr. Bones as well.

"Sheila, who is this weird-looking fool standing over there pointing his cane at you and looking like he is crazy? Is he a problem?" James is a suit-and-tie man because of his job but he comes from the streets, and he will not back down from anyone.

Sheila looked at James.

"James, you would not believe it if I told you. I can talk to you about him later but know he is the devil and is already defeated."

James looked back where Mr. Bones stood but he was gone.

"He is gone. Where did he go so fast? I was just looking at the man. Is he Houdini?"

Sheila shook her head.

"No, he is not Houdini. But he is a manifestation of the devil, walking about seeking whom he may devour then going somewhere else looking for another blind victim to deceive but he has no victory here."

"Spoken like a true warrior for Christ. Sheila, I have to go but I will be in touch, and I will keep you informed."

"Thank you James, for everything." She hugged him and squeezed his hand. James walked away. Sheila, her family, Grandma Harris, and baby Diana all got in the limo, and it drove away.

CHAPTER EIGHTEEN
The Nightclub

Victor was in his office at the club sitting on the sofa wearing two-thousand-dollar custom-made ostrich skin shoes, sixteen-hundred dollar tailored made pants, and a five-hundred-dollar shirt. It is Saturday night, and the club was full. The song, *A House Is Not a Home* by Luther Vandross, was playing. Sherry Wilson buzzed his office door. She is wearing burgundy color heels and a tight ivory color dress that comes to her ankles with a long slit on the side showing her well-toned pretty legs and a low cut in the front revealing much cleavage.

Victor walked to his desk checked his monitor and hit the button on his speaker to let Sherry in and he sat down at his desk.

"Come in Sherry."

She walked in and her every step exuded confidence and class.

"Hi Victor, yes I know you are busy, as always." She rolled her eyes at him. "But there is something I need to mention to you."

"Sherry, I have been looking forward to seeing you again, but it seems like you have been avoiding me." He stared at her thinking about their lovemaking, and it stirred him emotionally and physically. He felt his erection growing and could not wait to hold Sherry in his arms again. "You look very lovely as always." He walked over to her put his hands on her waist and pulled her into him.

Victor kissed her lips, cheek, and began caressing her butt. With one hand on her butt, he moved his other hand to her leg inside of her dress exposing her butt and revealing her thong, and continued kissing her passionately.

Once again Sherry found herself exactly where she desired to be, in Victor's arms. His touch was making her insides scream for more and she felt herself becoming wet. She desires to have him inside her so badly right now, but she must remain focused on her job. She moved her head away from him slowly.

"Victor, you know how much I care about you and desire your touch, but I need to talk with you. Please let me go."

He kissed her and stepped back.

"I appreciate the compliments and the feeling is mutual, but something is bothering you. So, let's sit on the sofa and you can tell me what it is."

They walked to the sofa and sat down.

Sherry exhaled and was glad for the break because she would have let him take her right there on the floor. She turned to look at him.

"Some men dressed in expensive suits came into the club yesterday making me feel very uncomfortable and they asked about you."

Victor's face and demeanor were serious as he looked at Sherry.

"How many men came in and what did they want?"

"Four men came in but only one did the talking. He was an ugly, fat guy in his sixties and he asked if you were in. I said no. He became irritated instantly and stepped

closer to me and said, where is he do not lie. I said I did not know where you were or when you would be back, but I would not have told him anyway. He got in my face with smelly breath, pointed his dirty finger in my face, and said, tell Victor to find his own yard to play in and for you not to make any plans for the future." She touched Victor's arm and caressed his cheek. "Victor, please don't lie to me. Are you in trouble? You know you can trust me, and I will always do whatever to protect you as you would me."

Her words touched his heart and he smiled thinking…*I must have put it on her good.* He kissed her lips.

"I thank you for telling me this and no, I am not in trouble. I know this man and he is a jealous business associate. Oh, I have something for you." He walked to his desk picked up some paperwork and sat back down next to Sherry and handed it to her.

"What is this Victor?" She began to look at the papers.

"You can read all of it later but it's my way of saying thank you. I made you part owner of this club and if anything were to happen to me, the club is all yours, debt-free. And one million dollars for continued working expenses."

She looked at Victor and put her arms around his neck kissing him passionately on the lips, then stared at him.

"Wow, I don't know what to say or how to respond. This is all so much, never would I think you would do this for me." She dropped her head and slowly lifted it looking at Victor with sadness in her eyes. "Victor, I don't want anything to happen to you so please be careful." She glanced at the papers, then looked directly at Victor and began to cry. "Oh Victor, you do care about me." She leaned forward kissed him and put his hand on her leg sliding it up her dress and rubbed his fingers between her legs so he could feel how wet she was. Sherry moved her panties to the side and slid Victor's finger inside her wetness and continued to passionately kiss him.

Victor leaned her back on the sofa and slowly began fingering her, then stopped. He pulled his finger out, licked and sucked it and kissed Sherry passionately on the lips, and then pulled away.

"Sherry, you are an amazing woman and as much as I would like to continue this, I must address the situation that you have brought to my attention, immediately. So, you will have to excuse me." He kissed her walked back to his desk and sat down.

Sherry looked at him with anger and confusion. Thinking… no, this is not happening to me again. I am so ready to put it on this man and he walked away again. He must have lost his damn mind. He sits here and fingers me, getting me hot as hell, and suddenly, he walks away talking about business. And I was just about to show him my supreme oral skills and blow his mind. Whatever! She got up with the paperwork in her hand and walked toward Victor.

"Thank you Victor, for everything, and please be careful." She pointed her finger at him. "You are going to stop teasing me and then walk away. Money is not everything Victor. Why are rich men so damn greedy?" She walked out of the door.

Victor watched her walk away. He wanted Sherry very badly, but his mindset never changed. Business will always come before ass because ass before business makes a man weak and broke. He reached for his phone on the desk.

"Playtime is over Mr. Elizar." He makes a call. "Is the line clear?...Very good...Mr. Case listen very carefully. I have an assignment for you. Mr. Elizar has become a problem and must be dealt with immediately. No witnesses and the details of this matter will be left in the usual place. Once you are there, eliminate everyone, and I mean everyone. You will remove all contents from the safe and be careful concerning the disk...Yes the usual $250,000, excuse me, $375,000. No problem and be careful, he is very well-guarded. Goodbye, Mr. Case." He hung up the phone and smiled. "Goodbye, Mr. Elizar."

Victor walked out of his office and began to look around his club at all the people dancing and having a good time. "No one will take from me what I have built, no one." He was thinking about Sherry and how close he came to having her again. "A.M.O.A, always money over ass. I will be tapping that sweet ass again, real soon," he smiled and continued to look at the people in the club then waved his arms in the air. "My empire!"

CHAPTER NINETEEN

Mr. Elizar's Time

Mr. Case is dressed in a black ninja suit revealing only his evil-looking eyes. He carried a large black bag while walking carefully through the woods which led to the back of Mr. Elizar's house. The house has an eight-foot fence around it and guards were walking around the house carrying automatic weapons, two guards in the front and two in the back.

Mr. Case stopped walking and bent down close to the fence and looked around and then reached into the bag and pulled out a crossbow, laying it on the ground. He pulled out arrows and throwing stars, placing the stars inside his ninja jacket pocket. He pulled out a pair of black gloves and grabbed a gun with a silencer on it and two throwing knives that he inserted into the waistband of his pants. He pulled out a long sword which he slid from its case a little to reveal the shining steel reflecting off the moonlight. He carefully held it in his hands and bowed his head to the flat part of the blade, then slid the sword back into the cover which had a sling on it, and he put the sword on his back. He removed a small black bag from the larger one and opened it pulling out C-4 plastic explosives with timers on them. After examining one of the explosives, he put them in the small bag and wrapped the bag around his waist. Mr. Case put the gun in his waistband and put his gloves on. He set an arrow in his crossbow and looked at the two guards walking in the back of the house.

Each man was at opposite ends of the house when Mr. Case aimed his crossbow through the fence at one of the guards. The arrow hit him in the back of his head and came out through his eye and he fell to the ground with his body shaking. Mr. Case reloaded his crossbow quickly and aimed it at the other guard as he turned around, the arrow hit him in the chest, and he fell to the ground. Mr. Case climbed the fence and ran quickly across the yard and around the side of the house, going to the front where he saw a guard walking carrying an automatic weapon. He pulled out one of his throwing stars and threw it, hitting the guard in his forehead. He was dead before he hit the ground. He walked across the front of the house when he saw the other guard walking carrying his automatic weapon. He walked quietly behind the guard and kicked him in his head. He dropped his gun and fell.

The guard shook his head and looked at Mr. Case.

"Who in the hell are you fool?" He stood up. "I don't know who you are, but you picked the wrong house and the wrong guy." He threw a kick at Mr. Case.

Mr. Case blocked the kick and caught his leg at the same time pulled his sword out and cut the man's leg off. Blood was pouring out and the guard was hopping on one leg.

"Oh my God, my leg, you cut my damn leg off." He screamed.

Mr. Case swung his sword quickly again and cut his head off.

The man's head hit the ground and rolled away but his body was still standing, and blood was squirting up from his neck. Mr. Case kicked the man's body and it fell close to his head.

Mr. Case continued walking silently across the front of the house to the other end and around the back of the house again. He reached a door that led to the kitchen and peeped in and saw a man with his back to him standing next to a table making a sandwich.

The man took a big bite of the sandwich and Mr. Case opened the door quickly and stepped in with his sword in his hand. As the man turned around with his mouth full of food, Mr. Case swung his sword and cut the man from the head down. His body dropped to the floor, in halves.

Mr. Case put his sword up when he heard another man coming and he removed one of his throwing knives. As the man walked through the door at the other end of the kitchen, he threw his knife and hit him in his chest, then threw another one quickly and hit the man in his eye. He fell to the floor and Mr. Case walked over to the body and stepped on it.

While all of this was going on Mr. Elizar was in his master bedroom upstairs with his lady friend Michele, and music was playing. Michele is twenty-four years old, five feet seven, a mixed heritage of African American, Puerto Rican, and Italian. Her face was beyond beautiful, and her body was flawless with curves that would be considered car wreck dangerous. Mr. Elizar was lying on his bed on his back with his feet at the foot of the bed and he was wearing nothing but his boxers. Michele stood at the foot of the bed wearing a robe and high-heeled shoes. Moving slowly and seductively, she smiled at him.

"Do you like what you see Mr. Elizar?"

"Oh yes, from what I can see but I need to see it all before I give you my full report. Now take that robe off and let me see what you are working with."

Licking her lips at him she was thinking…*I am going to rock this old man's world. If it were not for pills like Viagra, his old ass would not last five minutes with me. And if it were not for his money, I would not even be here. Look at him, thinking he is all that. Fat, ugly pig and I felt the little skinny four-inch dick he is working with. What in the hell am I going to do with that? Oh well, for what this fat slob is paying me I am going to fake an orgasm and act like he got a big dick. I hate this fat ugly little dick bastard.*

"It will be my pleasure baby to show you what I have under this robe." She untied her robe letting it fall to the floor. She wore a pink bra and a pink matching thong. Michele turned around giving him a full view of her gorgeous curvaceous body that she kept fit from all the hours spent in the gym.

"Would you like a closer inspection?" She asked while caressing her breasts, small waist, and hips and smiled at him.

Mr. Elizar has been with more women than he can recall but this woman was amazing and when she turned around, he saw the tight round ass she was working with. He knew she was worth the ten thousand dollars a night he would be paying her, plus extra just for that amazing body.

"Truly a woman who knows a man's weakness is the lust of his eyes and a beautiful lady such as yourself get us every time. Now come here, the spirit of Delilah." He grinned at her.

She put one of her fingers in her mouth sucking it slowly while looking directly into his eyes.

"Even Samson and all his strength could not resist what Delilah had." She removed her shoes and climbed on the bed while still sucking on her finger for his pleasure.

While Mr. Elizar was being seduced, Mr. Case walked through the house. He removed his gun and continued to walk when he reached the den and saw three men sitting at a table playing cards. They do not see him until he intentionally exposes himself to them standing only a few feet away from the table. Each man had his gun lying on the table in front of them and when they looked up and saw Mr. Case, they jumped a little in their seat from being startled by his presence but one of them pointed at him.

"What in the world, who in the hell are you supposed to be and how did you get in here?"

Two of the men moved their hands slowly toward their guns. The man who pointed at Mr. Case spit in his direction.

"I don't care who he is, just kill the creepy bastard." He reached for his gun slowly and the other two men grabbed their guns, stood up quickly, and aimed them at Mr. Case.

Mr. Case shot the two men in the head, and they fell to the floor. The other man sat at the table looking at his gun and then at Mr. Case. Mr. Case shot his gun and it slid off the table.

"What the hell do you want fool? Do you have any idea whose house you are in and how much trouble you just got yourself into?"

Mr. Case put his gun away and stood there looking at the man.

The man at the table is six feet three, two-hundred forty pounds of ripped muscle. He smiled and stood up pulling out a KA-BAR knife with a seven-inch blade from behind his back. This knife was issued to people in the special forces of the military. He pointed it at Mr. Case.

"You just made a big mistake ninja man. I didn't spend ten years in the Navy Seals for nothing, time to die boy." He moved toward Mr. Case and swung his knife at him.

Mr. Case stepped out of the way and punched the man twice in the face with incredible hand speed. The guard stumbled back but did not fall.

"Lucky punches ninja man." He spat blood out of his mouth. "Try that again boy, if you…" Before the guard could finish his sentence, Mr. Case punched him again in the mouth and kicked him in the stomach and face. The guard fell to the floor, but he was still holding his knife. He looked up at Mr. Case and spat more blood out of his mouth.

"Okay, so you got a little training, and you are fast, but you are still going to die ninja boy."

Mr. Case moved toward the guard, but he stood up quickly and swung his knife, cutting him on his arm, then punched him in the jaw and kicked him in the face. Mr. Case fell to the floor.

The guard looked down at Mr. Case and smiled.

"I told you, ninja man, ten years of Navy Seals, nothing but the best. Time for you to die." He stepped toward Mr. Case.

A cloud of smoke appeared suddenly in the room and Mr. Bones stood there dressed in all black, with his cane in one hand and holding some small bones in the other.

The guard turned his head in Mr. Bones' direction and pointed his knife at him.

"Who in the hell are you and where did you come from?"

"You have already answered your question." He looked at Mr. Case. "Don't concern yourself. They call me Mr. Bones and we serve the same master. I came on the scene because you needed my help."

With a bewildered look on his face, the guard looked at Mr. Case and Mr. Bones.

"I don't give a damn how you two fools are dressed or who you serve. You bleed just like everybody else. It's bleeding time." He stepped toward Mr. Bones and swung his knife.

"Fool!" Mr. Bones mumbled some words and threw his bones at the man. When the bones hit him, he immediately erupted into flames and started screaming.

Mr. Bones pointed his finger at Mr. Case.

"Get up fool and finish him." He yelled.

Mr. Case shook his head and jumped up quickly and removed his sword and walked over to the man still on fire and cut his head off, then looked at Mr. Bones.

"Don't look at me, finish the damn job." He tapped his cane on the floor and disappeared into a cloud of smoke.

Mr. Case looked at where Mr. Bones was and shook his head in total disbelief and then put his sword back in its cover. He continued walking through the house and up the stairs to Mr. Elizar's bedroom. He reached his bedroom door and listened and then pulled out his gun.

Inside the bedroom, Mr. Elizar laid on his back and Michele was performing oral sex on him. He has received blow jobs from women across the country, but this young girl's head game was superb. He lifted his head to look at Michele with a big smile on his face.

"Damn your mouth feels so good Michele, you can suck a dick. A woman like you can charm a man right out of his clothes and out of his money. That's right, suck all this dick, slob on it. Ahhhh baby, that feels so good."

Michele gave him a fake smile and thought...*I better stop before he cum too quickly. Ain't much to suck no damn way, little boy limp dick.* She stopped sucking and looked at him.

"All for you baby, because a real woman knows when to keep her clothes on and when to take them off." She got off the bed and removed her bra and panties.

Mr. Elizar sat up mouth dropped open as he stared at her.

"Damn, you are fine. Come here and get all of this dick."

Michele had to bite her lip to keep from laughing and speaking her thoughts out loud...What dick? I have seen Vienna sausages bigger than his dick. A Little skinny baby dick you can hardly see because of his big fat ugly stomach.

"Relax baby, the lessons are just beginning." She rubbed between her legs and caressed her breasts.

Mr. Case bursts into the room and points his gun at them.

Michele turned her head quickly toward Mr. Case and screamed. He put his gun away quickly and retrieved a throwing star from inside his suit jacket and threw it, hitting her directly in the mouth. Then with the speed and agility of a cougar, he jumped high in the air toward her, grabbed his sword while still in the air, and cut her head off. It fell on the bed and her body collapsed. Blood squirted everywhere and some of it splattered on Mr. Elizar's body.

Mr. Elizar screamed and backed up on the bed.

"No!" He yelled and jumped off his bed.

Mr. Case moved quickly toward Mr. Elizar and hit him twice with a left and right hook to his face, then kicked him with a spinning hook kick in his neck. He hit the floor and Mr. Case pulled his sword out and aimed it at him.

Mr. Elizar boxed for years back in the day, but he has never been hit so hard in his life like he was just hit. He wiped the blood from his mouth and saw three of his teeth on the floor. He stood up holding his mouth and pointed at Mr. Case.

"Wait!" he yelled, "what do you want and who are you?"

Mr. Case pointed his sword toward the wall and then back to Mr. Elizar.

"What! You broke into my house, and I know my bodyguards are dead or you would not be here. You came into my bedroom and killed my lady, all for some money. Do you have any idea who I am, you stupid idiot?"

Mr. Case cut his ear off and then stepped back.

"Ahhhhhh," he screamed, "my ear, you cut my ear off. Who are you?" He grabbed his head and blood was all over his hand. "I know what you want but whoever is paying you it's not enough. I can double, no triple, whatever you are being paid."

Mr. Case pointed his sword toward the wall again, then back at Mr. Elizar.

"All right, I got it, you can't be bought. Don't swing that damn sword again." He held the side of his head where his ear was, blood came from this wound in clots. He walked over to the wall and pulled a picture away revealing a safe.

Mr. Case put his sword away and pulled out his throwing knife while Mr. Elizar had his back to him.

Mr. Elizar opened his wall safe dripping blood everywhere and saw his gun inside. While his back was to Mr. Case, he reached for his gun slowly.

"I don't know who you are, but you made a mistake." He grabbed his gun and turned around quickly.

Mr. Case has been an assassin for years and knows the mind of his prey. He was prepared for Mr. Elizar to do something stupid. He threw his knife, hitting Mr. Elizar in the neck, then pulled out his gun and shot him several times.

Mr. Elizar grabbed his neck and made gurgling sounds as blood came out of his mouth, he fell to the floor dead.

Mr. Case put his gun away and walked to the wall safe and saw money, the disk, and an envelope. He looked around the room and saw a briefcase. He dumped its contents onto the floor, walked back to the wall safe and put the contents in the briefcase then walked over to the bed and put the briefcase on it. Mr. Case reached for the black bag wrapped around his waist, pulled out the C-4 explosives, set the timer, and left it on the bed, and grabbed the briefcase. He pulled his gun out and walked downstairs. When he reached the kitchen, he put the briefcase on the counter and pulled out another C-4, set the timer, put it on the counter, grabbed the briefcase, and ran out of the house. He climbed the fence and walked through the woods. There was a loud explosion as the house blew up. Mr. Case stopped walking and looked at the inferno, then walked away with the briefcase in his hand.

CHAPTER TWENTY
Victor and the Detectives

A two-toned Grey Mercedes Benz stretch limousine drove up in front of the club early Sunday morning. Victor and his five bodyguards are in the limo wearing tailored Italian suits. Victor and three of his men got out and walked toward the front entrance of the club but before they could walk inside, an unmarked police car drove in front of the Limo quickly.

Victor pulled out two 357 Magnums and aimed them at the car. The driver of the limo got out and pointed his automatic weapon at the car. Another guard stepped out with two handguns and aimed them at the car while the other three guards did the same with their automatic weapons. When the police car stopped, Detective Rick Matthew and his assistant Detective Steve Anderson stepped out of the car quickly with their guns in one hand and their badges in the other pointing them at them.

"Police put your guns down, put them down now." Rick shouted.

"Put them down, put your guns down." Steve shouted.

Victor lowered his guns and then looked at his men.

"Lower your guns gentlemen."

His bodyguards lowered their guns but kept them by their side. Victor looked at the detectives and smiled.

"Detective Rick Matthew and Detective Steve Anderson, it's Batman and Robin in the flesh. You can put your guns down now gentlemen before this situation becomes deadly, real fast."

Victor's bodyguards aimed their guns at the detectives. The two detectives looked at each other then slowly lowered their guns and put them away. All the bodyguards lowered their weapons.

"Mr. Augular, are you preparing to participate in more of your drug business?" Rick asked and stepped closer to Victor.

"Mr. Matthew, you and your partner will never know just how close you came to this day being the last day of your life."

"Save your idle threats for someone you can scare. I know all about you Mr. Augular. You appear to be a successful real estate tycoon, but you are nothing but a drug dealer and I know about your business associates." He looked at Victor's bodyguards and then at Victor. "Your bodyguards are ex-military special forces. They have training in explosives, weapons, communications, and martial arts. All are expert killers. Now, why would a law-abiding businessman need such an elite security force? Are you afraid someone is going to get you?" He laughed.

Victor stepped toward Rick.

"Detective Matthew, I don't have time to play games. I am a businessman, nothing more, nothing less. But even if I were doing something wrong, you could not touch me. I am well covered." Victor turned his head and looked across the street.

Mr. Bones stood there dressed in all black with his cane in one hand and shaking his black pouch in the other.

"As I said, I am well covered." He looked at Rick and smiled.

Rick looked at Mr. Bones and then at Victor.

"Who in the hell is he supposed to be, a witch doctor?" He looked across the street again, but Mr. Bones was gone.

Victor laughed.

"Did you see someone detective?"

Rick stepped closer to Victor and pointed his finger at him.

"Let me get directly to the point. We know you are dirty, and we know what kind of dirt you deal in. It is people like you the devil is using to corrupt the legal system and the world. The sad part is crooked politicians allow it and even help people like you bring this walking death into this country. You are nothing but a dope dealer and we are going to get you. No one is untouchable, no one. Remember that dope dealer."

Victor looked at his men and then took one step back. He pointed his finger at Rick.

"Be careful boy. You have me mixed up with someone else. I am a simple, successful, hardworking businessman and I am offended by your accusations."

Rick moved closer to Victor and pointed his finger in his face.

"You be careful. Your kind makes me sick. Now you and your Armani suit-wearing killers get the hell out of here."

Victor caressed his suit jacket and then looked at Rick and Steve.

"It's a nice suit, is it not? One that you low-budget cops will never be able to afford." He laughed and caressed his suit jacket again.

Rick pointed his finger at Victor.

"You remember this, your day is coming, and you will fall. Now get out of here." He said with anger.

Victor walked past Detective Matthew and intentionally bumped his shoulder into him as he passed by and then looked at his men.

"Gentlemen, let's go for a ride." He and his men got in the limo, and it drove off. Victor was in the back of his limo with three of his bodyguards and the limo phone rang.

"Hello, Mr. Case, I have been waiting to hear from you sir. How was your trip? Very good, I expected nothing but the best from you. I understand your desire to relax but some urgent business has come up in Miami. I am on my way there now and your assistance will be needed. That is not a problem. Yes sir, I will give you a call." He hung up the phone and looked at his bodyguards.

"Detectives Matthew and Anderson may become a problem. If they do, I want them dead, but it must be done right."

One of the bodyguards nodded his head.

"No problem Mr. Augular, no problem at all." He looked at the other men who had a look of death in their eyes.

The limo phone rang again.

"Hello, Miss Walker, it is good to hear from you again. I am on my way out of town, but your suggestion just gave

me an idea. How fast can you pack?" He smiled and then laughed. "Yes, well I figured you could. I am on my way to BWI airport, and my private jet is waiting. Can you meet me there? Business is calling, but afterward, we can spoil each other. Good, and don't be late." He hung up the phone nodding his head. "I will be tapping that ass in Miami." Victor looked at his bodyguards and laughed.

CHAPTER TWENTY ONE

Attorney Reed's Office

It is Monday afternoon. James Reed sat at his desk in his office talking with Detective Rick Matthew. Rick sat in a chair in front of him.

"Detective Matthew, I appreciate you talking with me about this case. David O'Neil was very dear to me and so are his wife and children. I promised myself and his wife that David's killer would be found no matter what. That promise must be kept sir. Hopefully, we can help each other so this case will not go unsolved."

"Mr. Reed, I am a simple guy. Call me Rick."

"No problem and call me James."

"Now that we have gotten that out of the way, I have no problem with us working together on this case because you are considered one of the good guys in my book. A pencil pusher but a good guy all the same."

"I thank you sir. You know we pencil pushers do what we can to make a difference. Now, what else have you found out about the circumstances surrounding David's death?"

"The lab did some testing on the clothes he had on at the time of his death. The dirt on his boots matched the dirt at the construction site where he worked, but that same dirt is found all over Maryland. We talked to the people he worked with but there were no leads."

"What about a motive for killing him? I know about the lunch box full of drugs and money. His wife told me about it."

"Don't get emotional but maybe you didn't know your friend as well as you thought. People fall into hard times and drugs are big business, fast money."

"No way, David loved the Lord, his wife, and family. He would not jeopardize all that to get involved in drugs, no way." He said leaning forward in his chair and raising his voice.

Rick waved his hand at James.

"Wait, hold on. Remember, do not get emotional. I am a detective, and it is my job to look at all angles so relax. Okay, so he brought the wrong lunch box home, and someone killed him for it, and we need to find out who. We do know the construction company David worked for is owned by none other than, Mr. Victor Augular."

"This is becoming more interesting. Mr. Augular is very rich and very well connected in Maryland and many other places. Yes, I have heard the rumors of him being deeply involved in drugs, but nothing has ever been proven. He is well protected by people in high places and his political connections run long and wide."

"Yes, he is rich and politically protected but no one is above the law, not even Victor Augular who I recently ran into. Talk about covered. I did a complete background check on him and his men. Mr. Augular's mother died of cancer and his dad was shot down in the streets by police. That case was investigated but some reports disappeared. This changed Victor's life forever. Fast forward to the here and now, he has a very elite bodyguard team working with him. Ex-military Special Forces trained in weapons, communication, explosives, and martial arts, expert killers who are licensed to carry any weapon they desire."

"Wow, all of that would make anyone very bitter but why would a simple businessman need that type of protection? Sounds like a hit squad and speaking of hit squads. That was some massacre concerning Mr. Elizar and his men. I know the inside information, people were dismembered."

"It was a nightmare and cops threw up at the scene. It was a professional hit, C-4 explosives were used, and Mr. Elizar was a business rival to Mr. Augular. Mr. Elizar has been under investigation for drugs and real estate scams."

James shook his head.

"Mr. Elizar is not a business rival anymore. Professional hit, C-4 explosives, and drugs. It all seems to point to one man, Mr. Victor Augular, and his elite bodyguards."

"I knew you were smart and speaking of Mr. Augular, the department has received a reliable tip about a large shipment of drugs coming into Miami. Mr. Augular was leaving town and heading to Miami in his private jet. We checked his flight plans today."

"And you feel there is a solid connection there, which it could be, but I also know Mr. Augular has businesses in Florida and all over the country."

"True, he does but I know this man is dirty and so does the DEA and FBI which is why my partner and I are going to Miami along with others to see what happens." Rick stood.

James stood and walked around his desk to shake his hand.

"Rick, I thank you again for your time and help. Be careful in Miami. If Mr. Augular is behind this, you know he will be very well covered."

"Yes, he will but we will be ready for Mr. Augular and anybody else. History has proven no matter how big, rich, and politically connected you are, in time they all fall. Al Capone, Pablo Escobar, Rayful Edmond, and John Gotti were all rich and powerful at one time. But in time, every one of them was brought down one way or another and so will Mr. Victor Augular." They shook hands again and he walked out of James' office.

CHAPTER TWENTY TWO
Miami Airport

Four hours nine hundred forty-eight miles later, Mr. Augular's jet landed at Miami International Airport. The weather is warm ninety degrees with a slight breeze. A black stretch Benz limo drove up next to the plane. The driver stepped out and stood beside the car. The jet door opened, and Victor's bodyguards, Stephanie, and Victor walked out. Mr. Charles Redding has been Victor's private pilot for a while and Mr. Robert Jackson is his assistant pilot. Charles approached Victor while his men removed the luggage from the plane and into the limo.

Charles walked closer to Victor.

"Mr. Augular, will you need the plane today?"

"No, but I will later. Charles, you and Robert have your usual accommodations at the hotel. Anything you need, you can get. The hotel concierge will take care of it personally with no problems."

The pilot smiled because this is the part of his job he has always enjoyed while working for Mr. Augular. Whatever he and his assistant want, they can get. Luxury cars, fine women, lavish hotel suites, and the best foods from around the world. But he never forgets working for Victor comes with a huge price. It is his way, all the time, or death.

"Thank you sir, enjoy your stay in Miami."

Victor walked over to Stephanie who wore dark brown heels, tan Prada shorts hugging her hips and butt, and a brown Prada top, unbuttoned just enough to reveal her cleavage. He kissed her on the lips and put his arm around her waist. They walked towards the limo and the driver.

The driver of the limo and Victor's bodyguards were standing next to the limo. The driver is twenty-five years old, five eleven, and one hundred ninety-five pounds. He is dressed in a black chauffeur's uniform.

"Mr. Augular, are you ready to go sir?" He stepped closer to him.

Victor frowned.

"Who are you and where is my regular driver?" He stepped away from Stephanie and unbuttoned his suit jacket.

"The regular driver called in sick. My name is Luther." He extended his hand toward Victor.

Victor looked at the man's hand like it was garbage.

"Luther, I don't know you, so you will not be my driver." He reached into his pants pocket, pulled out a wad of money, peeled off three hundred-dollar bills, and handed them to the driver. "This is for your time. Now go find you something else to do." He pointed to one of his men. "Drive the limo."

The bodyguard stepped toward the limo.

Luther took the money but stepped in front of the bodyguard and extended his arm.

"No sir, I can't allow that because this is my shift, and I am responsible for this car."

Victor's bodyguard pulled his gun out and put it to Luther's stomach. Victor stepped toward Luther, pulled out his 357 magnum, and pointed the barrel at his eyes.

Victor loves the fear in this man's eyes right now because he craves for people to fear him. No mercy. The police did not show any mercy when they shot his dad in the street like a dog. Victor's eyes reveal anger as he leans closer to Luther.

"Relax boy, this limo ain't worth going to hell over."

Luther was so scared his body shook, he dropped the money, and pissed on himself. He remembered what his grandmother told him just yesterday. She said, *baby it is time for a job change for you.* Right now, he agrees.

"No sir, take the car, take it." He said while trembling. Victor pressed his gun into the man's eye.

"That's a wise choice young man." He put his gun away, looked down, and saw the piss by the driver's feet, and smiled because other people's fear satisfied him.

Victor's bodyguards put their guns away and he pointed to one of his guards then pointed to the money on the ground.

"Get my money. That fool does not deserve it." The guard nodded his head and picked the money up. Everyone got in the car and the limo drove away. Luther fell to his knees with his hands together, looking up, praying.

CHAPTER TWENTY THREE
The Police Meeting

At the Miami-Dade County police department, a meeting was taking place in the conference room. Detectives Rick Matthew, Steve Anderson, the head of the narcotics task force, FBI agent, and the chief of police for Miami are present. Everyone sat in front of a long table and the chief of police stood up.

"I thank everyone for being here. Let me get directly to the point. A large drug shipment is coming into my city which must be stopped. This shipment is said to belong to Victor Augular who arrived in town today on his private jet. Detective Matthew and Detective Anderson are part of a multi-jurisdiction national drug task force, and their assistance has been vital, so I welcome them. Gentlemen, this shipment must be confiscated at all costs and all parties involved in prison. Now, I will turn this meeting over to the FBI," he turned toward the agent, "sir, the floor is yours." He sat down.

"I thank you chief and all of you for being here as well. Time is short so I will be brief. The bureau has been keeping a close watch on Mr. Augular and his activities for some time. We know he is dirty, but we have never been able to prove it or catch him in the act. He always seems to be one step ahead of us every time. We know there is a leak somewhere that can see and hear our every move, but we do not know who or where."

Mr. Bones was dressed in a police uniform in a closet that is close to the conference room. His cane was in one hand and a black pouch in the other. He stood inside a circle made up of small bones. He mumbled some words.

"Stupid fools, there is no place I cannot go or anyone I cannot hear. I am the prince and power of the air. I am Mr. Bones and Victor will know about this." He mumbled some words and began tapping his cane.

Back in the conference room, the FBI agent is slowly walking around.

"It's crucial that we handle this operation with extreme care. Mr. Augular has some powerful political connections on the state and federal levels. That is why only the people in this room know of this operation. The other assisting personnel will be told at the very last minute. We now know when and where this drug shipment is coming in and we will be there to intercept it. Now, are there any questions?"

Rick halfway raised his hand.

"I have no questions and you may already know this, but I wanted to mention Mr. Augular has an elite team of ex-military Special Forces as his bodyguards. They are trained expert killers, and we need to be prepared for them."

The narcotics agent stood up.

"I know about Mr. Augular's bodyguards. My task force is not the military, but we are also well-trained and good at what we do. We will be ready for anything." He sat down.

The FBI agent cleared his throat to get everyone's attention.

"Good, now let's discuss the details of this raid."

Back in the closet, Mr. Bones stood in the circle of bones shaking his pouch and mumbling some words.

"Fools, no one can defeat me. They are so blind and deceived just the way I like it. The stupid government made laws that help me take people straight to hell. Oh, I loved it when the law was passed to take prayer out of school," he smiled and laughed. "Prayer moved out and my evil spirit moved in and took over. Now, look at the kids killing each other in schools because my spirit is in them causing havoc. I never could stand all that stupid praying. I hate people with great faith, always talking about loving your neighbor. To hell with your neighbor, don't love your neighbor, fuck your neighbor's wife." He laughed while tapping his cane on the floor then disappeared in a cloud of smoke.

CHAPTER TWENTY FOUR
The Hotel

Stephanie, Victor, and his bodyguards are at the Setai, a lavish hotel in South Beach with private access to the beach. Victor and Stephanie have the Penthouse suite at $20,000 a night. He sat at a table looking at some paperwork. Stephanie walked out of the bathroom wearing Carine Gilson lingerie, where thongs start at $240. She wore a black thong, matching bra, and a black robe that was almost see-through that hung just below her butt. She walked toward Victor and stopped.

"Victor, since you enticed me over the phone, carried me away in your private jet to lovely Miami, and have me here in this beautiful room. What are you going to do with me?"

Victor stared at Stephanie and was always amazed by her beauty and raw sexuality.

"Stephanie, you are a very sexy, erotic lady who does believe in advertising what you have been blessed with. This reminds me of an old saying, if it is not for sale take the sign out of the window." He said this to irritate her.

She frowned and waved her hand toward Victor.

"Victor don't insult me. I get paid very well for advertising and we both know everything is for sale, directly or indirectly." She walked over to the bed and sat on the edge of it facing him and spread her legs slowly, looked down then looked back at Victor. "You need to take this time to enjoy what you have in front of you. So how much time do you have until you have to go?" She caressed the bed with her hand, looking directly at him.

Victor licked his lips and stood up.

"It depends on if I can just cover part of what I see or the complete package." He walked over to Stephanie and got on his knees and placed his hands on her legs caressing them as he lowered his head between her legs, kissing and licking from her knees to her inner thighs. Then moved her panties to the side and began licking her wetness slowly and delicately.

Stephanie leaned her head back using her hands to balance herself on the bed.

"Oh Victor, you know how good that feels, and you better not stop, ohhh, it feels so damn good."

Mr. Bones walked through the lobby of the hotel wearing dress shoes, a light-colored dress shirt, and dress pants. He has his cane in one hand and a briefcase in the other. He walked to a courtesy phone and called Victor's room.

The phone on the table rang.

Stephanie leaned forward and slapped Victor's head with her hand.

"Damn you Victor, I know you are going to answer that damn phone, I am sick of this." She stood up and pushed her way past him and walked away and then turned around and stared at him. "I am tired of you teasing me Victor. Suck me or fuck me, just stop teasing me. I am getting dressed and going shopping so I will see you later." She walked back into the bathroom and slammed the door.

Victor walked over to the table and answered the phone.

"Hello."

"Mr. Augular, you know I don't like talking on phones, but I am trying to blend in, for now. You have company but we need to talk, immediately."

"Mr. Bones, your timing is not good, but I know this must be important or you would not be calling me. Where are you?"

"I am aware you and Miss Walker were preparing to commit some fornication. You were trying to get your lick on, nasty man. I am in the lobby of the hotel where you are and as soon as Miss Walker finishes getting dressed and leaves, I will be up to see you."

"Mr. Bones, you do get around. Use the door to come in because your smoke entrance and exits can be overwhelming."

"As you wish Mr. Augular, and this will allow me to tempt more people to sin." He hung up the phone laughing and walked away.

Two attractive ladies were walking toward Mr. Bones, as they passed him, he purposely brushed against one of them while mumbling some words and tapping his cane on the floor. One of the ladies touched her friend on the arm.

"I just had a wicked thought come to me. My husband has been neglecting me sexually. He has become all business, a five-minute man in bed, and no oral sex. To hell with that. Remember that guy at the bar who was flirting with me so hard, and gave me his room number? Well, I am going to his room tonight, give him one of my

husband's Viagra pills I started carrying around in my purse, and let him sex me in any position he wants, however, he wants. In my mouth, my vagina, and my butt, I am going to be a total sex freak."

They both laughed and continued to walk.

Mr. Bones stopped walking and looked back at the two ladies and walked away smiling.

Victor sat at the table looking at paperwork when Stephanie walked out of the bathroom wearing a form-fitting tailored $15,000 Coco Chanel dress that comes two inches above her knees with a V-cut in the front showing a little of her breasts, a $12,000 Cartier watch, and $20,000 Hermes Birkin small purse in her hand. And she put a touch of Clive Christian *Imperial Majesty,* perfume at $215,000 for a 16.9 oz. bottle, in the right places on her body.

Victor stood up staring at her.

"Stephanie, you are going to give a man a heart attack looking so damn good." He walked closer and kissed her neck. "Baby you smell so good." Kissing her lips and caressing her hips. He turned her around to look at her butt. "Damn, you got a fat ass. Do you have any underwear on?" He slid his hand under her dress.

Stephanie pushed his hand away quickly and backed away from him.

"Every woman likes to be complimented but production beats conversation any day. If you want to know if I have any underwear on, push me against the wall and come get this." She rubbed her ass and stared at him. "Victor, underwear or not, make love to me. I want it good, hard, and deep and stop playing games with me." She walked out of the room and out the door with her hand on her ass caressing it with each step she took. Victor stared at her as she walked away.

"She got a mouth on her along with that, come fuck me body." He walked back to the table and sat down.

There was a knock on the door, and it opened. Mr. Bones stood there holding his cane and briefcase.

Victor waved his hand at him.

"Mr. Bones, please come in, your timing is perfect."

He walked into the room but did not close the door and walked over to Victor.

"Mr. Augular, I know you have urgent business so I will be brief."

Victor pointed to the door.

"Mr. Bones, you neglected to close the door."

"Childs play," he tapped his cane on the briefcase and the lights in the room became dim and the door closed, "oh yes, this is the way I like it, dark." He mumbled more words and a chair slid across the floor directly behind him and he sat down. He threw his briefcase in the air over his head, and it turned into small bones that floated down to his hand. He took his other hand off his cane and it stood by itself. Victor feared Mr. Bones greatly, but he would never show it.

"You never cease to amaze me Mr. Bones. Now tell me what has brought you to Miami."

"The police know about your drug shipment. They know when and where. Also, Detectives Matthew and Anderson are in Miami. The FBI, the narcotics team, the

ATF team, and plenty of police will be there. I suggest you contact Mr. Case for his assistance, and I will be there as well. No one can beat the bones." He opened his hand and the bones floated six inches above his hand and hovered in the air for a few seconds, then fell back in his hand.

Victor stared at Mr. Bones. Deep inside he knew he was dealing with the spirit of evil. He has never seen anyone like him. He greatly dislikes being around Mr. Bones, but he needs his services.

"Mr. Bones, one day you must tell me how you can do the things that you do. Thank you for this information and your assistance. Now if you excuse me, I will call Mr. Case."

Mr. Bones stood up.

"No problem." He pointed his cane at him. "Just remember my services are not free, everybody must pay a price, even you! My home is being enlarged because of greedy evil people like you but I love it." He mumbled some words and tapped his cane on the floor twice making the floor vibrate. A thick vapor appeared, and Mr. Bones disappeared, but the vapor was still present. It moved toward the door, and it opened and then the vapor went through the door and the door slammed shut. The lights in the room go back to normal.

Victor's hand is on his chest feeling his accelerated heartbeat.

"That man is the devil himself, but I will find a way to beat him. Even Satan himself was kicked out of heaven, so Mr. Bones can be beaten." He picked up the phone and made a call, "Mr. Case, I need you in Miami immediately.

Yes, that is true but there will be uninvited guests. You want three hundred and fifty thousand dollars. No problem. Yes sir, the details will be in the usual place. I will see you then." He hung up the phone and stood up. "It's show time in Miami." He smiled.

CHAPTER TWENTY FIVE

Show Down in Miami

There are many boats in the shipping area but there is one large cargo vessel that's dockside being unloaded. The full moon tonight and the lights from the buildings provide enough light to see.

A forklift carrying large pallets is being driven from the cargo vessel to inside a tractor-trailer that is parked close to the cargo vessel. Several people are working to get the cargo vessel unloaded. Three people are working on the boat, one driving the forklift, four people at the end of the ramp with two on each side. There are four people at the end of the trailer, two on each side watching the trailer being loaded. The driver was in the truck. Thirteen people are working hard and fast to accomplish this task.

There are large warehouses on both sides of the entranceway of the dock. There was a man on one of the roofs on both sides of the warehouse with a Browning M2-50 caliber machine gun aimed down at the street, capable of firing 750 rounds per minute. All the men working wore gloves and coveralls with automatic weapons underneath, and they have on headsets to communicate with each other. Parked at the other entrance close to the warehouse are two grey vans. The last pallet was loaded on the trailer and the doors to the truck were closed.

Three black vans directly behind the other, approached the entranceway slowly where the men are on the roof. Inside the vans are Detectives Matthew and Anderson, FBI agents, narcotics squad, ATF team, and DEA agents. There are eight men in each van. Detectives Matthew and Anderson are in the first van along with the squad leader for the ATF, FBI, and the narcotics team. The leader of the FBI team began talking with the leader of the ATF. The FBI leader sat in the front seat of the van, he turned his head toward the back.

"I am glad we were able to get the information on this big drug shipment. There are enough drugs on this ship to supply the whole state of Florida and I hope Mr. Augular is stupid enough to show up. The bureau wants him badly."

The ATF leader shook his head.

"I understand how you feel. I have heard about Mr. Augular's elite bodyguard team, I hope to run into them so I can find out what they are about because I am tired of hearing all these Superman stories about them. Anyone can be stopped. How big is this shipment anyway?"

The FBI leader waved his hand in front of his face.

"It has been verified that there are ten thousand kilos on this ship, purchased at ten thousand dollars per kilo, makes it a full one hundred-million-dollar deal that would go in someone's pocket, but not today. Now everyone get ready to roll out, we are almost there."

As the three vans approached the middle of the warehouses, Mr. Bones appeared in a cloud of smoke standing directly in front of the vans wearing all black with his cane in one hand and his bones in the other. The first van stopped and the other two did the same.

The FBI leader pointed at Mr. Bones.

"Who the hell is that?" He said yelling.

Mr. Bones pointed his cane at the van.

"You foolish people, no one can beat the bones." He mumbled some words and tapped his cane on the ground twice, then threw his bones on the ground directly in front of the first van.

Fire erupted on the ground and immediately stretched from one warehouse to the other, then traveled ten feet in the air.

The FBI leader turned to the driver of the van.

"Back up, back up, and get the hell out of here." He yelled.

All three vans backed up quickly and Mr. Bones disappeared, but he appeared again in a cloud of smoke behind the vans. He did the same thing, and another wall of fire was behind the vans. Now, the vans were caught between two walls of fire ten feet high. Mr. Bones disappeared again.

The men who were working by the truck on the loading dock and the ship unzipped their coveralls pulled out automatic weapons and ran to the wall of fire. Seven of the men lined up in front of the wall of fire kneeling on one knee and aiming their weapons at the vans. The other four men stood directly behind them and aimed their automatic weapons at the vans. The other two men who were working ran towards the two grey vans parked at the other entrance and got in.

The driver in the tractor-trailer drove to where the two grey vans were parked and stopped. The agents in the vans, except the van in front, stepped out of the van. The two men on the roof opened fire with their .50 caliber guns on the vans and the men as they stepped out. Their bodies were splattered with gunfire and bullets penetrated the vans like paper, wounding, and killing the men. The police were screaming and falling on the ground, and chunks of flesh, blood, and body parts were everywhere. Arms and legs were shot off by the police like snapping twigs.

The eleven men in front of the vans opened fire, shooting the men as they stepped out. This attack was brutal and precise. The police never expected such immense direct firepower and were caught off guard and they never expected someone like Mr. Bones. This was a well-planned slaughter by Victor.

The eleven men stopped shooting and ran toward the two grey vans. One of the agents in the first van, who was shot, screamed to the driver to drive through the wall of fire. Although the driver was shot, he managed to put the van in gear and drive.

As the van drove through the wall of fire, Mr. Bones appeared in a cloud of smoke in front of the van. The agent screamed to the driver to run him over. Mr. Bones mumbled some words, tapped his cane on the ground twice, and threw his bones at the van. When the bones hit the van, smoke erupted immediately inside the van and when it cleared, a lot of snakes were inside. The snakes were biting the men repeatedly all over their bodies.

The driver slammed on the brakes and the men rushed out of the van with snakes still attacking them.

Mr. Bones tapped his cane again on the ground twice, turned around, and threw some bones high in the air. A large black cloud of smoke formed in the air and when the smoke disappeared, a helicopter was in the air. Mr. Bones tapped his cane on his shoe, and he disappeared in a cloud of smoke.

Victor was in the passenger seat of the helicopter and Mr. Case sat in the back dressed in his ninja suit with his sword on his back, holding an automatic weapon. A rope hung from the helicopter. Victor turned around to Mr. Case and pointed at him.

"Mr. Case, it's time for you to earn your money. Finish this job and go get my drugs. I will see you back in Maryland."

Mr. Case nodded his head and slid down the rope, shooting the men coming out of the vans. When he hit the ground a cloud of smoke appeared in the back seat of the helicopter and when it disappeared, Mr. Bones sat there.

"Hello Victor, time to go." He mumbled some words and tapped his cane twice on his shoe and a large black cloud covered the helicopter. When the cloud disappeared, the helicopter was gone.

Mr. Case saw an agent running in circles trying to get the snakes off him. He dropped his automatic weapon and ran over to him. The agent looked up and saw Mr. Case coming towards him and reached for his gun. Mr. Case pulled his sword out and cut off the agent's hand that held the gun and before his hand hit the ground, he cut his head off and cut his body in half. His body fell to the ground in three pieces.

Another agent was running around screaming with a snake wrapped around him. Mr. Case runs over and cuts him from the top of his head down, splitting him in two. His body fell to the ground in two halves, away from each other. He saw Detectives Matthew and Anderson lying on the ground, but they were not dead. He walked toward them and pointed his sword at their head and then he runs to the tractor-trailer and got in.

The two men on the warehouse roof climbed down and ran toward the two grey vans, shooting their guns at the agents at the same time. They reached the vans and got in and the tractor-trailer and the two vans drove away. Mr. Bones appeared in a cloud of smoke in front of the van that drove through the wall of fire which was still burning.

Detective Matthew sees Mr. Bones and helps Detective Anderson off the ground and they both limp away from the van toward the warehouse.

Mr. Bones tapped his cane on the ground twice and the van in the middle exploded. He tapped his cane again one time and the van in front exploded. He began laughing, raised his arms with his cane in one hand and his pouch of bones in the other.

"Death to the world, no one can beat me, no flesh is any match for the bones." He yelled and continued to laugh as the vans burn, and then exploded.

CHAPTER TWENTY SIX
The Party

Victor was on his three-level, two-hundred-and-sixty-foot yacht named *Victor's Reign,* valued at one hundred twenty million dollars. The yacht is fifty miles out from the beaches of Aruba, and it could make a return trip across the Atlantic without refueling. He was having a party celebrating the success of his hundred-million-dollar drug deal. The money has been dispersed in various secret offshore accounts around the world in countries with no extradition treaty with the United States. No name accounts, private numbers, and select codes to access it, along with fingerprint verification. Victor has acquired over eight hundred million dollars so far since he has been in business. For him, this is just the beginning.

There are fifty close friends and business associates of Victor on board helping him celebrate. Everyone wore shorts or bathing suits except Victor, who wore light-colored pants, a short-sleeved shirt, and sandals. His bodyguards were strategically positioned throughout the yacht with specific instructions to kill and throw overboard anyone who caused any disturbance. He has ten other guards on board as well, with the same instructions. Attractive ladies walked around serving drinks wearing various revealing bathing suits. Stephanie wore sandals and a revealing tailored dark blue $2,500 one-piece bathing suit that left little to the imagination. Music by

Sam Cooke was playing, and people were dancing and others talking.

Victor was in the lounge talking to an incredibly attractive slim lady from Cuba with a tight body wearing a revealing black Knotty Swimwear bathing suit. She stood close to Victor touching his cheek while flirting with him. Stephanie walked into the lounge and saw this lady whispering in Victor's ear, kissing his cheek while rubbing his butt. Stephanie walked toward Victor and stood behind the lady.

"Mr. Augular, you need to relax and let me take care of you." She continued to rub his butt.

Stephanie becomes instantly angry and slapped the woman's hand away from Victor's butt and stepped closer to her.

"That job has already been filled and you are not qualified. So, get your bony, no-ass away from here. I am bipolar so I would not be responsible for taking a glass and cutting your face from ear to ear." She stared at the lady with cold, evil eyes.

The lady looked at Stephanie like she was crazy and walked away.

Stephanie walked closer to Victor and got in his face.

"Do you want her? That bony, no breast having, no ass bitch, you want that?" She stared at Victor and then rolled her eyes at him.

"Miss Walker, are you jealous." He started laughing.

"Don't fool yourself and I am far from jealous. If you want her, you can have her, but I thought your taste was better than that bony, flat ass, fake lips, dick-sucking slut. I

know she sucks a lot of dick because that's the only way she can get a man off. She is nothing but walking bones with fake lips."

He continued to laugh at Stephanie.

"You are something else. I need to talk to you about something. Please, join me below in my suite?" He smiled at her.

Stephanie turned her head, giving Victor a look of disgust.

"I don't feel like talking and I am not in the mood for anything else or playing games. So, go find your pancake ass slut and talk to her."

"I also don't play games and I desire to talk with you now and I will not ask you twice." He looked at Stephanie with eyes of controlled anger.

"Fine, it is your yacht, and we are out in the middle of the ocean. I don't have much of a choice."

"You are a smart lady." He caressed her butt and put his arm around her waist, and they walked off.

A lady walking toward them wearing a thong bikini spoke to Victor and he rubbed her on the butt. Stephanie pinched Victor on his side. They reached Victor's master suite, and he opened the door for Stephanie then smacked her on the butt as they walked in. As soon as the door was closed Stephanie turned around quickly and slapped him.

"Let me tell you something Victor. I am not one of your cheap sluts you can order around and do with as you please. I do not need your money. I am well paid, and I am not afraid of you, and you are not going to disrespect me. If you want to rub women on their ass, then go ahead and do that, but don't do it around me." She said with killer venom in her voice showing no fear of him.

Victor rubbed his face and smiled.

"You are very interesting."

"What the hell are you smiling about and what do you mean, very interesting?" She put her hands on her hips.

He walked over to the dresser by the bed and opened a drawer and pulled out a small thin case and put it in his pants pocket, then walked back to Stephanie.

"I am smiling because you are very sexy when you're upset. It turns me on." He moved closer to her.

She held her hand out toward him.

"Hold it right there Victor. I don't know what kind of game you are playing but I am not in the mood and don't you touch me."

He pulled her closer to him.

"You talk too much, and I am not playing any games. My business in Miami is complete and it's celebration time for us, but you are trying my patience and not making this easy."

"If you want easy, go get that bony, no ass slut you rubbed on. If you are trying to seduce me, start begging and I might reconsider if you beg me right." She licked her lips and smiled at him.

"Weak and poor people beg. I stopped begging a long time ago but maybe this will change your mind." He pulled the case out of his pocket and opened it, revealing a thin necklace with diamonds all around it. "This was made just for you. I hope you like it."

Stephanie's mouth dropped open.

"Oh my God, Victor it is beautiful." She removed the necklace from its case and held it in her hands admiring it. "I have seen a lot of lovely jewelry, but this is gorgeous," she looked at him, "this necklace has to be worth a fortune."

"Stephanie, it is my gift to you and the price does not matter. What good is money if you have no one special to spend it on? But I know you want to know," he thought...*high-class gold digger you are*, "the necklace was appraised at $1,200,000 but it was insured for $1,600,000, it is all yours." He removed the necklace from her hand. "Now may I see how good it looks on you?"

She looked at him for a moment, smiled, and turned around so he could put the necklace on her as she faced the mirror. Victor purposely pressed his body on her butt as he put the necklace around her neck.

Stephanie felt Victor's erection growing but desired to play hard to get. She looked at herself in the mirror.

"Victor, I have no words to describe how I feel right now or the beauty of this wonderful gift you have given me. Now I want to hear you say, I apologize, and maybe..."

Victor cut her off before she could finish her sentence by picking her up in one smooth motion.

"I talk too damn much. I've had enough of your mouth."

"Victor no!" She yelled.

"Be quiet." He carried her to the bed and dumped her on it removed all his clothes grabbed Stephanie by her ankles and pulled her closer to the edge of the bed.

Stephanie did not expect this from Victor, and she does not like him being in total control.

"Victor, what are you doing? You are not being a gentleman, stop." She said this but did not mean it because she wanted to see how far he would go.

"To hell with being a gentleman, I am tired of your mouth." He snatched her heels and bathing suit off, moved on top of her, and kissed her lips, and sucked them. Then moved to her neck, throat, shoulders, breast, and stomach kissing, licking, and sucking along the way with much desire. He roughly grabbed her legs moved them apart and placed his head between them until his tongue reached her wetness. And then slowly slid his tongue from her wetness to her ass and began kissing and licking back and forth sticking his tongue inside her as far as it would go, feeling her getting wetter and enjoying her sweet juices.

Stephanie was surprised at his attitude and actions which increased her sexual desire for him.

"Oh Victor, damn you better not stop, this feels so good. You are going to make me cum baby." She could not hold it any longer. "Victor, I am cummming, don't stop, don't stop, suck it baby, suck my pussy, I am cummming, ohhhh Victorrrr, it feels sooo good."

Victor intended to teach her a lesson for her mouth and nasty attitude. He was rock hard with anticipation, and while she was still climaxing, he grabbed her legs pushed her knees back to her head, and slid inside her.

Stephanie enjoyed her first orgasm from Victor's excellent oral skills, and then she felt him push his hard

dick inside her. She had desired this from him for a long time.

"Victor, oh my God, you are finally giving it to me just the way I like it, slow and easy baby." She does not want it to be slow, but she needs time to adjust to him.

Victor thought...*slow and easy, yeah right. She knows she wants to be dicked down.* He pushed her legs back some more and began sliding inside Stephanie faster.

"I am tired of your mouth, take this dick." He was thrusting in and out knowing she was close to climaxing again, so he thrusts faster and deeper into her.

Stephanie was so turned on she grabbed Victor's butt and helped him thrust inside her faster.

"That's it baby, harder, I want it harder, punish this pussy, it's yours, I am going to be good, oh Victor, fuck me harder, fuck me harder. I will be good, ohhhhhh."

Victor loved the words coming out of her mouth and it made him desire her more. He slid out of her slowly then thrust back in, making her body and the bed shake. Stephanie could not take it anymore. It is too good.

"Victor, that's it, that's my spot, I am cumming on your dick. Don't stop baby, please don't stop, I am cummming Victor, fuck meeee, ohhhhhh fuck this good pussy, ohhhhhh Victorrrrr."

Stephanie's orgasm was so hot and intense, it triggered his. He was pounding her at this point just the way he knew she wanted him to.

"Damn Stephanie, your pussy is so good. I am cumming baby, you are making me cum, ohhhhhh

Stephanie." He continued thrusting until he knew she was totally done, and so was he.

They lay on the bed next to each other relaxing. Stephanie lay on her stomach and Victor looked at her butt and smacked it.

"I told you I was going to get that mouth, now get up and take a shower with me." He got off the bed and walked towards the bathroom.

Stephanie relaxed on the bed as she watched Victor walk away and thought…*if he is going to fuck me like that then I will continue to give him attitude.* She felt the necklace around her neck then got off the bed and walked towards the bathroom. Stephanie stopped walking and looked at herself in the mirror.

"I am wearing a one million six-hundred-thousand-dollar necklace. I get what I want at any cost. Only fools and stupid women fuck for free. The power of the pussy. Damn, I am good!" She smiled and continued walking to the bathroom.

CHAPTER TWENTY SEVEN
(Seventeen Years Later)

It is August the thirteenth, a bright summer day. Sheila was having a birthday cookout at her home for her son because it was his seventeenth birthday. Ron is a clean-cut handsome young man at five feet ten, one hundred eighty muscular pounds. He graduated from high school. Christine and Sandra are there. They are twenty-four and twenty-three years old. James Reed, Grandma Harris, and Diana Brown were there as well.

Diana worked for Mr. Reed as his paralegal. She is nineteen years old, five feet seven, one-hundred thirty-eight pounds, and incredibly attractive with a curvaceous figure. She hides her hips and round butt by dressing conservatively. There were a lot of people at the cookout from the church. Ron worked for the same construction company his dad worked for, against his mom's wishes. Some people were in the front yard sitting in chairs and others were in the backyard and gospel music was playing. Christine and Sandra were in the backyard by the grill and Sheila and Ron were in the kitchen. Food was everywhere.

Sheila looked at Ron and smiled and walked toward him.

"Ron, are you enjoying yourself today son?"

"Yes, I am, and thank you for all of this, but my money helped pay for most of this anyway, so I am going to eat my share and a few others."

"Boy don't get smart because being seventeen does not make you a grown man. God is still on my side, and he will give me the strength to knock you down. You are supposed to pay for your food. You work, don't you? God said, if a man doesn't work, he doesn't eat." She looked at him and smiled.

"Mom, I know God's word and you can't go around using God like an attack dog on people." He said with a sarcastic tone and attitude.

"What did you say boy?" She looked up. "Help me Lord, don't let me slap him down to the ground on his birthday."

Grandma Harris and Diana walked into the kitchen.

"What is going on here? What is all this noise about? Let me know what is going on so I can get my shout on." Grandma Harris said as she clapped her hands.

"Amen grandma." Diana said and touched her arm.

Sheila pointed at Ron.

"This boy thinks he's grown, and I had to call on the Lord so I wouldn't swell his lips on his birthday. Split, swollen, and busted lips on his birthday wouldn't look right."

"Sheila, don't swell his lips on his birthday, that wouldn't be right," she pointed her finger at Ron, "Ron are you disrespecting your mother?"

"No Grandma Harris, I am not." He said and looked at his mom with attitude.

Diana stepped closer to Ron.

"You shouldn't disrespect your mother, Ron. I can't believe you boy." She stared at him and rolled her eyes.

Grandma Harris waved her hand in Ron's face.

"Back in my day, if you disrespected your parents, you got slapped and knocked out but this new generation, child they are something else. God said if you spare the rod, you spoil the child, but Ron does love the Lord."

Ron walked over and kissed her on the cheek.

"Thanks Grandma Harris."

She playfully pushed Ron's face away from her.

"Wait boy, don't kiss me, I wasn't finished talking. Do not get your lips swollen and split on your birthday. Anyway Sheila, I think you spoiled the boy. Did you breastfeed him too long?"

"Grandma Harris, please don't be nasty." Sheila said and rolled her eyes at her.

Grandma Harris walked over to Sheila and hugged her then looked at Ron.

"Ron, if you stay with the Lord, God will bless you with my Diana for a wife." She looked at Diana and smiled.

"Grandma, please! I am too young to be thinking about marriage and if a man does not love my Jesus and cannot get a prayer through, I do not need him. And I do not want a pretty boy who is filled with himself thinking he is all that." She stared at Ron and stuck her tongue out at him.

Sheila, Diana, and Grandma Harris started laughing.

"I hope everyone is having fun at my expense. That's why I will be glad when Keith gets here."

Keith and Ron met years ago at vacation Bible study in church. Keith stopped coming to church, but he and Ron remained very close and became best friends.

Sheila stepped toward Ron.

"Ron, I know he is your friend, but you should not spend so much time with him. God said, *have no fellowship with the unfruitful works of darkness but rather expose them.* I feel one day he is going to get you in serious trouble. That expensive car he drives, the girls I see him with, and the way they dress, wearing those tight shorts revealing their butt cheeks. Their miniskirts are too short, and they show too much of their breast. Ron, you know that ain't the Lord baby."

"Those are the only kinds of girls Keith like, whorish nasty looking girls that spend time on their back. Nothing but Jezebel's and Delilah's and I do not like him. I tolerate him because of you Ron. I like you." She stepped closer to Ron and kissed him on the cheek and walked away.

Grandma Harris and Sheila looked at each other and spoke at the same time.

"Thank you Jesus." They looked at Ron and laughed.
Ron walked away following Diana outside to the backyard, but she ignored him when she saw him coming and walked away. Ron walked over to his sisters who stood by the grill. The girls are attractive and the same height and weight, five feet seven one-hundred forty pounds but shaped a little different. One has more hips and butt than the other.

"Christine, Sandra it is great to see you two again. I don't see enough of you two since you moved out."

Christine kissed him on the cheek.

"Hi Ron and don't exaggerate. You see us all the time in church."

Sandra kissed him on the cheek as well.

"Hi Emmanuel and happy birthday to you again, my brother."

"Hi Christine, hi Sandra, and I asked you not to call me that."

Sandra walked closer to him.

"Why not?" She asked with attitude. "God gave you the name Emmanuel, which means, God with us. God has chosen you to do his work, so make sure you keep yourself clean and pure. Stay away from Jezebels and Delilah's."

"You sound just like Diana, always calling a girl a Jezebel or Delilah because she's not a Christian."

"I like Diana, she is committed to the Lord, and she does not dress showing her butt cheeks and butt crack in public. I know she likes you, so you better stay faithful to the Lord, and you would be very blessed to have Diana as your wife."

Ron waved his hand in her face.

"All of this talk about a wife. I am only seventeen years old, and I am not thinking about getting married. But there is nothing wrong with looking at all the fine ladies in this world."

"Boy, you better keep your eyes on God and wait on your chosen wife Diana, and don't lust over her either." Christine said and pointed her finger at him.

"I know, *wait on the Lord, be of good courage and he shall strengthen your heart.* That sounds good but don't you get tired of waiting. I mean you do look at men and you do have needs, you are human," Ron said with a little attitude.

"Hold it." Sandra held her hand out toward him. "I know where you are going with this. Yes, I find men attractive, and we have needs and are human. We are your blood sisters so you can talk to us about anything, but we are also your sisters in Christ so do not say anything foolish or nasty and disrespect us. Do not get double-slapped on your birthday. I will slap you on the right," she pointed to Christine, "and she will slap you on the left and we will slap you down to the ground." They slapped hands and laughed.

"Great, everybody is a jokester today, pick on Ron day, no problem." He said and nodded his head.

Grandma Harris, Diana, and Sheila walked in the backyard toward Ron and his sisters. Sheila walked over hugged and kissed both of her daughters on the cheek.

"How is everything going girls?"
Before anyone could answer, very loud music with heavy bass was heard coming from the front of the house. Grandma Harris makes a face.

"What in the world is that noise?"
Diana looked at Ron frowning.

"Keith Washington and his car and he probably have one of his Jezebels with him, nothing but a dog in heat."

Ron's face lit up when he heard Keith's music. "Keith, my man." He kissed Diana on the cheek and quickly walked away to meet him.

Diana turned in Ron's direction.
"Ron, wait!"
Grandma Harris touched Diana on her arm.

"Keep praying for Ron baby and give him time. God will have his way, don't you worry."

Sheila walked toward Diana.

"Amen, pray for him baby."

"Thank you Mrs. O'Neil."

Sheila walked away and began talking to other people.

James walked around talking to people and then he walked toward Diana.

"Diana hi, it is good to see you outside of the office scene."

"Hi Mr. Reed, it is good to see you also, and for once you don't have a suit on."

"Diana relax, we are not in the office so please call me James I only wear suits to the office or church, but now I am enjoying the people here and all this good food. Where is the birthday young man?"

"He went out front to meet his buddy," she turned her head and whispered. "Nothing but a dog on two legs."

James laughed.

"I heard that, and I can assume you do not like Ron's friend."

"You have assumed right. I will admit he is nice-looking, polite, and well-mannered but his lifestyle is all wrong for Ron to associate with. His fancy cars which I do not know how he can afford. He's always flashing a lot of money, and he keeps those slutty Jezebel girls around him, the ones that always show the crack of their butts when they dress."

"Now Miss Diana Brown, it sounds like you have feelings for Mr. Ron, and you don't want him talking to other ladies."

Diana frowned at him.

"Mr. Reed, please. Ron can have any girl he desires and if he desires those slutty jezebels that Keith hangs out with that show the crack of their butt in public, he can have them. Just don't talk to me." She walked away mumbling.

James laughed as he watched her walk away and then walk toward Sheila.

Keith was leaning against a dark Grey 2011 Corvette with black interior, with chrome and gold custom rims. His girlfriend, Stacy Copeland was standing next to him. Keith is twenty years old, five feet eleven, and two hundred ten muscular pounds, a clean-cut handsome young man. He wore a platinum chain around his neck worth $10,000, a Patek Philippe watch worth $39,600, and a platinum and diamond ring on his right pinky finger worth $19,800. He wore ostrich skin shoes, brown triple pleated pants with a quarter-inch cuff, an ostrich skin belt to match, and a short-sleeved white Egyptian cotton shirt.

Stacy is twenty years old, five feet eight, one-hundred forty pounds, and gorgeous. A true *FULL SEVEN,* she is very pretty in the face, slim in the waist, got hips, full lips, pretty painted fingertips, a big round butt, and a pretty smile. Her body is very tight. She has a brown skin complexion with a very erotic look like she belongs in any rap video. Every day, when she walks down the street, men and women try to talk to her because she is so attractive. She wore black heels and a light purple low-cut dress that revealed her ample breasts. It hung just above her knees and hugged her body, showing the curves of her hips and butt.

Ron stood in front of Keith.

"Keith, how is everything, and introduce me to your lady friend."

"Pastor Emmanuel, my man. Everything is fine, my brother. I am still enjoying the beautiful creations of God," he looked at Stacy from the feet up and smiled then looked at Ron, "Pastor Emmanuel, this is Stacy. Baby this is my best friend, Emmanuel O'Neil whom God has chosen to deliver me from my sins but hold off on the deliverance because I have a lot of sins left to commit." He looked at Stacy and licked his lips. "A lot more sinning," he laughed and looked at Stacy again and stared at her butt, "damn!"

Stacy punched Keith on his arm.

"Keith, you need to stop and grow up. You are being very disrespectful, but I will deal with you later," she looked at him and scowled then extended her hand to Ron. "Hi, I'm Stacy and you need to ignore Keith but since you two are best friends, you should know how he is. Is Emmanuel your name and are you a pastor?"

Ron shook Stacy's hand.

"Hi Stacy, it's nice to meet you. No, I am not a pastor, but I am a Christian and yes Emmanuel is my middle name and Ronald is my first, but everyone calls me Ron, which is my preference. You and Keith come on in."

Stacy turned and looked at Keith with attitude.

"Keith, I hear gospel music, you set me up. You told me we were going to a house party, not a church cookout. I am dressed like I am going to a nightclub, and you know how church people are, especially older ladies who think if you are not wearing a dress to your ankles and up to your neck, then you are not Holy. I know I am not living according to the word of God, but that does not make me trash."

Keith clapped his hands and looked at Stacy.

"Hallelujah, amen sister, go ahead and preach." He laughed.

"Keith, you shouldn't play with God like that." Stacy said, giving him a look that said, that is enough.

Ron pointed his finger at Keith.

"She's right, you need to stop doing that. Anyway, let's go get something to eat."

They walked toward the house and Stacy walked in front. She can see and feel how people stared at her, making her feel uncomfortable. So, she decided since they would judge her anyway, she might as well give them all something to look at. She purposely made her butt and hips shake extra when she walked. An older married couple sat in the front eating and as the man was about to put some food in his mouth, he saw Stacy walking. He stopped all motion. His eyes were bulging, his mouth was open, and he dropped his food and stared at her.

"Lord have mercy child." He was drooling and wiped his mouth.

His wife looked up to see what her husband stared at so hard when she saw Stacy. She turned and slapped her husband.

"Stop looking at that home hell-wrecker Jezebel." She looked at Stacy when she walked into the house. "That is a nasty, trashy girl, showing her body like that. It's a shame before the Lord. She going to hell for sure. No stops."

Stacy saw all this while she walked and laughed hard to herself, and this motivated her to shake her body even more.

Keith and Ron walked side by side behind Stacy and they saw how everyone stared at her. Keith walked directly behind Stacy looking at her hips and butt shaking. He tapped Ron on his arm and nodded toward Stacy's butt and smiled.

"Damn Stacy, you got sexy hips and a fat ass that's jumping." Keith said laughing.

Stacy kept walking but turned her head a little to the side.

"Keep looking at my hips and ass Keith, you and Christian Ron. Put it on video baby."

Ron could not keep himself from looking at Stacy with lust and thought...*this girl is the finest woman I have ever seen, good God, she is erotic and hot.* He caught himself, forgive me Lord.

All three walked through the house toward the backyard approaching Sheila and James. Sheila saw them coming and tapped James on the arm to get his attention.

"Hi Keith, we heard your music as you drove up. Do you think it was loud enough baby, and who is this pretty young lady with you?"

Keith walked up to Sheila and hugged her.

"Hi Mom and yes it was a little loud, but you know how it is when the right song comes on. You got to turn it up, so you can feel that bass. Anyway, this is my lady, Stacy. Stacy this is Ron's mom, Mrs. O'Neil, my second mom."

Stacy extended her hand to Sheila.

"Hi Mrs. O'Neil, it is nice to meet you."

"Hi Stacy," shaking her hand as she pointed toward Reed, "this is a family friend, Mr. Reed."

"Hi Stacy." James said but he had to control his thoughts when he looked at Stacy. She was hot, make a man dig in his pockets.

Sheila stepped toward Stacy.

"Keith, you must have been conducting yourself like a perfect gentleman to have this very attractive lady by your side."

"Mom, I am always a gentleman." He looked at Stacy.

Diana walked up behind Keith.

"I am sure you are Keith," she extended her hand to Stacy, "hi, I am Diana," she stared at Stacy and thought...*just as I thought, a Jezebel. Could she show any more of her body? Don't make any sense, lust walker.*

Stacy shook her hand.

"Hi Diana." Stacy could tell by the way Diana looked at her that she was being judged. She cannot stand being judged by people who do not even know her. She heard

from Keith that Ron and Diana were supposed to be close, so she decided to irritate Diana on purpose for judging her.

Ron clapped his hands together.

"Now that all the introductions have been made, let's go eat, I'm starving."

They all walked toward the grill with Ron and Diana walking next to each other. Stacy stepped between Ron and Diana making sure her hips brushed against Ron, and she grabbed his arm while they walked, getting close to his face.

"Ron, you and Keith have been friends for years. Tell me how he really is." With every step, she brushed her hips against him, noticing the evil look Diana gave her. She loved it, serves her right for judging me.

Everyone sat or stood around eating. While they were eating two older women sat close by who watched Stacy and talked among themselves.

"Will you look at that child over there? A pretty young thing but that dress is skintight with her breasts hanging all out and will you look at the butt on that girl. She got that big high booty butt. Look like something you sit luggage on."

"Amen sister. It is a shame before God. Look at her. She got that Jezebel spirit all over her. I am glad my husband is not here. Young girls like her with those tight bodies and big butts, make men go crazy."

"I know that's right sister. If my husband were here, I would have to slap both of his eyes to keep him from lusting over that girl. The word of God is true, *For, she has cast down many wounded, many strong men have been slain by her.* Just like Delilah brought Samson down, Jezebels like her bring a good man down."

"Amen to that sister."

"Amen! See, women like her cause a good man to sin by showing all that big tight booty. You know men cannot take all that in their face. Their minds snap. Then, they take one of those penis pills and try to have sex all night. If not, they want to go out and find them a young tramp like that child over there and do some hard nasty fornicating. Lord have mercy."

"I know that's right. That is why you must feed your husband well at home. Keep him weak sister, weak and tired. Speaking of home, we need to go home and feed our husbands and put this mashed potato on them good, all night long. Thank God for Viagra, Levitra, and Cialis. Sister, those pills make you run from your man."

"I know that's right. Feed them and drain them, time to go, yes Lord."

They got up and stared at Stacy's butt, then looked at each other and shook their heads but kept walking.

CHAPTER TWENTY EIGHT
Attorney Reed's Office

James was in his law office and Diana sat at the receptionist's desk wearing a dress that came below her knees. James sat at his desk. Rick Matthew walked in.

"Detective Matthew, good morning sir, Mr. Reed is expecting you. I will let him know you are here." She picked up the phone, "Mr. Reed, Detective Matthew is here, yes sir I will." She hung up the phone. "Mr. Matthew, will you follow me?" They walked toward his office. As Rick followed Diana, he saw the sway of her hips and butt-shaking under her dress. He thought...*damn this young girl got a body, a heart breaker in the making.* He shook those thoughts off. They reached James' office and Diana knocked on his door and Rick walked in.

James stood up behind his desk.

"Rick, come in sir." He looked at Diana. "Thank you Diana."

As she walked away, Rick stared at her butt and shook his head. James noticed the way Rick looked at Diana and he developed an instant attitude. He stood there and looked at Rick with a scowl on his face. Rick closed the door and walked over to shake James' hand. James pointed his finger at him.

"You should be ashamed of yourself, a grown man looking at that baby like that."

Rick held his hands up in front of James.

"Hold up counselor, relax. I understand she is a close friend of yours, but you need to get real. She is not a baby.

What is she, twenty, twenty-one? That young lady had a body on her for days, and she put older women to shame. Damn, I wish my ex-wife was built like that. I would have never left her nagging, torn-up body. Now, can we get down to business?" He extended his hand to James.

James looked at Rick's hand and then shook it.

"I guess you're right. I am protective of her. It is good to see you again, it has been a while. Have a seat. You've aged well, looks like you've been working out." They both sat down.

"After my wife left me, I took my heartache to the gym and have been doing it ever since. Anyway, I know it has been a long time. It has been seventeen years and so much has happened for all of us. Victor Augular was something back in the day but now he is mega-wealthy and has more international political connections than ever before. But we will catch David's killer. Seventeen years later I still have nightmares about what happened in Miami. I have never in my life seen anything like that."

James leaned back in his chair.

"I know it's been a long time; a day doesn't go by I don't think about David's killer still walking free. I will never forget what happened to you and Detective Anderson. It sounds unbelievable, something from a horror movie and if I didn't know it was true, I would say you were drunk and made it up."

"I wish I had. I was filling out paperwork for days trying to explain how out of twenty-four people only two survived that slaughter. I have never seen so much blood in my life. Those two men dressed in all black. The ninja

man with his sword and the man with his black cane. Those two got to be from hell."

"The man with the cane I remember seeing at David's funeral. He was there, then he just disappeared but the slaughter in Miami was almost identical to what happened to Mr. Elizar and his men seventeen years ago. People were dismembered in both cases but none of this makes any sense."

Rick exhaled and rubbed his chin.

"I've had a lot of time to think about all of this and have come to one conclusion. Victor Augular, it was rumored long ago he engages in voodoo which I always thought was garbage but after what I saw in Miami, I believe it. I saw a man appear and disappear, a wall of fire came up from the ground and black smoke appeared in the air out of nowhere. Then a helicopter appeared behind the smoke. It was all unbelievable."

"Very unbelievable, you and your partner were the only survivors. I do agree with you concerning Mr. Augular being behind this entire nightmare but in my business, the court will not accept voodoo, only proven facts."

"You are right counselor, but Victor Augular is bigger than ever now. He probably has connections in the White House. I don't give a damn about witchcraft, voodoo doctor, or whatever. Victor Augular will go down at all cost."

"Yes sir, he will go down, no one is too big for God. I made a promise to Sheila that will be kept."

"It's only a matter of time and speaking of time. You have done very well for yourself. You are one of the biggest defense attorneys in Maryland and a good guy. In this business, that's rare."

"I thank you sir but I have learned in this business, that the people you work with don't care too much for you being a good guy. It is always the ends that justify the means, but I don't feel that way."

Rick stood up.

"Very good for you counselor, you keep your hands clean, and you will continue to do well. Oh, there is one more thing. In my business, I have dealt with all kinds of people doing all kinds of things but how do you deal with a voodoo doctor who I know is real because I know what I saw?"

James stood up and looked directly at Rick.

"There is only one way to beat the devil and that's through God. You need him on your side. Prayer from a clean vessel, *the effectual fervent prayer of a righteous man availeth much.* The power of God can beat the devil."

"James, I can't argue with the truth. It is past time for me to get my life right with God. He spared my life in Miami. Death was standing over me. I remember saying to myself at that time, Jesus help me, then the ninja man walked away. God saved me."

"I can say no more." He extended his hand to Rick and smiled. Rick shook his hand.

"I will be in touch counselor and thank you sir for your time."

"Yes sir, and I thank you."

Rick walked out of the office towards the front door and saw Diana over in a corner standing up on her toes stretching to put a book on the shelf. Her dress moved up above her knees hugging her hips and butt. Rick stared at her while he walked and whispered to himself.

"Damn, she got hips and ass on her. Just give me one night and I would rock that young tight body. Forgive me Lord." He shook his head and continued walking out of the door.

CHAPTER TWENTY NINE

The Deal with the Devil

Ron was home alone in the living room, kneeling on the floor by the sofa praying when the house phone rang. He stood and walked over to the phone.

"Hello, what's up Keith? What is wrong with your car? Yes, I still have the company truck and I can come and get you. Where are you? Hustler Park, no problem I will be there to get all four of you. Yeah, I am on my way, I said I'm on my way." He hung up the phone and walked outside and got in a heavy-duty white pickup truck that seats five and drove away.

He reached the park where Keith and his three friends were. All of them wore sweatsuits and held gym bags in their hands and stood by Keith's Corvette. When Ron stopped, they ran to the truck, three of them got in the back seat and Keith got in the front. Keith hit Ron on his arm.

"Pastor Ron, my man, boy it's good to see you. Praise the Lord son."

"I told you about your foolishness and not to call me that. Don't play with the Lord Keith." He gave him a serious look.

Keith started laughing.

"Alright, I was just having a little fun. What's up Ron? Anyway, my three friends in the back are Chuck, Rico, and Prince. They are going to help me load up the construction supplies after we make this stop first."

"Keith, how did your three friends get to the park? All of you could not fit in your Corvette."

Keith pointed back to his friends.

"They got dropped off by a friend and he left."

Chuck leaned forward toward Ron.

"What's up man, are you really a preacher?"

"I am no preacher in the church, but all Christians are a preacher for Christ." He drove away.

Rico leaned toward Ron.

"No offense Ron, but before you start preaching, I want to dabble in sin and some female flesh a little while longer. The girls in this day are stupid and give that ass up quickly. And I am trying to slide inside as many as I can. Especially the freaks, you know the ones that walk nasty and are small in the waist, thick in the hips, and got a fat round ass."

Keith nodded his head.

"Amen to that my brother but let me get my share."

Ron looked at Keith.

"Tomorrow is promised to no one, remember that. Aids and STDs are killing people by the thousands, which is why I will continue to obey the Lord."

Keith hit Ron on his arm.

"Look Ron, people don't care about none of that. It is simple, put a condom on your dick, put her legs in the air, and wear it out homie. Just because you ain't using what God gave you, do not try to stop me from making the ladies say my name, oh Keith, oh Keith." He said laughing.

Prince hit Keith on the shoulder.

"Now that's what I'm talking about. Make that bitch say your name when you put that meat inside her, doggy style, holler when it feels good." He began jumping up and down in his seat laughing, "Ron, no offense but you can have God, let me keep sinning, fucking these hoes, and making this money. Remember, in the real world we live in, a broke man is a joke man, and a man with cash can get that ass." Prince said. He, Chuck, and Keith laughed.

Ron gave Keith a look to let him know he offended him with his language and attitude.

"You think that's funny? No respect for women at all, referring to them as bitches and hoes. Would you want someone to call your mother that? No, you would not. All of you enjoy your sin for a season because payday is coming and the wages of sin are death, physically and spiritually, remember that."

Prince leaned forward and tapped Ron on his shoulder.

"No offense brother Ron, but you never had a girl, never smelled it, tasted it, or hit it for about ten minutes. My brother that is sad. If you ever got some good, tight, hot, wet pussy you will be hooked for life especially if she knows how to throw that ass back. And if her head game is tight and she can slob that knob, she would drain your pockets, quickly."

"Yeah, if you say so." Ron knew not to waste his time responding to what Prince said. They drove in silence until Ron reached the auto store and he parked across the street.

Keith pulled out a roll of money and showed Ron.

"I have a surprise for Stacy. You passed a jewelry store, I am going to buy her a platinum necklace before I

get the part for my car. Let me school you like my man was trying to do. She gets the necklace, I get the booty. And do not front my brother. Christian or not, you saw how fine Stacy is and that banging body she is working with. Small waist, hips, and ass for days, damn!"

Prince hit Rico on the arm.

"She is too fine. I do not care what anyone says. No matter what, you have to pay for the booty, married or single. A broke man can't get too much pussy."

Keith raised his hands.

"Amen my brother, you got to pay for that booty. Fact is, the better she looks, the fatter the ass, the more money you have to keep spending to get that ass."

"All women are not gold diggers. There are women out here with true loving hearts. Keith, one day you are going to really need God and I pray he does not turn a deaf ear to you at that time." Ron shook his head. "I will sit in the truck until you all get back and don't take all day. I have other things to do than play chauffeur."

Keith nodded his head and waved his hands in the air back and forth.

"Yes sir Pastor Ron, yes sir."

Keith and his friends left the truck laughing and carried their gym bags and walked to the jewelry store. Before going in they looked around then reached in their bags and pulled out masks, put them on, pulled guns out, and walked into the jewelry store.

Ron sat in the truck singing to himself. Moments later, he heard gunfire and police sirens. He looked back and saw two people running out of the jewelry store with mask on and carrying gym bags. A police car drove up in front of the jewelry store and two policemen quickly jumped out with guns aimed at the two masked men. One of the guys stopped running and threw his hands up. The other one ran toward the truck and the officers shot at him, but they missed. He stopped running, turned around, and shot one of the officers, he fell to the ground. The guy continued to run toward the truck. The guy with his hands up shot the other officer and he fell to the ground. A man ran out of the jewelry store with a shotgun and shot the guy with the mask on. He fell back ten feet, dead. The guy who ran toward the truck jumped in the back and began banging his hand on the side of it yelling at Ron.

"Drive man, drive."

Ron stared at him in total amazement.

The guy in the truck removed his mask and it was Keith. He hit the side of the truck hard and repeatedly.

"Drive this damn truck Ron, get the hell out of here."

Ron drove away quickly until he reached the park and stopped close to Keith's Corvette. Keith jumped out of the truck with his gym bag and gun in his hand then he put the gun in the bag. Keith leaned on the truck and wiped the sweat from his head and exhaled heavily.

Ron got out of the truck and stood in front of Keith. He waved his arms up and down.

"Are you crazy Keith? he screamed. "I cannot believe you did this. You robbed a jewelry store, shot a police officer, and got me involved in this. Have you lost your mind?" He stared at him.

Keith shook his head.

"You don't know half of it. The man's wife in the store pulled a gun on us and shot two of my partners but one of them shot her. All three of them are probably dead now. You saw the man coming out of the store with that shotgun blow my other partner away. That was the lady's husband. I never thought it would lead to this. This job was supposed to have been easy, in and out."

"Easy! Yeah right. The devil is a master deceiver. You play his game; you pay his price. I don't understand why you did this." He said screaming.

"Ron, I know you are upset but stop all that damn screaming like some little girl. What's done is done. I did this because I had to, my life was on the line. I sold drugs for a while. Weed at first, a few pounds here and there. Then twenty pounds at a time. I recruited my three friends that you met to help me move the weight and make this money. We were doing well but I wanted more. I received three kilos of cocaine in advance and then everything went bad. Two kilos got messed up and my neck was on the line, so my partners and I hit the jewelry store. Damn, they are all dead now." He stared at Ron and lowered his head.

"Why did you get me involved in this mess? Why?"

"I needed a driver, someone I could trust, and I never thought it would end up like this. You were never supposed to know. It was supposed to be in and out," he held up the gym bag. "But we did get paid," he put the gym bag on the ground and opened it, showing Ron a lot of money and jewelry. "Look Ron, I know all this looks bad, really bad, but we came out on top. I specifically picked this jewelry store on this day because I knew a lot of dope boys cater to it bringing in nothing but cash. It's over four hundred thousand dollars cash in this bag and I know it's a million dollars' worth of jewelry in here, street value." He stepped toward Ron and grabbed his shoulders, shaking him. "We are paid my brother, paid in full."

Ron pushed Keith away and stared at him.

"Keith, you are crazy. People are dead and all you can talk about is this blood money. I should have listened. All my life I have obeyed the Lord, now look at me. I am going to prison for armed robbery and murder, and maybe get the death penalty Why? Because of my continued transgression of the word of God. I knew you were living foul but not this foul. Lord have mercy on me."

Keith stepped closer to Ron.

"Ron, relax and don't go Jesus crazy on me now. We need each other partner. The police are a small part of my concerns. The man who I work for, his boss makes Pablo Escobar look small, so just give me a little time to pay my people. After that, you can pray and call on God all you want." He grabbed Ron's shoulder. "I need you, don't turn your back on me now, please. Promise me you will not betray me. Please keep my name out of it."

Ron stared at him.

"I gave you my friendship a long time ago and I don't know what compels me now to protect you, but I will." He looked at the bag. "You can keep that blood money; I don't want any of it. Even now, my trust is in the Lord."

Keith hugged him then let him go.

"I know you may not believe this or even want to, but if you stick with me on this, you are my friend for life. We

will rise to the top, so you keep on praying and stay strong. I know this is bad timing, but I got to go." He extended his hand to Ron. "So, are we friends for life?"

Ron stared at Keith then shook his hand.

"Yeah, friends for life Keith, but what price will I pay? Only God knows, and may he have mercy on my soul."

Keith hugged Ron again.

"Yes sir, my brother. Remember this day Ron. Now I have a prophecy for you. One day you are going to need me and because of your friendship and loyalty to me, I will not turn my back on you. I will help you make more money than you can count, drive the finest luxury cars money can buy. And nothing but FULL SEVEN'S throwing themselves at your feet ready to suck your dick first thing in the morning. I am talking about ladies so fine my brother, you would want to lick that pussy from the back." He started laughing. "Oh, I forgot who I was talking to. You never had any pussy." He grabbed his gym bag and walked to his car and jumped in and drove next to where Ron stood. "Stay strong Ron, now I have to go. Oh, just for the record, I know you love the Lord, but damn my brother you need to bend Diana over and hit that, she is so fine and got a fat ass." He quickly drove away.

Ron kicked Keith's car when he drove away, then fell to his knees and lowered his head.

"Lord, what have I done? Have mercy on me in court." He began crying.

CHAPTER THIRTY
The Courtroom

$\mathbf{R}$on's court date has finally come. He wore a $2,000 dark Grey wool, Gucci suit, a $250 white Armani shirt, a $105 John Bartlett tie, and $540 Dolce & Gabbana, black calfskin leather loafers. All compliments of Keith. He was in the courtroom and sat at the defense table next to James. James wore a $3,000 Oxford blue pinstripe suit, a $375 blue and white Armani shirt, a $150 Forzieri tie, and $2,000 Stefano Bemer shoes. Sitting behind them were Sheila, Grandma Harris, Diana, Stacy, Keith, Sandra, Christine, and Pastor Cleo Williams. Sheila and Grandma Harris sat next to each other. The courtroom was packed with church members. The prosecuting attorney was Mr. Hammerstein who was extremely hard on criminals and does not believe in making any deals, which was why he turned down James' plea for a deal. He wanted this case to go to trial.

James leaned closer to Ron and whispered to him.

"Are you okay? You look very tired."

"I am tired because I have not gotten much sleep, and I still have nightmares of the police interrogating me for hours at the station."

"Yeah, I know about all of that which could prove to be a blessing for you later, but for now, let's focus on this day."

Ron nodded his head and looked around the courtroom at his family and church members.

"Okay."

The bailiff walked into the courtroom with the judge walking behind him.

"All rise. This court is now in session. The Honorable J.P. Woodard is presiding."

Everyone in the courtroom stood.

The judge sat down and looked around the courtroom.

"I see we have a packed courtroom today, full of Mr. O'Neil's church members. Let me make one thing clear. I am a church-going man myself, so I respect the house of God." He leaned forward in his chair. "This is not the church but a court of law and there will be no loud outbursts in my courtroom. You all may be seated."

Everyone sat down. The judge looked at the papers on his desk and then looked up.

"Is the prosecution ready?"

Mr. Hammerstein stood.

"Yes your honor." He sat down.

"Is the defense ready?"

James stood.

"Yes your honor." He sat down.

"Very well, the defendant, through his counsel has requested a bench trial instead of the jury. This means I will hear the prosecution and defense arguments. After I hear arguments from both counsels, this case will be decided by me today and the defendant will go free or go to prison. I have read the extensive preliminary reports on the defendant and the issues surrounding this case." He waved his hand at James, "Defending counsel, impress the court."

James stood and adjusted his tie.

"Your honor, since you have read all the reports pertaining to this case, I will not prolong the court's time but get directly to the issues at hand. A crime did take place. The jewelry store was robbed and tragically one of the store owners was shot and killed along with three robbers. Two police officers were shot and critically wounded and are in intensive care. This crime was pre-planned by the perpetrators, but Mr. Ronald O'Neil did not take part in this criminal conspiracy, nor did he take part in the commission of this crime. In fact, Mr. O'Neil had no knowledge a crime was being committed until he heard gunshots and saw two men wearing masks running out of the store. He was an innocent bystander in all this. The only thing Mr. O'Neil knew was he was taking a co-worker to the auto parts store and the other three men were friends of his coworker. Mr. O'Neil is also a victim of all of this and should not suffer any more than he already has. I ask the court to find Mr. Ronald O'Neil not guilty. Thank you, your honor." He sat down.

Mr. Hammerstein stood.

"Your honor, my colleague did such a good job discussing the facts in this case, my job is almost done, so I will be brief. The fact that was not mentioned was the fourth perpetrator. Who did participate in this crime, who did shoot and critically wound a police officer as he ran away from the jewelry store. This person jumped in the back of the truck Mr. Ronald O'Neil drove. Mr. O'Neil did drive away with this fourth perpetrator in the back of the truck. This fourth perpetrator's identity is still unknown,

only because the defendant has refused to give his identity. It is this main reason why the prosecution strongly feels Mr. O'Neil is not the innocent bystander and victim the defense counsel has portrayed him to be in this courtroom today. And it is why the prosecution asks the court to find the defendant guilty. Thank you, your honor." He sat down.

Judge Woodard stared at Ron.

"The court also wants to know why Mr. O'Neil has refused to identify the fourth perpetrator involved in this crime."

James stood.

"Your honor, the defendant did not know this fourth person. Mr. O'Neil has stated he was a friend of his coworker who was killed and whose name he never knew. When this fourth perpetrator jumped in the back of the truck with a mask on, he pointed a gun at Mr. O'Neil and said drive. My client, in fear for his life, did as instructed and drove away until they reached the park where this fourth perpetrator quickly jumped out of the truck and ran away with the money and the jewelry. He was introduced to the defendant as the mechanic, but he did give a detailed description of this individual to the police. Which means your honor, the defendant has done all he could to assist in this case." He sat down.

"Prosecution, do you have anything different to add?"

Mr. Hammerstein stood.

"No, your honor." He sat down.

Judge Woodard leaned back in his chair.

"I have listened to both counsels and the facts have been presented to the court. The court is fully aware of Mr. O'Neil's spotless record, his strong family ties, and his church support, which is obvious in this packed courtroom today. I have one question for the defendant. Mr. O'Neil, stand up please. I want you to openly address this court. I understand you are a deeply religious man."

Ron stood.

"Your honor, I am a born-again Christian, Holy Ghost filled, and Jesus Christ is my Lord and master God manifest in the flesh."

"Amen, amen, amen!" The church members yell.

Grandma Harris stood.

"Testify for the Lord baby, testify." She waved her hand in the air and sat back down.

Judge Woodard banged his gavel.

"Alright, enough of all that. I said there will be no loud outbursts in this courtroom. Now, Mr. O'Neil, my question to you is, and this same Jesus that you confess to as being your Lord will be your judge right here, right now." He leaned forward and stared at Ron hard. "Mr. O'Neil, do you know the identity of this fourth person who was involved in this crime?"

Ron lowered his head.

"Yes, your honor, I do."

You heard all the whisperings and ohhhs and ahhhhs of the church members when Ron said that.

Judge Woodard frowned at Ron.

"Mr. O'Neil, I thought you did. Now, we are getting somewhere. Who is this third person?" He said with attitude.

Ron looked up thinking...*Lord forgive me for what I am about to say.* He began to cry.

"I can't your honor, this guy threatened to kill my entire family. I already lost my dad, and I will do whatever I must, to protect my family. I just can't." Ron sat down slowly.

Judge Woodard folded his hands in front of him and then cleared his throat.

"Mr. O'Neil, I am aware of your father's murder from the reports and his killer has yet to be caught, which is a shame. I understand protecting one's family under the circumstances for which you have stated here today. But this is a court of law son, and in this court, we must go by the law. One last time Sir, who was the fourth person who took part in this crime?"

Keith has never been so scared and nervous in his life, wondering if Ron would hold out and not give him up. If he did talk, he knew his life would be over.

Ron stood and looked at the judge.

"I have to protect my family, your honor. My dad would, at all costs, and I must do the same even if it means my freedom. I am sorry your honor." He lowered his head again and sat down.

Keith did not realize he held his breath while waiting to hear how Ron would answer the judge. He finally exhaled slowly thinking...*my brother, we are friends for life, and I will have a hump in my back, wearing Stacy out tonight just for you homie.* He looked at Stacy, squeezed her hand, and smiled.

Grandma Harris and Sheila were holding hands, silently praying ever since Ron sat down because they knew the judge was about to sentence him.

Judge Woodard looked at Ron with disgust for making a mockery in his courtroom.

"Mr. O'Neil, you leave this court no choice but to sentence you accordingly. Mr. Ronald Emmanuel O'Neil, stand up."

Ron and James stood.

"This court sentences you to…I sentence you to…" he rubbed his head, "I can't seem to sentence you, Mr. O'Neil."

Sheila whispered to Grandma Harris.

"That is my Jesus, yes Lord. Hold his tongue."

A deputy walked in the courtroom and handed the bailiff a note, then stood next to him. The bailiff handed it to the judge. He read it, and then looked directly at Ron with pure anger on his face.

Sheila's body shook then leaned toward Grandma Harris and whispered in her ear.

"I felt a very strong evil spirit."

Grandma Harris touched Sheila's arm and whispered back to her.

"I thought it was just me, but I felt that same foul spirit."

Judge Woodard continued looking at Ron with hatred in his eyes.

"Mr. O'Neil, I just received word one of the police officers who were shot during the robbery has died. Now, we have the murder of a police officer. The court has lost its patience with you sir. Mr. O'Neil, due to this new event, do you desire to identify the fourth person who participated in this crime? Think about what you are doing son."

Ron stared at the judge.

"I can't your honor, I have to protect my family."

Judge Woodard shook his head.

"Sounds like you made a deal with the devil son. Very well, Mr. O'Neil, this court sentences you to twenty-five years to life. May God have mercy on your soul son. Bailiff, handcuff him and I will give him three minutes with his family."

Diana's heart felt like it was ripped in two and she could not hold back her tears.

The deputy who gave the bailiff the note began to walk out of the courtroom. Sheila and Grandma Harris watched him leave and as the deputy reached the exit doors, he changed quickly into Mr. Bones. He was dressed in all black, holding his cane and black pouch. He stopped walking, looked back at Grandma Harris and Sheila then quietly tapped his cane on the floor while mumbling some words they could not hear. He looked at the ceiling and looked at Sheila and Grandma Harris and pointed his finger at the ceiling.

Grandma Harris and Sheila looked up, the words began appearing, *No one can beat the bones*. Mr. Bones smiled and walked out of the courtroom.

Sheila looked at Grandma Harris and whispered.

"Lord have mercy, that devil will not leave my son alone. Lord Jesus, help him."

Grandma Harris touched Sheila's arm and whispered to her.

"You hold on baby. God cannot lie and he will bring him out no matter how much time he has." Her body shook. "Lord, Sheila, God just told me starting from this day, he will bring Ron out in five years."

Pastor Williams stood.

"Your honor, May I address the court?"

Judge Woodard frowned.

"Sir I have already ruled on this matter but who are you?"

"My name is Cleo Williams. I am Mr. O'Neil's pastor."

"Usually my answer would be no, but I will allow you to speak Mr. Williams but make it very brief."

"Thank you, your honor. I know this is a very serious case but you just gave that man more time than what he can do, but I know for a fact, starting from this day, my Lord Jesus will bring Ronald O'Neil out of prison, in five years."

Judge Woodard laughed.

"Mr. Williams, there is no court in the land that will overturn this court's decision today based on the circumstances. No power in this world will allow Mr. O'Neil to be released from prison in five years. The fact is, he will do a minimum of twenty-five years, no matter what."

"God has all power in heaven and earth and his word will not return unto him void. Mr. O'Neil will walk out of prison in five years." He smiled.

"Not in this lifetime sir. This court and the law are the power. Bailiff, remove Mr. O'Neil from this courtroom. This court is adjourned."

Ron's family and friends hugged him and said goodbye. As Ron was escorted out of the courtroom, he looked over at Keith and Keith nodded his head at him.

CHAPTER THIRTY ONE
The Nightclub

Victor was in his office at the club and sat at his desk. Jazz music played. He wore a $6,000 blue Brioni suit and custom-made gator shoes. Victor thought about how fortunate things have been for him these last seventeen years, with Mr. Bones and Mr. Case's help. Month after month, one-hundred-million-dollar drug deals, and other business transactions have increased his wealth all over the world, along with other investments. Victor has amassed over thirty billion dollars in cash. He has invested his money in businesses throughout the world. Gas companies, real estate, car manufacturing companies, legal pharmaceutical companies, oil companies, large research hospitals, part-owner of various NFL and NBA teams, and some of the largest hotel-casinos in the world. He owns the largest private farm in the world, over sixty thousand acres of land growing and producing various foods.

His latest endeavor was a custom-built Robotic factory in a remote village in an undisclosed overseas location. He has the best science team specifically handpicked by him, producing robots that resemble humans in every way. He desires to have his robots working in every business and home in the country replacing many jobs that people perform. He wants ten million robots ready for distribution in three more years. The robots never sleep, never stop working, and are one hundred percent controlled by him. His plans are to lease the robots to anyone over eighteen years old for twenty years at three thousand dollars a year, which comes to thirty billion dollars a year, times twenty years. Six hundred billion dollars. This deal alone would make him the wealthiest and most powerful person on the planet, by far. In Victor's mind, this would make him untouchable by anyone. To him, he would be a God.

The club was full, and Stacy was on the dance floor, she wore two-thousand-dollar, custom-made suede heels, and a nine-thousand-dollar tailored off-the-shoulder dress that fit her body like a glove. Every head in the club stared at her because of her beauty and dangerous curves. She danced close and provocatively with a man who approached her.

Keith wore custom-made crocodile shoes and an Armani suit. He sat in Victor's office in front of his desk. He looked around the office and then looked at Victor.

"Mr. Augular, it is a pleasure to finally meet you, but I don't know why I'm here."

"You are about to find out. You were in court today and Mr. Ronald Emmanuel O'Neil is truly a rare person and a true friend to you. He protected you from life in prison and possibly death row. I know all about you. You are a drug dealer, thief, and robber. Welcome to the big time Mr. Washington."

"I'm impressed. So. what can I do for you Mr. Augular?" He asked with a smirk on his face.

"Very direct, I like that, but it's what we can do for each other. You are a small-time criminal. I am going to make you a successful businessman. I will pay you one million dollars for the jewelry you stole. Half of that belongs to your friend and it will be in your best interest to put his money someplace safe. You will be supplied with all the drugs you can handle. You will be given a legit business to support your lifestyle and please, get rid of that toy car you drive. Purchase a businessman's car and your lady friend Stacy, watch her very closely. Now, what kind of weight can you handle?"

"I don't want to overload myself in the beginning, but I will take thirty pounds of the best weed you got and twenty kilos of cocaine and see how it flows." Keith was ready to jump out of his seat he was so happy, and he thought...*Finally, I made it to the big leagues, dealing with serious businesspeople.*

"Wise move. The price per kilo is ten thousand. Also, get yourself a new address. Someplace nice but conservative. It makes no sense to drive an eighty-thousand-dollar car and live in the projects. Do the right thing concerning business and me, and everything will flow smoothly. Above all, never contemplate the thought of crossing me. I am covered far greater than you could ever imagine, no matter where you go, I can reach out and touch you. If you ever betray me, I will kill all your friends, family, and you, in a very painful way. Do we have a clear understanding?"

Keith's temper was boiling, listening to this man threatening him, and he thought... *who does he think he is? I fear no man. If I did not need him, I would shoot his ass right now.* He calmed down.

"Crystal clear understanding but there is one more thing. My man Ron is the best friend in the world to me

and I owe him. I would not want anything to happen to him while he is in prison, so can you cover him twenty-four-seven? Can you make that happen?"

"It seems Mr. O'Neil is already protected. But yes, I will put the word out he is not to be touched. He received a twenty-five-year to life sentence, but it was prophesied he would walk out in five years, for some reason, I believe it. Now, is there anything else?"

Keith shook his head.

"No sir, everything is lovely."

"Very good. Now you and Stacy enjoy your night and stay out of trouble." He stood and extended his hand to Keith.

Keith shook his hand.

"Mr. Augular, I thank you for your time sir, and now it's time to celebrate and spend some money."

"Have fun Mr. Washington and be careful."

Keith buttoned his suit jacket and walked out of the office and through the club. The music was loud, and many people were dancing. He saw Stacy on the dance floor dancing provocatively and close to some older, big muscular guy. His immediate anger caused him to have thoughts of murder...*She is going to make me catch a charge in this place.* He unbuttoned his suit jacket and walked over to Stacy and tapped her on the shoulder.

"Excuse me, Stacy, I am finished with my business and it's time to leave."

Stacy looked at him like he was crazy and yelled at him over the music.

"Baby, I am having fun and I am not ready to go yet."

The guy she was dancing with stepped closer to Keith.

"You heard her. Now go find you something to do boy before I slide you across this floor."

Keith snarled and pulled his gun out and stuck the barrel in the man's stomach.

"Don't be a hero fool over someone who does not belong to you. Now back your big ass up before I make your body leak."

He stared at Keith thinking should he try him. Stacy felt this guy wanted to be a hero, so she was going to shut this scene down. She reached under her dress, pulled out a razor quickly put it to the guy's throat, and got close to his face.

"I was dancing with you. I was not going to fuck you. So, calm your big ass down and live."

Keith grabbed Stacy by the hand, and they walked out of the club. Stacy put her razor inside her bra and Keith put his gun away.

The guy was scared thinking he was going to get shot or cut and said out loud.

"Thank you Lord, thank you." He walked off the dance floor towards the bar.

Keith and Stacy got in his Corvette and drove away.

Stacy stared at Keith with mixed emotions right now. She loves him deeply and will always protect him right or wrong, but she does not appreciate being treated like she is his property, and she is extremely upset. She pointed her finger in Keith's face.

"I don't know who you think you are, but you are not going to disrespect me anytime you feel like it, and just for

the record, I am not your property. I am your lady, and I am with you by my choice, so do not get it twisted. I am not your slave. It will benefit you to remember that. Now, where are we going?"

Keith glanced at her and smiled.

"Thanks for having my back but relax baby, all is well. Things are about to change for the better. I am moving and would like you to come with me." He looked at her. "Your choice of course. I am selling my Corvette for something bigger and better. We deserve the best."

Stacy looked at him and frowned.

"You are my man Keith, and I will always have your back because I am a true ride-or-die and a warrior to the end. You know this. I hope you know what you are doing but let me say this to you. I am no dummy! You are not going to use me and layup with every slut in town." She waved her hand in his face. "We are not married but I love you until death do us part. I will take care of you in every way a real woman should. Yes Keith, sexually I am all yours. I will make love to you, fuck in any position you want, however you want. Pussy, mouth, and ass if you want it, but if you cheat on me and I find out, I will cut your dick off while you sleep, so do not play me. Don't you ever disrespect me, don't you ever call me out of my name." She slapped him and then kissed him. "Don't you ever call me a whore or slut," she slapped him again, "and don't you ever call me a bitch. I hate that, I am not a female dog. When you get paid, I get paid. If you ever physically hit me, beat me, or mistreat me, that is the first day of the rest of your life, believe that. Since you are a big baller now. I want a new wardrobe, twenty thousand dollars, and the rest we will take one day at a time. Oh, and one more thing. I like sex a lot and I get very horny, often. So, when I say I want some dick or want you to bury your face between my legs, you better get busy. Pop one of those dick pills, I don't give a damn but if you fall asleep on me, I will be waking you up sucking your dick, riding you, or sitting on your face. Give me something, dick or tongue, bottom line, make me cum. Damn, all that conversation." She said all this and never cracked a smile, letting Keith know she was serious.

Keith looked at her like she was crazy.

"I know you better not slap me anymore; you are crazy. What you asked for is not a problem and you can consider it done but remember this. Never ask me about my business, my business is my business." He laughed. "Oh yeah, I will be giving you all the dick and tongue you can handle, believe that. Now, where do you want to go, my queen?"

Stacy kissed him.

"Queen, I like that. I love you Keith. From this day forward nothing but the best. I believe it's celebration time. Take me to a luxury hotel," she stared at him with seriousness in her eyes. "Keith, do you know how you are going to treat me?"

He looked at her.

"Yes, I do, old school big boy style. Spend money on you, treat you like the queen you are, and show you much respect. Keep hard-stiff dick in you regularly, and keep my

face buried between your legs and that fat ass of yours, licking, tasting, sucking, and fucking."

Stacy punched him on the arm.

"Boy, that's so nasty and is a street mentality."

He looked at her.

"Am I wrong?" He rubbed her leg.

Stacy smiled and thought…*all that sounds so good.*

"No baby, you are right, very right." Keith's words sexually turned her on. She reached under her dress and slid her finger inside her panties feeling how wet she was then rubbed her finger across Keith's lips. "This juicy pussy, my serious oral skills, and my heart will motivate you to give me anything I want."

Keith smiled and grabbed her hand lightly and sucked on her finger.

"I knew the day I saw you; that we would be exceptionally good together. The luxury hotel here we come." He caressed her leg and then looked at her, "Yeah, I knew you were the one." He continued to drive.

CHAPTER THIRTY TWO
Stacy and Keith

Keith and Stacy were at the Willard Hotel, known as the Crown Jewel of Pennsylvania Avenue in Washington, DC. They were in a large, gorgeous suite and R&B music was playing. Keith wore a burgundy silk pajama set and leather bedroom slippers. He walked around the room lighting candles. Stacy stepped out of the bathroom wearing heels and a silk, black robe just above her knees. She looked at the candles, then stopped and looked at Keith.

"Baby, all this is very romantic, and I will get used to it, so you can't stop," she stared at him and smiled. "You look very nice."

"I thank you, but this is just the beginning, so get used to it. You look very lovely, but I would like to see what is under that robe."

"I am sure you would, but good things come to those who wait."

"Come over here Stacy." He waved his hand at her.

"The wrong statement," she looked at him seductively. "You come to me."

"I ain't too proud to beg." He walked over to Stacy and kissed her lips and neck softly. Then slowly moved his body around hers until his growing erection was pressed against her butt and his arms were around her waist. Keith kissed her neck on both sides as his hands slid up her robe.

Stacy turned around to face him and backed him against the wall with her hands. She unbuttoned his pajama shirt and let it fall to the floor. Seeing his muscular, tight body always turned her on. She put her hands on his shoulders and kissed his lips, neck, and chest. Stacy saw the bulge in his pants and grabbed his dick and moved her face within inches of his.

"Shut up and don't say anything. This dick in my hand is all mine and I am all the woman you will ever need, Keith. If you put *my dick*," she squeezed it harder, "inside another woman, I will kill her and you, real slow and I mean every word I just said." She kissed him and their tongues tasted each other, and she loved it.

Keith felt the coldness in Stacy's words and knew he could never cross her, and live.

Stacy sucked on Keith's neck while massaging his dick at the same time, feeling it become rock hard in her hands. She stopped, walked away from him toward the bed, and turned around.

"I told you good things come to those who wait. Well, you have waited long enough." She untied her robe and let it fall to the floor. On her flawless body were burgundy color thongs and a matching bra. Keith stared at her with such a degree of lust, that he seemed to be in a trance.

"Damn Stacy, you are one fine woman. Your body is incredible," he licked his lips, "I got to lick that pussy from the back." He laughed, walked over, and passionately kissed her, "You look good baby, and your lips are so soft."

Stacy slid her finger between her legs and put it in her mouth. "You haven't gotten to the best part yet, now shut up and let your mouth do the talking." She took one step back from him and spread her legs apart.

"It's been said, I ain't too proud to beg." He stepped to her and dropped to his knees, placed his hands on her butt, and began kissing and licking her thighs and hips and reaching her crotch, he pressed his tongue against her underwear and felt her wetness, and licked it.

Stacy moaned but backed away from him and walked to the bed. She got on the bed on her hands and knees slowly with her butt facing him, turned her head, and looked back at him, smiling.

"Well, what are you waiting for? You said it, now start licking."

"No doubt! Real men do real things."

Stacy laughed.

"Shut up and get over here." She lowered her head, waiting for Keith.

Keith took his pants off, revealing his tan silk boxers. He walked to Stacy and placed his hands on her hips, kissing and licking her lower back, working his way down to her butt. Stacy removed her bra and panties then rolled over on her back, spreading her legs apart, stretching her arms out to him.

"Keith, I want you to take your time and make love to me very slowly and passionately, and then, I will take anything you can give me."

"My pleasure baby, just remember what you said." He removed his boxers and laid on top of her gently and

kissed her lips very slowly and softly. Keith loves Stacy very much and he wants to touch her in ways she will never forget. He took his time pleasing Stacy's entire body, front and back, top to bottom. No body part goes untouched. He used his hands, fingers, lips, tongue, and mouth to please her. Kissing, licking, sucking, biting, and tasting her face, lips, neck, shoulders, breasts, nipples, stomach, legs, back, and butt. Just to tease Stacy, he purposely avoided licking between her legs, saving that spot for last. Finally, he slid his tongue across her wetness very slowly.

Stacy was so turned on by everything Keith did to her, and so wet because she had climaxed twice. But when she felt his breath and mouth between her legs, kissing and licking her, then felt Keith pushing his tongue inside her, she could not help but place her hands on his head, pulling his face into her even more.

"Oh Keith, baby you are making love to me so good, your mouth is so warm don't stop, suck it, suck this pussy and make me cum again in your mouth, ohhhh Keith."

Keith slid his hands underneath Stacy's butt, lifting her up, pulling her body into his face even more, and moved his tongue in and out of her, back and forth. Then wrapped his arms underneath and around her legs so she could not go anywhere because he knew what was about to happen. He put his lips, mouth, and tongue on her clit, sucked on it, not letting go as he gripped her tighter, and pulled her toward him.

Stacy felt like she was about to pass out because the pleasure she received from Keith was so intense. But when his lips and tongue gripped her clit, she leaned her head back against the bed, arched her back, and climaxed so hard, her entire body shook. She squeezed her thighs hard against his face.

"Ohhhh Keith, baby I am cumming, oh Keith, I'm cummming baby, don't stop, ohhhhhh. Eat this pussy, ahhhhhh Keith I am cummmin." Stacy finally relaxed but her body trembled lightly from the mini orgasms she had after all the pleasure from Keith. She lay there not able to move.

Keith moved closer, looked into her eyes, and smiled, knowing his oral skills were what legends were made of, but for him, it was just the beginning. He touched her arm.

"Baby, are you okay? Don't go to sleep yet." He pulled her closer to him and kissed her lips. He was rock hard and lifted Stacy's legs up and slowly slid inside her. She felt so hot and wet he could bust inside her right now, but tonight he will make his mark in her heart and on her body. Keith slid inside Stacy back and forth with slow deep thrusts.

The moment Stacy felt Keith inside her she climaxed again.

"Oh Keith, I love you. Damn, your dick feels so good inside me. You better not cheat on me. Do not make me kill you. Ohhhhhh, I love this good dick." She wrapped her legs around his waist and held on tightly.

CHAPTER THIRTY THREE

Sheila's House

At the time Keith and Stacy were enjoying their moment of sexual bliss, a different scene took place at Sheila's house. Sheila, Grandma Harris, and Diana were in the living room. Sheila and Grandma Harris sat on one sofa and Diana on the other.

"Lord, I can't believe this day. My son is gone. First, the devil killed my husband, then my girls moved out, and now my only son is in prison with a twenty-five-year to life sentence. Lord, how much more am I supposed to take?" She started crying.

Grandma Harris put her arm around Sheila.

"Sheila, I know everything seems all wrong, but God has all things in control. The Lord knows the end to all things, and we must trust him no matter what. Remember the Lord said he will bring Ron out in five years, and he will be on fire for God at that time."

Diana shook her head and exhaled.

"Grandma, I know God cannot lie and his word always comes to pass, and I do believe Ron will walk out of prison in five years. But I do not understand why this happened to him. Why?"

"Baby, I know we all do it, but we cannot question God. His word says, *trust in the Lord with all thy heart and lean not unto thy own understanding.* Keep in mind this is not the work of God but the devil. He is behind this, but his time will come."

"I understand why Ron did not reveal who else robbed that jewelry store, but the price he must pay to protect his family. I am proud of him but angry at him as well. I don't understand that foolish boy." Sheila wiped tears from her eyes.

Grandma Harris kissed Sheila on the cheek to comfort her.

"Well, I don't understand either, but it was good the Pastor and so many church members were in court today to show support. Thank God for using the Pastor to confirm his word and I am glad Keith was there. He is a nice-looking young man, and his girlfriend Stacy was by his side. She loves that man."

Diana got up from the sofa and began to walk around.

"Okay Grandma, Keith is nice looking but looking good is not everything and I still don't like him at all, or her. I am wondering could Keith be involved in this mess somehow. And speaking of Keith, while my Ron is in prison, Keith is probably with Stacy partying and doing God knows what while Ron is suffering." She sat down and looked out into space.

CHAPTER THIRTY FOUR

Keith and Stacy

Back at the hotel, Stacy was on her hands and knees close to the foot of the bed. Keith stood at the foot of the bed behind her. He slapped Stacy lightly on her butt and put his hands on her hips and pulled her back as he slid inside her. The moment Stacy felt Keith inside her she screamed from pure pleasure.

"Yes, that's it, don't stop, please don't stop. Give it to me. I have wanted this so badly from you and it feels so good. Oh Keith, fuck me, fuck me hard. Ohhhhh you better not cheat on me, with your good dick self. Ahhhhhh baby, it feels so good, don't make me kill you, ohhhh don't stop. Fuck me Keith."

Keith slapped both sides of her butt.

"You better stop threatening me. Do you like this dick? Then throw that ass back and fuck this dick like it's yours." He gripped her hips tighter, pulled her into him, and slid in and out of Stacy. "Damn Stacy, you are going to make me cum, this pussy is so wet and tight, ohhhhhh it's so good."

Stacy has never experienced love making this good in her life and she wanted more but felt herself ready to explode because Keith was fucking her so well. As she was ready to climax, Keith surprised her. He pulled out and flipped Stacy on her back, pushed her legs back, and slid inside of her. He moved fast, just the way he knew she wanted it at this time.

Stacy felt so vulnerable in this position, so exposed but she would not trade it for anything in the world right now. She loved his hard dick in her, fucking her brains out.

"That's it Keith, give it to me, fuck me. Your dick is so hard." She began pounding the bed with her hands. "Keith I am cummming, ohhhhhh baby. Damn you are fucking meeeee so good. Ohhhhhhh I am cummming, ahhhhhhh Keith."

Keith could not hold it any longer and pushed her legs back further, thrusting his dick into her.

"Stacy, this is my pussy, take this dick. Oh Stacy, I am cumming baby, ohhhhhh Stacy, say my name."

Stacy slapped the bed with her hands.

"Ahhhhhh Keith, Keith, Keith."

After giving her all he could, Keith lay next to Stacy knowing they were exhausted from all their lovemaking. Keith got up and walked to the bathroom and got a washcloth, wet it with warm water, and wiped himself. He rinsed it and brought it back to the bed. He wiped Stacy slowly and very gently. She moaned because the warm washcloth felt good and relaxed her. Keith put the washcloth back in the bathroom after washing it and lay next to Stacy. Minutes later Stacy got up and went to the bathroom, took care of her business, took a quick shower, and then came back to bed and kissed Keith. They faced each other in bed and held and kissed each other until they fell asleep.

Hours later they woke up still facing each other. Keith was rock-hard again and wanted Stacy. He rolled Stacy on her back and began licking between her legs very slowly until she was wet. He got on top of her, held himself up with his hands, kissed her lips, and then penetrated her very slowly.

"I love you Stacy." A tear fell from his eye.

Stacy wrapped her legs around his waist and pulled him into her.

"Oh Keith, baby I love you so much just keep loving me as you do." Tears flowed from her eyes and hit the pillow, but she continued to take all Keith gave her. Slow, passionate, and softly they made love. Stacy knew this was her man and loving him like this was a must.

"Oh Keith, you have my heart baby. Please do right by me so I don't have to wear that black dress at your funeral."

He slid inside Stacy slowly and sucked on her neck while holding himself up. Keith looked into her eyes and smiled.

"Damn Stacy, this loving I'm giving you must be superb because you keep threatening me." He laughed but continued thrusting inside her.

"Don't play with me Keith or my heart. Ohhhh it's so good. So damn good." Stacy wrapped her arms around his neck and kissed him with such intensity it felt like her emotions would cause her to explode. Their lips were locked together, and she held on tightly as tears flowed from her eyes.

CHAPTER THIRTY FIVE

Sheila's House

Sheila, Diana, and Grandma Harris sat at the dinner table. They just finished eating.

"Mrs. O'Neil, dinner was good as always and I understand why Ron is spoiled. A house full of love and cooking like this, who would not be spoiled? I miss him a great deal."

"Only God knows how much I miss my son, but I know he will be alright because he's in the master's hands. Diana, earlier when we were talking about Ron being in prison. You used the phrase, my Ron. Diana, how do you feel about my son?"

Grandma Harris smiled and looked at Diana.

"I have been waiting for this. Don't be shy, go ahead and tell us how you feel about Ron, and don't leave anything out."

"Well first, I am not shy but anyway Mrs. O'Neil, I have always had deep feelings for Ron, but it was necessary to keep them suppressed. I know he was chosen by God to do great things. I have never told Ron this, but in my spirit, I know we will be as one, but this situation of us being separated is breaking my heart." She said with quivering words.

"I knew you had feelings for my son but not to that degree, even though you two are three years apart, you practically grew up together. Hold on baby, although the devil has tried to destroy my son since his birth, God is in control."

"Amen to that Sheila. Diana, baby, you hold on. God has a good man for you but more important than that, you stay humble before the Lord and prayerful. Keep your hormones in check and keep your underwear on."

"Grandma please," she lowered her head, "not in front of Ron's mother, it's embarrassing." She rolled her eyes at her.

"It's all right baby, it's natural to have sexual desires. God made us this way, but we must not transgress his Holy word."

"Mrs. O'Neil, I'm not going to transgress the word of God for Ron or any man." She looked at Grandma Harris and rolled her eyes and smacked her lips. "And grandma, don't worry about me and my underwear. They will stay where they belong," she rolled her eyes and turned her neck, "on my body."

"No, you did not roll your eyes and neck at me. Diana, I know you are heartbroken over Ron going to prison but do not get smart and do not disrespect me. Don't make me bust your lips." She balled her fist up and shook it at Diana.

Diana thought...oh God, here she goes again. Always talking about busting somebody's lips and then talking about Jesus, but I love her. "Grandma, forgive me, I wasn't getting smart, I was..."

A cloud of smoke appeared suddenly in the room in front of the table and Mr. Bones appeared dressed in all black with his cane in one hand and his black pouch in the other. He shook his entire body and wiggled his head.

"Alright, I've heard enough about busted lips and Diana's stupid underwear problem."

Diana hit the table with her hand.

"In the name of Jesus."

Mr. Bones pointed his cane at Diana.

"Shut up about him, I hate that name, and he can't help you."

Grandma Harris pointed at him.

"What do you want devil? God already defeated you."

"Shut up old woman. I came here to brag and boast. No one can beat the bones." He pointed his cane at Sheila. "Look where I sent your precious chosen boy Ron. I am going to make him suffer greatly in prison by sending demonic spirits his way. Spirits of loneliness, lust, depression, fear, guilt, despair, hate, and revenge. I am the prince and power of the air, and I can go anywhere, and attack anyone."

Sheila hit the table with her hand.

"Enough of this, you are no match for my Ron, he is truly born again, Holy Ghost filled, and you are the father of lies."

Diana stood.

"Devil, you can deceive and beat anyone in this world except my Lord Jesus and his mighty Holy Spirit."

Mr. Bones slammed his cane on the floor so hard, the entire house shook.

"I told you to shut up about this Jesus, he is dead and still in the grave." He pointed his cane at Diana. "I am

going to send someone your way to get inside your underwear and put some strong lustful spirits inside of you. Then a freaky Jezebel you shall be. You got a fat ass. I hate you born again Holy Ghost-filled people."

Grandma Harris stood.

"Enough of this foolishness devil, you have said enough, it is time for you to leave."

"Shut up you wrinkled old woman. I ain't going nowhere. You are no match for the bones, prune face."

Sheila stood and stepped closer to Mr. Bones and pointed her finger at him.

"Hold your tongue devil and get out of my house."

Grandma Harris stomped her foot.

"Enough! Sheila, Diana, in the name of Jesus, James 4:7 say it with me."

All three quoted the scripture simultaneously.

"Submit yourself therefore to God, resist the devil and he will flee from you, in Jesus name."

"Noooo," Mr. Bones yelled, "I told you I don't want to hear anything about no Jesus, and you can't beat me, you stupid females. I am the bones." He mumbled some words and tapped his cane on the floor twice. The lights in the house started blinking off and on, windows started cracking and shattering, furniture started moving and the table began to rise. Mr. Bones held his arms out wide, mumbled some words, tapped his cane twice, and began rising slowly in the air.

Sheila pointed her finger at Mr. Bones.

"In Jesus name, peace be still."

Everything stopped moving and Mr. Bones floated back to the floor.

"Noooo," he yelled again and began to shake. "I will get all of you as soon as you become weak. I will be back and get you and your son. I hate you people and I wish this gospel of Jesus Christ was never preached." He screamed very loudly, tapped his cane once on the floor and mumbled some words.

More windows cracked and smoke appeared, and Mr. Bones disappeared, but the smoke lingered. The front door opened, and the smoke went out, and the door slammed shut.

Grandma Harris, Sheila, and Diana begin shouting and praising God.

CHAPTER THIRTY SIX

Keith and Stacy

Keith and Stacy just left Euro Motors car dealership in Bethesda Maryland. Keith spent $160,000 on a new 2012 Palladium Silver Metallic S600 Benz with Sahara beige/black leather interior. He paid for the car with one of his business credit cards. They drove to Hyattsville and parked in front of One Independence Plaza, a high-rise condominium complex. Keith wore wearing a conservative but expensive business suit and Stacy wore an expensive blouse, five-hundred-dollar designer jeans that fit her body like a glove, and heels. They sat in the car and music was playing quietly. Stacy turned to Keith.

"Baby I don't understand why you chose this area and this place. I mean it is nice but with the money you are making, we could do much better. Like Potomac Maryland."

Keith leaned forward and kissed Stacy on the lips.

"You are so sexy and have soft kissable lips."

Stacy kissed him back.

"Thank you baby, but stay focused and answer my question, please. I know I put it on you, and you're sprung now and can't wait to get more of my lovin but focus baby." She touched his leg, "Stay focused." She started laughing.

Keith leaned back and looked at her.

"What! You got it backward. I made love to you so good and put my tongue and dick game down superbly.

When you climaxed, I thought you were having convulsions and I needed to hurry and call 911. You even threatened to kill me. That is deep because everyone knows, when this happens, the woman is sprung. Hypnotize to the dick and tongue." He started laughing hard.

Stacy hit him on his chest.

"Stop all that damn laughing Keith. I did not threaten you. I made a statement of fact, believe that. Women like me are rare. And if you betray me over some nasty slut showing her ass," she pointed her finger in his face, "You damn right, I will rock your ass to sleep."

Keith leaned toward her.

"I told you about putting your finger in my damn face, don't get shot." He looked at her like she was crazy.

Stacy leaned forward and kissed Keith softly on the lips.

"I know what you do want in your face," she slid her tongue across his lips, "now back to business. Why did you pick this area and this place?"

Keith stared at her thinking she might be a little unstable, but he loves her.

"Yeah, okay. No doubt my paper is long and growing and we can live anywhere, including Potomac Maryland. But I wanted a convenient place, a nice area but not too lavish. I do not want or need attention at this point. This area is nice, and it is within walking distance of everything we need. A grocery store, Prince George's Mall, restaurants, a subway station up the street, a library down the street, and a movie theater across from the condo.

What more do you need? Yes, we could do better, but this is good, and I like it. So be happy."

"You made some good points, and it is a very convenient area and within walking distance of everything. Keith, I know I like nice things, who doesn't but I would be happy with you no matter what because I love you, not the material things. I could hustle and get my things if that is all I wanted out of life. Material things do not hug you or love you back. I need a true friend, someone who loves me for me. Remember that. Now let's go in and see this condo. It better be nice for what they are asking for it."

They got out of the car and walked into the building. Keith stared at Stacy's butt. He thought…her look was flawless, and she has an amazing body. I got to stay on point always. Guys will be trying to step to her daily and make me catch a charge. I do love her, but she got a foul ass mouth. No problem, treat her good, keep my face buried between her legs and ass and keep some hard, stiff dick in her and make sure my pockets stay swollen. I got this.

They walked inside the building and saw the guard at the desk.

"Hello, my name is Keith Washington. I have an appointment to see a condo."

The guard viewed his appointment book.

"Yes sir, I will call Miss Smith and let her know you are here." He picked up the phone to call her.

The elevator door opened, and Miss Smith stepped off and walked toward the security desk. The guard waved at her.

"Miss Smith, I was just about to call you." He pointed toward Keith. "This is Mr. Keith Washington, and he has an appointment to view a unit."

Miss Smith extended her hand.

"Mr. Washington, good afternoon sir and this must be your lovely fiancée."

Keith shook her hand.

"Miss Smith, it is nice to meet you and yes this is my soon-to-be better half, Miss Stacy Copeland."

Miss Smith shook her hand.

"It is very nice to meet you both, now, if you follow me, I will show you the condo."

They walked toward the elevator and got in and Miss Smith looked at Keith and Stacy.

"Normally after an application has been filled out there is a waiting period to do background checks, but I saw on your application you work for Mr. Victor Augular. I received a call from him, and he spoke very highly of you and asked me to show you my best. Well, who am I to turn down such a gracious offer from one of the richest men in the nation?"

"Mr. Augular is a good man to work for." Keith gave her a fake smile.

They stepped off the elevator walked to the condo and walked in.

Miss Smith turned to them.

"Well, this is it, and it is the best we have left. It is what you asked for, two bedrooms and two baths and plenty of everything else."

Stacy looked around.

"Baby this is nice." She walked around. "Keith this is beautiful, and I want it."

Keith walked over to Stacy and stood close to her.

"Say no more, we will take it."

Miss Smith looked at them and smiled.

"Very good, now if you two will come to the office we can take care of the paperwork. Did you like the size of the master bedroom?"

"Yes, we did, it will do just fine," he looked at Stacy and caressed her butt when Miss Smith was not looking. "Just fine."

Stacy pushed his hand away and whispered to him.

"Stop it Keith." She looked at him and frowned.

They walked out of the condo and to the office where Keith spent about an hour filling out paperwork. Then he and Stacy left the building and walked to his car. As they walked, Stacy held his hand, but she stopped walking and turned to face Keith.

"Keith, what is this fiancée stuff? Why did you tell her that? You have not asked me to marry you and there is no ring on my finger. I am not going to pretend something exists when it does not. I'm the real deal and I don't fake anything, you know that, so don't play me."

He looked at her trying to keep his temper intact.

"Stacy, you are trying my patience today. Is anything ever good enough for you, damn? Mr. Augular told her that, not me, so relax and stop pressing me and be grateful."

Stacy felt bad now because she assumed Keith was trying to play her, but she was wrong and is incredibly

grateful for all the things he does for her, but she refused to back down and appear weak.

"I made a mistake, and I am very appreciative of you and all you do to build a life for us, so don't come at me like that."

He stepped closer to Stacy and stared directly into her eyes and his facial expression was all attitude.

"Who are you talking to like that? Look, if you do not like the way I treat you and if you think you can do better, then go do what you have to. You got too much mouth." He backed up.

Stacy knew she crossed the line with Keith and never want to lose him. She realized she needed to tone it down a little because he would not go for all her mouth and attitude. She moved closer to him and looked into his eyes with care and love.

"Forgive me. I do not want us to argue, and I never want to lose you. You know how much you mean to me." She put her hands on his waist and kissed his lips with warmth and passion, then looked into his eyes again. "Do you forgive me?"

Keith wanted to say something smart, but he felt her sincerity and hated when they argued. "Yeah, I forgive you." He kissed her lips and whispered in her ear, "Since you run your mouth so well, you need to do something with it and make me smile." He caressed her hips.

"Baby, I will be glad to put this mouth on you. Make you stutter. But the love in my heart is so much stronger." She kissed him, and they walked to the car and drove away.

CHAPTER THIRTY SEVEN
The Nightclub

Victor's stretch Benz limo drove up in front of his club, but it was not open yet because it was three o'clock on a Wednesday afternoon. He and his men got out and all of them wore Kiton single-breasted suits at $6,000 apiece. They walked into the club and saw Mr. Bones standing there holding his cane and black pouch. Victor's bodyguards pulled their guns out and aimed them at Mr. Bones. He waved his hand at them.

"Mr. Augular, tell your men to put their guns down before I take them home with me and they can see their slut mothers."

Victor looked at his men.

"It's alright. Mr. Bones is always welcome. Gentleman, I will be in my office."

His men put their guns away. Victor and Mr. Bones walked to his office. He sat at his desk and Mr. Bones stood in front of it.

"Mr. Bones, what can I do for you?"

"I came to brag." He put his cane on top of the desk and he sat down. "How do you feel about what I did to the O'Neil boy and where I put him? Twenty-five years to life prison sentence."

"As always Mr. Bones, your work is outstanding, but I have one question. Why is Ron O'Neil not dead?"

"Don't get smart Victor, some things take time, and these born-again Holy Ghost people are the hardest people to destroy. But his day will come, he will lose faith, and then it's my turn."

"Mr. Bones, it sounds like there is someone who has more power than you." Victor enjoyed irritating Mr. Bones, what few times he could.

"Shut up," he yelled, "no one is any match for me." Mr. Bones cane began to vibrate on the desk.

Victor jumped up quickly from his desk.

"What the hell is going on?" He pointed to the cane. "What is that?"

Mr. Bones waved his hand at him.

"Relax Victor. It's a message for me." He shook his black pouch and dumped the bones in his hand and stared at them. "Detective Anderson will be walking in here to see you, but I will be around." He mumbled some words and his cane stood up, tapped itself on the desk, then it disappeared. Smoke appeared where Mr. Bones stood and when the smoke cleared, a large Rottweiler dog stood in front of Victor's desk. It walked over to the corner of the room and laid down.

Victor looked at the dog and pointed his finger at it.

"One day, I am going to find out what you are and how you do what you do."

The dog lifted his head and growled at Victor and then lowered his head down.

Detective Anderson walked into the club holding his badge up. Victor's bodyguards were sitting down but they stood up quickly pulled their guns out and aimed them at Mr. Anderson.

Steve pulled his gun out.

"Relax you clowns. I am here to see Mr. Augular, now, where is he? Never mind I already know." He put his gun away and walked past them to Victor's office and walked in, but he did not see the dog in the corner. Victor sat on his desk.

"Detective Steve Anderson, it has been a long time, but it is always a pleasure to see one of Maryland's finest, well-paid civil servants."

Steve pulled his gun out and aimed it at Victor.

"Shut up. I should put a bullet in your head right now." The dog stood and looked at Steve. Victor pointed to the dog.

"Be very careful Mr. Anderson, my friend doesn't like you becoming so emotional."

Steve looked at the dog then at Victor.

"I see you are becoming more paranoid, still scared someone is going to get you." He lowered his gun. "You are a murdering piece of garbage and I have one message for you. You are going down. I know you were responsible for what happened in Miami. Twenty-two fellow officers lost their lives because of your dirty drug business. No matter what it takes, I am going to get you. I should shoot you right now." He aimed his gun at Victor again.

The dog growled and Steve turned his head to look at it and then he lowered his gun slowly while he looked at the dog.

Victor pulled out his two 357 Magnums and aimed them at Steve's head.

"Cowards like you never have the nerve to do anything. Now get the hell out of my office."

Steve looked at the two guns aimed at him, turned to look at the dog again, and put his gun away.

"Your day will come, and I will spit on your grave." He walked out of the office.

The dog walked back to the corner, growled, and metamorphosed back to Mr. Bones. He stood there holding his cane and pouch.

Victor's body trembled from fear.

"I will never get comfortable with your creepy abilities," he pointed at Mr. Bones, "I want him dead. No one threatens me and lives."

"Relax Victor. I have something special in mind for Detective Anderson. Now call Mr. Case and I will fill you in on the details."

Victor picked up the phone.

CHAPTER THIRTY EIGHT

The Police Station

Four hours later, Mr. Bones stood outside of the police station wearing a police uniform and carrying a suitcase. Police officers walked in and out of the station. Detective Anderson walked into the station and the bathroom and entered one of the stalls.

Mr. Bones walked into the police station and then into the bathroom as well. He mumbled some words and his clothes changed into his all-black gear, his cane and pouch are in his hands.

Steve opened the stall door and saw Mr. Bones standing directly in front of his stall, staring at him. He pulled his gun out quickly, stepped away from the stall, and aimed his gun at Mr. Bones.

"Who in the hell are you and where did you come from?"

"Actually, I came from heaven, but I was kicked out. Now I rule the earth and take people like you to hell with me. Your sorry life was spared in Miami but today you are going to hell." He tapped his cane on the floor and the lights in the bathroom went out. Seconds later they came back on, and Mr. Case stood directly behind Detective Anderson, dressed in his ninja suit with his sword in hand.

Mr. Bones tapped his foot on the floor.

"Thank you for living a sinful life, it makes my job so easy." He tapped his cane on the floor twice and the gun Steve held turned into a snake.

He dropped it and Mr. Bones turned to Mr. Case.

"Mr. Case, do this fool."

Mr. Case swung his sword and cut Steve's hand off that held the gun, and then he cut Steve's head off. His head hit the floor and rolled towards Mr. Bones' feet. He mumbled some words and kicked the head toward the wall, but before the head hit the wall, it exploded into pieces in mid-air. Bone matter and blood splattered on the walls. Steve's body fell to the floor. Mr. Bones tapped the body with his cane and the entire body turned into worms.

Mr. Bones pointed to Mr. Case.

"It is time to go."

Before they could leave, a police officer walked into the bathroom and pulled his gun out, and aimed it at them.

"Jesus, nobody moves!" He looked around the room. "What in the world happened in here and who are you two?"

"Ah yes, another hypocrite and a foolish one at that. You never accepted Christ in your life, and you were getting your freak on last night but not with your wife. Shame on you married man for telling that young girl with the big breasts and booty to back that ass up. And she was backing it up too. But your adulterous days are over. You are coming home with me." He stepped closer to the officer.

"I said freeze, don't move or I will blow your brains out."

Mr. Bones opened his mouth very wide.

"Shut up all that stupid hollering." He slid his right foot across the floor. The lights in the room went out and

came back on but Mr. Case stood directly behind the officer with his sword in his hand. With one swing, he cut the officer's head off, cut through his waist, and cut his legs off. The body parts dropped to the floor and then turned into worms.

Mr. Bones laughed.

"I do like the way you swing that sword. Time to go, but I want to leave them something." He spat on the floor and snakes appeared all over the floor and then he raised his hands. "Fools, no one can beat my power. I am the king of this earth." He tapped his cane once on the floor and smoke appeared and then disappeared and he and Mr. Case were gone, but the snakes were still there.

CHAPTER THIRTY NINE
The Club

It's Thursday night and ladies' night at the club. Victor and his men stood in front of the club all wearing Armani suits. There was a long line of people waiting to get in. Victor and his men walk in. Many people speak to Victor as he walked around the club. Sherry was waiting for Victor wearing a pair of $750 grey, leopard print, calf hair ankle-strapped platform shoes, a $2,500 dark blue Prada skirt that hugged her hips and butt, and a light blue midriff top revealing her flat tight stomach. She walked over to him.

"Hi Victor," she kissed him on the cheek, "You look nice, as always."

Victor looked at Sherry and licked his lips and leaned closer to whisper in her ear.

"You are trying to get me to hurt somebody tonight. You and that tight skirt hug your hips and ass wonderfully. I should take you to my office right now and make you scream my name."

Sherry smiled and playfully bit Victor's ear.

"You are not ready for all of this." She backed away from him.

He nodded his head at her.

"So you tell it, but I remember differently. You look beautiful." He hugged her and kissed her on the cheek then caressed her butt. "Very nice Miss Wilson. By the way, I am expecting Miss Stephanie Walker to show. When she does will you let me know, please?"

Sherry wanted to say when hell freezes over, but she can't.

"I know about Miss Walker and you. Don't hold it against me if I happen to forget to let you know," she frowned at him. "A detective Rick Matthew has been waiting to see you."

"I don't have time for this clown right now, I have to leave town. Where is he?"

Sherry pointed to the bar.

"Over at the bar sitting down."

"I will take care of it. I will be in my office so call me when Miss Walker comes in." He hugged her and walked away.

Victor and his men walked over to the bar, but one of his bodyguards tapped him on the shoulder.

"Mr. Augular, would you like for us to handle him for you?"

Victor stopped walking and turned to face his men.

"No, I will talk to the clown in my office, but we must leave town tonight. If he tries to take me downtown, make sure he fails. Don't kill him, just some hospital time, and make sure my plane is ready."

"No problem sir, we will take care of it. Two of them walked away.

Victor and his men continued to walk toward the bar and approached the detective.

"Detective Matthew, what can I do for you? I am a very busy man so don't waste my time." Mean mugging him.

"Mr. Augular, you really must be scared." He looked at Victor's men and smiled. "Victor Augular and his babysitters, never leave home without them. You must be living real foul, Mr. Victor Augular, a drug dealer and a cop killer."

Victor pointed his finger in Rick's face.

"You need to be careful what comes out of your mouth. Someone might take it personally. We can finish this conversation in my office."

Rick stared at Victor with hate.

"Don't put your nasty finger in my face again or I will take it as an assault and arrest you. Let's go to your office." He looked at the bodyguards and then back at Victor. "Don't forget to bring your babysitters." He laughed.

Rick followed Victor to his office and the bodyguards walked behind them. He walked into his office and sat at his desk. Rick walked in and closed the door behind him and the bodyguards waited outside the office.

"Detective Matthew, make it brief, I'm very busy and I do not have time for games."

Rick walked toward the desk.

"No problem, I hate being around you anyway. I know you were responsible for Mr. Elizar's and his bodyguard's deaths, the slaughter of the agents in Miami, and for the gruesome killing of my partner and the officer in the bathroom at the police station. I do not know how you did it, but you did it. I know you deal in voodoo and Satan is your Lord. Remember this, devil worshiper. *Whatsoever a man soweth that shall he also reap.*" He stepped closer to the desk and hit it hard, "You killed my partner. I am going to make sure you reap yours; I promise you that. I should shoot you and send you to hell right now."

Victor stood and leaned toward Rick.

"Do it now coward, do something. Cowards like you never do anything but talk. I should teach you some manners, coward."

Rick pulled his gun out and aimed it at Victor.

"You try it, go ahead tough guy, so I can blow your brains out, you stinking murderer."

Victor's bodyguards came into his office with their guns aimed at Rick.

"I suggest you put your gun away or get shot full of holes."

Rick looked back at the men and put his gun away, then looked at Victor and pointed his finger at him.

"Your day will come, and I will be there, Satan lover."

Victor pulled his gun out walked up to Rick and pointed the gun at his eye.

"Don't ever threaten me." he looked at his men. "Gentlemen, Detective Matthew has become very emotional, escort him out of my club and if he falls, step on him, several times."

The bodyguards escorted Rick out of the office and through the club. Stephanie walked into the club wearing a dress that fit her like a glove and is almost see-through.

Rick saw Stephanie as he walked out and shook his head. Stephanie walked toward the bar where Sherry sat.

"Hi Sherry, how are you doing this evening?"

Sherry looked at Stephanie and frowned at such a nasty image she was portraying.

"Stephanie, you must be starving for attention wearing that see-through dress. So, what brings you to town?"

Stephanie stepped closer to Sherry.

"Don't be a hater and why are you looking at me so hard dear? I do not do women. Anyway, I travel a lot, but Maryland is my home and Victor appreciates my company whenever we have time to spend together."

"I am sure a lot of men appreciate your company and time," giving her a smug look. Sherry thought...*I hate this bitch. Can't Victor see she is nothing but a gold-digging high-priced slut.*

Stephanie's fingers tapped the top of the bar.

"You're a sad case. You wouldn't be so uptight if you got some good dick, in the ass." She laughed at Sherry.

"I don't have time for this or you. Victor is in his office, and he is waiting for you. It wouldn't be wise to keep him waiting."

Stephanie leaned closer to Sherry with their lips almost touching.

"The best is always worth waiting for and Victor loves my best and how I taste." She grabbed Sherry's neck and kissed her hard on the lips and then walked away quickly toward Victor's office, and walked in.

Sherry was shocked and angry Stephanie did that, but she will deal with her when she comes back.

Victor sat at his desk.

"Miss Walker, don't you believe in waiting to be asked to come in before you walk through someone's door?" He stood and walked to the front of his desk.

Stephanie stopped in front of Victor.

"You have waited long enough. Show me how much you miss me."

Victor stared at Stephanie and was lusting hard because he can almost see her body in her thin, tight dress.

"Stephanie, you and that dress are going to get someone hurt." He pulled her into him and kissed her.

Stephanie wanted more of Victor's time, and she knew Sherry tried to get her claws on him. So, she made up her mind before she came to the club tonight what she was going to do to him.

"You do miss me, but I want more, much more, and I want it now." She kissed him passionately and felt his erection on her thigh, which was what she wanted. She put her hand under her dress, pushed her panties to one side, and slid her finger inside her, then rubbed her finger across Victor's lips. And then dropped to her knees and unzipped Victor's pants quickly, pulled his dick out, and slid her mouth on it. Not giving him time to react, she began sliding her mouth back and forth on his dick.

Victor was caught completely off guard by this, but her skills are too good for him to stop her. He looked down at her.

"Damn Stephanie, you must miss me. Ohhhh, that's good baby, don't stop, suck it."

Stephanie looked up at Victor with his dick in her mouth and she thought...*I am going to get you hooked on me.* She began sucking him faster and kissed, licked, and sucked his balls. She put his dick back in her mouth and sucked on him like his dick was the last she was ever going to get. Never releasing him until she felt the vein in his dick getting bigger, knowing he was about to cum. Stephanie knew she was blowing his mind with her skills. She gripped his dick with her hand and locked her mouth on the tip, sucking it with expert skills, never letting go or releasing the pressure she has on it.

Victor experienced many blow jobs in his life, but this has to be the best. He could not hold it any longer.

"Ahhhhh Stephanie I am about to explode, ahhhhh I am cummming Stephanie it's so good, don't stop, damn Stephanie."

Stephanie has him just where she wanted him. She never stopped sucking until she felt his juices flow into her mouth, and she kept that vacuum pressure on his dick.

Victor's head was back, and he felt light-headed because Stephanie sucked him so good.

"Ohhh you are so damn good." He finished exploding in her mouth and stood there with his dick hanging out.

Stephanie licked and kissed his limp dick and then wiped her mouth. She put Victor's dick back in his pants and zipped his pants up and stood directly in front of him.

"Think about that the rest of the day, lover," she kissed him on the lips and walked toward his office door, stopped, and turned around and looked at him, "I will see

you in Atlantic City, Victor. Don't disappoint me." She walked out of the office.

Victor was bewildered as he looked at Stephanie walk away.

"Damn, that woman can suck a dick."
Stephanie continued to walk through the club when she saw Sherry standing behind the bar. She walked over to the bar and stood in front of her.

Sherry waited for her, so she leaned closer, prepared to curse her out and slap the taste out of her mouth. But Stephanie was too quick for her, she leaned forward and grabbed the back of Sherry's neck, pulled her forward, and kissed her hard on the mouth.

Sherry tried to smack Stephanie, but she moved her head. Sherry had a disgusted look on her face and wiped her mouth with a napkin.

"What the hell is wrong with you? I knew you were a twisted bitch," she pointed at Stephanie, "If you ever touch me again, I will cut your throat, you sick bitch."

"Shut up, you know you liked it. By the way, now you have tasted Victor and me because I just finished sucking his dick, swallowed every drop of his cum. You jealous slut." She blew a kiss at Sherry and walked out of the club with a smile on her face completely satisfied she accomplished what she came for.

Sherry walked in front of the bar and watched Stephanie leave the club. She was so angry she could kill. The music was loud, and Sherry watched the people dance and grind all over each other. Suddenly, she became very horny in a nasty sort of way. No romantic thoughts, just straight fucking.

Victor walked through the club on shaky legs and saw Sherry standing in front of the bar and walked over to her.

"Sherry, you know where I will be, so if you need something or if anything transpires you can't handle, give me a call." He leaned forward to kiss her, but Sherry moved her head.

If looks could kill Victor would be dead because Sherry looked at Victor with hate.

"I can't believe you Victor. You have some damn nerve. I cannot believe you would touch that sorry bitch, then try to kiss me." She stepped closer and got in his face. "You let her suck your dick. I cannot believe you. I do not care who you are, no one disrespects me like that. I could slap you blind. Don't you ever, ever touch me again, you sorry, nasty, dirty bastard."

One of Victor's bodyguards was close by, and Victor waved him over and whispered in his ear to go and clear out the closest bathroom. The guard looked at Sherry and walked away and entered the bathroom with his gun in hand. Three people were in the bathroom but when they saw the guard come in, they left in a hurry. The guard walked out and stood by the door so no one could enter.

Victor grabbed Sherry's hand and pulled her along the way as they walked to the bathroom. He kicked open the door and pulled Sherry in and pushed her against the wall.

Sherry never experienced being manhandled by any man and she was thrown off by it. She did not know how

to react, and her defense mechanism kicked in and now she was fighting mad.

She slapped Victor twice, but he laughed. He grabbed her waist and pulled her into him, kissed her hard on the lips, then bit her neck. The only thing Sherry felt right now, was rage.

"Victor stop it. What is wrong with you? Have you lost your damn mind? Get the hell off me Victor." She yelled.

He enjoyed feeling Sherry's anger and this increased his sexual excitement at the same time, so he decided to take it to the next level.

"Be quiet, you know you want me." He moved her closer to the sink, pushed her body against it so her butt was pressed into it. He lifted her skirt and ripped her thong off, kissed and sucked on her lips making his dick stand up.

Sherry tried resisting him, but her body was giving in to his touch. Her emotions and love for him betrayed her. She allowed his tongue to penetrate her mouth and enjoyed it so much she began sucking on it. But she emotionally recovered quickly and smacked his face so hard you heard the sound echo in the bathroom.

"No Victor, stop it."

Victor looked at Sherry and smiled.

"I knew you had fight in you, and I like it." He turned her around fast, bent her over the sink and kneeled, and placed his hands on her hips. Then pressed his face between her legs, and licked her ass and pussy back and forth, making her wet. He stood, unzipped his pants, pulled his dick out, and put his hand on Sherry's back, and bent her further over the sink, and slid inside her.

The moment Victor pushed her against the sink Sherry began losing control, but when he pressed his face between her legs, she lost it. Her mixed emotions of anger, irritation, and strong sexual freaky desires caused her to crave Victor but still tried to resist him. Until he slid inside her with force just the way she wanted and needed right now.

"Yes Victor, that's it, give it to me, you nasty bastard."

Victor grabbed her hips, thrusting inside her fast and deep.

Sherry moved her butt into Victor, meeting him thrust for thrust and she grabbed the side of the sink for support and leverage, getting what she wanted.

"That's it, ram that dick in me Victor, harder, fuck me harder, damn you, ohhhhhh it feels good, get this pussy, but I hate you." She said this knowing it would irritate Victor and cause him to fuck her with more aggression.

Victor smacked Sherry on the butt and pulled out, then slid back in, slowly and deeply. He pulled out again and licked her ass and pussy with passion and sucked her clit.

Sherry's body shook, and she climaxed fast because Victor caught her off guard when he started licking her ass and pussy again. He put his dick back in and started fucking her hard just the way she wanted it.

Sherry could no longer control herself and exploded with all her emotions and juices on Victor.

"Ohhhhh Victor, fuck me, fuck me, I am cummning, ahhhhhhh I need this good fucking, it's so damn good, harder, ahhhhhhh fuck me Victorrrrr."

Sherry's orgasm rocked her from the inside out and she trembled, feeling her juices flow out onto Victor.

Victor could not hold it any longer and erupted inside Sherry hard, giving her every drop of his seed. When he was done, he smacked Sherry on the butt.

They cleaned up and walked toward the bathroom door, but Sherry stopped and turned Victor around to face her. She smacked his face hard, turning his head.

"That was for touching that nasty dog, Stephanie. You let her suck your dick and she kissed me before leaving, just to flex on me. Well, you have licked my pussy and ass, deeply. Now go kiss her on the mouth and let her taste my pussy and ass. Nasty walking bitch she is." She stared at Victor and then walked out of the bathroom.

Victor rubbed his face and watched her leave then laughed.

"I knew she had fight in her, they all do." He walked out smiling.

CHAPTER FORTY

Atlantic City

Stephanie, Victor, and his bodyguards walked through the lobby of the Carrington Hotel in Atlantic City. Victor and his men wore Hicky Freeman suits. Stephanie wore heels, a Maxstudio blouse, and a mini skirt. The weather was sunny with a mild breeze. The owner, Mr. Frank Cantina, had two men with him as he approached them.

"Mr. Augular, my name is Frank Cantina, I am the owner of the hotel. Are you and your guests enjoying your stay?"

"Mr. Cantina, yes sir, we are. The accommodations you provide are very satisfying but there is some business I would like to discuss with you."

"No problem, if you are not busy, we can go to my office now and talk."

"Now is a perfect time." He turned to one of his men. "See to it Miss Walker is taken care of and I will call you later."

"Yes Sir Mr. Augular."

Victor kissed Stephanie and hand her his American Express black card.

"Enjoy yourself and I will see you back at the suite."
Stephanie looked at the card and smiled, she thought…black card, with his money, I could buy Atlantic City. See what giving a man a great blow job will get you. And women suck dick for free, fools.

"I look forward to it and you do know how to get my attention. The stores are calling me." She kissed him then walked away with two of Victor's bodyguards by her side.

Victor gave a hand gesture at Frank.

"Mr. Cantina, lead the way sir."

Frank nodded his head.

"Yes sir."

Frank walked away and his bodyguards followed him. Victor and his three bodyguards followed Frank and his men to the elevator. They reached the floor where Frank's office was, and they walked off the elevator toward the office. Frank told his men to wait for him down the hall. Frank entered his office and sat at his desk and Victor sat in front of the desk with his bodyguards standing outside of the office.

"Mr. Cantina, I know you are a busy man so I will be brief. Your hotel and casino are in deep financial trouble, so here is my proposition. I will give you ten thousand kilos of uncut cocaine. In return, you give me your hotel. When you have the product, we will sign some papers. You move out and my management team moves in."

"Your offer is interesting. Yes, my casino and hotel are in financial trouble, but I am not in the drug business." He stared at Victor with serious dislike.

"My source tells me otherwise and my source is never wrong. I can find out anything about anyone at any time. So, are you interested, and let's not waste each other's time? Time is priceless, so think very carefully."

Frank has become instantly irritated with Victor and the look on his face showed it.

"Mr. Augular, there have been rumors about you for years concerning your involvement in voodoo. The story of what happened to Mr. Elizar and what went down in Miami is still being discussed. Twenty-two agents were killed, a man appeared and disappeared, walls of fire came from the ground, ten thousand kilos of cocaine drove away, a helicopter appeared in the sky, and men's heads were cut off. It has been said you were responsible for all of that."

Victor laughed.

"I am sure a man of your intelligence knows not to embrace such ridiculous rumors. Now, what is your answer to my very generous offer?"

"There are others I have to consider but I will have an answer for you in twenty-four hours." He already knew he would never do business with Victor because he hates this man.

Victor stood.

"Thank you sir and I look forward to us doing business."

Frank stood and they shook hands.

"Mr. Augular, enjoy your stay in Atlantic City." He stared at Victor. "My city, I will be in touch."

"Yes sir, your city. I will see myself out." He walked out of the office and turned to his men. "I am going to kill that clown." They all walked away.

Victor and his bodyguards were sitting down in his hotel suite talking.

"I made that clown Frank Cantina a very generous offer which I hope he accepts. He mentioned giving me an

answer in twenty-four hours but in this business, you should expect the unexpected. In the morning we are leaving, and tonight, if Mr. Cantina decides to become ambitious, then he dies tonight, and I get it all."

One of his bodyguards cleared his throat.

"Mr. Augular, we are exceptionally good at what we do but I checked on Mr. Cantina, and he is very well covered here. It would be extremely hard to take him out on his turf."

Another bodyguard looked at the one who was talking and shook his head.

"Mr. Augular it would be hard but not impossible, nothing is impossible when it comes to killing someone."

"Very true, nothing is impossible, and anyone can be killed. It would be difficult, but history has proven you can kill anyone. I hope it does not come down to that, not yet." Victor said.

Stephanie and the two bodyguards entered the suite, and everyone carried shopping bags.

"Victor hi, I did not know you would be back so soon, but I can sit my bags down and leave." She and the guards put the bags down.

Victor stood.

"Stephanie, we just finished talking," he looked at his men, "gentlemen, tonight or in the morning, whatever happens first."

All of Victor's bodyguards left the room.

Victor walked over to Stephanie, hugged, and kissed her.

"I missed you."

Stephanie grabbed his crotch.

"And you should miss me and my great skills. I missed you also. Does this mean your business is complete and the rest of the day is ours?"

"My business is complete. The rest is up to someone else making a wise choice. For his sake, I hope he does but tonight is your chance to spoil me."

Stephanie kissed Victor and bit his lip.

"Your way of thinking is backward, my lover. You are going to spoil me, which you have done financially and now it is time for you to spoil me physically. I want a lot of personal attention, tongue, and dick." She wrapped one of her legs around one of his bit him on his neck tenderly and kissed the same spot.

Victor laughed and pulled away from her.

"It's obvious what kind of mood you are in, you bit me." He picked her up.

"Victor Augular, what are you doing? Put me down." She laughed.

"I will, but in the right place." He carried her to the foot of the bed and put her down. "Relax and let me give you what you want." He pulled her miniskirt and panties off and bent Stephanie over the bed. Victor removed his shoes, his pants, and slid his underwear off. He got on his knees and buried his face between Stephanie's legs, kissing and licking her.

Stephanie was surprised at what Victor was doing but she loved his actions greatly.

"Oh Victor, that's it, lick this pussy."

Victor licked Stephanie into a quick orgasm. Then slid inside her pumping in and out with great passion and animal lust until she screamed when she climaxed so hard.

Stephanie relaxed on the bed, fully satisfied and tired. She watched Victor walk away to the bathroom to take a shower. As she lay on the bed many thoughts came to her mind but there was only one main thought right now about Victor. "Damn, I love me a handsome rich, freak."

CHAPTER FORTY ONE

Sheila's House

Keith drove up in front of Sheila's house in his S600 Benz. Sheila and Diana were in the living room watching TV. Keith wore gator shoes, five-hundred-dollar jeans, and a two-hundred dollar tailored long-sleeved shirt. He has on a Rolex watch and a gold and diamond pinky ring. He got out of the car and rang the doorbell. Diana answered the door wearing a knee-length dress that fits the contours of her body.

"Hi Keith, come on in." She stared at him and thought…*he does look good and dresses nice, but I really dislike him.*

"Hi Diana and thank you." He stared at her butt while they walked. "You look nice tonight in that tight dress. But I'm telling Ron you are out here showing your hips and butt trying to catch." He laughed knowing his words irritated her, but she does have nice hips and a fat butt.

Diana stopped walking and turned around to face Keith.

"Keith Washington, your spirit is so foul and filthy. I expect you to think like that. You can tell Ron whatever you like. I know how I am living, and you can keep your flirtatious ways to yourself, Jezebel lover." She walked away from him.

Keith walked toward Sheila.

"Hi Mom, how are you doing tonight?"

Sheila looked at Keith up and down and thought...*how does he afford to dress so nicely working a construction job?*

"Don't hi mom me, come over here so I can hug and pray for you boy. I know you ain't living right." She hugged him and then placed her hand on his head. "Lord, I pray for your grace and mercy for his soul and deliver him from darkness and into your Holy light, Amen."

Keith lowered his head.

"Thanks Mom." He stared at her.

"Don't get the wet eyes on me. Repent and come to the Lord. Now come and sit down." She grabbed his hand and they walked to the sofa and sat down.

Diana looked at Keith and waved her hand at Sheila.

"Mrs. O'Neil don't go for his sad puppy-dog look. Keith, tell her how you were flirting with me, and I am going to tell Ron."

Sheila looked at Keith.

"Keith, were you flirting with Diana?"

He looked at Diana and then Sheila.

"No! Diana, it would help if you did not scandalize my name. I was not flirting with her mom. I complimented her and said she looked nice, but she acts as if I asked her to go to bed with me. Diana is the one wearing that tight dress, trying to show her body. I am telling Ron that."

Sheila shook her head and laughed.

"You two are something else acting like two little children. Keith, watch your mouth boy, do not get your lips busted. Keith, I am glad you have been blessed with a good job, especially in these tough economic times but I need to ask this. You drive an expensive car, and you wear expensive clothes and jewelry. How can you afford all this working construction? My husband worked construction for years, he made good money but he could not afford the things that you have."

Keith lowered his head and then looked at Sheila.

"Mom, I have taken care of myself since I was twelve years old when my mom and dad were killed by a drunk driver. Yes, I ran the streets doing whatever to survive. I worked in construction at an early age as a laborer learning the trade, and I sold weed for a while, but I saved my money for years until I had enough to invest in my own small construction company. Later, I found out my parents had life insurance, and I used the insurance money to invest in my company as well. I also received a business loan. The rest is history. I am a real businessman and a natural money hustler. I learned never to put all your eggs in one basket. I also buy old houses fix them up and sell them. I have also received some big city contracts to build low-income housing. I own two barber shops, two hair salons, an urban clothing store, and three laundromats." He turned to look at Diana. "Satisfied?" He gave her a dirty look.

Sheila rubbed Keith on the back.

"You have suffered a lot to be so young. I am proud of you for wanting to do the right thing and I hope all of your businesses do well." She smiled at Keith but thought...*I am not stupid; he still can't afford all that he has. He is probably still selling drugs.*

Diana sat down.

"Keith, I did not know your parents were killed so tragically, I am so sorry. I do not condone selling drugs of any kind, but I do understand you had to survive. You have done very well to be so young." She smiled at him but knew he was not telling the complete truth about what he does. "Keith, have you seen Ron recently?"

"Yes, he is doing well and asked about you. Ron has gained weight pumping iron, so you better keep your eye on my man when he gets out Diana. Clean-cut young man and he loves the Lord. Any lady in her right mind would love to have him." He stared at Diana. "You need to go see him."

"For once Keith I have to agree with you. Any lady of quality would love to have a man like him and if it is the Lord's will, we will be together, but I cannot see him in prison. I just cannot. It would hurt my heart too much to see him in a cage like an animal."

Keith leaned forward and looked at Diana and Sheila.

"Diana, Mom, let me say this. A lot of things are the Lord's will, but we miss our blessings by not applying our work where our faith is. Diana, if you want Ron, then you better start showing it. He is a good man, and you will not visit him. That is real foul. You could never be my woman. I need a ride-or-die lady, a warrior. You need to show love, not talk about it. Some friend you are."

"I know Ron is a good man", she raised her voice, "but I don't want to see him in prison. Oh, and just for the record, I would never want to be your woman, Jezebel lover." She stared at him.

"Diana, do you love Ron?"

"Yes, I do Mrs. O'Neil."

"Have you ever told him you love him?"

Diana lowered her head and then looked at Sheila.

"No, I have not. The time was never right."

"He will be out in five years because God said he will. So, Diana you better get busy and when I pick him up from prison you better look good. I know you are born again but you don't have to wear something that's sweeping the floor and up to your neck, Miss Diana." Keith looked at Sheila. "Right Mom."

Sheila looked at Keith.

"True! Holiness is not in the clothes. Keith, there is hope for you yet son."

Diana pointed her finger at Keith.

"Let me get you straight Keith. I know holiness is not in clothes but in the spirit of the person and I do not dress like that anyway. Ron's feelings for me are in his heart not in my clothes. However, I am not going to dress like some Jezebel or Delilah just to get a man, and what do you mean, when you go, pick Ron up?"

"Keith, it's nice you want to be there when Ron gets out, but it's up to him who he wants to be there."

"So much for what you said Keith, Delilah lover." Diana rolled her eyes.

"Slow your roll Miss stuck-up Virgin Jesus lover. Ron already asked me to be there. But don't worry Diana, Ron might want you when he gets out, maybe. If you act right."

Sheila pointed her finger at Keith and Diana.

"Alright, that's enough from you two. Keith, if you want to keep seeing out of both of your eyes and keep the

swelling down from your lips, don't talk so disrespectfully. I love the Lord, but God doesn't like ugly. So, don't get your pretty eyes knocked out, and if you disrespect my Jesus again, I am going to beat all the black off you boy."

"Wow, I thought you loved me. The Bible says, *be angry and sin not*, but you are talking about knocking my eyes out and beating the black off me. Maybe I am in the wrong house." He threw his hands up, "Lord help me, I am going to get my eyes knocked out." He said laughing.

"Keith, you are truly something else, but you are right, I should not have said that." She kissed him on the cheek.

Keith placed his hand over his heart.

"I feel better now, and I forgive you Mom. Diana, you keep praising the Lord." He stood and walked toward Diana. "You hold on to God's unchanged Holy hand," he raised his hands, "God said in Malachi 3:6, *I am the Lord and I change not.* So, you hold on to the Lord and my man Ron, yes Lord, hallelujah, do it Lord, do it." He started laughing.

Diana stood up.

"Stop that Keith," she yelled, "stop playing with God."

Sheila stood up and walked toward Keith.

"Keith, you are impossible, now get out." She pointed her finger toward the door. "Get out of my house. One day you are going to get serious with the Lord and bow down before his mighty Holy hand, now get out."

Keith was laughing and covered his face with his hands.

"Don't hurt me, don't knock my eyes out, help me Lord, don't let her beat the black off me, save me." He continued to laugh.

Sheila stepped to Keith.

"Get out of here boy."

Keith hugged and kissed Sheila quickly on the cheek then walked toward Diana with his arms stretched out.

"Hug me, I'm sensitive." He had a fake smile on his face.

Diana held her arm out.

"Don't you touch me Keith Washington. I don't know where your lustful, dirty hands have been."

Keith grabbed Diana's hand and pulled her into him, and then hugged her and kissed her on the cheek.

Diana swung at Keith but missed because he ducked and ran toward the door. When he reached it, he turned around and waved his arms.

"Thank you Lord, thank you. You saved me from knocked-out eyes and a change of skin color, thank you Lord Hallelujah." He opened the door to walk out and then turned around. "I love you Mom, and Diana, I love you too with your stuck-up, nasty attitude self." He bowed toward them and walked out laughing.

CHAPTER FORTY TWO
The Nightclub

Keith was busy with his drug business and made a lot of money. He and Stacy were going on shopping sprees every week for months. Spending fifty and a hundred thousand dollars like it was nothing. Money was flowing like water. He has a meeting with Mr. Augular tonight at the club. Stacy was persistent about them going out, so he asked her to come with him.

Keith wore a four-thousand-dollar Armani Collezioni suit, twenty-eight-hundred-dollar pair of Tistoni alligator shoes, and a twelve-hundred-dollar, tailor-made shirt. Stacy wore twenty-five-hundred-dollar suede Manolo Blahnik shoes, blue three-thousand-dollar Escada couture jeans showing the curves of her body well, and an eighteen-hundred-dollar Italian blouse revealing much cleavage. Keith drove in front of the club in a different S600 Benz. He went back to Euro Motors and purchased another S600 that was white with a tan interior. There was a long line of people waiting to get in. The moment he and Stacy stepped out of the car, all eyes were on them, and Stacy loved it. Keith hands the valet his keys. Stacy held Keith's hand when they walked to let all these gold-digging women looking at him like he was their next meal, know he was very much taken. They walked into the club, and it was packed, and the music was pumping. The dance floor was crowded with people gyrating, bumping, and grinding on each other. Seeing this made Stacy want to dance and show them how it was done. She loved to dance, and dancing also made her very horny. Security was tight and Keith saw some of Victor's bodyguards and extra security as well. He pulled Stacy off to the side so he could talk to her.

"You look so good tonight baby. Every guy in this place is fantasizing about having you. I have to meet with Mr. Augular for a while, so I will find you when I am finished." He pulled her closer. "Don't let me catch a charge in here because you are shaking your ass on some dude."

"Keith, relax please, and go to your meeting. Damn you are sprung." She thought...*I truly got it going on to have someone like Keith, who can have any woman he wants, all up on me. I love it.*

"Yeah okay, I will see you when I am finished." He pulled her into him, kissed her lips with passion and possession, and then grabbed her hips. Stacy loved the way he kissed and how he made her feel every day. She took his hands and placed them on her butt, caressing it.

"This is all yours baby, you know that. You and your diamond dick and pearl tongue are all that," she whispered in his ear. "I got something I want you to lick and taste later." She rubbed his hands on her butt, slid his hand down her butt cheeks then kissed him.

He stared at her and smiled.

"Yeah okay." He smacked Stacy on the butt lightly and walked to Victor's office.

Victor's bodyguards let Keith in. Victor stood close to his desk doing dumbbell curls. He wore casual shoes,

slacks, and a tank top. He has on two shoulder holsters with his two 357 magnums in them. Keith saw a bottle of wine on Victor's desk and wine glasses. He stood in front of the desk.

"Mr. Augular, how are you doing sir, did you have a nice trip?"

Victor put the dumbbells down and looked at how Keith was dressed. He admired this young man's expensive taste in clothes.

"I am doing very well and yes I had a nice trip in more ways than one." He wiped his head with a towel and sat on the edge of the desk. "I see you are spending your money well, nice clothes. This is how real men dress, not the foolishness I see daily with people wearing pants hanging off their butt. Only idiots and clowns dress like that. If these young men only knew how stupid they look, they would change. So much for that, let's get down to business. Based on the reports I have received about you, all is well, but you tell me. How is business?"

"Business is great and flowing well. The product is so pure, I have to put some cut on it, or it would kill people on the spot. They love it, can't get enough of it."

"Very good Mr. Washington but be careful with everything you do, and I will handle the rest." He pours himself a glass of wine and he sat on his desk. "Do you like wine?"

"No, drinking is not my thing. It was drinking that caused my mom and dad's deaths from a drunk driver."

"I can understand that."

"Mr. Augular, business is so good, I need more product. I would like one hundred pounds of weed and a hundred kilos of cocaine.

Victor gave Keith a look of approval.

"Ambition, I like that Mr. Washington. But remember, when much is asked, much is required. Never forget that. If you do well on this deal, on the next one I will front you one hundred pounds of weed and a hundred pounds of cocaine. You can pay me for the extra weight when you regroup from the streets."

Keith nodded his head.

"That's some serious weight to handle, but I have the manpower to move it, so it is not a problem."

"Good, now there is one more thing. If you ever get caught with all this weight, legally it will look like an impossible situation, but hold your peace and do not panic. If you have a bond, I can pull you in twenty-four hours no matter what it is. If you do not have a bond, it will take me one week to pull you. But relax, keep your mouth shut, and trust no one. Now is there anything else?"

"Yes, there is. When my man Ron gets out of prison, I will need to spend some time with him. He's a true friend and I owe him."

"And you should. A true friend is hard to find but be careful and keep your business and him separate."

"No problem. Ron loves Jesus so much he would die for him and that is his life, but my business is my business, and he has his. Unless you have something else to discuss, that's it for me sir."

"I heard you bought two S600 Benzes, went clothes shopping, and moved in that nice complex in Hyattsville I called in for you and your fiancée Miss Stacy Copeland. Very good sir."

"I thank you for your assistance and for setting me up in my own construction company but is there anything you don't know."

"My eyes are everywhere. The details of what you want will be given to you by one of my business associates very soon, and he will be your contact for all future dealings."

"Again, I thank you. Now it's time for me to step."
Victor walked over to Keith and shook his hand.

"Take care of yourself and, *my business*," he touched his chest when he said that. "Mr. Washington."

"No question sir." He walked out of the office and through the club looking for Stacy when he noticed a crowd of people standing around on the dance floor looking at something. He stepped closer to find out what was going on, unfastening his suit jacket just in case he had to shoot somebody. As he walked closer to the dance floor, he thought…*Stacy better not be dancing her ass up on some guy because this time I am going to shoot him.*

When he reached the dance floor and moved his way through the crowd, he saw Stacy and three other girls showing off dancing like the floor was all theirs. The girls dancing with Stacy were very nice looking, and their moves were hot, but Stacy's body seemed to be moving in slow motion, every move was smooth, full of erotic energy and lust. Winding her back, and hips like she was working a pole in a strip club. The way she dropped all that ass and made it shake should be illegal. Keith stared at her, damn she could dance. He walked towards her, and Stacy saw him coming. She wrapped her arms around his neck, pressed into him tightly, and kissed his lips like they were the only ones in the entire room.

"I missed you baby, now dance with me." Stacy turned around and backed her butt up on him and began grinding hard into Keith.

Keith loved the attention he was getting from Stacy. He grabbed her hips pulling her into him tighter and moved right along with her.

CHAPTER FORTY THREE

Five Years Later

It's Ron's fifth year of incarceration. He was in his two-man cell doing pushups with no shirt on when his cellmate, Zechariah Brown, walked up to the cell door. Zechariah is an older black man whom Ron has become close to in five years. He is a handsome African American man at six feet two, clean-cut, two hundred forty muscular pounds, his body is ripped with muscles from years of working out.

"What are you trying to do today, add another inch on your chest before you walk out of prison?"

Ron did a few more pushups and then stood up and faced Zechariah.

"Mr. Brown, praise the Lord and I am keeping in shape what God gave me."

"Well, you have done a good job my brother."

"I know the Bible says, *body exercise profit little*, but it did not say neglect it and so many Christians do. That is why they are so fat, have health problems, and are out of shape."

"I have to agree with you. Many people are lazy, and their attitude is, I am going to heaven and do not need to take care of my body. No question, no marriage or relationship should be based on sex or physical looks, but neglecting your body does cause major marriage problems, but the church doesn't discuss this as it should."

"Well, I can't change the world, but I can take care of what God gave me."

"True indeed, now put your shirt on so we can go for a walk in the yard. Chosen one with muscles." He laughed, "Emmanuel."

"Only you can call me that." He put his shirt on. "Now we can walk."

They walked through the prison and reached the yard and continued to walk.

"You know Zechariah, society puts a lot of pressure on women and how they should look but that same pressure is not put on men. We all need to step up."

"I agree my brother. It has been a long road in here for me. I was in Raleigh North Carolina in this club when I met this fine sexy lady, and you know the rest. We were intimate and afterward, she started crying and told me I was her first. She was eighteen and I was nineteen. We slept together again, and when I woke up, she was gone, and I never saw her again."

"That's a sad story. You are not going to start crying, are you?" He laughed and hit Zechariah on the arm.

"No, I did my share of crying about that years ago, many times over, but that's not the end of it. About a year later she called me, saying she had a baby and that I was the father. She was in Harlem, New York living with her mother but she did not want to see me and gave me no address. I came to Harlem trying to find her, which I did, but I was too late. She was killed in a car accident. I tried to find her mother and the child, but they had moved and left no forwarding address. I never found them."

"And I heard about the rest. You were with the wrong people at the wrong time. They robbed a store, but you did not know it and the store owner was killed. You drove the getaway car and got a life sentence. Our stories are almost identical."

"Yes, they are, and we met by no accident. I came here when I was twenty-one and twenty-five years later, I am still here, but God has blessed me. I answered Jesus Christ's call on my life at twenty-five, and although I am still here, I have never given up on God because he has never given up on me. Well, once again I am about to see his mighty hand with you."

Ron raised his arms.

"Yes Lord, I went to prison on July the 29th and tomorrow is July the 29th, five years later. I have not heard anything about going home, but God cannot lie, and his word shall come to pass. Tomorrow I will walk out of this prison."

"Amen, my brother Ron. God has great things in store for us."

As they were walking in the yard another inmate rushed toward them with a knife in his hand and Ron saw him first.

"Zechariah, watch out." Ron yelled.

The man stabbed Zechariah in his stomach, and he fell to the ground bleeding, holding his stomach. He turned towards Ron and swung his knife. People are all around them and the guards were coming, but Ron moved from side to side trying not to get stabbed. The man advanced toward Ron, and he moved out the way of the knife and hit the man in his jaw, his stomach, and an uppercut to his chin. He stumbled backward and then the guards tackled him to the ground and took the knife away and put handcuffs on him. Ron tried to get to Zechariah, but the guards pushed him back and one of the guards checked on Zechariah.

Zechariah looked at the guard.

"I am dying, get Ron O'Neil, please."

"Ron O'Neil," he yelled, "who is Ron O'Neil?"

Ron pushed his way through the crowd.

"Right here," he rushed toward Zechariah and kneeled beside him. Ron touched him on the shoulder.

"Zechariah, you are going to be alright, hold on brother."

Zechariah raised his hand to touch Ron's shoulder.

"Ron, just listen. I have no fear of death because I would rather be absent from the body and be present with the Lord. Heaven will be my home, but you know you're calling, so obey the Lord my brother." He gave Ron a big smile.

Ron shook him.

"Zechariah, Zechariah."

The guard checked on Zechariah.

"I am sorry son, but he's dead."

"No, Lord, no!" Ron screamed.

The captain and his men were coming and moved through the crowd, to the fight scene. The captain looked around the yard.

"Move these men off the yard, now. And lock this place down, I want total lockdown." He looked at the man

in handcuffs and then at the man on the ground and recognized who it was. "Zechariah, damn man."

The guard kneeling beside Zechariah looked up at the captain.

"He's dead Captain, stabbed in the stomach."

The captain walked over to the man in handcuffs and grabbed his shirt collar very roughly.

"You stupid idiot. I am going to make sure you get the needle for this." He turned to his men, "Take this garbage away." He walked over to Zechariah and kneeled close to his body and looked at him and shook his head, then stood up. "Bag him and take him away."

Ron stood and faced the Captain.

"Captain, before you take him away, can I pray for him sir."

The captain looked at Ron.

"Mr. O'Neil. I know of you and Mr. Brown's faith and walk with God, but son he is dead. Prayers can't help a dead man."

"I want to pray for him Captain, please." He stared at him.

"It will do no good son but make it fast Mr. O'Neil."

Ron kneeled beside Zechariah and prayed.

"Father, in the name of Jesus, if you have called him home, then let it be oh Lord. If not, then manifest your Holy word unto me, oh God, and let thy will be done." He laid hands on Zechariah. "Zechariah, come forth."

Zechariah opened his eyes and Ron stood up.

"Hallelujah, by the mighty hand of God." He yelled.

The captain walked over to Zechariah and looked at him.

"Good God almighty. I don't believe it, I see it and still don't believe it, a miracle."

Zechariah stood up and ripped his shirt open, rubbed his stomach, and wiped the blood away but there was no mark where he was stabbed. The other inmates looked at Zechariah and could not believe their own eyes.

"Lord, I thank you, hallelujah. I was dead but now I am alive, only by the mighty hand of God, hallelujah." Zechariah jumped up and down.

The captain reached out and touched Zechariah, still not believing what he witnessed.

"Zechariah, you are truly a walking, talking, and breathing miracle. Unbelievable."

Ron pointed toward Zechariah.

"Zechariah, Jesus said, I am the resurrection and the life, he that believeth in me, though he were dead, yet shall he live, and one more time God proved he has all power over life and death."

Zechariah raised his arms and looked up.

"My God, my Lord. God has all power, all power." He and Ron raised their hands and shouted, "Hallelujah, hallelujah, all power, thank you Lord, thank you."

Early the following morning Ron and Zechariah were in their cell asleep when the Captain and two guards approached the cell, the Captain kicked the door.

"Ronald Emmanuel O'Neil, wake up son."
Ron and Zechariah sat up and Ron jumped out of bed and walked to the front of the cell.

"Good morning captain." He rubbed his eyes.

The captain stared at Ron.

"A fax came in concerning you. Son, you have twenty-five years to life sentence, but some judge has terminated your entire sentence due to some constitutional violation in your case. As soon as I take care of your paperwork, you can walk out of here a free man and I still do not believe this, truly unbelievable." He and his men walked away.

Zechariah jumped out of bed and stood in front of Ron.

"It's your time Ron, it's your time." He stared at Ron and hugged him.

CHAPTER FORTY FOUR

The Limousine Ride

Grandma Harris, Sheila, Christine, Sandra, Diana, and Keith were riding in a 2011 pearl white stretch Maybach limousine with light grey interior. This limo sells for $799,500 but you can rent it for $1,500 an hour, an minimum of four hours. Grandma Harris, Sheila, Christine, and Sandra wore long dresses, Diana wore a blouse and a skirt just above the knee with a short slit on the side. Keith wore an Armani suit. Sheila looked at Keith.

"Keith, I don't know why I let you talk me into this. My car would have been fine."

Christine looked at her mom and shook her head.

"Mom, this is very nice, and I could get used to this."

Sandra tapped Keith on his knees.

"I know I could. Keith, it's a shame you are living foul." She stared at him and smiled. "God wants to use you."

Diana looked at Sandra then at Keith and thought...*I know Sandra is not trying to push up on Keith. She must be forgetting about his crazy girlfriend Stacy.*

"I saw the way you looked at Keith, Sandra. You do not want him. He may look good, but he is living foul, but I could get used to traveling like this. Wow, this is some car." Diana rubbed the car seat.

Keith pointed his finger at Diana.

"I am tired of you telling me how foul I'm living like you are all that. You are always judging me. Don't hate the player, hate the game baby. Pray for me, do not judge me. Ron deserves the best of everything, and he may as well start now. Diana, you look nice, and you are showing a little leg, bless your little heart. You might have it going on."

Diana slapped Keith on the head.

"Shut up Keith with your filthy, dirty mind. You make me pray hard for you." She rolled her eyes at him.

Grandma slapped Keith on the head.

"Keith don't pick on my baby. I know that pretty girlfriend of yours would not want to see you with black eyes and cracked lips and do not let a lust spirit jump on you. So, keep your eyes off my Diana's legs and get right with God, boy."

Keith rubbed his head.

"I love all of you, but all this slapping me on my head needs to stop." He looked at Grandma Harris, "You are right Grandma Harris and I am trying to, but it is very hard."

Diana pinched Keith on the leg.

"Stop lying Keith, you are not trying. You love your dirty, sinful lifestyle."

Sheila smiled and looked at Keith and reached over and lightly caressed the side of his face.

"Keith, it is only hard for people to come to the Lord because they have not made up in their heart to fully surrender to him. When a person has said in their heart, Lord Jesus forgive me of all my sins and come into my

heart, there is no demonic force in this world that can stop them from receiving Jesus as their Lord and master."

Grandma Harris began stomping her feet on the car floor.

"Amen to that Sheila, Lord have mercy. I feel a shout coming on. Oh glory, hallelujah, thank you Lord, thank you."

Keith leaned back in his seat.

"Lord help me, I didn't know I was going to church this morning and hear a sermon."

Sandra caressed Keith's face.

"Call on the Lord Keith, and he will change your life, you and the whole world."

Christine clapped hands with Sandra.

"Amen sister."

Keith covered his face with his hands.

"As much as I like this car, I can't wait to get out."

"Oh hallelujah, but we and the Lord have you now," Diana said and raised her arms. "Touch him now oh Lord."

Everyone began to laugh, except Keith.

CHAPTER FORTY FIVE

An Open Door

Zechariah and Ron were in their cell and Ron was gathering his personal belongings to put in a bag. Then he and Zechariah kneeled to pray.

"Lord, we thank you for what you have already done. Your word says *the king's heart is in the hand of the Lord, as the rivers of water he turneth it withersoever he will.* Lord your hand has touched the judge's heart in my favor." Ron said, exhaled, and smiled.

"Yes Lord. I thank you for showing favor to Ron. Your word says, *so shall my word be that goeth forth out of my mouth, it shall not return unto me void, but it shall accomplish that which I please, and prosper in the thing whereto I sent* it. Lord, you spoke it and it came to pass. We thank you."

The captain and two guards approached Ron's cell, the door was open, and the captain kicked the cell.

"Mr. Ronald Emmanuel O'Neil, time to go."

Ron and Zechariah stood.

The captain touched Ron's shoulder.

"Son, you and Mr. Brown are walking miracles, no matter what anyone may say. I have seen the impossible become very possible. Mr. O'Neil, your family is waiting outside for you, and they brought you a change of clothes. It's time to walk, Mr. Brown you can walk with us to the change-out room."

Ron grabbed his bag and they walked through the prison and reached the change-out room. Ron walked in and changed clothes and walked out wearing ostrich skin shoes, a grey Armani suit, a white-cuff link dress shirt, and a grey and white tie. His bag is in his hand.

Zechariah stared at Ron.

"That's a nice suit. I have not seen a suit that nice ever. I will see you again, so I will not say goodbye. Stay with the Lord Ron, no matter what. You have everything to be thankful for."

"Without a shadow of a doubt, but I have one question before I go. The young lady you got pregnant, what is her and the child's name?"

Zechariah rubbed his chin.

"It's funny you asked because I dreamt about her. She gave the baby her first name and my last name, Diana Brown."

Ron gave Zechariah a huge smile.

"Your time will come Zechariah, hold on to the Lord." They hug.

The captain touched Ron on the shoulder.

"It's time to go Mr. O'Neil."

"I know God will bring you out of prison. Keep calling those things which be not, as though they were. God bless you Zechariah Brown." They shook hands, hugged again and Ron walked off with the captain and his men. They reached the gate and stopped walking. The captain turned to face Ron.

"Mr. O'Neil. I have been in this prison system for over twenty years, and I have seen many things, but you and Zechariah are walking miracles. son. He got stabbed and dies, you lay hands on him, and he comes back to life. You

walk out of prison in five years on a twenty-five-year to life sentence. Son, only God could have done this. Seeing these things and your life has changed me. I gave my life to the Lord last night. Do not ever turn your back on God. Take care of yourself son. Open the gate." He yelled.

The gate opened and Ron walked out and saw the stretch Maybach limo. Grandma Harris, Sheila, Christine, Sandra, Diana, and Keith stood by the car.

Ron raised his hand and smiled.

"Praise the Lord, everybody." He dropped his bag and fell to his knees, "thank you Lord, I thank you." He stood up.

Sheila walked toward him and stood directly in front of Ron, and stared at her son.

"Lord, I thank you for bringing my baby out." She hugged him and began to cry and then stepped back to look at him. "Let me look at you. Boy, you have gained weight and you put a lot of muscle on your skinny little body. You look good son, and that suit looks great on you." She hugged him and kissed him on the cheek.

"Hi Mom. I have missed you so much and your great cooking."

Grandma Harris walked toward them.

"Alright Sheila, let the boy go. I want my hug too. I helped to change his stinking, dirty diapers many days." She hugged Ron.

Christine and Sandra walked toward Ron. Christine hugged him.

"Praise the Lord Ron, you look good."

Sandra hugged him.

"Praise the Lord Emmanuel and you have gained some weight, but it's all muscle and you do look great." Ron hugged them both at the same time.

"Praise the Lord to you both." He kissed them on the cheek.

Keith walked toward Ron.

"Mr. Ronald Emmanuel O'Neil, even prison couldn't hold the chosen child." He held his arms out, "act like you love me, preacher man."

Ron pointed his finger at Keith.

"I told you about that preacher man stuff." He hugged Keith.

Diana stepped slowly and emotionally toward Ron.

"Praise the Lord Ron, you do look nice, strong tight body and that suit fit you well. You look very handsome."

Ron stared at Diana.

"Praise the Lord Diana. You have always looked good to me."

Keith waved his hand in the air.

"You two are something else. Diana, you know you miss and love the guy, so put the body on him and hug him and stop being so uptight."

Ron pointed his finger at Keith.

"Be cool Keith."

Keith threw his hands up.

"Oh no! Are you flipping on me, preacher man?"

Grandma Harris pinched Keith on the arm.

"I told you about your lips. They look nice so don't get them cracked and busted."

Christine pinched Keith.

"Keith, don't get double-slapped."

Sandra pinched Keith.

"I know that's right, Jezebel lover." She and Christine slapped hands and laughed.

Diana looked at Keith and rolled her eyes at him, then looked at Ron.

"You look fine baby. I am going to keep my eyes on you and watch out for all the Jezebels that are going to try and get their hands on you."

Ron stepped closer to Diana and kissed her on the cheek.

"Thank you, but you are the only one I want to touch me."

He turned and looked at Keith.

"You have been a man of your word Keith."

Keith raised his hands.

"Finally, I get some love thrown my way, about damn time."

Ron hugged and kissed Diana on the cheek and then kissed her on the lips, for the very first time, their tongues met and taste each other. Ron pulled Diana closer to him and kissed her passionately.

"I have missed you so much baby." He kissed her lips again.

Keith moved closer to Ron and touched his shoulder.

"Now that's what I am talking about, put the body on her son, and slob her down."

Sheila slapped Keith across his head.

"I told you about your mouth, boy."

Keith rubbed his head and stared at Sheila.

Diana stared at Ron trying to hold back her tears.

"You will never know how much I prayed for and missed you Ron." She hugged him and began crying.

Ron stepped closer to Diana and looked her directly in the eyes.

"If you missed me so much, then how come in five years, you never came to see me, not once Diana?"

Diana lowered her head and then looked at Ron.

"Ron please, let's not talk about this now."

Sheila tapped Ron on his hand.

"Ron, let's get away from this place baby."

Grandma Harris put her arm around Sheila.

"Amen to that sister."

Ron waved to get everyone's attention.

"I thank all of you for being here. Keith, the clothes are nice my friend, great suit."

Keith nodded his head.

"For you partner, nothing but the best. You have not seen anything yet. This is just the beginning, Emmanuel."

"Thanks for everything Keith." He looked at the limo. "Very nice limo." He looked at Keith again. "I know you did that, thanks again." He turned to look at the prison and tears fell from his eyes.

Diana hugged him and wiped the tears from his face and then kissed him.

Keith picked up Ron's bag and they walked toward the limo.

Ron's arm was around Diana's waist, and then caressed her hips and butt, and whispered in her ear.

"Girl, you got hips and a fat butt on you, Lord have mercy."

Diana removed his hand.

"Your eyes and hands should not be on my hips and butt we are not married yet so keep your hands to yourself, Emmanuel."

They looked at each other and smiled.

They all got in the limo, and it drove away.

CHAPTER FORTY SIX

Sheila's House

Sheila was having a welcome home dinner for Ron. Grandma Harris, Sheila, Christine, Sandra, Diana, Ron, Keith, Stacy, James, and Pastor Williams sat at the table. Food was everywhere and gospel music played. Ron and Diana sat next to each other, and Diana wore a blouse and skirt and everyone else was casually dressed.

The pastor stood.

"Praise the Lord everyone. I am not going to preach but brother Ron, you have been blessed beyond measure. The devil is not finished with you but stay focused and follow God always son and remain prayerful. God bless you and the family." He sat down.

Sheila stood.

"I want to say, I thank God for my son being home and for keeping him through it all. Ron, I love you baby." Sheila sat down with tears in her eyes.

Ron looked at Sheila and smiled.

"I love you to Mom." He stood up. "I want to thank everyone for being here, for your prayers and love for me, and for being real. I will never forget this moment. Mr. Reed, I owe you so much for everything you did on my case to get me out. I know you are a big-time attorney now, but you never forgot where you came from, and I respect that a great deal. Again, thank you sir." He sat down.

"Ron, I am glad I was able to help you. I was not sure at first if I could which is why I did not talk about it but thank God for his favor. And it's my pleasure to be here and your experience has truly brought me closer to God."

Sheila looked at James.

"James, I must be missing something. What are you and Ron talking about? How did you help him get out?"

James cleared his throat.

"Well, when Ron turned himself in, he was interrogated by the police for hours. Even after he repeatedly told them his counsel instructed him not to talk and he wanted his lawyer. His Miranda rights were never given to him. This was a direct violation of *The Fifth Amendment of the U.S. Constitution*, so I filed an appeal on Ron's behalf but even with the constitutional violation, it was very difficult because of the nature of the case with police getting hurt and one of them dying. Your case was high-profile, and no judge wanted to overturn the case. But in the end, the law is the law and finally, the court of federal appeals overturned his conviction, and here he is. Truly the favor of God."

Grandma Harris stood.

"Praise the Lord for his awesome spirit of favor. Now God can bless you with a good, clean Holy woman to be your wife if you live right. Lord, I thank you." She sat down smiling.

Keith raised his hand.

"No disrespect intended, but before you all start having church in here, Ron, I have a surprise for you." He reached into his pocket and pulled out a small box and threw it to Ron.

Ron opened it and saw some keys.

"What are the keys for?"

Keith stood.

"Walk with me and I will show you. Diana, you can come too and keep Ron company." He winked at her.

Diana stared at Keith.

"I am still praying for you Keith Washington." She gave him a, I do not like you look.

Ron stood and pulled Diana's chair out and Keith did the same for Stacy.

Everyone walked to the front door and Keith pointed to a new 2012, black S600 Benz.

"Ron, it's all yours, my brother." Keith said.

The pastor touched Ron on the shoulder.

"Wow, that's some car son."

James bumped into Ron.

"I know plenty of attorneys who would be envious of you driving a car like that."

"That's some car. I don't know what to say." He hugged Keith and they walked toward the car leaving the others standing in the yard.

Keith hit Ron on the chest.

"Open the trunk my brother."

He opened it and saw a briefcase.

"What's in the case?"

"Open it and find out."

Ron opened it and it was full of money.

"Lord have mercy Keith." He looked at Keith. "What have you done now?"

"Nothing, so relax." He leaned closer to Ron and whispered in his ear. "It's one million dollars in there and it's all yours."

He stared at Keith and became instantly irritated.

"No, it's not. This is money from a poison tree. It's blood money." He closed the briefcase and closed the trunk. "Keith, we need to talk but not now."

The others came and looked at the car.

Sandra touched Keith's shoulder.

"This car is very nice Keith." She turned to look at Stacy. "Stacy, you better keep your eyes on him."

"I always do." She said with attitude while staring at Sandra and thought...*especially from sneaky, horny church-going girls like you, trying to slide up on my man.*

"It is nice. Big baller type of car and I know it cost a lot of money." Christine said as she looked at Ron and Keith.

Sheila walked up to Keith and put her arm around his shoulder.

"Keith, this is nice and expensive, and you bought this for my son. I don't know what to say."

Diana stared at the car and looked at Keith.

"I do. I want to know how he got it. I know he told us about the businesses he owns, but that's an expensive car."

Stacy stepped closer to Diana.

"Yes, Keith owns businesses, not an employee like you. So, what are you trying to say?" Stacy locked eyes with Diana and anger was building within her.

Diana got in Stacy's face.

"Exactly what I said. I want to know how he got it."

Sheila stepped between them.

"Alright you two, enough of that, nothing is going to spoil this day. God has moved and my baby is home, so you two relax." She looked at them with attitude.

Stacy was angry and wanted to slap Diana so badly right now because of her holier-than-thou attitude. If she only knew how close she came to getting dragged across the yard and beat down and cut.

"Yes, God has moved in a mighty way so don't let the devil in your home to cause disturbance and ruin this wonderful moment." The pastor said and looked at everyone.

"Thank you Pastor and Mom, but I am not a baby." Sheila's mouth dropped open and she pointed her finger at Ron.

"What! I know you are older and put some muscles on your skinny little body, but you will always be my baby, so don't get smart and get your lips smacked and cracked fresh out of prison."

Grandma Harris stomped her feet.

"Amen to that sister."

The pastor laughed.

"Don't you all be too hard on the young man, show him love."

Christine rubbed Ron's cheek.

"If he acts right, he might not get cracked lips."

"Don't get your lips smacked and cracked, Ron." Sandra said as she looked at him and laughed.

Pastor touched Ron's shoulder.

"Ron, it looks like you are outnumbered."

James walked closer to Ron and laughed as well.

"Do you need legal representation, sir?"

"If God can be for us, then who can be against us." Diana said as she walked up to Ron and put her arm around his waist.

"Amen baby. *Who can find a virtuous woman, for her price is far above rubies?"* Ron put his arm around Diana's waist, and they walked back into the house.

Grandma Harris watched them walk away.

"Lord, will you look at that. My, my! Now, Mr. Reed, you need a good woman. What is wrong with you? How come you are not married? You are a good-looking successful man. You like women, don't you?"

Sheila and Pastor Williams walked over to Grandma Harris and stood next to her.

"Yes ma'am, I love women, but I am waiting for the right lady."

"Well, what do you like? Those skinny ones with big fake plastic breasts and a flat bottom, or those ladies that drive you men crazy, you know, with hips and a big booty butt?"

"Grandma Harris please, don't be nasty." Sheila said and looked at her scornfully.

James looked at Grandma Harris and laughed.

"Miss Harris, you are too much. Yes, I like women with curves and meat on their bones, along with a kind, warm, loving heart, and soul."

"Miss Harris, you are something else and I thank God for you because you are an inspiration to everyone." Pastor said.

"What, I didn't say anything wrong. I may be old, but I know what you men like, even a dog like meat on his bones."

Sandra laughed.

"Oh, no she didn't say that."

"Grandma Harris, you are one of a kind." James hugged and kissed her on the cheek.

She pushed his arm away.

"Don't hug and kiss me. I am too old for you. You need a young woman, but oh glory, back in my day; I would ring my husband's bell. I kept him strong, and the sun will rise daily if you know what I mean, but he had a heart attack and died, poor baby."

Stacy laughed.

"Grandma Harris you need to stop."

"Oh hush child. You, young people, do not know what you are doing. I never told my husband to stop, oh glory." She walked away and into the house.

Keith put his arm around Stacy.

"She killed the man baby, with sex." He whispered to her.

Everyone walked inside the house, but Keith and Stacy walked together behind everyone else.

"I like Grandma Harris a lot but little Miss Virgin Diana, I can't stand her, Miss Perfect, but I know what she needs." Stacy said.

"I know what she needs too, and I would put it on her."

Stacy stopped walking and slapped Keith on the right and left side of his face with both hands, then grabbed and kissed him.

"Don't let your mouth get your body a toe tag, Keith. The day you put your dick in her, is the day I cut your throat while your face is buried between my legs. Believe that." She walked away and into the house. Keith stared at her butt as she walked, then rubbed his face.

"She's going to make me shoot her one day, but damn, she got that illegal lovin. Lovin' is so good, it should be illegal." He walked into the house.

When Keith entered the house, Ron walked up to him.

"I need to talk to you so let's go in my room." They walked into the room and Ron closed the door.

"Keith, God has blessed me in a mighty way, and I am more determined than ever to do his will, above all. What happened to us is in the past and that is where it will stay. I know you have not changed your evil ways, you have increased them by selling more death and destruction and I want no part of it."

Keith stepped back from Ron and looked at him like he lost his mind.

"What do you mean you want no part of it? You are part of it. We are partners and I have big plans for us."

"There is no us. My plans are with the Lord, and I will never be used by you or the devil again. As painful as this is because we grew up together and have been friends for a long time. Since you are still living for the devil, we can no longer be friends and you are no longer welcome in my mother's house."

Keith stared at Ron.

"I can't believe you would turn your back on me after all this time. You are the only true friend I have and can

trust. I have no mom, no dad, no family, nobody and you want to turn your back on me. I don't have anyone else." He lowered his head.

"You will never know how hard this is for me Keith, but my disobedience to God cost me five years of my life in prison. I will not turn my back on you because the Lord would not, but light has no fellowship with darkness. Your choice is darkness, mine is light, walking with the Lord."

"Don't quote any bible scriptures to me. I probably know the bible better than you."

"This may be true, but it's not how much word you know, but if you are living it. God said, *if you love me, then keep my commandments.* I am not judging you Keith, but your lifestyle is foul. So, we can't hang out anymore."

He pointed his finger at Ron with a nasty scowl look on his face.

"So, it's like that? You remember this, Emmanuel, what I spoke to you before you went to prison, it will come to pass, and we will have it all."

"I already have it all, and *if God is for me, who can be against me?* Keith, I love you as if you were my blood brother, but you need to leave, and you can take the car and drug money with you. I will be fine."

"I am not taking anything back, it is yours. You earned it, and if you don't want it, give it to the church." Tears began to run down his face. "Now I don't have anyone, but me."

"You can always have the Lord Keith." He stepped closer to him.

Keith pushed Ron away and looked at him with hate.

"I don't need you or your Jesus." He stared at Ron. "My best friend is me and my money, the hell with you preacher boy." He bumped into Ron purposely as he walked out of the room as tears ran down his face.

Sheila saw Keith as he walked out and walked toward him.

"Keith, are you all right?"

He hugged her.

"I love you Mrs. O'Neil. You have always been like a mother to me." Tears fell from his eyes.

"Keith, what's wrong? What happened between you and Ron?"

"Ron said we can't be friends anymore."

Stacy walked up behind Keith, placed her hand on his back and Diana was behind Stacy.

"Baby, what's wrong?"

"Nothing," he put his arm around her waist. "Time to go." They walked out of the house and got in his Benz.

Stacy stared at him because she had never seen Keith like this.

"Keith, please tell me what's wrong, what happened?"

"Ron had to make a choice. He chose God and said we cannot be friends anymore. He was my best friend for years." He lowered his head.

"Baby, I am so sorry." She hugged him.

He pulled away from her.

"It is what it is. Forget him and his Lord. I got me, my money, and my world. Ron will be sorry he turned his back on me. So, what's up?" He looked at her. "Are you still riding with me or are you going to jump ship too?"

Stacy knew he was hurting, and this was not a time to get smart.

"Keith, I am not Ron so don't insult me. Ride or die until the end. You and I, against the whole world baby. Warrior to warrior, you know that." She hugged and kissed him.

Keith stared at her and nodded his head.

"Yeah, that's right. You and me against the world. I am tired and need a change of scenery. How about we go somewhere tropical?"

Stacy rubbed Keith's leg.

"Anywhere you want to go baby." She continued rubbing his leg to comfort and distract him.

Ron was still in his bedroom. Sheila and Diana walked in.

"Ron, are you alright? What happened between you and Keith?" Sheila said.

He turned around and tears were running down his face.

"I lost a friend. I had to choose between Keith and the Lord. God has to be my choice always, so Keith and I can't be friends anymore."

"I know it hurts but you made the right choice." She hugged and kissed him on the cheek and walked out, closing the door behind her.

Diana moved closer to Ron.

"Ron, I don't know what to say. I never liked Keith, but I know you two were best friends and that's hard to find."

Ron hugged and kissed her cheek, lips, and caressed her butt, and pulled her into him.

"I need you."

Diana pulled away and looked at him.

"Ron, please stop."

"I need your closeness and warmth Diana, is that too much to ask?" He caressed her hips, grabbed her butt, and pulled her dress up.

She pulled away again.

"Ron please! I know you are hurting, and I have feelings too, but I cannot comfort you like that. You know I want you just as much, but I can't lose my salvation for you or any man."

He stared at Diana and became irritated because he needed her and she rejected him. She would not be there for him, and she was acting very uptight.

"I didn't ask you to lose your salvation, so stop exaggerating. I needed your support and for you to visit me in prison. I got no love from you. Not one damn visit in five years, nothing. I need you now Diana, for comfort and support, but once again, I get nothing. But you love me. Yeah right. Miss me with that one. Strange love." He looked at her with contempt in his eyes.

Everything Ron said hit Diana hard and she knew he was right. She was torn emotionally right now, and of all people, never desired to cause him any pain.

"Ron, I am so sorry for not coming to visit you, but you have to understand it would have crushed my heart to see you in a cage. Please forgive me." Her eyes spoke volumes of love and compassion as she looked at him.

Ron stared at Diana because her words touched his heart.

"I forgive you Diana, but I need you now." He put his hands on her waist and pulled her into him. He smiled as he slid his hands underneath her dress, grabbed and then caressed her butt, feeling her flesh because she wore thong panties. He kissed Diana and slid his hand inside her panties, and reached between her legs from the back, felt her wetness, and kissed her passionately.

Diana enjoyed Ron's touch greatly but mentally snapped when she felt his hand inside her panties. She pulled away and slapped him harder than she meant to.

"Stop it Ron!" She yelled and backed away from him, "What's wrong with you? I know you are hurting but I cannot believe you would disrespect and violate me like this. You know how I feel about you, but I will not be disrespected by you or any man. So, stop!" Diana was so angry at what he did she wanted to hit him again. "Has prison corrupted you Ron? Do you have a lust spirit?"

He rubbed his face.

"You did not have to slap me so hard because I grabbed your butt and no, prison has not corrupted me and no, I do not have a lust spirit. But you are right, and I apologize for disrespecting you. Anyway, before we leave the room can I have another hug?"

"As much as I enjoyed being in your arms, I don't think hugging you right now would be a good idea." She looked between his legs.

Ron looked down and saw the print against the pants of his erection, then looked at her.

"Yeah, I guess you are right, but I did find out four things about you."

"I know I should not ask but what are the four things Ron?" "You wear thongs, your skin is very soft, you have a round tight ass, and you get very…"

Before he could finish his sentence, Diana put her hand over his mouth.

"Stop! I know what you were about to say. Ron, I do not want a man who wants me just for my body. I want a Godly man and a true friend. Oh, and don't say ass." She kissed him on the cheek. "If you continue to live right and marry me, you will find out how much me and my body got it going on." She stared into his eyes. "Ron, if I am good enough for you to have sex with, then I am good enough to marry. I am not some jump-off or gold-digging slut. Remember that." She grabbed his hand and they walked out of the room, then stopped and stared at him. "Ron, just for the record, your hands did feel good on my butt." She kissed him on the cheek and walked away, shaking her hips and butt.

He stared at her while she walked.

"God don't like ugly, and you need to stop shaking your hips and butt like that if you don't want me to grab it, teasing me." He smiled and walked fast to catch up with her.

CHAPTER FORTY SEVEN
Vacation

When Stacy and Keith left Ron's house, they went home and showered. Keith put on dress shoes, a dress shirt, and slacks and Stacy put on a very pretty dress. They packed, not knowing exactly where they were going except someplace tropical. They eventually picked Antigua. Keith made one call and chartered a private jet to take them.

They chose St. James Club and Villas. A plush tropical playground that sat on a private one-hundred-acre estate, boasting breathtaking ocean views and two white-sand beaches. The moment they arrived at the airport at two o'clock in the afternoon, it has been five-star treatment. Stretch Benz limo ride to the hotel, assigned their tour guide, their luggage carried to their five-star luxury suite, and their clothes were carefully put away. The suite came with twenty-four-hour concierge services including a full body and facial massage at any time. Their room gave them a great view of the ocean.

They left the room and went for a walk along the beach, still wearing their dress clothes, but had sandals on. The weather was eighty-five degrees bright and sunny. The agreement was not to discuss any business at this time, just walk, hold hands, and enjoy each other's company. Kissing, running, and having fun. Stacy hopped on Keith's back while they walked. He found a secluded spot near some rocks, so he put her down and tried continually to put his hands underneath Stacy's dress, but she pushed him off playfully and ran away.

The sun was going down and the air was getting a little cool, so they walked back to their room. Both were tired so they showered and went to sleep on the king-sized bed.

Stacy wore one of Keith's T-shirts and nothing else. Keith wore a silk tank top and silk boxers. He woke up lying on his side and smiled when he looked at Stacy sleeping so peacefully with her butt pressed into him. He slid her T-shirt up gently so he could see her sexy butt and kissed the side of her face softly and caressed her butt. Stacy woke up to his warm gentle touch that always warmed her emotionally and physically. She loved this man so much and desired to give herself to him in every way possible, never giving him any reason to be with another woman for anything. His scent, his body, his touch, even his breath moved and aroused her deeply. She began grinding on him until she felt his erection growing. Stacy wanted action, not a lot of talk right now. She rolled over to face Keith and pushed him on his back and put her finger to his lips.

"Baby don't talk. Let me take care of you and be the woman I am."

Keith felt her strong desire and need to cater to him, so he relaxed and let Stacy do her thing. He pulled his tank top and boxers off.

Stacy loved looking at his muscular body. She slid her body down and grabbed his semi-erect dick and put it in her mouth, sliding it in and out, feeling it getting bigger and harder with each move of her hot mouth. She kissed, licked, and sucked him with passion, and she knew her oral skills were great but did not want him to cum yet. Stacy removed her T-shirt and kissed Keith deeply and passionately until their tongues made love in each other's mouths.

Keith's dick was fully erect and rock hard sticking straight up, so Stacy straddled his waist. She slid down on his erection slowly until he was completely inside her. She looked into his eyes and saw his pleasure.

The moment Stacy lowered herself on Keith he wanted to cum inside her because she was so hot and wet. He did not want to disappoint her, so he used discipline and grabbed the side of her butt, and started lifting her, pushing deeply into her. Up and down he pushed, increasing his tempo and feeling her excitement.

Stacy felt so good having Keith love her like this but she knew he was trying to flip this situation around so he could sex brag later, and she was not having it. Without pulling his dick out, she turned her body around with her back to him. Stacy leaned forward and rode him hard and fast; she knew the power of the ass visual. It was not the size of a woman's butt like so many men and women think, it was the visual of seeing the woman's ass when she rode his dick. She knew men loved to see their dick thrusting inside a woman and in this position, they had both, watching his dick thrust inside her, and watching her ass at the same time. The heat between them was incredible and Stacy knew she was close to climax, so it was her turn to tip the bragging scales in her favor. She

knew Keith loved looking at her butt, so she leaned over a little more to give him a full view of slamming her body down on his dick.

The tightness and heat of Stacy's pussy and watching her butt rise up and down on his dick was too much for him. He lifted her and pulled her back down on him faster and harder just the way she wanted him to.

Stacy rocked back and forth and stopped moving suddenly. She squeezed her pelvic muscles repeatedly on Keith's dick, making their fit tighter. She rose on him slowly until his dick was almost out, then lowered herself on him very slowly. Doing this repeatedly and Kegel exercises at the same time were too much for Stacy.

"Keith, ohhhh I am cuming, fuck me Keith, baby fuck me. Harder Keith, I'm cummming baby. Get this pussy."

Keith felt his nut coming from all of Stacy's work. He pushed into her harder and faster until he could not hold it.

"Yes baby, ride this dick, ohhhhhh I am cummming, damn you are making me bust this nut, ahhhhhhh Stacy, your pussy is so damn good, ride this dick baby, ride it."

Stacy climaxed so hard it felt like an internal eruption. Her body shook and trembled as she rode Keith hard and fast, and squeezed her pelvic muscles until her juices ran out on him. Stacy exhaled and rolled off Keith slowly and laid on her stomach, gripping the sheets hard, still shaking and trembling.

"Keith, I am still cumming, ohhhhh, I am cummming."

Keith was not finished with Stacy, but she did not know it. He knew his queen was a very erotic woman, so before she could relax, and while she was still hot and wet, he slid his body down and began licking and kissing her ass. Pushed her cheeks apart gently and licked her ass and pushed his tongue inside slowly in and out. He licked all over her ass, kissing and sucking it. Then slid his finger in her wetness fingering her.

Keith made Stacy feel so good it felt like her brain was about to explode. She desired to have this done badly and was very turned on when Keith licked and kissed her ass. She bit the pillow and gripped the sheets so hard that her hands hurt. Stacy wanted more of this good loving, so she raised her butt higher. When Keith pushed his tongue inside her ass, sliding it in and out, she started screaming and climaxed hard.

"Ohhhhhhh Keith, yes lick my ass, lick my ass, ohhhhhh finger this pussy baby, you are making me cum, ohhhhhh damn your tongue feels so good in my ass, ahhhhhh Keith."

Keith loved driving Stacy crazy and all of this made him hard again. He turned Stacy over on her back, pushed her legs back, and slid inside her. She was so hot and wet, he went in easy, but she was still tight. His desires were so lustful he wanted to fuck Stacy until they both collapsed.

Stacy has never been sexually pleased like this and it was overwhelmingly satisfying. Feeling Keith inside her again was more than she could ask for.

"Oh Keith, yes baby, I love you. I love you, this is yours, claim this pussy." She could not hold back the tears coming down her face, not just because of the physical pleasure but because she loved this man that much, regardless of his money. She was deeply in love with

Keith, and it was this strong emotional attachment to him that pushed her over the edge.

"Oh Keith, I am cumming again baby. Please put my legs down and hold me, don't fuck me, make love to me."

Keith let go of her legs and lowered himself over her, supporting his weight on his hands, he slid inside Stacy, slow and deep, feeling his nut coming. He kissed her with much passion, as he looked directly into her eyes and made love to her.

"Stacy, I love you, ohhhhhh you feel so good, making me cum, ohhhhh Stacy."

Stacy sucked on his tongue, wrapped her arms around his neck and her legs around his waist, and pulled him into her harder. All of this was beyond wonderful.

"Yes, oh yes Keith, I do love you baby, ohhhhhh I am cummming again. Push that dick in me, I love you Keith." Her tears flowed harder until there was a wet spot on the pillow.

They finally relaxed and Stacy held on to Keith, feeling his seed inside her and loving it. She would never tell him this because he would think she was trying to trap him for his money. She wanted his child because she loved him that much.

They got up, showered, and got back in bed, and kissed each other passionately for several minutes, and relaxed until Keith fell asleep. Stacy looked at him and thought...*Lord, I know what we are doing is wrong, but I love this man so much.* With tears slowly coming down her face, she kissed his lips wrapped her arms around him, and fell asleep.

CHAPTER FORTY EIGHT

Temptation and Desire

Christine and Sandra were in the car driving on a foggy road and Sandra was driving. The girls wore mini skirts and tops revealing their cleavage. Christine looked at Sandra.

"I can't believe I let you talk me into going to a nightclub. I felt convicted the entire time I was there."

"Yeah well, you may have felt convicted, but I know you had a good time because I saw you dancing. I did not know you could move like that. You were all over that guy with your butt all on him and that was no Christian dance."

"Sandra please, don't point the finger at me because I saw you too. The way that guy was grinding on your butt. I know you felt what he was working with."

"Girl, I sure did, and it felt good," she said laughing. "After the dance was over, he kept begging me like Keith Sweat, talking about, I want it. But you know I told him, ain't nothing happening, and walked away." She laughed.

"Girl you are crazy. I cannot believe the way some of those women were dressed. Breasts were exposed, some had a bra on for a top, and miniskirts so short, when they danced you could see their underwear, and some did not have any on. Lord have mercy, no wonder guys are going crazy over women, all that in their face."

"Christine, I saw you dancing about two feet from that guy, dropping it low in front of his face. He danced low trying to keep up with you and I know he saw your underwear, shame on you. I know what he wanted, and so do you. Girl, you were driving him crazy."

Christine laughed.

"You are so nasty, and I can't believe this. What happened to us? We do not go to church anymore or study the Bible and look at how we are dressed. Like two Jezebels, and now nightclubs and grinding on men. I don't feel the Lord's presence in me anymore at all." She lowered her head.

"We have been in church all our lives. We are having a little fun. It does not mean we do not love the Lord, and just for the record, wearing miniskirts, going to nightclubs, and grinding on men is one thing. Giving it up is another. I am not married, so I don't give up the booty." Sandra said laughing.

"I know where you are coming from sis, but we are not the same. Knowing God is not enough. The devil knows him and the Holy word and anybody can say they love God, but God said, *if you love me then keep my commandments*. When we allowed guys to grind on us on the dance floor, our mind was not on the Lord."

Sandra focused on the road as she drove but had a sad look on her face because she felt the guilty of her behavior.

"You are right, because when I danced with that guy, and he was grinding on my butt, and I felt his thang, my mind was not on God. My flesh wanted to have what I felt. Girl, his thang felt like a piece of hot, hard steel rubbing on me." She glanced over at Christine. "Christine, tell me the truth. Are you still a virgin?"

Christine lowered her head and thought...should I tell her the complete truth. I want to, I need some help. No! She cannot deal with my problems. I can't tell her; I can't tell anyone. But I will tell her some things.

"Yes, I am, but I started watching porn movies a few years ago, just a little. Now, I look at it every day, and the truth is, I want sex badly and I have a strong lust spirit because I have very dirty sexual thoughts often about men and women. I am so ashamed of this, but it is the truth. What about you?"

"Yes, I am still a virgin but oh my God, your story is the same as mine. I have been doing the same things. Watching porn movies, having dirty sexual thoughts, all of that. Dancing and grinding on men tonight felt so good." She looked at Christine. "God forgive me, but I want some dick, so bad."

They looked at each other and laughed.

A cloud of smoke appeared in their lane and Mr. Bones suddenly appeared on the road, dressed in all black, holding his cane and black pouch in his hand.

Christine looked up.

"Sandra, look out." She shouted.

Sandra saw Mr. Bones and turned the car quickly to avoid hitting him, but the car flipped over and caught on fire. Sandra was unconscious and Christine was badly hurt, but she got out of the car and dragged Sandra out and off to the side of the road. She sat next to Sandra and began crying and then prayed.

"Oh God. Forgive us for our sins. Lord, I know you allowed this to happen because we have turned our backs

on you and transgressed your Holy word, but Lord, I pray for your grace and mercy, don't let my sister die."

A cloud of smoke appeared in front of them, and Mr. Bones stood there dressed in all black holding his cane and pouch.

Christine raised her hand.

"Thank you Lord, I thank you."

Mr. Bones laughed.

"Wrong Lord. Shut up crying you hypocrite. A few minutes ago, you and your sister were talking about getting some dick. Now you want to call on God. I can send some dick your way if that's what you want," he laughed. "I have been waiting for you two for a long time. I knew one day you would get weak in your faith and turn from God. I have been watching. You stopped reading your bible, stopped praying, stopped going to church, and stopped fasting. You gave me room to move right in and put a strong lust spirit in you. Porno movie watcher. Shame on you two, grinding on those men like that," he pointed his cane at Christine. "You know they have names for women like you two. Dick teasers," he shook his hips, "shake what your momma gave you and she gave you a lot too. Both of you got hips and a fat ass," he stepped closer and pointed his cane at Christine, "You still want some dick, hypocrite?" He began laughing.

Christine was crying and waved her arms in the air.

"Oh Jesus, help me Lord. Help me, Father."

Mr. Bones slammed his cane on the ground, making it shake and sound like thunder.

"Shut up, just shut up, it's too late for you. I got the power, and I can attack anyone. Now look at you, stupid backslider. My home has been enlarged because I blind and deceive people like you."

Christine looked up.

"Lord, you are married to the backslider, and you know our hearts, in Jesus' name, Lord help me."

"I told you to shut up praying," he yelled. You were not thinking about praying when you and your sister had your asses grinding on those men's dicks on the dance floor." He turned around and stuck his butt in her face. "Remember, pull up to the bumper?" He shook his butt then turned around. "Don't pray now, keep talking about how you want dick." He tapped his cane on the ground repeatedly, "Dick, dick, yes, you dick wanting undercover slut. Your soul is mine, you have no more power to resist me." He leaned forward and got in Christine's face. "The freaks do come out at night, and you are an undercover, dick-desiring, ass-shaking on the dance floor, freak."

Christine stood.

"Oh yes, I can resist you. I rebuke you devil, and you must flee from me, in the name of Jesus."

"No, no, shut up speaking that name, shut up." He mumbled some words, tapped his cane on the ground twice, and threw his bones on the ground in front of her.

Smoke erupted and a dog appeared in front of Christine. He tapped his cane five more times and with each tap, smoke appeared on the road, then a dog appeared. He raised his arms and yelled, "I am the bones, and no one can beat the bones." He mumbled more words

and began metamorphosing into a large black cougar. It snarled at Christine.

Christine fell to her knees.

"Lord help me, don't let me be destroyed."

The dogs stepped closer, growling, and snapping at her.

She stood up.

"Devil, I rebuke you. *No weapon formed against me shall prosper* and I command you to flee from me."

The dogs on the road howled and ran away and the cougar transformed back into Mr. Bones.

"No, no, you could not have done this. You have no power. Somebody stood in the gap for you in prayer. Damn you. I hate you people. I am going to get your whole stinking, praying, fasting family. And I am going to get that old woman too. I will kill you all." He pointed his cane at her. "I will be sending some dick your way, some dirty dick. Oh, I hate you people."

"Shut up devil and in Jesus name hold thy peace." She pointed her finger at him.

"Noooo!" He yelled then mumbled some words and tapped his cane on the ground and disappeared in a cloud of smoke.

"Thank you Lord, thank you. Hallelujah Father, you saved my life and soul, thank you Jesus."

A car approached and Christine saw it, she raised her arms and waved to get the driver's attention. The car stopped and two people got out and rushed over to Christine.

"Thank you Jesus." And then she passed out.

CHAPTER FORTY NINE

Reaping What You Sow

Sandra lay in bed at Providence Hospital. Sheila, Christine, Ron, Diana, Pastor Williams, Grandma Harris, and Dr. John Hardy stood around Sandra's bed. Dr. Hardy looked at everyone and saw their worry and concerns.

"I am not supposed to allow all of you in here at one time, but this family is nothing but walking miracles and I had to let you in. But you can't stay long because she needs her rest."

Sheila touched Dr. Hardy's shoulder.

"Thank you Dr. Hardy."

He leaned closer to Sandra.

"Tell me how you feel Sandra."

"My head hurts, and I can't move my body."

"Doctor, why can't she move?" Sheila said.

"I was afraid of that." He looked at Sandra. "The x-rays showed the vertebrae in your neck are cracked, and your lower spine is also cracked, but we could not be sure of the overall damage until you became conscious and talked with us."

Sheila reached over and grabbed Sandra's hand.

"Lord have mercy. So, what does all this mean doctor?" Sandra said.

Christine began to cry.

"It's all my fault. I should have been more persistent in saying no and we would have never gone to that club in the first place."

Grandma Harris rubbed Christine's shoulder.

"Now is not the time to place blame baby."

Dr. Hardy looked at Sandra's legs checking for proper blood flow.

"Only time will tell of your condition Sandra, meaning your bones are not broken just cracked, and they should mend together in time and be just as strong. It's the nerves and tendons that were severely damaged from your neck down and we cannot be sure as to how they will heal, or if they will heal completely."

Pastor Williams stepped closer to the doctor.

"Dr. Hardy, will the surgery take care of it?"

"In this case, time is the best form of operation."

Sandra touched the doctor's hand.

"How much time Dr. Hardy?"

"That's something no one can answer. I will say this. After the bones heal, if your nerves and tendons do not completely heal, even an operation will not guarantee complete healing. The fact is, no matter what, it will take a miracle."

Sandra raised her arm.

"I believe in miracles. Jesus said, *if thou can believe, all things are possible to him that believes.* I am claiming my miracle now."

Sheila caressed Sandra's face.

"Amen baby, amen."

"I have to leave and check on other patients, but I will be back." He walked out of the room.

Sandra looked over at Ron.

"Ron, pray for me. We all know what you were called and chosen to do, so will you pray for me, please?"

"Yes, I will pray, and the will of the Lord shall be done."

Pastor touched Sheila's arm.

"While Ron is praying, let's all touch and agree in the spirit that the Lord's divine healing will take place."

Ron lowered his head.

"Let's pray. Oh heavenly Father, your word says, if two of you shall agree on earth as touching anything that they shall ask, it shall be done for them of my Father which is in heaven. Lord, let thy will be done."

While Ron was praying, Mr. Bones was in a closet close to Sandra's room, doing his evil work. In front of him on the floor was a circle of bones and in the circle of bones was a picture of Sandra. Mr. Bones tapped his cane on the ground and mumbled some words and dropped some bones on the picture. The picture caught on fire. He tapped his cane on the floor repeatedly.

"Die, die, die. Die Sandra, die!"

Back in Sandra's room, Ron continued to pray, suddenly Sandra's body jumped.

"Noooo," Sandra screamed, "help me Lord." She passed out.

Ron jumped back.

"What happened? What did I do?"

Sheila stepped closer to Sandra and shook her.

"Sandra, Sandra." She touched her face. "My God, she is burning up."

"Nurse, nurse," Diana yelled as she ran out of the room.

Christine looked at Ron.

"What happened to her?"

"How am I supposed to know? All I did was pray for her." He looked at Christine and frowned.

Pastor waved his hand in the air.

"Lord have mercy, this is not the work of God, but the work of the devil and I can feel his evil spirit in this room."

Grandma Harris turned towards the Pastor.

"And I know which devil Satan is using who is responsible for this."

Diana, two nurses, and Dr. Hardy rushed into the room and checked Sandra's condition.

"She is on fire and her blood pressure has jumped up. Everybody out!" Dr. Hardy said.

Everyone left the room and stood in the hallway.

"This is all my fault. I should have never touched her. Who am I anyway? I never asked for this calling, ever." He backed up and leaned against the wall.

Diana walked toward Ron.

"Ron don't say that. God did not do this. The devil did and this does not change your calling."

Sheila walked over to Ron.

"Baby, this is not your fault, so don't go there. Don't let the devil steal your blessings."

The pastor walked closer to Ron.

"Ron above all, God does not lie, so look past the situation and stand on his Holy, spoken word."

Dr. Hardy walked into the hallway.

"Dr. Hardy, what's wrong with my baby, and what happened to her?" Sheila said with tears in her eyes.

"I don't understand this at all and there is no physical explanation for it. Your daughter's blood pressure and temperature went up and then back down, with no explanation whatsoever."

Christine walked closer to the doctor.

"So, is she alright?"

"No, I am afraid she's not." He stepped toward Sheila. "Sheila, your daughter went into a coma and there is no way of telling how long she will remain in this state. I am sorry. I do not understand any of this. I have to go back inside and check on her. All of you are a praying family. Lord knows don't stop praying now." He walked back inside the room.

Ron hit the side of the wall with his hand.

"It's all my fault. She was fine until I touched her, and everybody here knows this."

Sheila rubbed his face.

"Ron don't do this. When you were praying, I felt a very evil presence enter the room. Son, you have seen the mighty power of God, so don't let the devil deceive you into thinking he has more power than God because the devil is the father of lies."

The pastor walked over to Ron and stood in front of him.

"My brother, I know this may be hard to see now, but I feel it very strongly in my spirit. God allowed this to happen to show a greater miracle. Think of Lazarus. Jesus allowed him to die but only for greater glory to God because he raised Lazarus from the dead after he lay in the grave for four days."

"Well, I prayed for my sister, and she went into a coma, and I am sick of this." Ron lowered his head and stared at the floor.

Diana stepped closer to Ron and grabbed his hand gently.

"Ron, God has just begun to use you. Please don't let the devil deceive you baby."

He snatched his hand from Diana's.

"No! I never asked for this good guy calling. I am tired of being a good guy. I was locked up for being a thief, well, that's exactly what I am going to be, but a rich thief." He touched the platinum chain with a cross on it on his neck. He snatched it off and threw it on the floor. "I don't want this anymore. I am going to be the biggest drug dealer this state has ever seen. Heaven help anybody who gets in my way." He yelled.

Diana hugged Ron and began crying.

"No Ron! Please, please don't talk like that, and don't do this."

He pulled away from her.

"No." He walked away and then looked back with a facial expression that looked evil and pointed his finger at them. "Heaven help anyone that gets in my way." He turned around and continued to walk away. Every step he took seemed as if he walked in slow motion.

Sheila began crying.

"Lord have mercy, help him oh Lord. Help us all."
Pastor hugged Sheila and then put his hand on her shoulder.

"It's not over sister O'Neil, believe God. He said in his word, *being confident of this very thing, that he which have begun a good work in you, will perform it until the day of Jesus Christ.* So, Ron will do the work of the Lord." He stared in the direction Ron walked away in. "But at what price oh Lord, what price?"

They all stared in the direction Ron walked away in.

CHAPTER FIFTY
Keith's Condo

Ron left the hospital last night angry, hurt, and confused. He caught a cab to Brookland/CUA metro subway station, but it was closed by the time he got there, so he walked around close to the station all night. He got on the subway when it opened at five in the morning going to Prince George's Plaza subway station in Hyattsville. He walked across the street to the mall and sat on one of the benches outside until the mall opened.

He went inside to the food court and ate at McDonald's, then sat there thinking. Ron's mind was made up. He was going to call Keith, but he knew Keith would try to talk him out of what he wanted to do. He continued to think. A few hours later he got up and walked down the street to Keith's complex. He walked inside the building and saw the guard at his desk. The guard looked up and saw Ron.

"Yes sir, can I help you?"

"Yes, you can, I need to see Mr. Keith Washington please."

"Is he expecting you sir?"

"No, he is not but if you call him and mention Ron is here, I would greatly appreciate it."

He picked up the phone.

"Mr. Washington, there is a Mr. Ron here to see you. Yes sir." He put the phone down. "He said for you to come right up."

"Thank you sir." He got on the elevator, then walked off and knocked on Keith's door.

Stacy was in the bed and Keith walked to the door wearing black, silk pajamas.

"Ron, come in and where have you been? Your mom called me last night and told me what happened. By the way, she interrupted me when Stacy was calling my name, loudly," he laughed. "My brother, we need to talk."

They walked over to the sofa and sat down.

"I didn't come here for any speeches; I came for business." He spoke with an emotionless look on his face as he looked at Keith.

"Look, I know you are highly upset and if you need a place to relax for a while, my home is yours. Even though you kicked me out of your house, you cannot run from what you were called and chosen to do. Don't let the devil fool you."

"Look who is talking." He laughed.

"I am not a chosen one, you are. I am what I am."

"We are all called to give our lives to Christ, but I didn't come here for any debate. My mind is made up and I am sick of this. I am going to be what the world wants me to be, only a whole lot bigger. Remember what you told me five years ago, Benz limo, money, and women? I want it all and you truly owe me." He stood and pointed his finger in Keith's face and yelled, "And I want it, now."

Keith shook his head.

"I know you are hurting but you don't mean what you are saying. Your mind is all messed up right now. Once you calm down, you will feel better and stop talking so

foolishly. Now the Christian wants to be a gangster. Yeah right."

"I don't have time for your mouth. Are you going to keep your word or not?" He pointed his finger at Keith. "You owe me big time, so pay me and stop wasting my time."

Keith stood up.

"Look partner, I know you are upset but I run this. I know you got bigger pumping iron in prison, but you ain't bulletproof. So, do not act crazy, preacher man."

Stacy walked into the living room wearing a short silk robe that comes just above her knees and it's wrapped tightly around her waist showing her curves very well.

"What's going on out here? Hi Ron, and what are you doing here so early in the morning? Shouldn't you be somewhere praying?"

"Hi Stacy and my praying days are over. It's time to get paid."

"Hi baby, and ignore him, he's upset. You do look nice." He walked toward her and put his hands on her waist, kissed her, and caressed her butt.

Stacy pulled away from Keith.

"Baby stop, don't do that in front of Ron."

"True indeed because I didn't come here to watch you two make no baby."

Stacy looked at Ron and frowned.

"Don't knock it until you try it, preacher man."

Keith pulled Stacy into him.

"A woman after my own heart." He kissed Stacy slowly while caressing her hips.

"Keith, I don't have time for this foolishness," he yelled, "rub Stacy's hips later, on your time."

He stepped away from Stacy and moved closer to Ron and felt his temper rising.

"What do you mean, on my time? It is my time. I told you partner, you ain't bulletproof, and don't raise your voice in my house, Emmanuel." He stared at Ron.

"You two need to talk." She kissed Keith. "Bye Ron." She made her butt shake unnecessarily as she walked back into the bedroom, to tease both of them.

Keith stared at Stacy walking then looked at Ron.

"Damn man, you could ruin a wet dream. Did you see how her ass shook when she walked? Pretty in the face, slim in the waist, thick hips, soft full lips, and ass for days. Damn!" He sat down on the sofa and looked at Ron. "What exactly do you want?"

Ron sat down on the sofa next to him.

"You said we were partners. Fifty-fifty, money, cars, women, I want it all. I am not just upset but serious."

Keith stared at him.

"Yeah, I can see that. My brother, you know nothing about the drug business, and you would not last a day. This is the most ruthless, violent, backstabbing, and cold-blooded business in the world. It is not all fancy cars, money, and sexy women. It is about death and destruction, and you never even had a woman. The first time you get some ass, you would go crazy. She would take everything you got in thirty days and leave you broke, busted, and disgusted. These female vultures out here can spot a

sucker like you a mile away. One shot of pussy and she would have you barking at the moon." He laughed as he pointed at Ron.

"We both know how I've lived, but that's behind me. The drug business is like everything else, you learn. I am no fool and the rest you can teach me. The car and money you gave me I put in storage. It's time to get it out."

Keith looked at Ron and laughed again.

"A fancy car and money don't make you a drug dealer. That makes you a mark for stick-up people and gold diggers. But since I cannot talk you out of it, you may as well learn from the best. We can do business and for you, real slow. Are you sure this is what you want my brother?"

"I have been walking and thinking all night. Yes, I am very sure, and I have some big plans. I am not talking about selling twenty pieces on a corner. Strictly weight from state to state."

"I knew we were made for business, but I am already doing that now." He stood. "But understand this, once you get started, there is no turning back, ever."

"You have heard the phrase, the point of no return, well I am there, so let's do this." He stood.

They stared at each other and then hugged.

"My brother, what I told you five years ago is about to come to pass, but first, you have to get you a woman and get some pussy. Oh, and the women love the tongue my brother, love the tongue, they go crazy, climb the walls, follow you around like a puppy. Why do you think Stacy is still here? Plenty of pipe and the tongue. I am nasty and there is no shame in my sex game. I put my tongue all over her body. Front, back, top to bottom. I suck and lick breasts, nipples, pussy, and the ass. I am a freak. I even lick and suck on my baby's toes. I make her eyes roll back in her head."

Ron waved his hand in front of Keith.

"That's disgusting," he frowned at him. "Stacy is super fine, but you lick her ass. Are you kidding me? That is nasty. You should have kept that info to yourself, and you need serious help."

"You better wake up homie. A real woman wants more than dick. You got to put your whole face between her legs, tongue, lips, and mouth. Move your face between her legs slowly and gently and keep sucking and licking. Oh, you got to lick and suck her clit better than any lollipop you ever had in your life." He looked at Ron and saw the disgusted look on his face and started laughing.

Stacy walked into the living room in her robe and pointed her finger at Ron and Keith.

"I heard that." She looked at Ron. "Take that bad look off your face because it's not nasty Ron. Real men do real things and enjoy pleasing their women, and I take no shorts. Keith, since you are telling everything, tell Ron how you climb the walls trying to get away from me. Ron, your miss perfect Diana, she cannot do that. So, you need to find someone else, someone that can move her body." She lowered her body, placed her hands on her knees, and shook her butt, then walked over to Keith, hugged, and kissed him. Stacy stuck her tongue out at Ron and walked back into her room shaking her butt.

Ron and Keith stared at Stacy as she walked away, and they spoke at the same time.

"Damn, she's fine."

Keith looked at Ron and frowned.

"Stop looking at my woman like that fool. You are lusting." He smiled. "She is super fine and those hips and fat ass, I am hooked. I would lick her from the back, every day."

"Yeah, okay but disgusting, she is fine and got you under control. Keith, get dressed and take me to get my Benz, playtime is over."

Keith stepped closer to Ron and put his hand on his shoulder and looked at him.

"Partner, when you get a woman that fine that treats you as well as Stacy treats me and the loving is so good, it should be illegal. That is as good as it gets on this side of heaven my friend. Anyway, enough of that, I hope you know what you are doing. Let me get dressed but call your mom. She is very worried about you."

"I will take care of that later, now get dressed."

"No sir. I am not doing anything or going anywhere until you call Mom. She doesn't deserve to be worried. Call her or no deal." He stared at Ron.

"So be it, but just for the record, nothing she or anyone can say will change my mind. I need a place to stay. Can you hook me up with a condo in this building? This place is nice."

"Yeah, you know I can take care of that. A man needs his own place and you got to have a place to bring the ladies to get your freak on. Let me say this, do not be one of those fake brothers with a fancy car and nice clothes but never get any pussy. No offense homie but Diana is *never* going to give that ass up unless you marry her, so you are going to have to find somebody else. Damn man, get a pretty but classy hood lady. Spend a few dollars on her, not a lot, do not be a sucker. Get her to slob your nob and fuck her for a few weeks, and then get rid of her. And whatever you do, do not catch any feelings. You can't turn a hoe into a housewife."

"Thanks for the sex speech but I am fine. The sex will happen later, but I want to concentrate on making money."

"Yeah okay, that's a no for you getting some pussy. You are going to make me look bad. Whatever homie, just call your mom."

"Keith, we will become bigger than you and the man you work for. Remember I said that."

"You do think big, but we could never become that large. It ain't just the money. We do not have the connections. I am talking about a continued supply of major weight at a cheap price, and the white man will never give us that."

Ron shook his head and frowned.

"I am sick of hearing this white man, black man slavery-like mentality. I am about to show you better than I can tell you. As soon as I handle this personal business." He pulled his cell phone out, exhaled, and then dialed. "Hi Mom."

CHAPTER FIFTY ONE

Sheila's House

It was three o'clock in the afternoon and Ron drove his Benz to Sheila's house. He wore black slip-on Bally shoes, a dark blue Hickey Freeman suit, and a blue dress shirt and tie. Sheila, Diana, and Grandma Harris were inside. Diana walked out of the front door and ran towards Ron. She wore a long dress.

"Oh Ron, praise the Lord. We have been so worried about you." She hugged and kissed him on the lips then stared at him. "Something is wrong. I can feel it and see it in your face." She smacked him. "Have you been with some nasty Jezebel? Did you cheat on me Ron?"

He rubbed his face and looked at Diana.

"You really are something and no I have not, and don't smack me again."

"Oh Ron, I am sorry." She kissed him on the side of his face that she smacked. "I had a moment, forgive me. You look exceptionally good in this suit." She looked at the Benz. "I thought you didn't want that car or anything to do with Keith. Please talk to me. I have waited so long for God to have his way in your life."

"I have to tell you something I have never told you and no matter what happens, always remember this." He stared into her eyes. "I love you Diana Brown, very much and always will, no matter what."

"I have waited so long to hear you say those words to me." She began crying. "And I love you, Mr. Emmanuel." She hugged and kissed him.

"You are the only woman I want to give myself to." He put his hands on her waist and pulled her into him and kissed her softly on the lips.

When Diana felt Ron's tongue against her lips, she opened her mouth, and their tongues tasted each other. This felt so good to her. Too good! Ron pressed his body tighter against hers, grinding himself slowly into her body. Diana felt the warmth between her legs and felt herself getting wet from his touch when she felt his growing erection. He placed one hand on her hip and the other on her butt and began caressing both as he kissed and sucked on her neck passionately.

Diana pulled away.

"Ron, please stop baby, don't do that. I can't take it." She lowered her head.

"Diana, I want you. After I finish talking to Mom, come with me, we can go anywhere you want. How about two weeks in Hawaii? We can live anywhere you desire."

"You forgot something. We are not married yet, and that did not sound like a marriage proposal to me. Where is my ring, Ron? I can't believe you." She frowned at him.

"Baby, we can do all that later, but right now I want us to be together." He pulled her to him and kissed her. "I know you feel how badly I need you. Don't you want me next to you?"

Diana's face rested against his and her hands were on his waist.

"Ron, don't do this to me." She looked into his eyes and stared at him. "You know I want you just as much, but we can't."

Ron wrapped his arms around her and pulled her tightly into him.

"Baby, I know you feel it. I want to be inside you so badly. I know you want this lovin." He slid his hands underneath her dress, grabbed her butt, squeezed, and caressed her butt cheeks. He kissed Diana passionately as he slid her panties to one side very slowly so he could put his finger inside her.

Diana gripped Ron's waist tighter because his warm hands felt so good, and she craved his touch. But the moment she felt his fingers slide her panties to one side trying to invade her most private area, she snapped again. Diana pulled away and smacked Ron so hard, that spit flew out of his mouth.

"Stop it," she yelled. "I love you, but we are not married. You are not going to disrespect me with that filthy mouth of yours. If all you want from me is sex, then you can go back to where you came from. You and Keith can have all the Jezebels you want. I can't believe you." She looked at Ron with intense anger.

Ron rubbed his face and wiped his mouth with his hand.

"You are going to get enough of smacking me. So be it. But as fine as I am and as swollen as my pockets are, I do not have to beg a woman for anything, especially sex." He walked toward the front door.

Diana ran in front of him and pointed her finger in his face.

"Let me tell you something, Mr. Ronald Emmanuel O'Neil. I do not know what demons you allowed to get in your head, but you better pray and stay with the Lord. And if you defile your body with some Jezebel, don't you ever touch me again." She pointed her finger in his face so close it almost touched his nose. "Bottom line is you can't touch me unless you stay with Jesus, so you better start praying."

"My praying days are over."

"What!" She yelled. "You have gone crazy. I am going to tell your mother and we are going to pray for you." She walked quickly away from him toward the house.

Ron saw the contours of her hips and butt-shaking well underneath her dress when she walked away. He smiled.

"Diana," he yelled. "I see your hips and butt-shaking under that dress. Girl, you got a fat ass. You need to let me hit that from the back."

Diana stopped walking, turned around, and walked up to Ron.

"Is that it now Ron? Is that all I am to you is hips and butt? Is that all you want from me is sex?" Tears began to flow from her eyes. "I thought you loved me, not just wanting to get into my panties. I have waited so long for you."

"You know I love you Diana, so stop with the drama, but damn girl, when are you going to let me bend that hot ass over and slide in." He laughed.

Diana smacked him so quickly and hard that she shook her hand afterward because it hurt from hitting him. She poked him in his chest and looked at him with eyes burning with anger.

"I am not a dog, and you are never, ever going to bend me over." She shook her hand repeatedly while looking at him. "I can't believe I fell in love with you." She walked away.

Ron rubbed his face again and thought...*if she smacks me one more time, I might hit her back*. He walked behind Diana.

Sheila and Grandma Harris were on the sofa in the living room when Diana and Ron walked in.

"Mrs. O'Neil, your son is here, and you need to pray for him and quick because Keith Washington has poisoned his mind. Grandma, he wants to take me to Hawaii for a honeymoon, without marriage."

"You will tell something won't you?" He looked at her. "But I am grown, and I can do what I want to."

Sheila walked toward Ron and hugged him.

"Praise the Lord son. I have been so worried about you. But you look nice, a little tired, but nice. Come and sit down with me so we can talk."

"Mom, I came here to let you know I am alright, but I have to leave and don't have time for long conversations."

Sheila emotionally snapped.

"What?" She yelled at him. "Who are you talking to like that? I know you are tired and upset but I am still your mother, and I will hit you in the head with two frying pans and knock you down, then repent, so don't get it twisted boy."

Grandma Harris walked toward Ron.

"Praise the Lord Ron."

"Hi Grandma Harris, how are you doing?"

"Yes Lord, just what I thought. You didn't even say praise the Lord." She turned to look at Sheila. "Sheila, I have seen this type of demon many times. His heart has turned from God, a rebellious spirit."

"Okay! Grandma Harris, everything in life is not a demon." Ron said as he stared at her.

Diana stepped closer to Ron.

"Boy, don't talk to my grandmother like that, with your disrespectful, arrogant self."

"I didn't come here to argue or disrespect anyone and if I have, I apologize. Now I have to go."

"Ron, you just got here, and where are you going? This is your home." Sheila said trying to hold back her tears.

Diana grabbed Ron's suit jacket.

"Ron is a big-money man now, driving his big Benz, new suits, and a bad spirit. I can't believe you."

Grandma Harris walked over to Diana.

"Diana, why are you so angry with him? What did he do to make you so upset?"

Diana looked at Grandma Harris then at Sheila.

"Mrs. O'Neil, your son told me he loved me, and it melted my heart. Then he told me he wants to take me to Hawaii and have sex, without marriage, nasty dog. Who does he think I am?"

"Diana, I do love you, no matter what you think, and it was not just sex."

She threw her hands up in the air out of frustration.

"If you love me so much, then why are you breaking my heart?" She began crying. "I have waited for you to

say that you love me and when you do, you have lust demons all over you and all you want is sex."

"Oh Lord, here we go with the demons again. I have to go." He turned to walk away.

Sheila grabbed his arm.

"Ron wait, we need to talk. Son, just sit here and I'll fix you a nice lunch and afterward, we all can sit down to talk and pray."

He pulled away from her.

"Mom, I have to go." He said with serious irritation in his voice.

Son, please stay, listen to your mother." Sheila wiped tears from her eyes. "Stay, prayer changes things and I know we can overcome this with prayer."

Diana walked in front of Ron.

"Ron, I don't care what forces of darkness are attacking you, I know deep in your heart, that you love the Lord. But if you walk out that door in your state of mind, you are turning your back on God, your family, and me. Please stay here and pray with us, please."

"No! And stop bugging me," He yelled. "I never asked for this calling, and I don't want it anymore, but I will always love my family and you Diana." He kissed her on the cheek. "Now I have to go."

Sheila grabbed his arm again.

"Ron, please stay, I can't lose you too."

Grandma Harris stepped closer to Ron.

"Sheila, Diana, let him go. His mind is made up and only God can bring him back." She pointed her finger at his face. "Ron O'Neil, you remember this. God cannot lie

and his word has gone forth concerning you and it shall not return unto him void. You will do the work of God, but at what price, I don't know."

Ron stared at Grandma Harris, looked at Sheila, and Diana, and then walked away and out the front door.

"No," Sheila screamed, "Lord, not my son, please not my son." She cried hard and fell to her knees hitting the floor with the palms of her hands. "Lord Jesus, please, don't let me lose my son."

Grandma Harris walked over and touched Sheila.

"Sheila, you hold on and give it to the Lord. He's still in control, no matter how it looks in the natural realm of things."

Sheila looked up at Grandma Harris.

"No, I can't take any more of this. First, my husband is killed, then my daughter goes into a coma and now my son turned his back on God. Why Lord? Why? Help me Jesus, Lord help me, not my Ron." She continued to cry.

Tears ran down Diana's face. Seeing and hearing so much pain coming from Sheila was heartbreaking.

"I can't take this, and I know how to stop him." She walked out of the house.

"Diana don't!" Grandma Harris said and fell to her knees. "Lord in the name of Jesus, quicken her spirit and touch her Lord. Don't let her be overwhelmed by the spirit of deception." She looked up with her hands clasped together and tears flowed from her eyes.

Diana ran up to Ron.

"Ron, wait!"

He stopped walking, turned around, and looked at Diana with tremendous sadness in his heart and eyes.

"Diana, I don't want to argue with you or hurt you any more than I already have."

She hugged and kissed him and then took his hands and put them on her butt and stared into his eyes.

"Ron, do you want me? Is this what you want?"

"What are you doing?" He looked at Diana like she lost it.

She pressed herself into his body and kissed him.

"You know what I am doing. Is this what you want? Tell me." She slid her tongue across his lips and passionately kissed him.

Ron kissed her back with equal passion.

"Baby, you know I do." He rubbed her butt with both hands and pressed his body into hers so she could feel his erection as he sucked and kissed her neck. He whispered in her ear. "I am going to make love and fuck you so good." He took her hand in his. "Diana, come with me." He stepped away with her hand in his.

Diana pulled him back toward her, kissed his lips, and looked at him.

"Ron, I know you are the man for me, and I love you deeply. Please baby, ask me to marry you, I will say yes, and I will give myself to you like no woman has given herself to any man." She rubbed his arms and stared into his eyes with the greatest of love and desire.

"Diana, you know I love you but right now I do not want to get married, it's too soon, but having you next to me in bed every night and being inside you would be wonderful." He kissed her neck and sucked on it. "Baby, I can't wait to fuck you doggy style." He grabbed her hand and walked off holding it.

Diana pulled him toward her and snatched her hand out of his.

"No!" She yelled and smacked him twice with her left and right hands, sending spit flying out of his mouth in both directions. "You make me sick. You are a nasty, dirty talking, filthy dog. I rebuke that spirit in you in Jesus' name. Oh, so I am good enough for sex but not marriage. I would never turn my back on God for you or any man. So, you run to your Delilah's and Jezebels, but you will never have me."

Ron rubbed his face and stepped closer to Diana and raised his hand in the air to hit her.

Diana got in his face.

"Go ahead and hit me Ronald Emmanuel O'Neil and see what happens to you. *Touch not my anointed nor do my prophet no harm.* You hit me and you will be cursed for years, tough guy."

Ron could not believe he considered hitting Diana, something he knew he would never do. He lowered his head and then looked at her.

"I would never hit you Diana. You know that but I asked you to stop slapping me, you are not crazy. Diana, you mean a great deal to me, far more than just sex. But I need to be held, touched, and loved. I need some warmth. So, if you do not want to give it to me, then there are plenty of women who will."

"I can't believe you would hurt me like this. You are crushing and breaking my heart." She lowered her head to hide her tears, then looked at Ron with fire in her eyes and pointed her finger in his face. "Ron, I pray every time you get close to a woman or try to have sex, your penis shrinks to the size of a prune. And you better keep your tongue in your mouth where it belongs." She stepped closer, looked back at the door, grabbed Ron by his suit jacket, and pulled him closer, within inches of her nose. "If you think about giving away what is mine when I see you again, I will slap your eyes right out of your head." She let him go and backed up.

"Oh, Christian girl getting violent," he smiled and pulled her close to him. "I knew you wanted this good dick. For the record, if my dick could not rise with someone else, my tongue would work." He stuck his tongue out, licked his lips, then licked Diana's lips and kissed her hard on the mouth.

Diana tried to smack him, but he ducked.

"You missed me." He leaned forward and got in her face to irritate her. "Confess it. You know you need me to bend that ass over and give you what you want." He leaned toward her and laughed.

Diana was so frustrated with Ron, that she responded from an emotional state of anger. She moved fast and smacked him hard.

"Stop it Ron! Stop playing with me and being so sick and disrespectful." She stepped close. "And you better not hit me."

He looked at her.

"I would never hit you Diana and I will always love you." He stared at her, and tears fell from his eyes, then he walked away.

"Ron wait, please don't go. I am so sorry."

Ron got in his car and drove away.

Diana looked up.

"Lord, deliver him Father, don't let him be destroyed. But am I ready, am I truly ready to be loved the way I say I want to be loved? Oh God help me and touch Ron Lord, please touch him." She fell to her knees crying out to God. "Don't let him be destroyed, oh God, please."

Ron drove a few minutes, then pulled over and stopped. He hit his steering wheel hard with his hand.

"Lord, I didn't ask for this calling and I don't want it anymore. I put my sister in a coma. Father, help me," he started crying. "Noooo," he screamed. "This is not my call. Help me Lord." He lowered his head and continued to cry.

CHAPTER FIFTY TWO
The Nightclub

It was one o'clock Saturday afternoon and Victor was in his office at the club lifting dumbbells. He wore sweatpants, gym shoes, and a tank top. His bodyguards were in the club practicing martial arts and their guns were on the table. Sherry walked into Victor's office with a bottle of water in her hand wearing gym shoes, tight spandex shorts, and a tank top.

"Now I am ready to finish my workout, you can never have too much water." She took a sip of her water.

"Or have too much money."

Sherry sat on the floor, put her bottle of water on the floor, and began stretching.

"See, that's your problem. You need to focus on more than making money and put your eyes on something much sweeter and more comforting."

Victor put the dumbbells down and walked over to Sherry.

"Money is very powerful and comforting, but do you know of something sweeter?"

"Victor, don't play with me," she smiled at him, "as a matter of fact I do." She stood and kissed him. "My lips are sweet and so is this." She took Victor's hand placed it between her legs and held it there. "This is even sweeter, but you already know that." She placed Victor's hand on her butt, and rubbed his hand all over it, and then pressed his hand between her butt cheeks. "And this, my love, is even tighter and oh so sweet, but I am a little hot and sweaty." She looked directly at him trying to entice him with her words and gestures.

Victor grabbed Sherry's hands and pulled her into him so she could feel his erection.

"Just the way I like it, hot, tight, wet, and sweet." He kissed her and whispered in her ear. "I miss you and I will never forget how tight and hot you are inside." He continued kissing her.

Stephanie drove up in front of the club in a new blue, 2013 Bentley Continental GTC. She stepped out wearing heels, a mini-skirt, and a low-cut top. She rang the club's doorbell.

Victor's bodyguards grabbed their guns quickly and two of them walked to the front door, opened it, and aimed their guns at Stephanie.

Stephanie walked in like she owned the place, and the guards lowered their guns. One of them stared at Stephanie.

"Miss Walker, the model of the year, please do come in."
When she walked past him, she caressed his chest with her hand.

"Very nice." She looked around and noticed they were working out. "The rest of you gentlemen don't stop working out on my account. Is Victor here?"

The bodyguard who complimented her stopped working out and turned toward her.

"Yes, he is but Mr. Agular has company and does not want to be disturbed."

Stephanie became angry immediately and wondered who Victor was spending time with.

"Who is Victor with?" She stepped closer to the guard and then waved her hand in his face. "Never mind, I will find out for myself." She stepped away from him with determination and purpose.

The guard grabbed her arm.

"I don't think that would be such a good idea." Stephanie tried to pull away, but the guard's grip was too tight.

"Take your hands off me, you idiot. Victor would not like you hurting me."

He stared at her and then let her arm go.

"Remember I tried to warn you."

She rubbed her wrist and then looked at the guard with eyes of death.

"If you ever touch me again," she leaned closer to him. "I will seduce you and cut your throat at the same time." She walked towards Victor's office.

Victor was on top of Sherry on the sofa kissing her when Stephanie walked in.

"Am I interrupting something?" She slammed the door behind her, took a few steps then stopped. Stephanie felt her anger and blood pressure instantly rise.

Victor and Sherry stood up quickly and adjusted their clothes and Victor pulled his tank top down to hide his erection from Stephanie.

"Stephanie, I didn't know you were in town."

"I am sure you didn't, and I see you will embrace anything." She looked between Victor's legs and noticed

his erection, and pointed towards it, and then pointed to Sherry. "You let this slut get you hard. I see you will let anything touch you."

"I am not anything, so why don't you leave so I can finish satisfying Victor like you never have." She smiled at Stephanie.

"I am beginning to enjoy this." Victor said with a grin on his face as he looked at Stephanie.

"Victor, you take me for a joke. You make me sick, and you Miss Sherry, will not be satisfying anyone ever again." She reached under her skirt pulled out a thirty-eight pistol and aimed it at Sherry.

"Stephanie, put the gun away before someone gets hurt." He raised his voice and pointed at her.

"Oh please, am I supposed to be scared? I knew you were a weak insecure bitch. If you were all that, Victor would not be screaming my name when I am riding his dick, you weak bitch."

Victor looked at Sherry.

"I don't think you should have said that."

"Shut up Victor, both of you shut up," Stephanie yelled, and spit flew out of her mouth because she was so angry. "Victor, I can't believe you put your dick in her," she pointed at Sherry, "because this worn-out slut would fuck a monkey. But I have a treat for you, Miss Sherry Wilson." She waved her gun at her. "Take your clothes off."

"Excuse me, I don't do group sex. I knew you were sick and a super freak. Have you had an Aids test recently? You nasty sick dog."

"Shut your filthy mouth up!" she yelled at Sherry. "I said, take your damn clothes off or I will shoot you where you stand, you sorry slut. Now get naked."

"Sherry, I think she means it." Victor looked at Sherry.

Sherry looked at Victor then at Stephanie.

"So be it. You're the model but you still can't touch this." She removed her shoes, tank top, and shorts. She wore a black bra and matching thong panties. She put her hands on her waist. "Miss pervert, do you like what you see?" She smiled and then frowned at Stephanie.

"I can't speak for her, but I like all I see." Victor stared at Sherry and then licked his lips.

"You have some nerve disrespecting me like this Victor, I hope you enjoyed it while it lasted." She walked over to Sherry and pointed the gun in her face. "I said get naked, you nasty rodent."

Sherry wanted to jump Stephanie badly, but she knew Stephanie would shoot her, so she figured it would be better to go along and wait until the timing was right. She took her bra and panties off and stared at Stephanie the entire time.

"Are you satisfied now? You sick, twisted, unstable bitch!"

Stephanie stepped closer to Sherry and smacked her, then put the gun to the side of her head.

"I don't like being called a bitch and you should never call someone names while they have a gun to your head." She turned her head and looked at Victor. "Victor, get over here now in front of this rat, rodent, bitch before I shoot her."

He moved closer.

"I'm here, now what do you want?" His temper was rising, and he disliked not being in charge.

Stephanie pressed the gun against Sherry's head harder to intimidate her and make Victor more uncomfortable.

"Victor, since you like tasting this rodent so much, I am going to give you a chance to taste her one last time." Stephanie looked at Sherry. "You better not move, you stank rodent." She stepped closer to Sherry and rubbed between her legs slowly with her other hand.

Sherry turned her head to the side and could not believe this was happening to her. She felt so degraded and violated right now. But what made it worse, she felt herself getting wet.

Victor stared at this scene and enjoyed every minute of it but did not know how it would end.

Stephanie looked into Sherry's eyes and saw the lust and felt Sherry getting wet and this gave her an idea. She wanted to embarrass her as much as possible. She slid two fingers inside Sherry and began moving them slowly back and forth while her thumb caressed her clit. Stephanie looked directly into her eyes and pressed the gun hard against her head. She continued to finger Sherry, knowing she was fighting her sexual pleasure and inevitable orgasm.

Sherry wanted to scream from emotional hurt, humiliation, and total embarrassment because she knew her body was going to betray her. She tried hard to fight it, but she felt her orgasm building. As much as she hated what was being done to her, Stephanie was hitting all her spots.

Stephanie knew Sherry was close to climax by her quiet moans and breathing, but she had one last thing left for these two.

"Victor do like I say, or I will put a bullet in this rat's head. Get behind her and start licking her from the back and hurry the hell up."

"You're the one with the gun, have it your way, dear." He walked behind Sherry got on his knees, placed his hands on her hips, and began licking and kissing between her legs.

The moment Sherry felt Victor's mouth between her legs she jumped because it felt good.

"Victor, please stop. Do not do this to me, not like this, please stop." She turned her head to the side to look back at him with tears in her eyes, pleading for him to stop and do something to help her.

Stephanie pressed the gun against Sherry's head.

"Shut the hell up. He cannot help you. I am the one with the gun. Spread your legs slut."

Sherry wanted to scream and cry at the same time for being so extremely disrespected, but she opened her legs more.

Stephanie enjoyed this greatly and slid her fingers inside Sherry harder and faster, still using her thumb to massage her clit.

Victor licked and kissed Sherry's butt and slid his tongue between her butt cheeks back and forth. He knew

Sherry enjoyed all this despite how much she hated Stephanie right now.

Sherry was sweating. Between Stephanie fingering her and massaging her clit, Victor's tongue kissing and licking her butt was too much for her. She exploded with an intense orgasm.

"Ahhhhhhh, I am cummming, damn you two, ahhhhhh it feels so good." Not thinking about it, she reached back and pushed Victor's head tighter into her butt and moved her pelvis harder onto Stephanie's fingers at the same time. Her body was trembling from such an intense orgasm. Afterward, she dropped her head in shame and embarrassment, but everything felt so good.

Stephanie pulled her fingers out of Sherry and was very satisfied at humiliating her.

"Victor, get up from licking this rodent's ass and stand beside her."

Victor did as she asked and stood next to Sherry.

"Victor, did you like that?" She looked at him with hate.

"Very much so." He was grinning at Stephanie.

"Good, here is some more of this rodent." She wiped her fingers roughly across Victor's lips. "Taste this nasty rodent, you sorry asshole."

Sherry looked at Stephanie with murder in her eyes.

"This is not over, and you are one sick twisted bitch."

Stephanie slapped her.

"Shut up. You are the dog." She looked at Victor. "Victor, was it good? Did she taste good to you?"

"Yes, she does, really good." He smiled and wiped his lips with his hand.

"You betrayed me Victor, you sick bastard, and I hate you and this rat rodent." She slapped Victor and Sherry.

"Go to hell bitch." She spat in Stephanie's face.

"You first, rodent." She shot her three times, in the head and twice in the body. Brain matter and blood splattered on Victor and Stephanie.

"Are you crazy?" Victor yelled and moved closer to her with fire in his eyes.

She pointed the gun at him.

"No, I am not crazy," she yelled at him. "I told you long ago not to ever cheat on me and your dick was mine. Did you think I was joking? As good as I make love to you, fuck you, and suck the cum out of your dick, and you still cheat on me. You are the crazy one. Now, look at what you made me do. Your lover is dead. I put holes in that rat rodent, slut bitch." She smiled.

Victor's bodyguards rushed into his office with their guns aimed at Stephanie and one of them stepped closer to her with his gun pointed directly at her head.

"Mr. Augular, say the word and she's instant toe tag."

"And so is he." She stepped closer to Victor and pressed her gun between his legs. "You shoot me, and my gun goes off and Victor becomes a bitch, instantly."

Victor waved his hand at his men.

"Stephanie this has gone too far. Put your gun down, now."

"No! You went too far. I told you not to cheat on me. Now tell your men to put their guns down and stand in

front of me, or I will blow your dick off." She pushed her gun between his legs.

Victor waved his hand at his men.

"Do what she says, she is very unstable."

The bodyguards lowered their guns and walked in front of her.

Stephanie looked at the bodyguards.

"Very smart." She slapped Victor twice. "I am not unstable. You men are all alike. You will say and do anything to get some pussy. You didn't say I was unstable when you had your dick in me, you bastard." She slapped him and grabbed the waistband of his sweatpants. "Now walk with me over to the door." She walked backward and pulled him along by his pants with her gun between his legs. She opened the door and pulled Victor through it and closed the door behind them. "Now remember this lover," she grabbed his dick, "you and your dick belong to me until I say different. If you ever cheat on me again, I will ride you like a horse and cut your throat while you bust that nut. You will come and go at the same time. Do you understand me?"

Victor nodded his head.

"If I didn't, I do now."

"Grab my butt."

"Whatever you say dear." He grabbed her butt.

"This is the only ass you will ever get and live. You remember that lover boy." She slapped him again. "I am not unstable." She kissed him hard on the lips and ran away.

Victor's bodyguards walked out of his office and one of them aimed his gun at her with a laser sight showing on the back of her head.

"Mr. Augular, I could drop her easily from here."

Victor placed his hand on the guard's gun.

"No, let her live, for now. She has some powerful friends in high places I am doing business with, so she may prove to be useful later. The woman does have heart, but I will kill her later." He looked back at his office thinking of Sherry lying on the floor, dead.

"Get that dead woman out of my club. She is of no service to me now."

Victor's bodyguards took Sherry out of the office through the back of the club where a van was waiting. They dumped her body in it and three of them got in and drove off while the others went back inside the club.

When Victor's bodyguards carried Sherry's body out of the club, it was necessary to keep his emotions in check. He knew Sherry loved him for him and not his money or power and that is a rare thing in life. He walked back to his office making sure to close the door. He walked over to his desk and sat down and looked into space. In the privacy of his office, it happened. Tears flowed from his eyes, and he felt the pain in his heart.

"Sherry, I will always miss you. Damn you Stephanie."

Stephanie was parked in front of the club and was very angry.

"I am not finished with you Victor Augular. No one cheats on me. I am going to destroy you no matter what it takes," she smiled, "and I know how. I am going to sick those two young wolves on you, Keith and Ron." She continued smiling then frowned and her face became almost distorted. "Yeah, I am unstable." She drove away.

CHAPTER FIFTY THREE
The Park

Three o'clock in the afternoon Keith was in the park leaning back in his white Benz listening to music. Ron drove up next to Keith's car in his black Benz. He got in Keith's car, and both wore tennis shoes and sweatsuits.

"Preacher man, good afternoon to you. I am glad to see you."

"Don't ever call me that. Those days are over, now it's time to talk business."

"I like that about you, always business. I have a gift for you. Reach under your seat."

Ron reached under his seat and pulled out a small briefcase and put it in his lap.

"What is it?"

"Open it and find out."

He opened it and stared at the contents.

"Lord have mercy. I have never touched a gun and there are two in this case."

"They come with the business, my gift to you and you will need it. One is a nine-millimeter, and the other is a 357 magnum. I had a case of special bullets made for our guns. Armor-piercing bullets. You shoot someone, and it guarantees a dead body."

Ron picked one of the guns up and a strange feeling came over him that he did not like but ignored it.

"This is beautiful, strong, and deadly. I have names for my new friends. The 357, I will call it Samson, and the nine, I will call it Delilah." He held both guns in his hands and smiled. "Yes sir, Samson and Delilah, S&D. I like that. From this day forward my name is S&D and I will go to the gun range and become an expert with these. Wherever I go, they go."

"I like that, S&D. Very nice, preacher man to the killer man. K&W and S&D. Look out world, we are taking over." They shook hands. "Now tell me this master plan of yours. Oh, let me show you how to load these monster guns." He took the guns from Ron, loaded them twice, and handed them back to him. "You got it partner?"

Ron nodded his head.

"Yeah, I got it," he loaded the guns twice, stared at them, and then put the guns in the case and put the case back under the seat. "My plan is simple. We become the grower, supplier, and distributor."

"What!"

"Relax Keith, let me finish. We buy some land in South America, build temporary housing there, recruit a small army from the streets here, and send them to South America to do the labor. We buy all the weapons we need. Then we grow, move, sell, and kill anyone that gets in our way."

Keith looked at Ron and thought...*what have I done?*

"Damn partner, I have created a monster and I can tell you are serious. I love it but you are talking about a huge operation my friend and a lot of money to finance this and going to war with other drug lords."

"I know all this, and I have thought about the details. But do you think we can do it? I mean really pull it off."

"With us working together, you are damn right we can do it, but we need a money goal, then we'll stop. Let's not get greedy."

"I thought about that too. We are partners so it will be a fifty-fifty split. A hundred million dollars apiece and we quit."

Keith rubbed his hands together.

"One hundred million dollars, damn that sounds good to me S&D. I have some money saved so getting started is not the problem, but we need a serious connection."

Keith's cell phone rang.

"Hello, Miss Stephanie Walker, yes, I know who you are. If you want to talk to me, I am in Hustler's Park. You should know where it is. Okay, I will see you when you get here." He put the phone away.

"Who was that?"

"Miss Stephanie Walker, the drug lord I work for, she is his lady. My brother, she is fine and has a serious body. As good as I lay pipe along with this pearl tongue of mine, if I had his money, she would scream my name like the Temptations, oh Keith, oh Keith." He started laughing.

Ron looked at Keith like he was crazy.

"You are something else, but Stacy would kill you. Anyway, what does this Jezebel want? I don't like it."

"She said it was important we talk and she's on her way over here, but I don't trust her either. It could be a set-up. You take S&D with you and move your car away from mine and watch my back." He hit Ron on the chest. "Ron, those guns you have are not water pistols. They shoot real bullets and people will die."

"I told you my name is S&D, and I don't have time for sad stories. It's time to make this money and get rich."

Ron grabbed the case, got in his car, and drove to the edge of the park where he could see Keith. He removed the guns from their case, laid them in his lap, and watched Keith.

Keith reached under his seat, pulled out his nine-millimeter, and put it in his lap. Minutes later he saw a blue Bentley approaching the park, driving up behind his car.

Stephanie stepped out wearing heels and a tight-fitting dress with a long slit on the side and a low-cut top. She walked towards Keith's car.

Keith got out with his arm behind his back holding his gun and walked toward Stephanie.

Stephanie extended her hand to him.

"Mr. Keith Washington, it is a pleasure to finally meet you."

Keith stared at her and thought...*this woman is fine.* He shook her hand.

"Miss Walker, I do like your whip, and you do know how to dress to get a man's attention. So, what can I do for you?"

"Well, for one, you can put your gun away and stop acting like a thug."

"It's all part of the business, pretty lady." He put his gun in the waist of his pants. "So, what's on your mind?"

"Business and revenge," she smiled and reached under her dress, and pulled out her gun and aimed it at Keith.

Ron was watching all this, and he got out of his car and ran towards them with his guns in his hands. He walked up behind Stephanie slow and quietly and pointed his guns at her back.

"Interesting places people keep guns. You have my attention, make your point."

"This is not what you think Keith. If I wanted to kill you, you would already be dead, right here, right now.

Ron walked closer to Stephanie and aimed his guns at her head.

"And so would you Jezebel, now drop the gun, or today is the first day of your soul in hell."

Stephanie looked back at Ron.

"Very nice work." She lowered her gun.

Keith removed his gun from his pants, pointed it at Stephanie and walked toward her, and took her gun.

"You are beautiful but dangerous Miss Walker. Do you have any more hidden, deadly surprises?"

"Search me and find out." She smiled at him.

"My pleasure." He put both guns in his pants and began patting her down. He rubbed her breasts and back and kneeled in front of her rubbing her legs. His hands moved inside her dress and inner thighs, purposely allowing his fingers to touch and press between her legs feeling her crotch. He rubbed her hips and butt taking extra time caressing and grabbing them because she wore thong underwear and her flesh felt good to him. He stood and stepped away from her.

"You have a tight body, and your ass is round and tight."

Stephanie smiled and laughed with her hands on her hips.

"Are you satisfied, and did you get your feel on? You would not last a weekend with me. Now if you do not mind, let's get down to business." She turned around and saw Ron pointing his guns at her. "Baby, you can put your guns down now. My, my you do look like you mean business."

"I do. Now, what is on your mind, Jezebel?"

She licked her lips and stuck her tongue out at Ron.

"You two are something else. Let's go for a walk."

Keith waved his hand in front of Stephanie.

"Let's do this."

Stephanie walked in front and Keith and Ron's eyes were focused on her body. They shook their heads and caught up with her.

"I want revenge on Victor. I want to destroy him. Keith, I know you have seen Miss Sherry Wilson, Victor's club manager."

"Yeah, I have, and she is fine. She could give you a run for your money. Pretty face and got a body for days."

"No, she can't, she's dead. I shot that rodent bitch. I caught Victor on top of her on the sofa in his office getting ready to have sex. No one cheats on me and does not pay the price, not even the great Victor Augular. My sex game is too good for a man to cheat on me. Victor is next in line to get his and we can help each other."

Ron looked at her.

"Why should we trust and believe you?"

"You will never see Miss Wilson again. I can help you move drugs all over the world because I have traveled all over the world. I know a lot of important people who owe me big favors." She turned and looked at Keith. "I know you got a big deal going right now and moving a lot of weight."

Keith looked back at her hips and butt while she talked and then grabbed her butt, caressed it for a few seconds, and smiled at Stephanie.

"I could not help myself. Damn, you got a tight, fat ass. Keep talking, I am listening."

She looked at Keith and gave him a look of disdain.

"Stay focused Keith, damn. I have not put this great lovin on you yet and you cannot stay focused. Typical! Keep your mind on business and off my ass, which you cannot handle. I want to help you two young wolves become extraordinarily rich and do something that has never been done by two young black men. Help you become drug Lords yourselves. I know some important people in South America who for the right price will let you buy some land, grow cocaine, and I will help you move it. I know people in the government who owe me major favors."

Keith smacked her on the butt.

"Miss Walker, we could possibly do business. But besides revenge, what else do you want?"

"You can't keep your hands off my ass, can you?" She gave him a look of irritation. "I want Victor destroyed and for him to lose everything he has. I want you to kill him

and I want one hundred million dollars deposited in my account. This is not negotiable."

Ron touched Stephanie's arm.

"I like your proposal, but everything is negotiable, and your price is too high. If you can deliver, we will pay you fifty million."

Stephanie stopped walking and stared at Ron and stepped closer to him. She caressed his face with the palm of her hand.

"You are very handsome but inexperienced. I have expensive tastes baby. One hundred million," she looked at Keith. "I will give you two the experience of a lifetime. Do you two know what, *the Devils three*-way is?"

Keith and Ron looked at each other and then looked at Stephanie and said at the same time.

"No!"

Stephanie looked at them laughed and thought...*these two are lightweights, especially Ron. And he looks like he needs some ass badly.*

"The *Devil's three-way* is the best threesome you could ever have. If you two agree to my terms and all goes well, you both can have me at the same time. And I do it all, the best threesome you will ever have in your entire life." She looked at them, licked her lips and smiled. She stepped closer to Keith and handed him a card. "Call me when you are ready to do some serious business." She leaned closer and whispered in Keith's ear, "I like it in the ass. Do right by me and I will let you have it." She kissed his cheek and walked away, got in her car, and drove off.

They watched her walk away.

"Damn, I got to get that ass." Keith said.

"What did that nasty Jezebel say to you?" And do you think she is for real?"

"She was flirting. Yeah, I think she is for real but let me check on her story and if everything checks out, we are in their partner."

"It works for me. Let's go back to your place so we can talk."

"No problem."

They walked back to their cars and drove off.

CHAPTER FIFTY FOUR

Keith's Condo

Ron and Keith sat on the sofa in Keith's condo.

"Partner, I know you don't like her, but Stephanie is fine, and her body is tight, the things I could do to her." He shook his head.

Ron stared out into space getting lost in his thoughts.

"Partner, did you hear me?"

He looked at Keith.

"Yes, I heard you, and yes, she is fine, but I think Stacy is better looking all the way around. She is unstable but you love her." He continued to stare out into space.

"That's my baby and all jokes aside, I would not trade her for anyone." He looked at Ron. "Ron, you have been quiet since we got back here and staring out into space. Talk to me. What's on your mind?"

Ron looked at Keith.

"I miss Diana, love her, and I don't want to lose her."

"I knew it. You are getting soft on me already and changing your mind, damn man."

"Relax, I am not changing my mind Keith. There is no going back for me, but I want Diana. You of all people should understand. You have the woman of your dreams in your life, and I don't."

"You are right, and I see you are serious. Well, the only way you can have Diana is to marry her. That's also the only way you will ever get that ass." He started laughing.

Ron punched Keith on the arm and laughed as well.

"Yeah, I know that's right. So, what do you think?"

He stared at Ron.

"If you love and want her that badly, then I say, go for it. But she will never go for you living this lifestyle and be with you. She is Jesus sold out."

"I have thought about that, and I know a way to have both, but I need your help."

"You know I got you. Let's put this in motion."

"I may pay a price, but I will deal with that when it comes. Diana loves me this I know for a fact. I need to get a nice house somewhere, something big and fancy. Marry her quick and sex her brains out. Get her away from the church a little and get her hooked on the lavish lifestyle and freaky sex. Turn her out and then she will be mine. What do you think?"

Keith looked at Ron.

"You know, it wasn't until now that I realized how much you love Diana. Your plan sounds like something I would do, if I were ready to get married, which I am not. Not even to Stacy and I love her greatly. Are you sure this is what you want to do?"

Ron stared at Keith.

"I have never been surer about anything in my life, but I have to get her to come to me, on my terms. Keith, I still have the million dollars you gave me, but I am going to need a few more, can you advance me?" He looked at Keith with anticipation.

"You are going all out to get that ass, damn." He laughed then stopped and looked at Ron. "Partner, if I got it, you got it, no problem. I just hope she's worth it."

Ron stared into space and then looked at Keith.

"Yes, she is more than worth it. Diana is my heart, and I will do whatever I have to for us to be together for life." He looked at Keith and stared into space again, smiling.

CHAPTER FIFTY FIVE
The Plan

Ron stayed at Keith's place last night, but he got up early and was busy all day. He went to the jewelry store and bought Diana a five-carat, Vintage Assher-cut diamond ring that cost twenty-five thousand dollars. He drove to Potomac and purchased a six-bedroom, four-car garage, nine thousand square feet house on two acres, for seven million dollars.

Arrangements were made to rent out Victor's club for the night. He called Diana and talked her into going out with him and the place would be a surprise, but when he mentioned Keith and Stacy were coming, he had to beg her to come.

Ron also asked Diana to wear something very sexy because he wanted to show her off, and she said no. However, she changed her mind when a limo, nine thousand dollars, and one of Keith's American Express credit cards were delivered to her to go shopping and for her to get a hotel room.

He did not want to pick her up at Grandma Harris' house because he did not want to see her or his mom. They probably would have talked Diana out of going with him and he was not taking that chance, not tonight. He said he would pick her up at the hotel and Keith and Stacy would be with him. He told Diana they were going someplace nice and expensive to eat, but he had a different plan.

Mr. Bones also had a serious plan. He heard Diana making reservations for a room at the Four Seasons Hotel in Washington, DC. She picked the lavish Royal Suite at $15,000 a night, compliments of Keith, and it has a great view of the city. Mr. Bones went to the room and lay on the bed, mumbled some words, rubbed his bones on it, spat on it, and spat in the shower. He spoke curses all over the room and then threw his bones on the floor and they turned into a cloud of light dust, that you cannot see. He left the room in a cloud of smoke.

Diana has never dressed like she was going to tonight, all for Ron, and hoped she would not regret it. She arrived at the hotel in time to take a nap, then got up to shower and felt very horny and nasty but did not know why. She dismissed the feelings and got dressed.

Keith, Stacy, and Ron rode in a light blue stretch Lexus limo on the way to get Diana. Ron was dressed to impress in his $1,500 shoes, $500 belt to match, $5,000 tailored Armani suit with an $800 collarless dress shirt. His $20,000 platinum neck chain accented the $35,000 gold and platinum pinky ring and his $25,000 Rolex watch. Keith wore $2,000 ostrich skin shoes, a $7,000 Italian tailored suit, and a $1,800 collarless dress shirt. Keith's $50,000 platinum neck chain mimicked Ron's *WTW* pendant, only his displayed R&D *(ride or die)*, a $40,000 Rolex watch, and the same pinky ring as Ron. Stacy wore $3,000 heels from France, a $9,500 low-cut, backless, tailored dress revealing ample cleavage and falling just above her knees hugging her lovely curves.

The limo drove up in front of the hotel and Diana stood out front. When they saw her, they stared and could not

believe it was her. Ron and Keith looked at each other with the same thoughts and spoke simultaneously.

"Damn!"

Stacy punched Keith on his arm also thinking, *damn!* She was shocked to see how Diana was dressed.

Ron stepped out of the limo and walked over to Diana and stared at her feeling his dream had come true.

Diana wore $4,200 grey heels, a black $12,000 off-the-shoulder dress with a long side slit that revealed her beautiful legs and hugged her curves. She had a great body and never wanted to display it, until that night. With her flat stomach, the dress accentuated her hips, butt, and beautiful breasts, so she decided to go braless to show her nipple prints. All this was for Ron. She wore perfume and lip gloss that made her full lips look even sexier. Her nails were painted red with white tips and her hair was perfect. She stood with her feet close together, holding a small black $9,500 Hermes purse.

"Hi Ron, your natural good looks and that expensive suit make you look extremely handsome. You look like a young, rich baller. That chain on your neck, what does WTW stand for?"

"Thank you Diana and I will tell you about that later, but you are breathtaking. I knew you had a body but this is blowing my mind. Damn, you are hot." He leaned closer, placed his hands on her waist, kissed her lips, and stared at her.

"Ron, stop staring at me please, you are making me feel self-conscious. You know I did this just for you. I would never dress like this." She hugged and kissed him.

"So, do you like how I am dressed?" She turned around so he could get a good look and smiled at him.

"You are kidding me, right? Diana, I love how you are dressed, you look so damn sexy and hot."

She pinched his lips.

"Ron don't cuss. Can you do me a big favor please?"

"Name it baby, whatever!"

"You know I don't do this, and I feel awkward, so will you please stay close and pay attention to me, and do not walk off and leave me tonight."

Ron thought…*if you only knew what I have in mind.*

"The last thing you have to worry about tonight is me not paying attention to you or leaving you," he stared at her breasts and nipples. "Baby, your breasts and nipples are visually erotic. I hope I don't catch a charge with fools acting stupid lusting over you." His continued staring caused an erection and he adjusted himself to hide it.

Diana noticed his erection and it sexually turned her on very quickly, but she had to maintain control, although this would be hard to do tonight. She questioned herself for not telling Grandma Harris or Sheila what she was doing. Hopefully, everything will be okay. She pointed between Ron's legs.

"You need to control yourself, although I want a lot of attention and affection from you tonight, you have to respect me, and I mean it Ron." She gave him a serious look.

"No problem Diana, relax, but you are making it hard on a brother, really hard." He exhaled and shook his head.

She stepped closer to him and put her arm inside his.

"I know I am baby, but you will be alright. Drink a lot of water." She kissed him. "Come on, let's go."

"Oh, you got jokes, no problem." He walked toward the car with her arm in his and put his hand on her butt, caressing it.

Diana decided she was going to allow Ron to express himself if he did not get carried away. His hand felt good on her butt, more than usual but she does not know why.

Keith and Stacy were kissing passionately but stopped when Ron opened the limo door. Ron and Diana stepped in and sat across from them, and Diana held the slit on her dress, so she does not show too much sitting down. She placed her bag on the floor.

The limo drove off. Diana felt Keith's strong lustful spirit as he stared at her, but it did not bother her as much as it usually does. Subconsciously, she enjoyed it but did not know why.

"Hi Diana, you look good tonight. I am impressed." Keith said with lust in his heart.

Stacy looked at Keith.

"Well don't be too damned impressed." She rolled her eyes at him then looked at Diana.

"Diana, I have to admit, girl, you look great."

"Thank you, Stacy and Keith, you two look great, you always do. Stacy your dress is a traffic stopper. Keith, you better hold on to her tonight." She smiled at him.

"I always do." He caressed Stacy's leg and kissed her lips slowly and passionately.

Ron cleared his throat.

"Can you two wait until we are not around to do all that?"

Diana pulled Ron's arm.

"Ron, leave them alone and put your focus on me and how I am dressed, thank you."

He was surprised by Diana's words but would not complain. Maybe she was trying to loosen up. Better for him.

"No problem." He turned to Diana and kissed her.

Diana opened her mouth to allow his tongue in, which felt great and caused her to desire him. Diana was so into kissing Ron that she did not realize her legs were open, revealing her panties to Keith and Stacy. She grabbed Ron's hand and placed it on her breasts, moved it around making her nipples hard, and made her wet.

Keith and Stacy looked at them in total amazement because they have never seen Diana like this.

"Talk about us, Diana, what has gotten into you? The way you are acting makes me think you are going to give Ron some ass tonight." Stacy said and looked at Keith.

"I did not want to say anything, but I thought the same thing." Keith said and looked between Diana's legs since they were open.

They stopped kissing and Diana adjusted her dress and body on the seat. She lowered her head in embarrassment and then looked at Keith and Stacy.

"I miss Ron so much but no, we are not having sex because we are not married, but if we were, as badly as I desire him right now. I would pull his dick out and sit on it

and ride him, and I would not care what you two thought. I love him." She stared at them.

Stacy and Keith looked at each other, then at Ron and all three shook their heads.

"Damn Diana. You said dick." Ron said.

They rode the rest of the way talking and kissing until they reached the club and stepped out of the limo. There was a long line of people waiting to get in.

Diana pointed at the club then stepped closer to Ron.

"Ron is this where you are taking me? Is this your surprise, a nightclub? I am not going in there. I can't believe you." Diana stared at him and became instantly angry.

Ron looked at her and felt defeated. Stacy saw the hurt in Diana's eyes and the disappointed look in Ron's, so for once she decided to help them. She walked over to Diana, grabbed her hand, and whispered in her ear.

"Diana relax and play your position. You look gorgeous tonight. Let Ron be himself and you enjoy being pampered. Think about all these thirsty skanks out here who would love to be in your position. He's your man, so you need to act like it."

Diana was surprised by this from Stacy because she always thought Stacy hated her. Stacy made some good points, and she is already here, so she may as well make the best of it.

"Thanks Stacy, you are right. I am with my man." She stepped closer to Ron, grabbed his hand, and looked at him. "I am all yours tonight and you better spoil me." She

kissed him and they walked into the club hand in hand with Diana's purse on her shoulder.

As they walked in Ron winked at Stacy.

Keith was surprised by Stacy and walked up to her.

"You are something" He kissed her.

"I have my moments, but I am not her and you can rub my ass. I will be getting some dick and tongue tonight, believe that." She kissed him and they walked in.

Ron did not know what to do concerning this part of his plan because he has never been to a club, so he let Keith handle everything.

This was the first club Diana had ever been in and did not know what to expect. She held onto Ron's hand tightly as they walked through the full club. Diana knew she looked good and was dressed very sexy, but when she saw how many of the women were dressed, it surprised her. Some of the women wore as little as they could get away with. Diana and Ron walked closer to the dance floor.

The DJ's music and skills were making people stay on the floor. He played Jamaican music with a lot of bass, which made the women drop it, wind it, and shake their bodies hard and nasty. Diana and Ron looked at each other and all the beautiful women dancing very provocatively. Some women wore panties and others did not. Ron has never seen so many sexy, beautiful women in one place in his life.

Some women were grinding equally as hard on each other as they did with guys. It looked like they were having sex on the dance floor. Keith and Stacy walked closer to Ron and Diana and saw the people doing their thing on the dance floor. Keith has seen a lot, but he had to use discipline on this night because he saw so many attractive women in all shapes and sizes. One couple caught his attention.

Two incredibly attractive women with curvaceous figures were dancing side by side, dropping it low at the same time. Every time they did, depending on where you stood, you saw butt cheeks and crotches because they wore crotchless panties. Pretty in the face, slim in the waist, and shapely derrieres.

This scene and watching all the dancing made Stacy hot and horny and wanted to get on the dance floor and grind on Keith. She never told Keith she was attracted to women, depending on how they looked. Some of these women had it going on. Keith walked closer to Ron and tapped him on the shoulder to get his attention.

"Let's go to our VIP section." He yelled to be heard over the music.

Keith and Stacy walked in front and his hand was on her butt caressing it. This turned Stacy on and she made sure to shake her butt with every step.

Diana looked at Keith caressing Stacy's butt and knew Ron looked as well. Who would not? This was having an unusual effect on Diana. It turned her on and she wanted Ron to pay attention to her like that. She gripped his hand harder. Feeling Diana's need for attention, he put his hand on her hip, caressing it firmly.

Diana smiled as she felt the heat from his hand, it made her insides jump. She put her hand on top of his and

moved it to her butt and slid it around. She was very horny.

They walked to another section of the club to a private room with glass doors. Keith closed the door behind them which drowned out a lot of the noise. The room was dimly lit and decorated well, with plush sofas and a table with tablecloths on them. Candles, champagne, and glasses sat on the table. They sat across from each other and Diana put her purse on the sofa.

"So Diana, what do you think of all this? You have to admit, it's very nice." Stacy said and rubbed Keith's leg under the table.

"Well, the music is loud and some of the women are almost naked, but yes it's nice. I like being with Ron." She looked at him and smiled.

"The feeling is mutual. Let's make a toast." He opened the champagne poured four glasses and passed them to everyone.

Diana held the glass and looked at Ron.

"You know I don't drink Ron."

Keith was losing his patience with Diana, treating her like she was going to break, so he was going to do all he could to corrupt her.

"Diana, this is a special occasion, and one glass will not hurt you." He gave her a fake smile.

"I guess you are right," she looked at Ron and smiled. "Ron, what's the toast?"

He raised his glass.

"A toast to new beginnings."

They all clinked their glasses.

"New beginnings."

They drank a little and started laughing. The talking and drinking continued, and they were playful with each other. Diana became more relaxed, allowing Ron to be affectionate, rubbing her leg and kissing her a lot.

"Ron, I have to go to the bathroom, come with me."

"No problem."

Stacy extended her hand.

"No, you stay here and talk to Keith, I will go with her." She kissed Keith and extended her hand to Diana. "Come on Diana."

She kissed Ron and grabbed her purse and Stacy's hand and they walked out of the room.

Keith moved closer to Ron so they could talk.

"Partner, your girl is looking good. Please tell me you are going to hit that tonight. She's allowing you to feel all over her, so don't slip."

"Yeah, she looks great, but I don't know about the sex thing. I do want to stick to the plan. Are we good?"

"Relax, I got it all covered my brother, just do you. The girls are gone, so do not lie. Tell me you saw all the fine sexy women in this place. Breasts, crotches, and ass is everywhere, damn man."

"You are right, this place is great, and the women make a man want to go get money, and we are."

"You are right." They dapped, stood up, and looked at all the fine women walking and dancing shaking hips and asses.

Stacy held Diana's hand as they walked through the club, and both got hit on by so many men and women. One guy walked behind them and grabbed their butts.

Instinctively, Stacy pulled her razor out from underneath her dress and turned around quickly, putting the razor to the guy's throat, and getting in his face.

"Don't you ever put your hands on me or my girl, fool."

He raised his hands.

"No offense. So that's you?" He nodded his head at Diana.

"You damn right." She grabbed Diana's hand, pulled her closer, and grabbed her butt, still holding the razor to his throat. "This is my ass, now get lost fool."

He backed up and walked away.

Diana was surprised by what happened and how Stacy handled the situation. But she was shocked when Stacy grabbed her butt and what she said. It felt good to be cared for and touched in this way, but she would never tell Stacy this.

They walked into the bathroom holding hands. They used the bathroom and washed their hands. Stacy was horny and looked at Diana with lust in her eyes. They were walking out when Stacy stopped walking and looked at Diana.

"Are you alright? You seem tense. Do not freak out about what happened. Some guys are pigs, and you have to put them in their place."

"I am good, you surprised me by what you did."

"Which part?" She said nonchalantly.

"The razor and how fast you pulled it out when you grabbed my butt, and what you said about it." She felt uncomfortable now and looked away from Stacy.

"I was trying to protect you boo. As fine as you look tonight, men and women in this club would love to have some of your pussy and ass."

"That's disgusting Stacy." She frowned at her.

"Not really." Stacy moved closer to Diana and pushed her against the wall and grabbed her butt with both hands. She kissed her and slid her tongue across Diana's lips.

Diana was shocked and pushed Stacy away.

"Stop, are you crazy? You had too much to drink."

Stacy stared at Diana and saw the look of curiosity in her eyes, so she was going to satisfy her curiosity.

"You did not like it?"

"Are you crazy? No, I did not. Let's get out of this bathroom, you are drunk."

"Liar!" She grabbed Diana's hand and pulled her into one of the stalls and closed the door. Diana almost dropped her purse on the floor but she put it across her body. Stacy reached under Diana's dress, grabbed her butt with both hands feeling her flesh since she wore thong underwear, and kissed her hard on the lips.

Diana tried to push Stacy away, but she had a tight grip on her butt and kissed her at the same time. This turned her on surprisingly and made her horny. The excitement, the alcohol, Stacy grabbing and kissing her, and feeling Stacy's fingers on her butt cheeks made her wet.

"Stacy stop, please stop."

Stacy looked into Diana's eyes.

"Tell me the damn truth. Does this feel good, and do you want Ron to fuck you tonight?" She moved her hand to the front of her panties and caressed her crotch and felt her wetness.

Diana leaned her head back and a moan escaped her lips. She looked at Stacy.

"This is so wrong, yes, it feels good and yes I want Ron to fuck me. I want his dick inside me so badly and I want to suck it. I am tired of being a virgin." She moved Stacy's hand and grabbed her butt and kissed her. They tongue kissed passionately while caressing each other's butt.

"That was very nice baby, very nice! Now, don't think about this, and let's go have some fun." Stacy said.

They fixed their clothes and walked out of the stall. Diana reapplied her lip gloss, giving some to Stacy and they walked back to the VIP room.

Diana was embarrassed by what happened but very sexually turned on. She kissed Ron hard, took a drink, and grabbed his hand.

"Come on, let's go dance so I can grind all this butt on you that I know you want. Oh, what about my purse?"

"Relax Diana, security will handle that."

They walked to the dance floor and Diana began dancing like she had been doing it for years. Shaking and grinding her butt on Ron with smoothness, and felt his erection, and enjoyed it.

Stacy and Keith were in the VIP room sitting down.

"What took you two so long and what's up with Diana? Acting like she's in heat or something."

"We had girl talk and she wants Ron to make love to her, but the virgin thing. Don't worry about her, you need to focus on me." She leaned back on the sofa, spread her legs, and placed Keith's hand between them. "Baby, I'm so wet for you, after we leave here, I want you to make love to me then fuck me and lick this pussy and ass good. Now, let's go dance."

They stood and Keith kissed her, grabbed her butt underneath her dress, and pressed his body into her so she could feel his hard dick. Stacy pulled away from him and laughed.

"Relax baby, all in good time and you can have it all."

Keith grabbed her hand and they walked to the dance floor and saw Ron and Diana doing their thing. They were surprised to see them dancing so well together to have never been in a club.

Stacy grabbed Keith's hand and pulled him on the floor and began showing off her dance moves like a seasoned pro, which she was. Bumping, grinding, winding her hips, and dropping her butt, shaking it like she was having sex with the air. Keith loved it and was in his world dancing with her.

Ron looked at Keith and nodded his head to him. Keith knew what time it was. He waved his hand high in the air repeatedly. The DJ watched them and knew what to do. He stopped the music and a spotlight shined on Ron and Diana. Someone walked toward them and handed Ron a mike. He cleared his throat.

"Good evening everyone. I hope everybody is having a great time."

Everybody screamed.

"Yeah."

"I have a special announcement to make." He turned around and looked at Diana.

"Diana, you mean a great deal to me. We have been through a lot in a short amount of time, but I know I want to spend the rest of my life with you. I love you very much." He reached into his pocket and pulled out the ring he bought and got on one knee. "Diana, every day I want to wake up and see your face for years to come but as my wife. Diana, will you marry me?"

Diana was in total shock. Never did she expect this, and tears flowed down her face. She covered her mouth with her hand and looked at Ron.

"Oh my God! Oh Ron, yes, yes, I will marry you baby. Oh, my God. Yes!"

Ron put the ring on her finger, stood up, grabbed her waist, and they kissed passionately.

Everybody started clapping their hands and the song began playing, "You Are My Lady" by Freddy Jackson. Ron and Diana continued to hug and kiss. Diana looked at the ring and her mouth dropped open.

"Oh my God, Ron this ring is beautiful. Oh my God!" She began crying again, hugged and kissed Ron as if her life depended on it. Music began playing and everyone started dancing.

Keith hugged and kissed Stacy then walked over to the happy couple and hit Ron on his shoulder. He turned around and they shook hands and hugged.

"Congratulation's partner, you followed your heart, and all will be well."

"Thanks Keith. I hope and pray so."

He stepped to Diana.

"Congratulations Diana."

Diana stared at Keith and smiled and gave him the tightest hug ever. She felt his erection when they hugged but overlooked it.

"Thank you Keith. Oh God, I am so overwhelmed by all of this. Look at this ring. Did you know anything about this?"

Keith looked at the ring.

"Wow, that's some ring." He hugged her again and whispered in her ear. "Be happy Diana and treat my man right and don't be stingy with the sex." He smiled.

Diana smacked him playfully and lightly.

"Yes Keith, I will treat Ron very well like God wants me to and put all this body on him."

Stacy stood behind Diana and pinched her on the side.

"I heard that girl you need some good lovin," she winked at her. "Congratulations Diana, I am so happy for you."

Diana's tears flowed from her eyes as she stared at Stacy. She hugged her.

"Thank you Stacy, I am so happy. All of this is an answered prayer," she extended her hand out to her. "Look at my ring."

Stacy looked at the ring and became jealous but would never show it.

"Oh my God, that's a gorgeous ring. You are so blessed." She hugged her and whispered in her ear. "From woman to woman, fuck that man every chance you get, and suck his dick regularly." She wiped the tears from Diana's face and kissed her on the cheek.

"You are something else Stacy, but I will take your advice." She hugged her again.

Ron hugged Diana from the back and pressed into her butt.

"Come on baby, let's go."

It felt so good being in Ron's arms and she does not want him to let her go. She turned around to face him.

"I am ready baby." She grabbed his hand.

A security guard walked up to Diana and gave her purse to her.

They said goodbye to Stacy and Keith and then left the club. Ron's Benz was parked in front of the club when they stepped out. He opened the door for Diana, and he got in and drove to the Four Seasons Hotel.

At the club, Keith and Stacy were on the dance floor showing off then they walked back to the VIP section and sat on the sofa. Stacy tried not to, but her emotions got the best of her, and right now, she was so envious of Diana. She did not know anything about all of this because Keith never told her. She looked at him.

"Keith, I am very happy for Ron and Diana, but how come you never told me anything about all of this."

He knew this was coming. He kissed her.

"A woman being proposed to is a big thing and in all the excitement I did not want you to let it slip out. I am

happy for my man, and I hope he can work it all out. Anyway, enough about them, let's focus on us." He pulled her closer, kissed her, and caressed her leg. "Baby, you look so good in that dress, you got every guy in this place drooling. You are one beautiful woman."

Normally this would have touched her heart but not tonight. Stacy thought about their future. She knew Keith was making a lot of money selling drugs and his legal businesses are doing great. She wondered when he was going to settle down and marry her since he constantly told her how much he loved her. Or is he just using her for the moment?

"Keith, you know for a fact how much I love you and you tell me and show me you love me. I am not trying to get into your business, but I am not blind either. I know you are making millions. When are you going to stop taking so many risks, settle down, and focus on us?" She stared into his eyes.

Keith knew all of this was coming. It's a woman's thing.

"Stacy, I have been doing a lot of thinking about my businesses and us. I have not reached my business goal yet, but I am working hard on it, and it will not take much longer. You know there is no one for me but you. I have the total package with you, and I love you Stacy, very much." He kissed her and slid his hand under her dress and caressed her thigh.

His touch always felt good, but she wanted answers right now, not affection.

"Keith, your touch always moves my heart, you know that, but if you love me so much, why have you not asked me to marry you? I do not want to be wifey in name only, I want to be, *the wife.* I am not trying to pressure you and I never would, but I want and need to know where I stand with you."

He held her hand and looked into her eyes.

"Stacy, I am asking you to trust me. I am not playing you and when the time is right, I got you baby, I promise you that. So please stick with me as I do you and continue to be my best friend." He stared into her eyes and kissed her lips softly and caressed her face with his hand. "I love you Stacy."

His words, his touch, and what she felt from him melted her heart and tears flowed from her eyes.

"You are a good man for me, and you have my heart. If you are playing me, I will send you someplace where it's very quiet." She smiled, kissed him, and rubbed his crotch. "Baby let's go, I want you."

Keith wanted to please Stacy right now. He grabbed a remote off the table and pressed a button and all the glass including the doors went opaque. He slid to his knees and pulled Stacy to the edge of the sofa, lifted her dress, pulled her panties down, spread her legs, and buried his face between her legs, licking her wetness.

Stacy loved Keith's oral skills and it did not take him long to bring her to the point of no return. She placed her hands on his head, pulled him into her, and climaxed so hard her body shook, and she was grinding her wetness on his face.

"Ohhhhh Keith." She yelled, not giving a damn who heard her.

Keith slid his finger inside her moving it back and forth and continued licking Stacy and could care less who heard her screams of passion.

CHAPTER FIFTY SIX
Fulfilling The Plan

Ron drove up to the hotel and they got out. A valet took his key to park the car. Diana held Ron's hand as they walked into the hotel and got on the elevator. She had her purse across her shoulder. Ron pushed Diana gently against the wall and kissed her and slid his tongue into her mouth which she gladly sucked on. He caressed her hips and butt. The door opened to her floor, and they walked to her room side by side with Ron's hand rubbing her lower back, hip, and butt. Diana's body was turned on, but she got nervous because she knew what Ron was expecting now. They stopped at her room door and Diana leaned against it.

"Ron, baby we need to talk, please."

He kissed her.

"No Diana, we don't have to talk at all." He leaned closer and began sucking on her neck and slid his hands under her dress, grabbed her hips and butt firmly, and pressed his body into hers so she felt his hard-on. His hands moved between her legs and his fingers touched the back of her thong, pulled it to one side, and started caressing her wetness. Ron slid one side of the top of her dress down with his teeth so he could lick and suck on her nipples and breasts.

Diana was moaning because all of this was driving her crazy.

"Ohhh Ron." Diana's body was on fire, and she wanted him so badly. She wrapped her arms around his neck and sucked on his lips, feeling her body giving in to his every touch making her so wet. Diana felt Ron's finger sliding slowly inside her. She jumped back and moved his hand quickly and pushed her dress down.

"Ron, baby please listen to me. You know how badly I want you right now and I am not playing games or trying to tease you. You have made me so happy tonight and I want everything to be right for us and a blessing from God. If I let you continue and you come in the room with me, I know I will not be able to resist you. I have waited so long, and we are so close. We can have a quick wedding if you want to. But please do not do this to me. I want to be a good, clean, Holy wife to you and myself. I promise I am worth the wait. After we are officially married, I promise to give you all the lovin' you can handle. Please baby, let's wait, please." Diana looked deeply into his eyes.

Ron stared at her, and as much as he desired to have her, he can wait and would stick with his plan.

"Damn Diana, you are driving me crazy, but you are right, and I will not pressure you. But what am I supposed to do with this?" He grabbed his hard-on.

Diana looked at it and she could tell he was working with something. She caressed his face.

"Oh baby, now I am feeling bad, but it will go down and you will be fine." She smiled and kissed him on the cheek.

"That is it, that is all I get, a kiss on the cheek? I am standing here with dick hard enough to break concrete and you kiss me on the cheek, damn!"

She laughed.

"Baby, I promise you I am worth the wait." She smiled and held in her laugh.

"Yeah okay, but you better be a closet freak. Sucking, licking, and throwing that ass back, good." He looked at her and laughed.

Diana leaned back and looked at him.

"Ron don't be nasty. But I will be whatever my husband wants me to be, husband. You get that, husband, not boyfriend?"

"I got it. I have a change of clothes in my car, and I am going to get a room here. So, will you be ready in the morning? I want to show you something. It's a surprise."

"After tonight, I am not sure if I can take another one of your surprises. You blew my mind tonight, but I will be ready."

He kissed her.

"Good, I will see you at eight. Sleep well." He hugged and kissed her and walked away.

Diana opened the door, walked into her room, put her purse on a chair, threw herself on the bed, and exhaled deeply. Minutes later she got up and took a shower. Afterward, she put lotion on her body grabbed a T-shirt from her bag, pulled the covers back on the bed, and laid down, and went to sleep quickly.

Mr. Bones was in the next room dressed in black with his cane and pouch in his hands stomping his feet.

"Damn, I almost had them, but somebody was praying for these two, but there is something I can do. She did not pray before she went to sleep, and this is good for me.

Now I am going to oppress her with more of my dirty deeds and spirits." He tapped his cane twice, mumbled some words, and transformed into a light mist. The mist moved underneath his door and traveled to Diana's room, slid underneath her door, and hovered over her, then fell on her body.

Diana began having a dream about many hands touching her body all over and being kissed and licked all over as well. She kicked the covers off, removed her T-shirt, and began caressing her body, pinching her nipples, and slid a finger inside her, fingering herself slowly, until she was wetter.

Mr. Bones' face materialized and hovered inches above her face whispering to her.

"Ass, pussy, dick, fuck, lesbian, lust, freak, slut, slut."

Diana continued to finger herself until she had an explosive climax and then woke up but was still fingering herself.

"Nooo," she screamed, "ohhhhhh yes this feels so good, ahhhhhh fuck me, fuck meeee." She slowed her pace fingering herself until she calmed down, then began crying and got out of bed and on her knees to pray.

"Oh God, what's happening to me? Forgive me Jesus for all my sins and cover me, oh Lord, with your grace and mercy." She got up took another shower and got back in bed and went to sleep.

The following morning Ron walked down the hall toward Diana's room. He wore dress shoes, dress slacks, and a dress shirt. He knocked on the door.

Diana opened it and embraced Ron, holding him tight kissing him repeatedly. She wore heels and a dress that fit her body but was not too tight.

"Good morning to you as well. I can get used to this type of greeting." He is smiled at her.

"I love your sense of humor. I missed you so much. I had a bad dream last night baby."

Ron looked at her with serious concern.

"Are you okay? This can wait and we can go later if you need more rest."

"No, I will be fine, and I am curious about this next surprise you have for me. If you will come in and get my bags, we can leave now."

"Oh, now you want me to come in." He said with a smile.

"Hush." She kissed him.

Ron walked in, grabbed her bags and they left the hotel and got in his Benz which was parked in front, and drove away.

They talked and laughed while riding until they reached Potomac MD and pulled up to this gate in front of a house. Ron clicked a remote and drove through reaching the circular driveway and they got out.

Diana looked around.

"Wow, this house is big. Ron, whose house is this?"

He grabbed her hand.

"Come on." He walked to the front double doors, unlocked it, and walked in.

Diana's mouth dropped open when she saw how large and beautiful the house was. Ron gave her a grand tour of

the house inside and out. It has a large full basement and enough marble throughout the house to supply two houses. They end up back in the master bedroom which is on the first floor.

She stood in front of Ron.

"Okay, I am blown away by this place. This is a dream house, now whose house is this Ron?"

"It's our house Diana."

"Ron don't play with me. For real, whose house is this?" She stared at him.

He kissed her and looked into her eyes.

"I am serious. It is officially our house. I purchased it and you can do all of the decorating if you want."

"Oh my God, this is our house, our house Ron. Oh my God!" Diana started stomping her feet and shouting she was so happy and kissed him. Then reality hit her. Her expensive ring, this house, his expensive wardrobe and jewelry, and all the money. Drugs!

"Ron, we need to talk."

"No problem. I can answer all your questions, but can we talk while we are in the car."

"Okay, but where are we going? I cannot take another surprise. You are too much."

"It's just the beginning Diana. We are going to see Grandma Harris and my mom."

"Oh God! Ron, do we have to do this today? It is too soon. I want us to have our time for a while."

"And we will, but the sooner we tell the family, the better."

"Okay, let's get this over with." She looked around the house. "This house is too much."

"So, you don't want it?"

"Boy, don't play, I ain't crazy. Yes, I want this house, but we need to talk first."

"Let's ride sexy."

They walked out of the room and Ron watched Diana's butt shaking.

"Diana, you got a serious body and round fat ass. Damn, I can't wait to get in that." She turned around and pinched his lips with her fingers.

"Ron, I asked you not to say ass, it sounds so dirty, but you can have all of this." She caresses her body. "When we say, I do."

"It works for me. The sooner the better." They walked out of the house and Ron had his hand on her butt, rubbing it.

Diana stopped walking, and turned around to face Ron.

"Baby, you want all of me badly, don't you?" She smiled at him mischievously.

"Don't play, you know I do."

She wiggled her finger at him.

"Come closer."

He leaned into her.

"What?"

Diana put her arms around his neck and whispered in his ear.

"When we are officially husband and wife, I am going to make love to you, fuck you, and suck your dick so good." She licked his lips and kissed him.

Ron looked at her and his dick became hard immediately. He grabbed her hips and pressed his body into her, so she felt him.

She hugged and kissed him.

"I can feel you baby, soon. Very soon, now come on."

They got in the car and drove away.

CHAPTER FIFTY SEVEN

Sheila's House

Ron drove up to Sheila's house and saw Sheila waving at him from inside.

"Ron, thank you for being honest with me and talking about the drugs and being out of that business. I trust you Ron, so please don't ever deceive me."

He felt bad because he was not honest with her, but in time she would understand, hopefully.

"Diana, you mean so much to me and I value what we share, you know that. Now let's go inside and get this over with." He kissed her and they got out of the car and walked into the house.

Sheila hugged Ron and kissed his cheek.

"Son, I have missed you so much and prayed so hard for you." She hugged him and stared at him while tears came to her eyes.

"I have missed you too Mom and thank you for all of your prayers."

Grandma Harris walked over to Ron.

"Okay Sheila, let the boy go. I want my hug too, all that praying I have been doing." She hugged Ron and immediately felt something was not right about him, but she does not want to spoil the moment, so she does not comment on it.

"You look good Ron," she looked over at Diana. "And you have my baby with you. Come over here child."

Diana walked over to Grandma Harris and hugged her.

"Hi Grandma. You know I always miss you."

The moment Diana hugged her, Grandma Harris felt a strong lust spirit and wondered did these two have sex. Diana's face was glowing.

Diana held her hand out.

"Grandma, look."

She looked at Diana's hand and put her hand over her mouth.

"Is that what I think it is? Oh my Lord, look at the size of that ring."

Sheila moved closer to look.

"Oh my God. Is that an engagement ring?" She turned to look at Ron. "Somebody better say something."

Ron hugged Sheila, then hugged Grandma Harris and walked over to Diana and stood behind her with his arms around her waist and looked at Sheila and Grandma Harris.

"Yes, it is an engagement ring. I surprised Diana last night and asked her to marry me. She said yes and we would like to get married soon. I know how you two think. No, Diana is not pregnant and no we did not have sex."

Sheila and Grandma Harris exhaled at the same time.

"I am so happy for you two. That explains the glow on her face. I was thinking you took my baby to some sleazy hotel, got her drunk or high and she gave up that kitty cat."

"Grandma Harris, you are something. Don't be nasty."

"What? Ain't nothing wrong with a woman giving up some kitty cat when she is married. She is supposed to knock her husband to his knees regularly. My husband never complained. Poor baby had a heart attack and died."

"Grandma, you are too much." Diana said and laughed.

"Diana, you are getting married, oh my God. There is so much to do." Sheila said.

Ron moved closer to Sheila.

"Mom, can we all sit down? I need to talk."

Sheila and Grandma Harris sat on one sofa and Ron and Diana sat on the other.

"Ron is something wrong?" Sheila said.

"No, I need to explain some things." He exhaled and looked at Diana, Grandma Harris, and Sheila. "Please don't interrupt me and let me get all this out. I love Diana as much as any man could love a woman and I want to spend the rest of my life with her. Keith was involved in drugs on a small scale and his drug business grew and he made a lot of money. I helped him with his business but all that is behind us. He told you about his legit businesses and they are making serious money. We are business partners and want to expand to owning a classy nightclub, but time will tell. I love the Lord and I have seen his great power and I want to live for him, I just don't know about this great calling I am supposed to have in my life. I purchased a house in Potomac and Diana has seen it. We plan to make it our home. Yes, I have done wrong, but when you do wrong and make a lot of money, then stop doing wrong, what do you do with all the money? Give it to the church. Yeah, right. I want to take it one day at a time, be blessed by God, and hope for the best. I am finished." He looked at them with anticipation.

Grandma Harris looked at Sheila, then Ron.

"You said a lot Ron and talked like a real man should. I want the best for my baby and you. I have two questions

to ask," she looked at Diana, "Diana, do you love the Lord and Ron?"

"Grandma, I love Ron but not with all my heart. I love God with all my heart, and that is how it should be. All flesh is the same. It will sin and let you down, but God is everlasting to everlasting peace."

Grandma Harris nodded her head.

"Son, thank you for being honest and I have to ask you this. Are you finished with your criminal life?"

"Yes Mom, I'm finished. I want to enjoy my life and my soon-to-be wife." He hugged and kissed Diana. "And she's fine too." He smiled at Diana. She pinched him on his side and then kissed him.

"Alright, that's enough of that. You two are not married yet, so control your hormones. Ron, you and Diana have waited this long, so don't sneak off someplace with my baby trying to get her kitty cat."

"Grandma Harris you really should be ashamed of yourself for talking like that."

"Sheila please. Ron and Diana's hormones are raging like wildfire. That boy knows he wants her little booty."

Sheila put her hand on her head.

"Oh God. You know I can't believe you sometimes."

"Enough about my body please. We have a wedding to plan."

"True that." Ron said smiling.

"So how soon do you two want this wedding?" Sheila asked.

Ron and Diana looked at each other and kissed.

"Soon." They both said and laughed.

Grandma Harris shook her head.

"Yes Lord, we need to hurry up and get these two married. They hot as firecrackers waiting to go off."

Ron and Diana laughed, and Ron lowered his head.

"What's wrong Ron?" Sheila said.

"I thought about Sandra. I miss her so much and want her at the wedding."

"I know baby, but God is still in control and it's not over yet." Sheila said.

"Amen to that." Grandma Harris said.

Diana looked at Ron and felt his sadness, knowing he blames himself for Sandra being in her coma.

"Ron, we both know God always finishes what he starts. This battle is not yours to fight baby. So, continue to believe in the master-builder King Jesus who has power unlimited and has never lost a fight. I could never serve a loser, and neither could you. I love you Ron, hold on baby, hold on." She stared into his eyes and kissed his lips softly.

CHAPTER FIFTY EIGHT

Coming Together

Sheila and Grandma Harris helped Diana decorate the house in Potomac, which Sheila continued to say the house was too big for two people. Decorations and furniture for the house cost five hundred thousand dollars. Ron sold his Benz and purchased two Bentleys for him and Diana. A $230,000 white 2012 Continental Flying Spur for him, and a $210,000 2012 silver Continental GT Coupe for Diana. He spent a total of five hundred thousand dollars on wardrobe for him and Diana and fifty thousand dollars on their wedding bands.

The church was full, and people were still coming in. Time went by so fast, but two months later and today is the day of Ron and Diana's wedding. Pastor Williams talked with them separately to make sure this is what they wanted and with no pressure. Keith took care of all the financial expenses, but Ron and Diana did not want a huge wedding. Instead, she wanted something simple, but nice. They decided Aruba for seven days for their honeymoon, and everything was first class, for twenty-five thousand dollars. The church decorations and miscellaneous items were another two hundred thousand dollars. The cake alone costs five thousand. All of this was compliments of Keith.

The bridesmaids were Christine, Stacy, and three of Diana's friends. Groomsmen were Keith, who is his best man of course, and four of Keith's friends. Ron chose grey and burgundy for his tux, tailor-made of course, and the groomsmen wore grey tuxes, and the bridesmaids wore burgundy dresses.

Sheila sat next to James and Grandma Harris. Music played as the bridesmaids and groomsmen walked down the aisle. Ron stood next to the pastor, more nervous than he has ever been in life. Now the moment everyone has waited for. The doors in the back of the church opened and the song began to play, *Just As Long As We Have Love,* by the Spinners. Everyone stood and Diana walked through the doors wearing a two hundred-fifty-thousand-dollar, cream-color wedding dress with a twelve-foot-long train and she wore a veil over her face. Diana prayed hard not to fall as she walked in her heels because she was so nervous.

Grandma Harris gave her away and she and Sheila cried the entire time.

Stacy looked at Keith and he winked at her. She smiled knowing her time was coming soon.

Ron and Diana exchanged wedding vows, did the placement of rings, and spoke their words to one another The pastor spoke and then said those words many desire to hear.

"I now pronounce you husband and wife. You may kiss the bride."

"Oh my baby!" Grandma Harris yelled.

Everyone laughed.

Ron lifted her veil and kissed Diana on the lips and hugged her.

"Hello, Mrs. O'Neil." Ron said and smiled at her.

"Hello Mr. O'Neil." And kissed him back.

Everyone stood and began clapping their hands. Diana and Ron held hands and walked down the aisle and to the room where the reception was being held. The wedding and reception were filmed, and many pictures were taken. The cake was cut, and Ron and Diana had their first dance and then others began dancing. Everyone began mingling and congratulated the bride and groom.

Keith stayed close to Stacy knowing how she felt. Later, Diana told Ron she was getting tired and was ready to go. It has been a long day. They hugged and said goodbye to everyone.

A cream color Rolls Royce took them home and they hugged and kissed the entire ride. Ron carried his bride through the front door of their new home. Neither he nor Diana spent a night in the house. They decorated it and spent their nights somewhere else.

CHAPTER FIFTY NINE
Worth the Wait

This was the night Ron and Diana looked forward to for many years. Two virgins coming together as husband and wife in Christ is priceless and they were nervous. They were in their master bedroom. While Diana was in the bathroom, Ron lit candles all around the room, and put music on that was preselected. He has a remote to change the selections. When Diana comes out, he wants the first song to be, *Between the Sheets* by The Isley Brothers, then *Freak Me* by Silk, and a mixture of Luther Vandross and Keith Sweat after that.

Ron wore tan silk boxers and a silk T-shirt. Diana walked out wearing black heels, a red camisole, matching thong, and her fingernails were painted light red with white tips. She looked around the room seeing all the candles and smiled.

"Ron, this is beautiful, the candles and the music are very romantic, and you look good. This may sound silly, but I'm nervous and you better not laugh."

"Okay," he looked at her then laughed, "you made me laugh. Baby, you look gorgeous and so very sexy. Absolutely beautiful.
Diana, kneel with me so we can pray please."

She looked at him and caressed his face with her hand.

"You are truly the man for me, of course baby."
They kneeled and held hands.

"Lord, we thank you for this day you made possible. Bless us, guide us, and bless our marriage, amen."

"Thank you Lord for so much, Amen."
They stood up facing each other and stared into each other's eyes with the spirit of love no words could express. Ron stepped back from her and stared.

"Keep the heels on Diana and turn to the side baby."

She turned to the side with her hands on her hips.

"Do you see anything you like?"

He continued to stare.

"Diana, you are radiant and you got a serious body. Pretty in the face, slim in the waist, hips, sexy lips, pretty painted fingertips, big butt, and a pretty smile. A FULL SEVEN! Girl, you got hips and ass for days. I can sit a cup on your butt."

Diana laughed and put an arch in her back to stick her butt out more and looked at Ron seductively.

"Is this what you want Ron? Is this what you can't keep your hands off?" She smiled at him.

Ron stood there staring at his wife, realizing how blessed he was to have her in his life and finally as his wife. He moved closer and put his hands on her butt and caressed it.

"All this ass is finally mine." He smiled at her.

Diana shook her head.

"You are something. I have heard that phrase before, so, I'm a *FULL SEVEN*, huh?" She smiled and looked at him. "Ron, I know I have lived somewhat of a sheltered life, and you have too, until recently," she kissed him, "but let's not ever judge each other. We are husband and wife now and I want you to be yourself and I will be myself in and out of the bedroom. You can say ass baby, but only to me and in a nice way."

"Woman I am grown. I can say whatever I want." He smacked her on the butt.

"Okay, Mr. grown man. Do you think your grown self can handle all of this grown woman?" She slid her finger between her legs and then across his lips.

"Let's find out." He walked over to the lampstand and pushed the remote, *Between the Sheets* began playing and he walked over to her.

"I like that and it's nice." She kissed him slowly.

Ron grabbed her hips, caressed them, and slid his hands on her butt cheeks, sliding his fingers between her legs. He took his T-shirt and boxers off and pulled Diana's camisole off and placed his lips on her neck and began sucking delicately. He kissed her lips and moved to her neck kissing and licking her breasts and his tongue appreciated her nipples with continued soft licks in the best way. His hand moved slowly inside her panties, feeling her wetness and desire which caused him to be more conscious of everything he did to please his beautiful bride. Ron turned Diana around and pushed her against the wall, sucking and biting the back of her neck, and slid his tongue down her back. He kneeled, placed his hands on her hips, and slid his tongue across her butt.

Diana put her hands on the wall and spread her legs.

"Baby, that feels so good."

He pulled her butt toward him and licked it slower and then pulled her thong off and began licking between her legs, tasting her juices, and licked all over her butt.

Diana was moaning and moved her butt slowly up and down on his face.

"Ohhhh Ron, I am close, it feels good. Do not baby me. I want you to make love to me, and then be nasty like you talk."

He stopped and picked her up, carried her to the bed and sat her on it, removed her heels, and pushed her back. He kneeled and lifted Diana's legs and licked his way from her ankle to her wetness. He slid his tongue slowly across it back and forth, and then stuck his tongue inside her, sucking her juices, until he buried his face between her legs, and sucked on Diana's clit while caressing and pinching her nipples gently.

She gripped the sheets and tilted her head back.

"Oh my God Ron, baby don't stop, it feels so good, you are going to make me cum. Ron, I am cummming baby, ohhhhhhh Ron it feels so good, ahhhhhhhh I am cumming."

He continued sliding his tongue across her clit sucking every drop of her juices as she climaxed, and then kissed the inside of her thighs. He moved up and they kissed as if they were trying to devour each other. Ron could not wait any longer and was rock hard, he penetrated Diana slowly.

The moment Diana felt Ron slide inside her she gripped his arms hard.

"Oh Ron, slow baby, go slow, but deeper. Make love to me Ron."

He stared into her eyes and kissed her passionately while pushing inside her. He slid in and pulled back and slid in until he was completely inside her.

"Diana, you are so wet and tight baby, damn you are tight and hot, you feel good." Ron began sliding inside her carefully until he felt her relaxing more.

Diana wrapped her legs around his waist and pulled him into her.

"Yes baby, deeper. Oh Ron, faster baby. Now fuck me baby. Fuck your wife, fuck this young tight pussy. Fuck me." She gripped his arms tighter.

Ron lifted her legs and was thrusting in Diana slow and easy.

"No Ron don't slow down. I can take it. I want you to fuck me baby. Give me all your dick. I am your wife, fuck your wife Ron."

After hearing this from her he increased his pace and was thrusting into Diana, faster and deeper until he felt his nut coming. He looked at his wife and began thrusting faster.

"Oh Ron you are making me cum, I am cumming again baby, ahhhhhh it's so good. Don't stop, ohhhh Ron." She wrapped her arms around his neck, pulled him closer, and stared into his eyes. "I love you Ron, this is so good," Diana's body was shaking and trembling as she held onto Ron tightly as wave after wave of mini orgasms hit her body.

Feeling and hearing Diana's passionate cries caused his emotional and physical response.

"Diana, I love you so much, you feel so good, ahhhhhhh pussy so good. Ahhhhhhh Diana." He thrusts faster, giving her all of himself until he relaxed and put her legs down. He kissed her and pulled out and laid next to Diana, holding her hand.

They laid on their back, looked at the ceiling, exhaling deeply, and had the same expression on their face and thoughts, *wow, so this is what all the conversation is about, oh my goodness.* Diana turned to look at Ron as tears flowed from her eyes.

"I love you Ron," she exhaled. "That was beautiful, a little painful at first but it got better. I am glad I waited. Being with you was everything I wanted it to be."

Ron kissed her.

"I wanted my first time to be special but being with you in Christ was so much more. I pray God continues to bless our marriage." He stared at her, and tears fell from his eyes. "I love you Diana."

He kissed her lips and pushed Diana on her back and began kissing and sucking her nipples, slowly dragging his tongue across them, until they stood erect. He moved his hand to her stomach caressing it, followed by his warm mouth and tongue. It felt natural for Diana to spread her legs and Ron licked her inner thighs and wetness. Ron moved the tip of his tongue very slowly across her clit repeatedly.

Diana did not think the first time he did this could get any better but feeling what he was doing now was incredible for her.

"Baby, your warm mouth, and tongue feel so good between my legs. Oh that's so good Ron. Just like that, nice and slow. Oh Ron, don't stop."

Her words gave him satisfaction and confidence and his tongue continued licking the tip of her clit and then moved his tongue very slowly between her legs, up and down, back and forth. Long, slow, and firm licks, then slid his finger inside her. Back and forth, in and out, moving his finger while he continued licking and sucking her clit.

This was too much, Diana screamed while arching her back.

"Ahhhhhh Ron, it's too good, it's too good baby. You better not ever leave me, ohhhhhh baby."

Ron made his tongue stiff and slid it inside her back and forth, sucking all his wife's juices and loving it.

"Oh God Ron, you are going to make me cry, ohhhhh yes, suck it baby, suck it." She hit the bed repeatedly then grabbed Ron's head and held it in place. "Ohhhhh Ron." Diana relaxed and let his head go and fell back on the bed, exhausted.

Ron was hard again and wanted her badly, so he moved up to slide inside her, but Diana turned her body to the side.

"Oh no," she laughed, "I can't take any more right now. You are trying to kill me. If I have one more orgasm like that, I might pass out. Come here baby and hold me, please."

Ron smiled and laid next to Diana.

"This is good, and I can wait. Tomorrow is another day, but I will be bending that ass over as good as your lovin is." He laughed.

Diana slapped him on the arm playfully.

"You are so nasty, but truth be told, I love you being nasty to me now that we are married. Wow, husband and wife. We are one, only by the hand of God. Come on, let's take a hot shower and get back in bed."

"Not a problem baby." They got up and showered, washing each other, kissing, and hugging the entire time. They got out, dried one another off, and walked back to the bedroom, and got in bed naked. Ron held Diana from the back, kissing her on the neck.

Diana moaned and pressed her body into Ron.

"This is so nice. Yes, tomorrow baby, tomorrow. Just hold me."

Ron kissed her and held Diana a little tighter and eventually they went to sleep in each other's arms.

CHAPTER SIXTY

Mr. Bones Revenge

Early the following morning, a dark cloud of smoke appeared in Ron's front yard, then it cleared, and Mr. Bones stood there in all black holding his cane and pouch. He walked around the yard and then stared at the house.

"Enjoy it while you can boy. I knew you would get weak one day. Now it is my time. My money got you this house and everything else you have is mine. You think you will not pay me, fool! Everyone pays me, nobody dances with me for free." He raised his arms. "No one beats the bones, no one. Watch how I work boy." He pointed his cane at the house and mumbled some words, black smoke comes underneath his feet surrounding his body, then he and the smoke disappeared.

Ron's cell phone rang, and it is Keith telling him he and Stacy were coming over to give him something before they leave for their honeymoon. This irritated Ron and made Diana angry, but he calmed Diana down by making love to her. They showered and got dressed wearing t-shirts and sweatsuits since they are not going anywhere until tomorrow when they leave for their honeymoon. Diana was so happy as she and Ron walked around the house smiling, hugging, and kissing each other.

Keith drove up to Ron's gate driving a 2012 $376,000 dark-blue Lamborghini Aventador Coupe. Ron exhaled his irritation and then let him in. He and Stacy wore sweatsuits, tailor-made of course, and Stacy's sweatpants hugged her body.

Ron opened the door with Diana by his side and they see the Lamborghini.

They walked into the house and hugged each other.

"Keith, I see you stepped up your ride. That car is a beast. Don't let it get away from you with all that power under the hood."

"The car is like my baby. Beautiful, strong, and powerful." He smiled and hugged Stacy from the back, kissing her on the neck.

"That is a beautiful car, serious attention-getter. Stacy, you have your hands full with Keith." Diana said.

"And I am loving every minute of it." She kissed him passionately on his lips.

"Okay, before you two get carried away let me give you the house tour." Ron said.

Once again, jealousy came over Stacy knowing this is how she and Keith should be living, but her time will come. Later, Keith and Ron were in the living room talking and Stacy and Diana were in her bedroom sitting on the bed talking.

"Diana, I am so happy for you girl, you got it all. Tell me one thing, I do not need details, but I must ask. Did you put it on him? Did you make love to him, or did you fuck him?"

Diana shook her head and looked at Stacy.

"You are so nasty. It was everything I wanted it to be and more. Ron took his time and pleased me, over and over." Thinking about it made Diana smile. "Oh, it was

good, very good. He made love to me and fucked me good but on our honeymoon, I will be fucking him, good." She laughed.

"That's what I am talking about. And suck his dick good, don't be scared, you are married now. Slob on that dick, put some spit on it."

They both laughed and continued to talk and then walked into the living room and saw Ron and Keith looking like they were going out.

"Ron." Diana put her hands on her hips and had an instant attitude. "I know you and Keith are not going somewhere one day before our honeymoon. I know you are not going to leave me in this big house by myself. Keith, I was beginning to like you, don't make me change my mind."

"Diana, I like you too. It is some quick business, and I will have your man back in no time."

Ron knew Diana was highly upset but business is business. He walked over to her and whispered in her ear.

"Baby relax, this is important, and it will not take me long and when I get back, I will kiss and lick your ass and pussy good, make you climax hard! And give you good, long time dick." He laughed.

Diana hit his chest and could not help but laugh after he said all of that.

"I am going to hold you to everything you said, and you better hurry and come back."

"Diana, I will stay with you until they get back," Stacy said as she looked at Keith, "Keith, don't take all damn day."

He walked over to her and stood inches from her face.

"Who are you talking to like that?"

"I am talking to you." She kissed him. "Hurry back, please."

Keith kissed her and caressed her hips and butt.

Diana looked at Keith's hands on Stacy's butt and it turned her on for some reason. She walked over to them.

"You two can save that until he gets back and stop feeling on her butt like that in front of me."

"Let's go Keith so we can hurry up and get back." He walked over to Diana hugged and kissed her and he and Keith walked out the door.

You could hear the deep rumble of the engine as the Lamborghini drove off.

Stacy looked at Diana and saw the sadness in her eyes from watching her husband leave so soon so she decided to make her laugh. She smacked Diana on the butt to get her attention.

"Girl, he is coming back so relax, and what do you mean by telling my man to stop feeling on my butt." She smiled playfully.

"Girl, please. Those tight sweatpants you have on showing the shape of your hips, butt, and camel toe," she pointed between Stacy's legs. "That's nasty and I don't want Ron seeing all that, and Keith grabbing your butt holding it, I don't want to see it either." She laughed.

Stacy stared at her.

"Don't hate. Besides, my baby likes it and that's all that matters but you can stare at it." She put her hands on

Diana's waist, pulled her closer, and kissed her while caressing her hips.

Diana pushed Stacy away quickly.

"Are you crazy Stacy?" she yelled and frowned at her. "I'm married now, and I love the Lord, so stop. Ron and Keith will be back soon. You must have lost your mind."

Stacy stared at her and then slid her hand inside her pants and touched her wetness and stepped closer to Diana, and rubbed her finger across Diana's lips, never taking her eyes off her.

"Suck on my finger Diana."

Diana stared into Stacy's eyes. Her mind said no, but she felt her body moving all on its own, feeling compelled to do what she knew was so wrong. She took Stacy's hand and sucked on her finger while their eyes were locked onto each other, and Diana moved closer to Stacy and caressed her butt. She stopped sucking on her finger and grabbed Stacy's hand, and they walked upstairs. With each step, Diana felt like she was in some type of evil trance being controlled. She heard voices in her head, giving her various sexual thoughts and images she was fighting but desired at the same time.

They reached one of the bedrooms and stood in the middle of the room and stared at each other. A force so powerful Diana could not resist, she removed all her clothes and watched Stacy do the same. They stepped closer to each other and kissed, then walked over and pulled the covers back on the bed and got in.

Stacy rolled on top of Diana and looked her deep in the eyes.

"Do you want me Diana?" She kissed Diana's lips very softly.

Diana does not understand any of this but her emotions and body did what her mind was saying no to.

"Yes, I want you, but this is so wrong and..."
Stacy kissed Diana's lips before she could finish talking.

"Hush, you are mine now, all mines." She kissed Diana very passionately then licked and sucked on her neck.

Keith and Ron drove into a large vacant lot and saw a stretch Benz limo. Keith drove close to the car and they got out. Victor and his bodyguards stepped out and walked over to them.

Victor looked at the Lamborghini.

"Very nice expensive car Keith. Enjoy it."

"Thank you and I will Sir."

Victor stepped closer to Ron and extended his hand to him.

"It's good to finally meet you, Mr. Ron. The man prison could not hold."

Ron shook his hand.

"Mr. Augular, it's nice to meet you Sir."

"Welcome to my side son. The dark side." He stared into Ron's eyes with hate and revenge in his heart.

Diana and Stacy were on the bed and the covers were on the floor and Stacy's head was between Diana's legs.

"Oh Stacy, don't stop. Lick this pussy and keep fingering me, it feels so good. Then lick my ass baby and finger fuck it. Ohhhhh."

Mr. Bones appeared in Ron's front yard in a cloud of smoke, tapped his cane on the ground, and pointed it at the house.

"I got you now Diana, you closet freak. My spirits are controlling your mind and body. No one can beat the bones. You and your husband made me wait, but both of you are weak now. It is my turn, and I am coming to get you. Playtime is over boy, it's time for my revenge and I am coming with the spirit of destruction and death." He laughed.

About the Author

 Ronald Gray was born in Washington, D.C., and attended high school in Maryland. After spending time in the military and living in various states, he came back to Maryland. He enjoys reading, traveling, and weightlifting.

Discovering writing was his blessing and passion, Gray looks forward to waking up just to write. This led to the formation of Black Wall Street New Dream Publishing.

This is his first book, but hardly his last. Some people write stories from their imagination, but Gray has lived many of the experiences he writes about. He knows what it is like to do supernatural things by the forces of darkness and then get delivered and walk in the awesome power of God. To see the so-called impossible become instantly possible... Miracles! Through this, he strives to be what God has called him to be. He refers to God as "King Jesus."

Get ready to be emotionally and spiritually blown away by his forthcoming books and movies that will positively affect so many people. You will see yourself as one of the characters in every story. His stories are for people who want the raw uncut truth. This is the world we live in!

Contact Gray

www.myproviderproductions.com

COMING SOON

"MY CALL II"
Mr. Bones' Revenge

This journey is not over. Sometimes in life, the very things you desire to have, are the very things that could destroy you. The journey continues but not without great love and pain that few ever realize until it is too late because of emotional distractions of what they have. So, they think!

Ron finally receives what he desires, but at what price? Will the power of love be enough to hold the relationships together when temptation becomes overwhelming coming from every direction, time, and place? Material possessions can be addictive.

Action, suspense, love, prayers, tears, sex, powers of darkness, and drama are intensified by greed and selfishness. Mr. Bones is out for pure revenge and will destroy anyone who gets in his way. So, get ready for what you say you want and what you will need to survive. If you can! Get ready for…

"MY CALL II"
Mr. Bones' Revenge

"MY CALL II"

Mr. Bones' Revenge

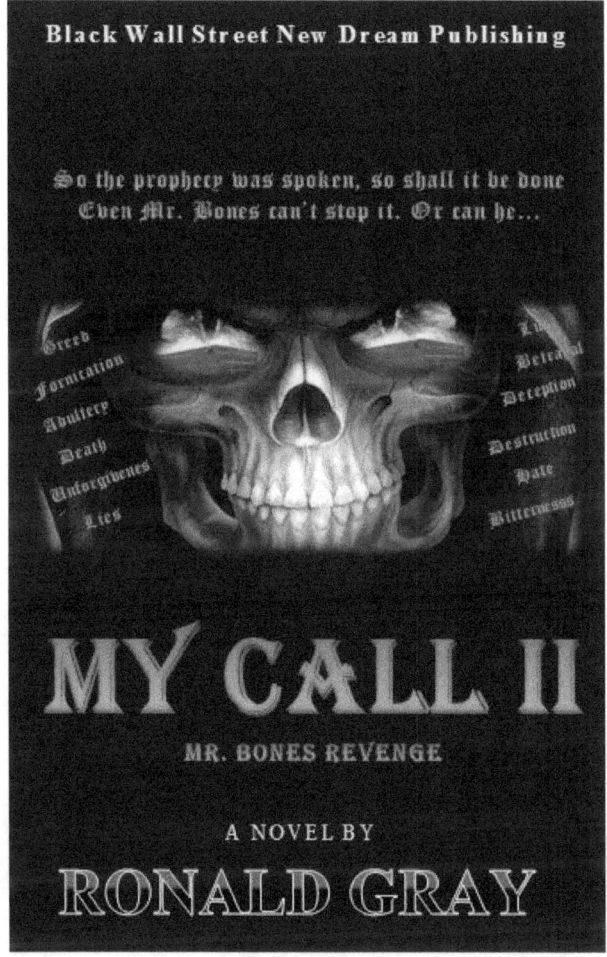